SULAND

VIOLETTA BOTZET LUETGERS

TATE PUBLISHING & *Enterprises*

Published by Tate Publishing & Enterprises, LLC
127 E. Trade Center Terrace | Mustang, Oklahoma 73064 USA
1.888.361.9473 | www.tatepublishing.com

Tate Publishing is committed to excellence in the publishing industry. The company reflects the philosophy established by the founders, based on Psalm 68:11,
"The Lord gave the word and great was the company of those who published it."

Book design copyright © 2010 by Tate Publishing, LLC. All rights reserved.
Cover design by Tyler Evans
Interior design by Joey Garrett

Published in the United States of America

ISBN: 978-1-60799-784-9
1. History / Native American
2. Fiction / Coming of Age
10.02.18

DEDICATION

I dedicate this book to the Native Americans who lived in Suland. They roamed free, worshiped their "Wakantanka" Creator God, and lived with honor.

INTRODUCTION

When I first began to study the history of the Great Sioux Uprising of 1862, I had no intention of writing a book. The more I read and studied the lifestyle of the Native Americans who lived in our "Big Woods" area of Minnesota, the more interested I became in these people and how they lived before and after the white man came into their lives. I have done my best to weave my fictional characters into the story with the very real people who lived this American tragedy. I hope you enjoy my story.

1839

PROLOGUE

Spotted Fawn opened her eyes slowly. Something had awakened her. She lay quietly and looked around the tepee in the darkness. She felt a slow, tightening creep across her stomach. A smile pulled at the corners of her mouth. She knew what had brought her back from her sleep. The pain was a welcome signal that her child would be born this day.

She lay quietly for some time and felt the pain slowly start again. Her eyes now accustomed to the darkness, she could see her husband across the tepee and hear his snoring. She and Running Elk had been together for many seasons, and now, finally, they were to have a child. She squeezed her eyes tight shut and whispered, "O Great Mystery, hear my prayer this day. Give us a son to grow into a strong hunter and warrior for our band."

As she lay on her willow mat, Spotted Fawn envisioned her dead father. All the while she had carried this child, she had stayed to herself as much as she could and had revived the memories of the strongest and best people of her family of Dakota. These thoughts would help the little one within her to absorb their strength and goodness.

Spotted Fawn opened her eyes and clumsily moved from her bed of soft buffalo robes. She reached toward the foot of her bed. Finding her soft doeskin skirt, she pulled it on, then tugged her shirt over her head and pulled on her moccasins. She struggled to stand and quietly moved to the skin flap that served as the door of their lodge. Pulling it aside, she stepped out into the cool morning air, sniffing the air and feeling its chill. The frost would come soon, for it was the Moon When the Calves Grow Hair. With slow steps, Spotted Fawn left her lodge and started the walk to the women's lodge, where she would give birth. She changed her mind, however, turning instead toward the small river. She would walk awhile to help the child to drop faster. As she walked beside the river, she listened to the water whispering over the rocks as it dropped toward the Great River. In the early morning light, she could see the little birds darting along the edge of the water, looking for bugs.

She strolled slowly to enjoy as much of the morning as she could. Where the sun was awakening, the sky had turned pink. She breathed the scent of dry leaves. Spotted Fawn followed the path as it angled away from the water through a grassy area. Suddenly she saw a movement on the trail ahead. She hurried her pace as best she could, glimpsing flashes of white as the animal scurried up the trail ahead of her. Then it stopped and turned to look at her. She paused and returned the stare. Her breath stopped, for never had she seen such a beautiful animal. It was a white fox with intense, bright-blue eyes.

The animal had a look of such intelligence it held her a prisoner of its gaze. A swift pain shot through her body, and she staggered forward. Instantly the fox leaped from the path and disappeared into the weeds. As quickly as she could, Spotted Fawn made her way back to the village and walked directly to the women's lodge. Other women of the camp would come to help and encourage her when they realized her time had come. For now, she would wait and bear the increasing pains alone. Her blanket wrapped tightly around her, she lay back on a willow mat and visualized holding her little one in her arms.

The sun had moved low in the sky before the child was born. It was a boy, and to the surprise of all, the little one had eyes the color of the sky. Within an hour, he followed his mother's movements with his eyes. She watched her son carefully and knew the Great Mystery had shown her his namesake in the early morning light. She named him White Fox.

White Fox came into the world in a small village where two rivers come together. These two rivers are the Clearwater and the Mississippi in the state of Minnesota. The white men later would call this area the Big Woods. The Dakota people called it Suland.

PART ONE

CHAPTER ONE

1847

It was during the Moon of the Snowblind. There was much activity around the camp. Running Elk sat close to the fire inside their lodge. He was replacing the point on his spear with a new one that he had chipped from glossy, black stone. He had gotten this one especially sharp. Running Elk looked forward to the trip to the small frozen lakes to spear muskrats and beaver through the ice. They would hunt the animals for their furs, but the meat would taste good too after the long winter season. Soon the women, children, and old men also would leave the campsite. They would move to the sugar camp, for the maple sap soon would be flowing.

On the other side of the fire, Spotted Fawn and Walking Woman were busy carving small troughs of basswood and basins of birch bark. The women could see White Fox behind his bed searching through his belongings. "What are you looking for, White Fox?" his mother asked.

"My blunt arrows," he replied. "Little Wolf has found a place where the chipmunks have awakened from their winter sleep. We are going to hunt them today." The boy's arrows would not stick in the tree but would bounce back to the ground to be reused.

"Are you ready?" Little Wolf called from outside the lodge.

"You boys be careful today," Walking Woman admonished as White Fox pushed aside the hide door and went out to join her son. No move was made to stop the two young hunters, however. The mothers knew that this game gave the boys good practice at hunting so that they would be good providers for their families someday.

As the two boys walked to the edge of the camp, Little Wolf turned to White Fox and said, "Your father and mother always make your things special in some way. I think it is because you are their only child."

White Fox realized his friend's word were true. His clothes were always trimmed with more quills and beads. His mother worked the hides of the doe until they were the softest and whitest. "I once asked my mother why I have no brothers or sisters," White Fox said. "She said that the Great Mystery had not sent any others." A grin flashed across his small, tanned face. "I think the Great Mystery picked you to be my friend because you have so many brothers and sisters to share with me."

Little Wolf smiled. "I think that is so," he replied.

Little Wolf came from a big family. His father, Long Legs, had a first wife, who had died many seasons ago. She was a sister to his second wife, Walking Woman. Long Legs had two tepees for his families. The one held the children from the first wife, and the second held his family with Walking Woman. Little Wolf was the eldest of the second family. White Fox was always welcome in this big family, just as Little Wolf was always welcome in his.

The boys continued on into the woods where the other little boys were gathering. Snake in the Hand always made the chipmunk call out of an oat straw. He could use it the best to lure the little creatures out of hiding. There were eight boys in all. There had been nine, but Moon Boy had gone to live in the Spirit World during the Moon of the Popping Trees. He had gotten very sick, and his old grandmother had thought she could cure him with her own herbs and medicines. She had not called the medicine woman, Straight Talker, until it was too late.

As the young hunters walked through the woods, they grew very quiet. They did not want the chipmunks to hear them. Finally they came to a place marked by many telltale little tracks. Snake in the Hand sat upon a log while the other boys each claimed a tree. They hoped every chipmunk would be foolish enough to climb their tree. Soon the boys were ready, and they stood motionless as Snake in the Hand began his chipping noises. He patiently continued to chip until the first chipmunk came scurrying across the snow. Then came another and another. Soon the little creatures were emerging from everywhere.

When it seemed that no more would come, Snake in the Hand gave the signal. The boys started howling loudly, sending the terrified chipmunks scurrying up the trees. Then they began shooting. Soon there were piles of little animals on the ground, and the trees were empty. Only a few brave chipmunks had made the big jump to the ground and escaped. The counting began. White Fox looked at his pile and was disappointed. He counted only five little bodies.

"I have eight of them," said Little Wolf.

"I have nine," answered Brave Boy.

"I have nine too," said Standing Calf.

White Fox did not say how many he had. There would be another time to win. He replaced his arrows in his quiver and turned back to the other boys when he heard a frightened scream. From beneath the roots of a fallen elm tree appeared a large black bear. A cub came out from behind her. Suddenly she emitted an earsplitting roar and lunged for the boys closest to her. White Fox watched, horrified, as the bear's claws ripped into the clothing of a boy's back. He turned to run, thoughts racing. He was far enough from the bear to make a run for the trail back to the village. Even so, he knew there would be no chance for any boys the bear caught.

It seemed to take forever to reach the camp, but finally he saw the smoke above the trees. He did not slow. As he entered the camp, he saw Long Legs, Little Wolf's father. "Uncle, Uncle, we need your help!" he cried. "A bear—a bear came from her den! I think she caught one of the boys!"

Long Legs shouted the alarm. From almost every lodge, a warrior emerged, weapon in hand. "The little boys have been attacked by a bear!" he yelled. "Hurry!" Most of the warriors kept their best pony close to their lodge. They mounted quickly. Long Legs reached down, grabbed White Fox, and sat the boy in front of himself. "Show me the way," Long Legs said urgently as the pony leaped into a gallop.

They rode out of camp on the trail that crossed the small river and led to the north. As they rode, they saw two boys running up the trail. Not far behind came three more. Little Wolf came next. "I think the bear got Standing Calf," Little Wolf yelled.

Long Legs kicked his pony again as White Fox pointed the way. They rode through the woods only a short distance when they saw the bear ahead. It was stomping and tossing its head from side to side. White Fox saw it pick up something and throw it into the air. Long Legs slowed his pony and gently lowered White Fox to the ground. "Go hide yourself, White Fox. We will take care of the bear."

As the men approached, the horses began to balk and dance. The warriors slid from their backs and moved cautiously toward the bear. She stood up on her hind legs and waddled toward the men. Long Legs was the first to pull his bowstring back and let the arrow fly. The bear grunted as the arrow buried itself deep in its chest. She continued moving toward the men until a flurry of arrows shot through the air, hitting their mark. The bear clawed the air and slowly fell to the ground, her cub scurrying into the woods.

The men walked toward the fallen elm tree. They leaned over something lying on the ground, and then White Fox heard a horrible cry come from one of the men. It was Standing Calf's father. He knew then that his childhood friend was gone. The men rode back to the village in silence. As they entered the camp, White Fox heard the wailing begin. The women came forward to see which of the fathers carried the bundle.

White Fox jumped from Long Legs' pony and ran to his

lodge. His mother was standing near and grabbed him. "All the boys are home now except Standing Calf. Is he the one?"

White Fox nodded. "He is the one." The boy pulled the hide flap aside and pushed his way into the tepee. Little Warrior wriggled in beside him. The boy sat by the fire and pulled his dog close. As he looked into the fire, he felt new tears running down his cheeks. The flap opened, and Little Wolf entered the lodge. "Your mother told me you were here." He pressed himself tight on the other side of Little Warrior. The dog's body was warm between them.

White Fox spoke softly. "Do you think they are together now?"

"Who?"

"Standing Calf and Moon Boy. Do you think they are together in the spirit world?"

"I think so," Little Wolf answered. "My mother told me we need not worry about the dead. Their ancestors meet them in the spirit world. She said we will live the perfect life there."

"I am happy here," choked White Fox. "I am not ready to go on to a new life."

"Neither am I," replied Little Wolf.

The two boys sat in the darkness of the lodge, the dog close between them, listening to the wailing of the women. They knew that Standing Calf's mother would probably cut herself and the other women would blacken their faces. Tomorrow the father and uncles would build a scaffold at the burial ground. They would wrap Standing Calf's body in a buffalo robe, together with his favorite things. He would need his bow, quiver of arrows, and his medicine bundle for the next life. Moon Boy's wrapped body was still on a scaffold too. At a later time, the bones would be removed and buried in the ground.

The boys did not fully understand these ceremonies and didn't want to ponder them. After a few minutes of silence, White Fox whispered, "I wish we could tell Standing Calf that we will miss him."

CHAPTER TWO

A week had passed since the accident, and the men left on the spring fur hunt. The women, children, and old men were preparing for the move to the sugar camp. White Fox and Spotted Fawn had made a skid for the hollowed-out log that would hold supplies and, later, sap. Spotted Fawn carried the large iron kettle from the tepee and packed it in the middle of the canoe. Around it she fitted the birch bark basins and the basswood troughs. White Fox hitched up his pony to pull the load.

The boy and his mother walked side by side. When the sun began to drop low in the sky, they reached their destination, a little frozen lake. The Dakota called this water Silver Lake because of the way the waves shimmered in the summer sunlight. It was a beautiful evening as they entered the maple woods. Soon they saw their sugar lodge. The people gathered around it and began an excited, happy chatter. The fun of the sugar camp would help them to put their grieving behind them.

Spotted Fawn disappeared into the lodge. She and Walking Woman began removing the leaves and debris that had blown in since the last sugar season. White Fox unhooked his pony and tied him to a tree until the animal became familiar with the new location. He unloaded the canoe. He and his mother and a few others would move into the bark lodge. The rest had brought their skin lodges and were busy setting them up. The people would have their new little village made in a matter of minutes.

White Fox and Little Wolf went off to gather wood for the evening fire. They were picking up dry sticks from around a fallen maple tree when a movement caught their eye. From out of the woods appeared a very old man with a huge bundle of red willow on his back. They could tell by his clothing that he was a Dakota. He looked stunned to see the boys. Then he approached them. "Greeting, little boys. Have I wandered close to your village?"

"We are not far from our sugar camp," replied Little Wolf. "We just made our camp near the Silver Lake."

The old man dropped his load to the ground. He had very white hair that hung loosely around his deeply wrinkled face. He studied the two boys intently. "You have the perfect weather for sugar making. I have traveled far to gather the red willow here."

"If you have a long way to carry your load, come to our camp tonight," Little Wolf invited. "Our mothers will start the evening fires as soon as we return with the wood."

"We have rabbit for the stew pot tonight," White Fox added.

The old man smiled. He sniffed the air as though he could already smell the rabbit stew. "I will come with you," he replied. He hoisted his load to his back, and the boys each bore as much firewood as they could.

Spotted Fawn looked up in surprise when she saw the old man enter the camp with the boys. "Mother," White Fox called, "I have brought someone to share our fire tonight."

The whole camp gathered around the old man to look him over. He nodded and smiled at them. "I am from a Sisseton village, in the Lac Qui Parle area. I have traveled far into Suland to find the special willow that I smoked in my pipe as a young man. The farther I came into the woods, the more I wanted to see the place where I lived in my younger days. I have been gone from home a long time, and I am sure my family thinks I will not return. But now I have collected my red willow, and I am ready to make the long walk home."

Spotted Fawn stepped closer to the old man. "Come and sit by the sugar lodge, and we will start a fire." A visitor was reason for a feast. Two of the old men entered the camp, pulling a doe between them. The women exclaimed happily and hurried after them. Soon they were busy skinning the doe and cutting the meat into pieces for roasting over the fire. The boys went in search of green sticks for this purpose. It wasn't long before everyone in the camp was gathered close around the fire. Each held a green stick with a chunk of venison roasting on the end.

Spotted Fawn broke the silence. "Tell us your name, elder, so we may know whom we are entertaining this night."

"My name is Cloud Man, and I find it a great privilege to enjoy your campfire and fine food." The flickering firelight emphasized the lines in his face as he smiled.

Spotted Fawn continued the introductions. "I too am of the Sisseton band from the Lac Qui Parle area, but I do not remember you. But I have been gone from that area for twelve winter seasons. My father was Dancing Bird. We lived at Fire Man's village."

The old man's face lit up. "I know who your father was. He was killed during a buffalo hunt. Our two villages hunted together that time." He paused. "That was many seasons ago."

Spotted Fawn grew exuberant and she nodded excitedly. "I was a young maiden when my father died. I have not had any news of my family for many winter seasons. Do you know anything of my brother? His name is Panther Man."

The old man furrowed his brow as he searched his memories. "I think this young man went off to the Canada country. I am not sure that he ever returned."

By this time, the old man had finished his meal and was visibly tired. His shoulder stooped and the skin on his face seemed to hang more. Even his eyelids were dropping. There would be more time for questions another day. Spotted Fawn smiled warmly at the elder. "Come, Cloud Man. I will make a bed for you inside the sugar lodge."

The people began drifting back to their skin lodges in the darkness. Soon the camp grew quiet. The morning dawned clear, sunny and warm. The sap was sure to flow this day. As White Fox stepped out into the morning light, he could see the women walking into the woods. Each had an axe in hand. They would strike a single blow to the tree trunk to see if sap would appear. Some of the trees would be ready to give up their sap; others would not. If a tree was ready to yield sap, the women would drive a hardwood chip deep into the axe cut. The sap would start to drip from the corner of this chip. The birch bark basins were placed underneath to catch the sap. The smallest boys would watch over these basins and use their bows and arrows to discourage birds and chipmunks from drinking from them. Every person had a job.

Spotted Fawn also would tap some birch and ash trees. The sap from these trees would give a bitter, dark-colored sugar that she would use for medicinal purposes. The box-elder sap would yield a beautiful white sugar. But none would produce as much sap as the sugar maple.

White Fox arose early to start his fire. He and his mother placed the large iron kettle over the fire and filled it with sap. It was the boy's job to keep the fire burning hot all day. Once they had good fires going, the children could visit and taste from everyone's kettles.

After many hours of cooking, the boiling sounds changed to a hiss. This sound told White Fox that the sap had changed to syrup and could be hardened in the snow patches that still remained around the camp. Spotted Fawn would take over and finish the sugar. This day, she would leave out much of the hardened syrup and watch it disappear as the children wandered by. Everyone in camp ate their fill that day, including the old man who had arrived the day before.

On the third morning, as White Fox stepped from the sugar lodge, he saw the old man walking into the woods, the willow bundle on his back. Spotted Fawn was watching him leave. She had talked with the old man many times over the past days to hear news of her home area. "Why is the old man leaving, Mother?" White Fox asked.

"He said he felt strong and happy this morning and must make his long journey home and back to his family," she answered. "I think he was glad he found our sugar camp. He left this for you and one for Little Wolf too."

Spotted Fawn handed her son a flute carved from bone. White Fox turned it over in his hand, joyfully inspecting it. He put the end in his mouth and blew gently, making the flute squeak. His mother smiled. "You will have time to practice today as you watch the sap boil."

This day, Spotted Fawn grew earnest about storing away the sugar. She used the birch molds to form the boiled sap into cakes of various shapes. She also put it into canes and hollow reeds, as well as the bills from ducks and geese. She pulverized some of the sugar and packed it into rawhide cases.

After three weeks of sugar making, the trees gradually quit giving their sap. Everyone was glad to go back home.

It was the Moon When the Cherries are Ripe, and White Fox and Little Wolf sat at the edge of the Great River, watching the water move by. Finally Little Wolf broke the silence. "My mother went to the women's lodge this morning. The little one will be born this day." He was thoughtful and quiet as he gazed at the water. "Let's walk to the women's lodge," he said after a time. The two boys walked to the lodge and settled themselves under an elm tree not far away. They sat quietly, listening, but no sounds came from inside.

"Have you ever heard the scream of childbirth?" Little Wolf asked. "It must cause a lot of pain to get the child out." White Fox shook his head in answer and sat quietly listening. Little Wolf continued. "I wish all of us could share the pain, so Mother would not have to feel it all."

Just then, Straight Talker, the medicine woman, emerged from the lodge and saw the boys. "Why are you here, little boys?" she asked sternly. "You are not to come so close to the women's lodge."

"We are anxious to know when the little one is born," Little Wolf answered.

"Why do the women suffer so much?" White Fox blurted out.

Straight Talker looked at them hard. "Smokey Day has a story he tells. Why don't you boys go to hear it today instead of bothering me?"

The boys had never seen Straight Talker look so stern, and they quickly trotted off to the lodge of the storyteller. They found him sitting outside his lodge whittling a piece of wood. Little Wolf spoke first. "Please tell us the story of why the women have to suffer to bear children."

"Sit boys. I will tell you the story," Smokey Day said, laying aside the wood and knife. "When the Great Mystery made Mother Earth, he made some of her land very hilly and some of the land flat. Some was hot, some was cold. He made land with the different seasons, like the place where we live. When he was done, he made many animals to live on the land.

"Then the Great Mystery made the people to live on this land. He divided the land and put one man and one woman on each piece. He showed them everything they would need to know. Then he gave them one rule that they must follow. They were required to stay on their own piece of land, and he showed them the borders so they would not get confused."

Smokey Day looked at his intent little listeners and continued. "After several years had gone by, the Great Mystery went to look for the people. He searched in the places where he had left them, but he found no one. Then he began to find them scattered in the forbidden places. The Great Mystery gathered the people together. He showed them how disappointed in them he was. 'Why did you disobey me?' he asked them. 'I provided everything for you on the land I chose for you.'

"One of the men spoke up. 'After we had lived on the land for some time, I went to the border you had given us. The land on the other side looked better to me. I took my mate and moved to the other side. After a time, we realized that we had made a mistake. But when we tried to return, we found we could not.'

"The Great Mystery could see the others nodding in agreement. They had all made the same mistake."

Smokey Day looked carefully at the two boys and saw that he still had their full attention. "Now the Great Mystery said to the people, 'I must punish you for not obeying my rules. From this day forward, the woman will suffer great pain when she brings forth little children. From this day forward, the man will find it difficult to provide for his family. You will not always find the fruits of Mother Earth in abundance, and you will suffer greatly when you cannot provide for your family.'"

Now Smokey Day looked at the two boys and asked, "Little Wolf, are you concerned for your mother?"

"I do not like the day when a new child is born, but all turns to joy when the child arrives."

Just then, Long Legs walked by, and the boys jumped to their feet. "Thank you for the story, Uncle," called the boys as they ran to catch up with Long Legs. He was walking toward the women's lodge.

Outside the lodge, Straight Talker stood holding a bundle. She handed it to Long Legs, and they heard her say, "Here is your new son. May he be a mighty warrior like his father."

Long Legs took the bundle in his arms and gently drew back the fur wrapping. A smile lit his face. He bent down so Little Wolf and White Fox could see the tiny face. It was wrinkled like a dry grape and the color of a red berry. The baby grunted softly and made a funny face. "He is another fine brother for you, Little Wolf," Long Legs said, "and one for you to share, White Fox. Now go to tell your brothers. You know what you boys must do."

As was the custom, all the brothers of the new boy must immerse themselves in water this day. As they ran past the family lodges, Little Wolf shouted, "We have a new brother!"

CHAPTER THREE

In the dim light of the skin lodge, the boy could see something at the foot of his sleep mat. He looked closer and saw it was a new, larger bow and a quiver full of arrows. He pulled one of the arrows from the quiver and felt the tip. It had a sharp point of stone. This was his father's way of telling him that now that he was seven winter seasons old, it was time for him to bring home bigger game. White Fox tightly clutched the bow and quiver to his chest and made his way out of the tepee.

The quiver had a rawhide strap, and he slung it over his shoulder and took off into the woods. White Fox moved down the trail to the sugar tree, but his friend Little Wolf was not there yet. The boy leaned his back against the tree and slid to the ground to wait. He looked carefully at the bow and saw that his father had carved a tiny fox on one end. White Fox smiled at the ownership mark. It was *his* bow.

Next he pulled the quiver off his shoulder and studied it. This was the work of his mother. The case was made of stiff rawhide and was trimmed with dyed porcupine quills. She had fashioned the sun, in yellow, with rays coming from it. Under the sun, she had stitched geometric designs of many colors.

A twig snapped and White Fox ripped his gaze from the weapon to the brown body barreling toward him. He was not fast enough, and the body collided into his. The two rolled across the path and into the base of another tree. White Fox was the first to regain his senses.

"I'll get you next time, Little Wolf!" White Fox's voice was harsh and low, but his grin contradicted the rough tone.

Little Wolf waved him off and laughed. "Yeah. You'll get me *someday*, but when that day will be, no one knows. It hasn't happened yet, *Slow* Fox."

The two boys were still grinning at each other like fools as they discussed where to hunt. White Fox and Little Wolf decided to go hunting and went deep into the woods, into an area that was new to them. Hunting was good. They got a rabbit and two squirrels in little time. They came upon a meadow. Little Wolf hesitated at the edge of the clearing, his eyes scanning the tall grasses. Slowly he stepped back behind a tree, touching White Fox's arm so he would do the same. "Look to the other side of the meadow," Little Wolf whispered.

White Fox looked far across the meadow and could see a man with a stick. He seemed to be moving some cut grasses. The boys could see two wood lodges on the far side of the meadow. They watched the man until he walked away toward the buildings. White Fox leaned toward Little Wolf. "Let's stay in the trees but go around to the far side of the meadow. I want to get closer."

When they reached the far side of the meadow, they saw two lodges that were made of logs stacked one on top of another. One had a smoke hole made of rocks. The boys stayed in the shadows of the trees and watched as the man disappeared into the lodge with the smoke hole. Soon a small girl came out and sat down. She had long hair the color of fall grasses. "Let's move as close as we can," whispered White Fox. "She is holding something on her lap, and I want to see what it is."

Just then a young boy came from the lodge. His hair was the same color as the girl's but was cut shorter. They watched as the boy went over to the girl and grabbed the item on her lap. As the little boy yanked it into the air, they could see that it was a doll. The boy ran off with the toy, and the girl chased after him, screeching angrily. The two Indian boys looked at each other and grinned.

Suddenly a woman came from the lodge. She shouted at the boy and started to chase him with a stick that had stiff grasses tied to the end. White Fox put his hand over his mouth so he wouldn't laugh out loud. Soon the girl had her doll, and all three of them disappeared into the lodge. "Let's sneak through the tall grass and look into the other lodge to see what is in it," suggested White Fox.

The boys moved stealthily through the tall grass. They could smell food and knew the family must be eating a meal. They moved to the far side of the second lodge so they would not be seen. Entering the large lodge through the window, the boys saw it had been built with partial walls enclosing small areas. They peered into the first small, enclosed area, and there stood a small pony.

"This is a strange-looking pony," said Little Wolf.

"Look at the long ears," said White Fox.

Little Wolf touched the animal's strange tail. "He has a tuft of hair on the end of it."

They were even more curious to see what was in the next stall. As they peered inside, they saw another animal that looked like a small buffalo, but with no hump. It had large, dark eyes. As the boys walked around it, they noticed a large sack to hold the milk for the young, much larger than that of a mother buffalo. They also saw another enclosure with a latched door. Inside they saw many large birds. The birds stood quietly looking at the boys, but soon began scratching the ground and making clucking noises.

"I think those boxes must be nests. See the grass sticking out from under the birds?" White Fox whispered.

Litte Wolf nodded in agreement. "I think there are eggs under those birds."

The boys were engrossed with the birds when a sudden, terrible roar sounded behind them. The boys spun around and stood face-to-face with a big man with black hair on his face. He held a stick over his head with metal spears on the end.

"Run!" shouted Little Wolf. One boy went on either side of the man, and they ran for the doorway. The man turned quickly and lunged at White Fox. He saw the sunlight glint on the sharp ends on the stick and knew his life was about to end. The sharp points snagged his buckskin jacket, and the boy felt his bow slip off his shoulder. Fear made his legs grow stronger, and both boys ran faster than they ever thought they could. Even after they knew the man was not behind them anymore, they kept running and did not stop until they were deep in the woods.

They both dropped to the ground, sucking in great gulps of air. They rolled to their backs and lay still until their breathing slowed. "I think we have just had our first meeting with the white man," said Little Wolf breathlessly.

"I hope it will be my last," gasped White Fox. "I lost my bow and arrows. But I am not going back to look for them."

"We have lost our game too," Little Wolf said, getting to his feet and brushing himself off. "We had better start back to the village. We have a long way to go."

Several times that summer, the boys sneaked close to the farm and lay in the weeds to watch the white family. Once they saw the big man playing with the children. With the black hair on his face, he looked frightening to the boys, but he laughed loudly when he played with his family.

"Why do you think the man got so angry at us?" White Fox wondered aloud to Little Wolf. "We did not hurt his animals." Little Wolf just shook his head slowly.

One day near the end of summer, White Fox saw the little white boy playing with his bow and arrows. He felt sad as he thought of the small fox his father had carved on the bow. But he knew he could not try to get it back. He had told his father about the incident the day he came home without his bow. His father had forbidden the boys to go back to find it. He would obey.

Early the next morning, White Fox awoke to see his mother

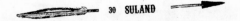

moving around the tepee. He saw that she was taking out her food-gathering bags. White Fox scrambled from his bed. "I will go with you to help with the gathering, if you wait for me."

Spotted Fawn's smile gave him his answer, and he hurried to put on his leggings, breechcloth, shirt, and moccasins. His mother took two of the rawhide bags for herself and handed the third to White Fox to hang over his shoulder. She pulled open the hide door flap, and they stepped out into the cool morning air. They left the village following the trail along the small river to the west. As they walked, White Fox asked, "Why do you prefer the turnips from the dry meadows when we can find them in the deep woods?"

Spotted Fawn slowed her pace. "The turnip grows slower on the dry ground, and the quality is better." White Fox nodded and they walked on in silence, enjoying the fine morning.Finally they came to a low area along the river. "There are onion here," Spotted Fawn said. White Fox followed her as she took off her moccasins and waded into the water.

She peered down into the water and then reached in, holding up her first onion. White Fox moved close. "Let me see what the top of the plant looks like." He studied it closely and then waded away to search for others like it. He soon found some and reached into the water to pluck them himself. "We will harvest only enough onions to fill the one bag," Spotted Fawn said.

When they had enough, they sat down under an oak tree to admire the size of their onions and to let the sun dry their feet. "I know of a meadow not far from here where the turnips grow," Spotted Fawn said. "We will go there next." The mother studied her son's face. He had grown since the warm season had come. She would have to enjoy his company now, for he would not want to come with her much longer.

"These lessons of gathering will serve you well someday," she told him. "You will go away on long hunts and even on the war-path, and you will need to live off the land." These things she said made her feel sad. She did not like to think of her little boy going off to war or traveling far to find the meat they needed.

They walked some distance before they reached the meadow

where the turnips grew. White Fox knew what the turnip plant looked like and soon was using a small antler to dig them up, filling the second bag. "Come over here," called his mother. "I have something to show you." She was on her knees, and he knelt beside her.

"See this mound of dirt?" she asked. White Fox nodded. She took a sharp stick from her bag and carefully started to dig the dirt away. He saw that she was uncovering the little storage rooms of a field mouse. "See the special storage pockets and see the good-tasting brown beans she has stored away?" White Fox recognized the beans from the soups his mother made, especially in the cold moons.

Spotted Fawn had her head bent low to the ground as she worked, and White Fox could hear her say softly, "You have been a hard-working little mouse. Mother Earth will give you enough good weather to refill your storage rooms. Thank you, little mouse." White Fox watched his mother as she carefully put the grasses back into place and covered the little mound with dirt. He knew that the other women did not put such effort into restoring the mouse's storage areas. His mother had a gentle heart, and he saw this in almost everything she did.

As they put the beans and turnips into the bags, his mother said, "We will leave some room for the root of the wild lily. I need it for my special medicine, and it is good to eat too." Spotted Fawn stopped suddenly and brought her head up, listening. White Fox stilled, watching his mother. There were voices.

They peeked through the tall grasses and saw two people coming from the woods. As they emerged from the shade of the trees, White Fox could see it was the white man with the hair on his face and his son. "Those are the white people Little Wolf and I saw before," White Fox whispered.

Spotted Fawn shook her head urgently to silence him. They crouched in the grass and watched. The man was carrying the long stick that White Fox's father had told him about. It shot balls out of the end and killed the animals. White Fox could see that the little boy carried his bow and quiver of arrows. "Mother, he has my bow and quiver," White Fox whispered. Again she shook her head for him to remain silent.

As they watched, the two walked along the edge of the meadow and disappeared into the woods. Spotted Fawn waited a little while, then stood up and pulled White Fox back into the trees. She began walking quickly back toward the village. "Mother, I thought we were going to search for the wild lily on the way home," White Fox queried.

"I am finished for today," she replied. "We will do that another day." White Fox could see that his mother was upset. That evening, she told Running Elk about seeing the white man. He got very quiet. There wasn't any storytelling around the campfire that night.

CHAPTER FOUR

1848

The Moon When the Cherries Turn Black had arrived, and the camp was bustling with excitement. Some of the hunters had gone to hunt buffalo far out on the prairie to the west. The rest of the Dakota people were preparing for the late-summer wild-rice harvest. People were preparing to leave for the rice lake, dismantling their tepees and loading their canoes. He lifted his head and saw his mother gathering her things. Spotted Fawn saw the boy looking at her and said, "You had better get up and out. The tepee is coming down soon." She paused and smiled. "I could wrap you up in the skins. Then you could sleep all the way to the rice lake." She laughed and went outside.

Soon they were ready to leave. White Fox climbed onto the skins piled in the canoe. His parents sat one on either end to do the paddling. It took a half-day of paddling up the Clearwater River to reach the rice lake. By the time the sun had reached its highest point, they were already paddling into the little lake. Already some of the men had chosen a campsite. Always they were careful to pick a place where their enemy, the Chippewa, could not creep too close without being detected.

Running Elk chose the place where he wanted their tepee to stand. As Spotted Fawn and White Fox unloaded the canoe, he went off into the woods to cut the poles. Looking up from his work, White Fox saw Little Wolf wave from one of the canoes that had just come around the bend in the river. Something jumped from the canoe and hit the water with a splash. A small head came to the surface, and White Fox realized it was Little Warrior. The little dog paddled eagerly to shore.

When Little Warrior's feet touched the sand, he ran directly to White Fox and ran circles around the boy as fast as his little legs would carry him. "Stop, Little Warrior." White Fox laughed. "You are making me dizzy."

Little Wolf approached them, laughing. "When we were ready to leave, Little Warrior was standing at the edge of the river howling and crying so sadly. Even Mother, who is not a dog lover, felt sorry for him."

That evening, the people built their fires by the lakeshore. The sun had gone down in a vibrant display of colors, leaving the fires to reflect on the calm water. The water birds had finally quieted down, accepting the people as their new neighbors. Only the black loon still wailed its mournful call. White Fox slept soundly that night and did not awaken until he heard Little Wolf call his name from outside the tepee.

"I talked to your parents as they were leaving," explained Little Wolf. "Your mother said to tell you that they would be tying the tops of the rice in bunches today. Do not expect them back until the sun is low in the sky." White Fox nodded. The boys looked out over the lake. The tops of the long rice grass wiggled as the canoes passed through. The boys knew that once the rice was tied it would be left to dry for a few days before the gathering would begin.

"Do you remember the burial mounds of the ancient ones that we found last ricing season?" asked Little Wolf.

"I remember. They were up on the hilltops overlooking the big lake," White Fox answered.

"Let's see if we can find them again," Little Wolf suggested.

White Fox thought about it for a while and then said, "I think that would be fun; we could make an adventure out of it."

The boys followed a trail that led away from the rice lake and gradually climbed uphill. Soon they came out of the trees and brush and saw the lake spread out below them. They stood quietly for a while, enjoying the scene. Then they continued on. The boys had gone quite some distance when Little Wolf stepped off the trail. White Fox followed. They continued until they came through the woods and into a clearing. Again they were overlooking the lake but now from a higher point. There before them lay the burial mounds.

The boys wandered slowly and silently around the mounds. Little Wolf stopped and looked out over the lake. "I understand why the ancient ones picked this place to bury their dead. It is beautiful and peaceful," he said. A light breeze came off the lake and touched their faces. They could hear it rustle the leaves as it passed into the woods.

"Do you know who the ancient ones are? Are they our ancestors?" White Fox asked.

"My father said that they were a tribe that lived here long before our people moved to this area."

The boys walked around each mound, thinking deeply and touching the mounds as though trying to get some feeling from the ancient ones buried beneath the ground. Little Wolf climbed up the side of one of the mounds. White Fox followed, and when they reached the top, they lay down, looking up to the sky. "I hope the ancient ones will not get angry at us," White Fox whispered.

"They will not mind as long as we do not disturb the ground," Little Wolf said with self-assurance.

The boys lay quietly, listening to the birds and the gentle breeze that swept the hillside now and then. The tall grasses around them swayed and swished softly as the breeze moved by.

Little Wolf broke the silence. "My sister Robin's Nest is being courted by Bald Eagle. At our home village, he has been coming in the evenings and playing the flute outside our lodge." Little Wolf looked thoughtful. "I think we should watch them closely during this rice harvest."

White Fox giggled. The boys knew that the wild-rice harvest was a favorite time for courtship among the young people. The little boys had the fun of watching, following, and teasing until they were chased away. During the next two days, while the rice was left to dry, the people spent time storytelling, running races, and playing games. The second evening, Sugar Boy ran through the camp shouting, "Canoe races! Canoe races!"

White Fox and Little Wolf were playing a pebble game and looked up the see the young men in their canoes out beyond the rice grass. There were ten canoes in all. "I should have guessed the races would be tonight," said Little Wolf. "I saw Robin's Nest making a long-grass necklace earlier."

"Look, Smokey Day is paddling out to the open water," said White Fox. "He will be the judge at the finish."

All the people of the camp gathered at the lakeshore to watch the contest. The boys heard Smokey Day call to the young men that he was ready. The first two contestants paddled forward. Someone gave the shout to start, and the race was on. "I think the one is Burnt by Fire, and it looks like the other is Grey Bird," White Fox said excitedly before letting out a great whoop in Burnt by Fire's support.

As the crowd recognized the young men, the cheers went up for their favorite. Little Wolf's brother Burnt by Fire was a favorite with many of the people, for he had a happy and helpful spirit. The boys could hear many calling out Burnt by Fire's name. They joined the cheering as Burnt by Fire pulled out in front and kept his lead. As he shot past Smokey Day, they could hear the storyteller shout out his name as the winner.

Burnt by Fire slowly paddled back to the middle of the lake to race again. The loser came to shore. White Fox elbowed Little Wolf and pointed at the young maidens. They had gathered together, and each held a necklace trimmed with wildflowers for the winner. White Fox grimaced. "I would not want all those gig-gling girls hanging necklaces around my neck."

Little Wolf laughed. "Neither would I."

"I think Burnt by Fire is racing again," said White Fox. "I can't tell who the other one is."

The canoes took off, both young men paddling powerfully for the start. Little Wolf burst out, "The other is Crooked Arrow." Both the little boys started jumping up and down shouting, "Burnt by Fire! Burnt by Fire!"

The two canoes were so nearly even as they crossed the water that the crowd went wild. White Fox and Little Wolf screamed and jumped. When Smokey Day shouted, "Burnt by Fire!" the crowd cheered wildly.

Suddenly a hush spread over the crowd. The little boys strained to see. Everyone was watching the two out on the lake. Burnt by Fire was paddling back to the middle of the lake, unaware that Crooked Arrow had turned his canoe and was following him. When Crooked Arrow got close enough, he reached out with his paddle and gave the other's canoe a hard shove. The canoe flipped over, and Burnt by Fire disappeared into the lake.

A trickle of laughter spread through the crowd. This sort of dunking was not uncommon during these contests. Burnt by Fire's head came up out of the water silently, his gaze trained on Crooked Arrow. He was swimming toward Crooked Arrow's canoe. Crooked Arrow had not turned away quickly enough, and he could see he was about to be dunked. He used his paddle to swat at the young man in the water. Burnt by Fire ducked as the paddle swung down.

A loud grumbling spread through the crowd. A dunking could be accepted as fun and part of the games, but this action by Crooked Arrow was not right. Crook Arrow brought the paddle down again. This time Burnt by Fire grabbed the paddle and yanked Crooked Arrow from the canoe. The crowd burst into cheers as Burnt by Fire swam back to his canoe and Crooked Arrow swam for his. The people grumbled and called out disap-provingly to Crooked Arrow as he came to shore and stalked past the crowd.

White Fox had not forgotten how Crooked Arrow had tormented him not so long ago, telling him that his father must be a white man. The first time had been the worst. It had been the first time White Fox realized he was different, but the realization had stuck with him ever since.

His curiosity had overpowered his fear, and he had cautiously crawled into the bush. He found Crooked Arrow sitting on the ground, smirking. "Little boy, do you know why you have eyes the color of the sky?"

White Fox had answered slowly. "Yes, I was named after the white fox my mother saw before I was born."

Crooked Arrow had sat silently studying the young White Fox. Finally he spoke. "Many of the white men have the sky-colored eyes like yours. I think you are the son of the white man." Crooked Arrow's smirk grew wider at the look on White Fox's face. The boy's bottom lip begin the tremble.

Suddenly White Fox jumped to his feet and exploded. "Why do you say such a thing? You know who my father is: Running Elk, a great Dakota warrior!"

Despite his arrogant words and youthful confidence, Crooked Arrow's words had hit their target. White Fox would never forget that he was not fully Indian as his friend. White Fox turned back to Little Wolf, "I wonder why Crooked Arrow has such a mean heart," he said.

Little Wolf spoke softly. "My father says that Crooked Arrow's father does not treat his son with honor. He mocks Crooked Arrow when he does not do well. He does not give him praise even when he does do well."

The boys were silent for a while. Then White Fox said quietly, "It is hard to imagine not being treated with respect by your own father."

The competition was coming to an end. Only two canoes remained on the lake. Burnt by Fire and Bald Eagle were the last two competitors. The canoes started out slowly, side by side. The young men put more and more power into their stokes. The faster they paddled, the louder the people cheered. They seemed evenly matched and stayed side by side right to the finish. At the last minute, Bald Eagle shot ahead of Burnt by Fire. The crowd heard Smokey Day shout Bald Eagle's name. Again the crowd went wild, cheering as the two canoes glided to shore.

White Fox leaned close to Little Wolf. "Burnt by Fire could have won. I know he is stronger than Bald Eagle."

"I think you are right. Why do you think he didn't try harder?"

As Bald Eagle stepped onto the sand, the young maidens ran to him. One after another, they stepped forward and put the pretty necklaces around his neck. The little boys watched, wrinkling their noses in distaste. "Look, Robin's Nest has waited until last," White Fox whispered.

As Robin's Nest put her necklace on Bald Eagle, the two little boys poked each other and giggled. She smiled shyly, and Bald Eagle returned her smile. Everyone watching knew something special was happening. The young girls giggled and carried on until the young couple walked away from the crowd.

The two little boys grinned at each other and jumped to their feet. Just then, Burnt by Fire walked by and grabbed the boys, each by one arm, and said, "Come with me. I was almost the winner tonight, so I will let you boys paddle me around the lake in my canoe." Neither of the boys argued.

The next week was spent gathering the rice. White Fox often went with his parents and watched as his father bent the tied bunches of rice grass into the canoe and lightly tapped the ends with sticks. The ripe rice dropped off the grass to rest in the bottom of the canoe. Sometimes his father let him help as Spotted Fawn paddled them through the rice.

Everyone was busy during this time of the harvest. This was a time of plenty for the people. Toward the end of the week came the harder work of drying and hulling the rice. If the rice needed extra drying, racks were built. A layer of grass was laid on the rack, and the rice was spread on top. A fire was built under the rack. Then it became a delicate job. If the fire was allowed to burn too high, the grasses would catch fire, and the rice would burn. Those tending the fires had to give the job their full attention.

When the drying process was done, the rice needed to be

hulled. The young men were expected to do this job. Each young maiden chose a young man and gave him a new pair of moccasins to use for the hulling. The rice was heated over a fire and then poured into shallow holes that had been dug ahead of time. Then the young men, wearing their new moccasins, jumped into the holes and danced on the rice until the hulls were loose. The men competed to see who could dance the fastest and thereby hull the most rice. When the hulls were loosened, the rice was scooped out of the holes onto hides. The young women held and shook the hides so that the wind would separate the chaff from the rice.

When all was done, each family decided how much of the rice they could conveniently carry back to the village and how much they would store there at the ricing lake. Each family chose a concealed spot, digging a cache and lining it carefully with bark and dry grass to keep the rice dry. These storage holes had to be disguised so that other passersby would not dig up the prized food stores. The rest of the rice was transported back to the village in rawhide bags and carrying cases.

The morning they traveled home, White Fox paddled in the front of the canoe, and his father steered and paddled in the back. Spotted Fawn sat in the middle on the pile of tepee hides and worked on a new pair on moccasins for Running Elk. He would be leaving on the autumn deer hunt in a few weeks. If the men decided to go far into the forest for the hunt, Spotted Fawn and White Fox would go along.

CHAPTER FIVE

1849

It was the Moon of the Grass Appearing, and the ice on the rivers had melted away from the shorelines. The creeks were swollen from the melting snows, making it easier for the big fish to get upstream in the little creeks and lay their eggs in the sandy bottoms. White Fox and Little Wolf were sitting with their heads together. "Feel how sharp I got the point," White Fox said, running his thumb over the point of the spear.

Little Wolf took the spear and ran his thumb back and forth over the stone point. "You have done a good job making this spear. Your stone points are more and more like the ones your father makes."

"I want to go back to that creek, the one with the birch tree tipped over it," White Fox said. "I think I can get one of those big fish with this new spear. Can you come with me today to look for the big fish?"

Little Wolf shook his head. "I cannot go today. My mother is making Robin's Nest's white doeskin dress, and I promised to watch over little Red Squirrel."

White Fox felt disappointment but said, "Maybe we can both go tomorrow."

Little Wolf nodded his agreement and got to his feet. "I must go back to our lodge. Have a good day looking for the big fish."

White Fox grasped his spear and soon was heading out of the camp on the trail following the Great River downstream. When he reached the place where the creek entered the Great River, he turned inland to follow the creek upstream. This creek came quite a long distance from the Silver Lake, and the hunters called it Silver Creek.

He had not followed the creek very far when he saw the birch tree leaning over the water. He laid the spear aside and grabbed a tree branch, pulling hard on it to test the fallen tree. It seemed stable enough. Yet it moved a bit as he crawled out over the fast-moving water. He gripped the branch with his knees but relaxed when the tree did not shift anymore.

A short distance downstream were some rocks, and White Fox fixed his gaze there. Soon he saw a nice fish wiggle its way over the rocks. He watched the sandy bottom below him and saw the shadow move past. *This will be easy,* he thought as he crawled off the branch to retrieve his spear. He worked his way back out again, clutching the spear in his one hand. He lay on his stomach with his legs wrapped around the tree. He balanced himself with his left hand and held the spear in his right.

Suddenly White Fox heard a splash downstream and turned his head in time to see a large fish wiggle over the rocks. His whole body tensed as he tightened his legs around the tree and brought back the arm holding the spear. When he saw the shadow slipping through the water below him, he jabbed the spear downward with all the strength he dared. He knew almost instantly that he had misjudged. He saw a swirl of scales as the point glanced off the fish.

Now White Fox was glad that he was alone. No one else had seen him miss. There was no hurry to get a fish, and he relaxed again, enjoying the warmth of the sun on his back. Suddenly the tree moved, and White Fox clutched tighter with his free arm. He tried to turn to see what had touched the tree, but as he did, the tree started to shake as if all of Mother Earth was moving. The shaking continued and intensified until White Fox dropped his spear and clung tight with both arms. Finally the whole tree tipped to the side, and the boy sprawled into the creek. The water wasn't deep, but it was so cold it took his breath away. He struggled to stand in the running water. Sand and water dripped from his face.

White Fox hurried to wipe the sand and water from his eyes. He could hear someone laughing. As his vision cleared, he could make out the image of a tall man. Fear knifed through him, but as he blinked his eyes to clear the image, he could see that the man wore clothing with Dakota designs. Relief flooded the boy's body, and he climbed out of the creek.

White Fox did not recognize the man. Slowly, his confusion faded as the realization dawned that this man must have shaken the tree, causing him to fall, and he began to get angry. But as the man continued to chuckle, White Fox looked down at himself and the corners of his mouth pulled into a smile.

"Are you all right?" the man asked. "I hope the big fish didn't bite you." White Fox just looked at him and tried to shake the sand and mud from his leggings. The man continued to speak. "I am on my way to a village upstream. Is that where you live?"

White Fox nodded.

"Take your spear and come with me. Leave the fishing for another day." The man spoke with such authority that White Fox didn't question him. He began to follow the man in the direction of the village. They walked in silence, the man leading his pony, until they could see the smoke of the village hanging over the trees in the distance. There the man stepped off the trail and sat on a large rock. He beckoned to White Fox. "Come stand by me."

White Fox moved close and stood in front of the stranger.

"You have shown me that you are a young man of good temperament. You did not show anger toward me for playing the trick on you at the creek. This good temperament will serve you well as you grow into manhood." The man looked deep into White Fox's eyes, and the boy returned his gaze. Then he continued, "I found something of value on the trail today, and I want to give it to you." He reached deep into a bag that White Fox recognized as a medicine bag and pulled out a feather.

"When I started my journey this morning, I saw a great owl watching me from a tree top. As I came near, it flew off and dropped this feather. It is not a big feather, but I know it is a gift of the great owl. I want you to have it, because I have seen the calm temperament of the great owl in you this day." He handed the feather to White Fox.

The boy took the offering and held it gently in his hand. It was a great honor for this man to give him a feather of the great owl. The boy reached inside his shirt and pulled out his small medicine bag. He looked at the man and said, "I will always treasure this feather and keep it in my medicine bag." White Fox looked even more intently at the man and added, "I want to know the name of the man who has given me this feather."

The man's face lit up in a smile. "My name is Panther Man. What is your name?"

"White Fox."

"Now that we know each other, let's be on our way," said Panther Man as he started walking again in his long strides. White Fox nearly had to trot to keep up. When they came to the edge of the camp, Panther Man slowed his pace until the boy caught up to him. "I have come to this village to find a special woman," Panther Man said. "Her name is Spotted Fawn, and her husband's name is Running Elk. Can you take me to their lodge?"

White Fox caught his breath. He nodded his head and took the lead, not wanting to show his surprise. He saw people stepping from their lodges or looking up from their work to watch them pass. He realized how strange they must look: a small, wet, muddy boy leading an unfamiliar Dakota brave through the camp.

White Fox's father was sitting outside the doorway of their lodge. As the two approached, Running Elk got to his feet. He looked intently at the stranger and suddenly uttered a joyful shout. "Panther Man, is that you following my son?"

The two men stepped close to each other and looked into each other's eyes. Then they clasped each other, and Panther Man said softly, "I have missed you, my sister's husband."

Spotted Fawn heard the commotion and stepped from the lodge. A look of surprise crossed her face when she saw the man. She cried out and ran to him, throwing her arms around him. After a long hug, she pushed him back to arm's length and said, "Brother, is this really you, or has your spirit come to visit?"

White Fox watched in surprise, for the Dakota women usually did not show so much emotion toward the men. He could tell that this meeting was bringing much joy to his parents.

"Come into our lodge, Panther Man," said Running Elk. "I see you have already met our son," he added.

Panther Man turned a surprised look on White Fox. "You did not say that you were Spotted Fawn's son."

"You did not ask," White Fox replied.

Panther Man smiled. "Your boy had a little accident and fell into the creek."

"Go to the river and wash off the mud," Spotted Fawn scolded. "We are going to eat soon."

White Fox ran to the river as fast as he could. He peeled off his shirt and leggings and hurriedly splashed the water on himself. The wind was cold on his wet skin. As he grabbed his clothes to dash back to the lodge, he came face-to-face with Little Wolf. "Who is the stranger?" Little Wolf asked.

"His name is Panther Man. He is my mother's brother, so I guess he is my uncle," White Fox answered breathlessly. "I must get back to the lodge fast, or I might miss out on some of the talk."

White Fox found his parents and uncle sitting around the fire inside their lodge. His uncle took a robe from White Fox's sleeping mat and wrapped it around the boy. "You must get warm. Here, take my bowl of soup. Your mother will get me another."

The lodge was warm and smelled good from the cooking and wood smoke. Everyone looked relaxed and happy. All was quiet as they ate, and White Fox could tell by the way she moved how excited his mother was. Finally Panther Man set aside his bowl and smiled at Spotted Fawn. She responded, "Tell me, brother, where have you been all this time, since I married and left our home village?"

Panther Man settled back and began to speak thoughtfully. "You remember that I had always had deep affection for Girl Who Walks with a Limp. During the warm season after you left, we were married. You remember the Black Robes at the Lac Qui Parle Mission? They were teaching our people their religion and encouraging them to farm the land, as the white man does. This meant giving up the roving life our people have always lived. I did not want that for myself or for my family, so we decided to leave. Our mother went with us, as did my best friend, Tall Bull, and two other families."

Panther Man had a faraway look in his eyes, as though he could see the story he was telling. "We wandered all through the warm season and ended up far to the north, in the Canada Country. We made our permanent winter camp along the Pembina River. We went into the first cold season with an abundant supply of meat and gathered foods. We lived a happy and plentiful life for eight winter seasons. We traveled in our hunts as far to the south as the James River and as far west as the Yellowstone. During this time, a son was born to us. We named him Sparrow Hawk. Your mother stayed well and strong during these times and enjoyed the life we lived."

Then Panther Man's face changed, and he seemed almost to age before their eyes. "The bad time came when Sparrow Hawk was five winter seasons old. We had become friendly with the French trappers in the area and did some trading with them. Three of these traders came to our village in the Moon of Making Fat. During the warm season, one of them had been sick, but he seemed to feel better after Girl Who Walks with a Limp made him some of her willow tea.

"It was just one sunrise after the men left our camp that our people started to get sick. It was the pock-face sickness, and none of our medicines seemed to help."

Panther Man looked at his sister with tears shining in his eyes. "They started to die, Spotted Fawn. First it was our mother and my son, Sparrow Hawk. Then Girl Who Walks with a Limp. I was with each one when they died. The Great Mystery did not grant my wish to take me too."

The tepee grew quiet with sorrow as the four sat gazing into the fire. Finally Spotted Fawn spoke softly. "I wish I had known you were suffering, my brother."

"There would have been nothing you could have done for me," Panther Man answered just as quietly. "I wandered the area alone for two seasons. Then I had a vision. The Great Mystery showed me that he was displeased with my wandering. So I returned home to Lac Qui Parle."

"How did you find us here?" Spotted Fawn asked.

"That is a story too, but a happy one," he said, smiling. "I was living at Standing Buffalo's village, near the Big Stone Lake, when a very old man walked out of the woods one day. He carried a large bundle of red willow and said he was on his way back to Lac Qui Parle."

White Fox looked at his mother and started to speak. She put her finger to her lips to silence him. Panther Man stopped talking and looked at Spotted Fawn. "It was you he spoke about, and when he mentioned your name, I felt joy in my heart for the first time in a long time. When I told him my name, he remembered you asking if he knew of me. Cloud Man and I smoked a pipe to thank the spirits. We knew it was the plan of the spirits that he should come from your camp directly to mine."

Panther Man paused and took a small puff from Running Elk's pipe. Then he continued. "The old man described his journey well, and it was not difficult for me to find the Silver Lake. From there, the trail is cut deep from the travois you drag with the sugar-making supplies."

Panther Man's eyes began to droop. Spotted Fawn moved from her place and started to prepare a place for him to sleep. As Panther Man watched her, he said quietly, "Do not feel sad for me, Sister. I had eight wonderful seasons living life the way it is best. The Great Mystery only offers us the perfect life after we go on to the spirit world."

White Fox crawled onto his sleeping mat and buried himself deep in the soft robes. The next thing he knew, someone was shaking him. "Wake up, Nephew. Today I will show you how to get that big fish to jump from the creek and stick himself on the end of your spear." Chuckling, Panther Man pulled White Fox from his warm bed.

White Fox found his shirt and leggings at the foot of his bed. He saw his uncle quietly gathering up his bow and quiver. White Fox found his spear, and the two stepped out into the cool morning air. The sky was clear, and the dawn was just beginning to break. Soon uncle and nephew were out of the camp and walking down the trail along the Great River. Panther Man pointed to the top of the river bluff. "See who is watching us leave our camp this morning?" In an old, dead tree sat the great owl. Its head turned as they passed below. "Do you ever wonder what the great bird is thinking as he watches us pass by?"

"I guess I have not thought much about what the birds and animals think," the boy replied. "My father has taught me to pray to the spirit of the animals that we hunt. I thank them for giving us their lives so we may live. Sometimes I do not like to kill the animals or to take the eggs from the birds. But Father says that Mother Earth has designed the animals to reproduce so quickly that they do not miss their young for as long a time as we do."

"Your father has taught you the right way. Mother Earth will take care of all her children, as long as we are not too greedy and take more than we need." When they reached the fallen birch tree, Panther Man directed, "Crawl out on the log with your spear, White Fox."

White Fox hooted. "I think it is your turn to try out the log,

and we will see how well you can hang on!" But as his uncle laughed, White Fox climbed out on the log.

Panther Man picked up a stick and walked downstream and stepped into the water. He ran the stick along the edges of the creek where the moving water had carved hollows under the bank. Suddenly he yelled, "Here comes a big one, Nephew! Don't miss this one."

White Fox saw the fish swish its shining tail and wiggle over the rocks. He clamped his legs tight around the tree, drew back his spear, and leaned over as far as he dared. When he saw the shadow passing below him, he jabbed as hard as he could. He lost his balance and fell headfirst into the water with a big splash. This time, as he struggled to his feet, he held up his spear. The big fish wiggled frantically on the end of it. "I've got him!" he yelled triumphantly. White Fox turned to look downstream and saw his uncle doubled over in laughter. He felt his cheeks grow hot but grinned broadly.

Panther Man had brought a rawhide game bag, and he lined it with dry grasses. White Fox watched as his uncle fit the fish into the bag. Panther Man turned to White Fox and smiled. "You have gotten yourself a big fish. But now you are wet again. We will go back to the riverbank and find a place in the warm sunshine. I will make a fire to dry your clothes and make us some tea."

Soon White Fox was sitting at the base of a large elm tree as Panther Man struck a rock against a flint stone to start a fire. A curl of smoke soon rose from the dry grasses and birch bark that his uncle had carefully arranged. The fire grew rapidly, and it wasn't long before the boy was warming himself next to it.

White Fox enjoyed watching his uncle. Panther Man placed some rocks into the fire to heat them. He then fashioned a basin of birch bark and filled it with river water. When the rocks were hot, he used two sticks to carefully transfer the rocks into the basin. He pulled a small pouch from around his neck. Opening the drawstring, he shook some leaves into the water basin. Then he too sat with his back to the tree and said, "Are you warm enough? It won't be long before your clothes will be dry."

White Fox nodded and asked, "What kind of tea did you put into the basin? It does not look like any of Mother's teas."

"At our village near the Big Stone Lake, we are not far from a trading post," Panther Man replied. "I traded with the white man to get this tea." He offered the basin to White Fox to sip and then drank some himself. "Hmm. This would be even better with some of your mother's maple sugar," said Panther Man. "Do you like it?"

"It does taste different, but I think I like it," White Fox answered. As White Fox sipped the tea by the fire, he felt the last bit of chill leave his body. "Tell me about the Canada Country, Uncle. Is it like Suland with many trees and beautiful rivers and lakes?"

Panther Man looked thoughtful. "No place is a beautiful as Suland," he said. "When we left our home village, we wandered north over the open plains. Twice in our journey north, we came across other bands of our people, and they joined our group. When we entered the Canada Country, there were thirty-eight people in our band. We settled in an area near the Turtle Mountains. We made our permanent camp along the Pembina River.

"We had no trouble finding enough game. We moved out onto the plains to hunt the buffalo. We trapped and hunted the fur-bearing animals along the rivers. We traveled to the white man's trading posts to trade furs for some of the items we needed."

White Fox enjoyed listening to his uncle because he had been to so many places and seen so many interesting things. White Fox could tell Panther Man was describing a good time of his life by the smile that was on his face. "Do you think that someday you could take me up the Canada Country?" he asked.

His uncle became solemn. "I could never do that, Nephew. There are too many spirits of the dead there to take the beauty of the land from me. I will never go back there."

Silence overtook the riverbank. Both man and boy dozed in the sun. White Fox awoke when a cool breeze touched him. He sat upright and looked at his uncle. He was still sleeping with a peaceful look on his face. White Fox leaned over and felt his clothes. They were dry. He pulled them on and rubbed off the sand that still clung to the buckskin. Panther Man stirred and opened his eyes. "It looks like you are ready to return to the village. Your fish will make a special treat for later on tonight," he said. White Fox replied with a smile.

When the two reached the village, they could see bustling activity. The little boys and some of the women were making a huge pile of sticks and dry wood in the middle of the council ring.

White Fox found his mother near their tepee and called to her, "Look, Mother, see the big fish I got." Panther Man loosened the ties on the bag and showed Spotted Fawn the fish.

"Your fish is fat and has lots of good meat. I think we will need it later tonight," she said. "We had your uncle all to ourselves last night. I think we are going to have to share him with the people tonight. It looks like we are going to have celebration."

As the sun dipped low in the sky, Chief Stone Man's son, who apparently had the job of teller of the news, ran through the village shouting, "Come to the feast to welcome our visitor!"

Many of the men and boys were already settled in the council circle when White Fox and his family arrived. After the women had stored the foods and all was quiet, Chief Stone Man spoke in a loud voice. "We welcome to our village a relative of Running Elk's lodge." All the faces turned to Panther Man. "This man has been separated from his family for many winter seasons and has brought much joy to his sister's lodge by his visit."

Just then, the chief's son entered the circle carrying a flaming torch. He handed it to his father. Stone Man touched it to the dry grasses under the pile of wood, and soon there was a bright fire blazing. As the fire grew, Stone Man reached for his rawhide pipe bag and removed his red pipe, made from the sacred stone from the pipestone quarries to the southwest. It was beautifully decorated with loon feathers, and the stem was wrapped with colored rawhide strips. He took his tobacco bag and filled the pipe with kinnikinnick. Taking a small stick from the fire, he lit the pipe. He inhaled deeply and passed it to Panther Man, who took a long puff and passed it on to Running Elk. The pipe was passed to each man around the council fire until it came back to Stone Man.

Panther Man reached for the pipe again and took his own tobacco bag from around his waist. From the pouch he took several pinches of a rich, brown tobacco and refilled the bowl of the pipe. He relit it and handed it back to the chief. Again the pipe traveled around the council fire. This time, each man grunted his approval of the good taste.

White Fox and Little Wolf sat as close to Panther Man as they could without interfering with the exchange that was going on. White Fox leaned close to his friend. "I wish that we were old enough to smoke." Little Wolf agreed, nodding his head emphatically.

Soon the smoking was finished, and Stone Man returned the pipe to its bag. Then he spoke. "Since Panther Man is our honored guest, we ask him to share one of his favorite hunting stories."

Everyone turned to look at White Fox's uncle. He smiled and nodded. He sat silent for some time as though deciding which of his stories to tell. Finally Panther Man started to speak slowly. "This story happened when I was a young man living at the village of our parents along the Minnesota River. One day I left the village to hunt alone and walked deep into the woods. When the sun was low in the sky, I sighted a big buck standing on a rise. It was the Moon of the Falling Leaves, and he was not as wary as he should have been. The scent of a doe must have been in the air."

The other men nodded their understanding.

"He stood broadside to me and made a good target. My arrow sank into the buck's shoulder. He took a few steps and fell to the ground." Grunts of approval could be heard around the circle. The men could appreciate the feeling of the perfect shot that Panther Man had described.

He continued. "I cut the animal's throat and took out his insides. It had gotten too late in the day to return to the village, so I hoisted the animal into a tree to keep it from predators and then made myself a bed of leaves and brush. It wasn't long before I heard the sounds of the night animals. It was not completely dark, and I could see a raccoon nosing around the area where I had buried the innards of the deer.

"I got up and gathered dry wood and started a fire. I knew it would lessen my night vision but decided I would need the fire to keep the bigger animals away. Then I lay back down and soon dozed off.

"I had been asleep for quite a while when I was awakened by a loud snuffling noise. I wasted no time! I grabbed my bow and climbed up the nearest tree until I found a branch that was high off the ground. It was as big a tree as I would have chosen if I had had time to choose." This brought some nods and chuckles from the listeners.

Panther Man's face showed the excitement he must have felt as he told of a big black bear stepping out of the darkness. "I wrapped my legs around the branch as tightly as I could. I brought my bow into a shooting position, but I knew it wasn't very likely that I could kill him with one arrow unless I hit his heart. I knew if I wounded him, it would only make my situation worse."

Panther Man paused and looked at his sister. "You were just

a young girl when this happened, but I am sure you remember it." Spotted Fawn nodded and smiled at him. He returned to his story. "I watched the bear go over to the tree where the deer was hung. He reached up and put his paws on the tree and pushed. He tried to shake the deer from the tree. But suddenly he stuck his snout into the air and sniffed. Then he turned and looked directly at me. He started toward my tree.

"I knew I had no choice. I pulled the bowstring back as far as I could and let the arrow fly. The arrow went into his chest all the way up to the feathers. He roared and grabbed my tree with such strength that he tipped the whole thing to the ground. From that time on everything seemed to move slowly."

Many of the older men nodded and muttered in agreement, as though they had experienced a similar situation. "Even before I hit the ground, I was in the bear's grasp," Panther Man continued, excitement shining in his firelit eyes. "He clutched me to his chest, and I remember his hot, foul breath and his yellow teeth as he closed his mouth on my neck."

Panther Man paused, remembering his terror. He took a deep breath and continued. "Suddenly I heard a scream like nothing I had ever heard before. Something flew out of the darkness and hit the two of use with such force that I was knocked away from the bear. I saw the bear stand up tall and sway back and forth. Then he fell, landing only a short distance from me.

"I lay still on the ground. I could feel the blood flowing from my neck and tried to stop it with my hand. As my heart began to quiet down, I turned my head and looked directly into the yellow eyes of a panther. He was watching me, ready to spring. I knew I was helpless, and I lay quiet. My mind became confused, and I couldn't think of anything to do. Finally, I spoke softly to the cat. 'You have saved my life, Great Cat. Do not take it from me now.' We stared at each other for what seemed a long time. I felt the fear slowly leave my body. Then the cat stood up and walked away."

White Fox could hear whispers around the circle. Panther Man spoke again. "After the panther disappeared, I managed to pull myself up to sit against a tree. I took a handful of wet leaves and pressed them to my wound. Then I waited for the sun to rise. By morning the bleeding had stopped, and I was able to make my way back to the village."

Everyone at the fire sat in awed silence, waiting for the end of the story. Panther Man pulled aside his deerskin shirt and revealed the scars on his neck. White Fox could hear many of the people suck in their breath. He sat close and easily could see where each tooth had punctured the skin. Then his uncle pulled a bear-tooth necklace from under his shirt. It was laced with the biggest teeth White Fox had ever seen. His uncle's eyes traveled around the circle. "This is when the people of my village gave me the name of Panther Man," he concluded.

The men got up from their places and came to Panther Man, clapping him on the back and admiring his necklace. "That is the best hunting story I have ever heard," Little Wolf whispered in awe. "You should be very proud of your uncle." White Fox nodded and smiled as he watched the people gather around his uncle. "Look, the young men are putting their big fish into the coals," Little Wolf said. "Where is the one you speared?"

As White Fox turned, he saw his mother carrying his fish to be added to the others. He could tell it had been cleaned and gutted, and he wished he had done that job himself, as the young men did.

To one side of the fire, some of the older men had gathered. The boys heard the steady *thump, thump* of the drums begin. A few of the young warriors started to move in a circle, tapping their feet to the drumming. White Fox knew the young maidens of courting age would let the young men dance alone for a while and then gradually join in.

The women were bringing to the men trays of cut-up venison and green sticks with which to roast the meat over the fire. Spotted Fawn brought a tray and set it in front of Running Elk and Panther Man. Soon the camp was full of the good smells of roasting meat. White Fox and Little Wolf found their friends Kicked by Pony, Little Bear, Sugar Boy, and several others back in the shadows, mimicking the young men's dance. White Fox and Little Wolf joined in dancing the slow, tap-foot-tap rhythm.

The boys heard giggles and turned to look. From the bushes came four little girls, Willow Girl, Little Sparrow, Red Bird, and Running Girl. The girls joined the dancing, mimicking the older girls who were now dancing near the fire. The only difference was that the little girls could not contain their giggles, and soon the boys moved away in embarrassment.

"Let's see if your father and uncle have left any meat for us," Little Wolf suggested. The boys got back to the fire in time to see Spotted Fawn set another tray of meat in front of the men. The boys moved in close to share. Spotted Fawn leaned down close to her brother. "You have made me proud this night. You have grown up to hold yourself with honor, and it makes me proud to call you Brother."

Panther Man smiled. "I can tell that you have the deep respect of the people of this village. I am glad I came here to find you and your husband. You can also be proud of your son. I can tell that he will grow to be a great warrior. He holds you and Running Elk in high regard and will take care of you in your old age." White Fox pretended not to hear the exchange between his mother and uncle, but it made him feel very good inside.

They ate in silence, enjoying the good food, until one of the young warriors stood to make an announcement. "I, One Who Runs, saw an enemy of the young boys in the forest today. I saw the nest of the Hornet enemy. We have not had a Hornet War for a long time. I think we should have a Hornet War to test the little braves in our camp."

White Fox and Little Wolf looked at each other and cheered. This would be their first real chance to show what brave warriors they had become. Both had heard about the Hornet fight from Little Wolf's older brothers.

Chief Stone Man nodded his approval and announced, "Tomorrow, when the sun is halfway to the highest point of the day, all of the boys who are not yet warrior hunters will meet here at the village circle. You will dress only in loincloths. Each of you shall choose someone older, who knows about these wars, to help you prepare for the contest. Make your choice at this time and then go back to your lodge to get your sleep. You will have a big day tomorrow."

Little Wolf turned to White Fox excitedly. "I am going to ask Burnt by Fire to help me. Who are you going to ask?"

White Fox thought a moment. "I think I will ask my uncle."

With this decided, Little Wolf jumped up. "I will see you tomorrow."

White Fox waved at his friend and then started to work his way closer to his father and uncle. He waited for his chance to break into the conversation. "Uncle," he said, seizing his opportunity, "would you do me the honor of being my helper tomorrow at the Hornet War?"

Both men turned to look at him. Panther Man answered solemnly. "I would be honored to help you with this contest."

With a yip, White Fox went racing back to his family's lodge to crawl into his sleeping robes. He did not see the looks of concern exchanged by his parents. Nor did he see the looks of dread on the other mothers' faces.

CHAPTER SIX

White Fox woke with a start. Although it was becoming light outside, the adults were still in their beds. The boy was excited about the coming day and squirmed in his sleeping robes. He raised himself up on his elbow and looked over to where his uncle slept. He saw two large, dark eyes looking back at him.

"Are you awake, Nephew, and ready to prepare for war?" Panther Man asked.

White Fox nodded. He crawled from the warm robes and dressed. Panther Man also crawled from his robes and started to dress. As he did, he watched White Fox. *This nephew of mine has good looks. He is not tall for a Dakota boy of ten winter seasons; but he is strong and energetic, and he has a handsome face. Someday many young women will want to make his moccasins for a lifetime.* This thought made Panther Man chuckle.

White Fox looked at him and asked, "What are the thoughts that make you laugh, Uncle?"

"These are private thoughts, Nephew. But don't be concerned. They are not about your Hornet War. I take that very seriously," he answered with a grin.

Panther Man pulled back the door flap and saw that it was going to be a beautiful day. Already people were moving by the lodge, walking to the little river for their morning swim or cleansing. Several young maidens walked past and looked at him with open interest. Panther Man returned their looks as he stepped from the tepee. He followed them to the river and then turned upstream to the place where the beavers had partially dammed the water, forming a small lake.

This place too was already occupied. Some women were busy washing their hair. Two cradleboards hung from the low branches. Panther Man stopped and looked at the babies. Toys hung from the handles, and the babies looked content. Basins of water stood nearby, warming in the sun, and he knew that the little ones would soon get baths too.

Panther Man felt a sudden tightening in his chest. One of the women resembled Girl Who Walks with a Limp, and the baby hanging near her could have been his Sparrow Hawk. The women were laughing and splashing, and it seemed he had seen this scene before. He stepped back and shook his head to clear his thoughts, turning to walk quickly up the river until he could not hear the laughter anymore.

Finally, he found a place where he could be alone. The water looked deep and cold. He shed his clothing and leaped into the water. He swam until his body tingled from the cold and then pulled himself up onto the bank. He stretched out in the sun to dry. Panther Man thought of how his people were trained from a young age to keep themselves clean. In his travels, he had seen other tribes who lived in dirty conditions. They didn't seem to notice the little body biters that they carried. He didn't understand how anyone could not notice being dirty.

When Panther Man was dry enough, he dressed and went to find his nephew. As he walked back to the village, he came to a place where many little boys were swimming. The little brown bodies shot through the water looking like a bunch of otters. One of the boys shouted, "Look, White Fox. There is your uncle."

One of the brown bodies separated from the rest and came to the shore. "Are you ready to help me prepare for the battle, Uncle?" asked White Fox.

"I am," Panther Man answered. "The first thing we must do is find you a special coup stick."

"Will the willow stick work the best?" asked White Fox. "The willow swamp is not far from here."

"You will want to strike many times without breaking the stick. The willow will work well," his uncle answered.

White Fox finished dressing and led the way to the willow swamp. "Go and find your own weapon," Panther Man said. "Then we will test it for strength." The boy disappeared into the willows. Panther Man could see the branches waving as the boy moved through looking for just the right stick. Presently, the boy emerged, holding a long red willow stick. It was thick at the base and looked sturdy.

Panther Man smiled at his nephew and nodded his approval. The little boy seemed to realize that the Hornet Warriors would not be easy to hit with too small a stick. This one would be perfect. The pair walked back to the village to decorate this worthy weapon.

They went to the tepee to find that Running Elk had laid out some of his precious war paints. Spotted Fawn, back from her early morning walk, handed them the paints and White Fox's medicine bag. She said nothing but watched as her son sat on a rock and opened his medicine bag. He withdrew a long blue-jay feather and laid it beside him. Next, he used his knife to cut a slit in the blunt end of the stick and inserted the feather. "This is to give me the aggressive nature of the blue jay," White Fox said proudly.

Panther Man nodded his approval. "It looks like the war colors of your father are black, green, and red," he observed. "We will decorate the coup stick with these colors. Then we will paint you for the war dance."

White Fox sat still as his uncle painted his face with the colors

of his warrior father. His mother watched the proceeding, looking very serious. Then the drumming began, first one drum and
then two. They were being called to the council ring. Panther
Man stroked on one last stripe of color and leaned back to look
intently at his nephew. He smiled. "You are ready to join the war
dance. Let's go!"

White Fox looked back at his mother as they started toward
the council ring and waved at her. She gave him a small smile in
return.

As the two males approached the council ring, White Fox
saw that Burnt by Fire was one of the drummers and Little Wolf
was already dancing. White Fox joined the dancing, and Panther
Man squatted down with the adult men to watch. Gradually
more boys came and joined in until there appeared to be about
twenty, big and small, who were going to take part in the battle.

They danced for some time as the sun inched up toward the
highest point of the day. These boys did not need to be taught
how to do a war dance. They had watched the warriors for years
and could mimic them to perfection. Finally, One Who Runs
came into the ring, and the drumming ceased. "Are all the warriors present? I have come to lead you to the Hornet's lodge."

One Who Runs started up the path to the river bluff. Chief
Stone Man fell into line, and all the boys followed in single file
behind him. The helpers got to their feet and followed. As they
marched off to war, White Fox realized that the light breeze
was blowing into their faces. It was good to be approaching the
enemy against the wind, he thought. He was proud of how quietly they were making their way through the forest. Each boy
had been taught from the time they first entered the woods with
their fathers how to walk without breaking twigs and rustling the
loose leaves.

They had walked for quite a distance when One Who Runs
stopped and pointed to a tree in a small clearing. On one of
the lower branches hung the hornets' nest. The boys gathered
around One Who Runs. "I have brought you to the enemy," he
said. "Now it is your job to choose your war chief and decide on
a strategy." With that, One Who Runs went back to join the

helpers, who were finding themselves vantage points from which to watch the battle. All of them could hear the humming in the hive. Even though it was a sunny day, it sounded like plenty of the enemy were still within the lodge.

"We must pick a war chief to lead us into battle," said Kicked by Pony.

"You are the biggest boy in our group," Little Wolf spoke up. "I think you should be our leader."

All the boys nodded their approval. Kicked by Pony was Chief Stone Man's son, and he seemed naturally to take the lead in their games. The boys liked him and found him to be fair-minded.

Chief Stone Man had been watching the proceedings and stepped forward. "Now you have chosen your leader, and he will decide the strategy. But these are the rules of the war: anyone who cries out in pain during the battle has lost his scalp to the enemy and must quit fighting. The rest of you cannot stop until all the enemy has been killed." With this, Chief Stone Man turned and walked back to join the onlookers.

Kicked by Pony looked from one boy to another. "Listen, my warriors, this is my plan. I will give the hornets' lodge the first blow and hope to bring it down. The more enemies that stay in the lodge when it falls, the quicker we can destroy them and the fewer scalps they will take. Now we are ready." The boys nodded confidently.

Kicked by Pony let out a scream and rushed the hornets' nest. With a big swing of his coup stick, he struck the nest. In his excitement, he did not hit it directly, and it swung but did not fall from the tree.

Panther Man could hear the angry humming from the hive. He could see the boys closest to the nest starting to swat at their own bodies. The war was on. White Fox's friend Little Wolf stepped forward. With a great swing, he hit the nest and sent it flying from the tree. The boys rushed forward and attacked the nest, each of them trying to count coup while they could. So far, the cries from the boys were war cries, but Panther Man knew that some would turn to cries of pain.

Some of the boys continued to beat on the nest. Others were

swatting at the enemy on the wing. Panther Man saw White Fox beating the ground where a cluster of bees must have fallen. The boy swatted his own body too, and unconsciously the uncle began to rub his own arms.

Just then a small boy came toward the nest with his stick and gave it a swat. Panther Man had noticed this little fellow at the warrior dance and had thought he was too small to take part in a Hornet War, but no one who wanted to participate was ever turned away. Suddenly the little fellow was rolling on the ground crying out in pain. His old brother left the onlookers and went to rescue him. The little boy already had lost his scalp, so there was no need to suffer any longer. As the brother returned carrying the little one, loud sniffling could be heard, but no one looked at him.

"Don't cry, Little Wounded One, you were too small for this war game," his brother consoled him. Panther Man smiled, knowing that this new name would stick with the little fellow until a day when he would earn a new one.

The action in the clearing showed no sign of lessening, and the boys were swatting their own bodies as much as they were using their coup sticks. The enemy was indeed a worthy one this day. After a long time, the angry buzzing grew less and less, and the helpers knew that at last the warriors were beginning to win the battle.

Panther Man saw that White Fox was sitting on the ground, but he had not heard any more cries of pain. As White Fox got back to his feet, Panther Man could tell that his nephew was having a hard time seeing and realized that his eyes were probably swelling shut. The war was almost over, and if White Fox could stay on his feet until the end, he would share the victory.

Finally the buzzing ceased, and Kicked by Pony let out the victory yell, with all the boys joining in. The helpers stood up and went to their little warriors. Panther Man walked up to White Fox. "I am here, Nephew. You fought a good war. How many scalps did you take?"

"Many, I think," White Fox answered. "But the enemy was shooting very painful arrows this day."

Panther Man saw that his nephew was trying to smile, but his face was swelling quickly. Tears were squeezing out of the corners of the boy's swollen eyes, but White Fox quickly wiped them away. "Would you lead me?" he asked softly. "I cannot see very well."

Panther Man took his arm gently, looking for a place that did not look red and swollen. This was the war game that gave the boys the best training for the real wars, but Panther Man did not enjoy seeing their pain.

Chief Stone Man stepped forward and spoke. "You have done well this day. Only one scalp was lost to the enemy. Even though we have some wounded ones to help on our walk home, you will enter the village as victorious warriors and will hold your heads high in honor." With this, the chief led the walk home. All the little warriors were praised and acknowledged by the band on their return.

Night came to the village. White Fox sat on his mat by the fire with a mudpack on his face and arms. Spotted Fawn's herbs and medicines already had reduced some of the swelling. She had made a special brew for him, and he was sipping it, wrapped in his buffalo robes.

Running Elk and his good hunting friend, Long Legs, had not returned from the hunt. They knew they were not needed in their lodge this night and probably were enjoying the stay in the woods. Panther Man sat on his mat near the fire.

"Tell me about the eagle feather you wear, Uncle. It is different than any I have seen on the other warriors."

Panther Man spoke as he worked. "Your father has probably explained to you why we use the eagle's feathers to signify deeds of bravery in war."

White Fox nodded. "He told me a long time ago. I'm not sure I remember all of it."

"The eagle is the most warlike bird and the most kingly. Also, his feathers are very sturdy to work with. When a man wears a single feather, it represents a special coup. A coup means the touching of the enemy's body after the enemy falls. But you know this. You practiced counting coup today on the Hornet enemy. It is easier to kill an enemy from a distance than to count coup on him during a battle. A warrior who wears an eagle feather must have counted coup and had it verified by the other warriors present."

Panther Man looked intently at White Fox. "Now these are the things to remember: if the warrior is wounded in the battle when he counted coup, he wears the feather hanging down. If he wears a feather with a round mark, it means he slew the enemy. When the mark is cut into the feather and painted red, it means he took the scalp. A brave who has been successful in ten battles is entitled to wear a war bonnet. Those who have counted many coups may trim the ends of the feathers with bits of white or colored down.

"My eagle feather is tipped with a strip of weasel skin, which means I had the honor of killing, scalping, and counting the first coup all at the same time."

"Tell me, Uncle, the story of the battle that your feather signifies," White Fox begged.

Panther Man smiled at the boy, who looked at him with his own battle-scarred face. Spotted Fawn also looked up from her work. She was busy beading a new pair of moccasins that she had cut from elk hide. Panther Man knew they were for him. He had seen her measuring his old ones when she thought he was asleep. Now she leaned forward and pushed the water basin onto the hot rocks around the edge of the fire to make tea.

Panther Man settled back, leaning against the backrest on his sleeping mat. He got a faraway look in his eyes. "When we lived in the Canada Country, we lived the nomadic life as you live here," he began. "We moved great distances to hunt the buffalo."

Panther Man shook off his sadness. He slipped the rawhide band with the feather back on his head. "Now, White Fox, you know the story of my eagle feather. It is time for you to go to sleep. Let the medicines take the rest of the hornets' poison from your body."

Suddenly White Fox did feel very tired, thanks to the herbal tea he had been sipping. He snuggled into his buffalo robes and closed his eyes. Wisps of steam began to rise from the water that Spotted Fawn had put onto the rocks earlier. She pulled the basin aside and sprinkled some crushed leaves into the steaming water.

Brother and sister sat in silence, watching the fire curl and leap. Shadows flickered and danced on the tepee walls. Finally Panther Man broke the silence. "Has this been a safe place for you to live?"

"We do not live far from the Chippewa territory. But Chief Stone Man has been a careful chief," his sister replied. "He always has young men watching from the bluff overlooking the two rivers. They can see in all directions up there."

"Have there been many raids by the Chippewa?"

Spotted Fawn poured some tea into a pair of small clay cups. "We had more trouble years ago. The warriors were raiding back and forth almost every summer season. Now the Chippewa must be moving closer to the white man's trading posts, as so many of our people have done." Spotted Fawn sipped her tea and added, "Lately we have seen the white man moving into our woods and cutting down the trees to plant corn. We hope the deer will eat it all, as did they when we tried to raise it. Then the white man will move away."

"Is that why you have no cornfields here?" asked Panther Man. "We grew much corn along the Minnesota River."

Spotted Fawn shrugged. "There has been no real need for corn here. We have an abundance of game and gathering foods, and we do not need to go far to harvest the wild rice."

"We could not raise the corn up in the Canada Country either," Panther Man responded. "The warm season was not long enough. Like here, there were other edibles to take its place."

Brother and sister talked long into the night.

One morning, White Fox saw his mother gathering her tools to harvest roots and water lilies. "I will go with you today to gather food," he volunteered. White Fox had not gone with his mother

to gather food for a long time, and she wondered if there was a reason for the help she was to get this day. As the two of them walked through the forest, Spotted Fawn saw that her son looked thoughtful. Finally he spoke. "Mother, Uncle is talking about going from our village soon. Has he spoken to you about this?"

"He has spoken to me about returning to the village at Lac Qui Parle," she replied.

"Have you asked him to live here with us?"Spotted Fawn stopped walking and turned to him. "You know I would like that, White Fox, and your uncle knows it too. But it seems he met a young woman when he visited our home village. She is a woman alone, having lost her man. They have much in common, and if she is still free when he returns, he plans to talk with her about marriage." White Fox's face fell.

"This would be good for him, for he is still young and needs to have another family," Spotted Fawn continued. "You want that for him, don't you, White Fox?" White Fox bowed his head. He hadn't been thinking of his uncle's feelings, only of his own. He did not want his uncle to leave. Spotted Fawn interrupted his thoughts. "You will see your uncle again, since we know where he will be living."

The day arrived when Panther Man was ready to leave. He had his buffalo robe rolled up and tied to his pony. His medicine bag and knife were tied to his waist. He swung his bow and quiver over his shoulder. He was leaving with only the things he had come with, except that Spotted Fawn had gradually replaced his clothes with new.

White Fox saw his mother come from the lodge and hand Panther Man a parfleche of pemmican and tipsinna cakes. The boy had seen her put some special maple candies in the bag too. White Fox thought of running into the woods to hide. He did not want to say good-bye to this man. He could see the tears in his mother's eyes as she hugged her brother. He watched as Running Elk stepped forward and clutched his brother-in-law in a bear hug.

Panther Man turned to his nephew. "Come here, White Fox. I have made something for you." He stepped into the lodge and emerged holding a warrior's shield. "I have made this for you to use in the future. For now, you may hang it in the lodge over your bed to remind you of the day when you will be a great warrior."

White Fox had watched his uncle make this shield from start to finish, from the round vine hoop to the dried and stretched buffalo hide. He had watched Panther Man paint the dark clouds and lightning bolts on the one side, the moon and stars on the other. "White Fox, you watched me make this war shield and paint it, but you didn't know it was for you. I have never seen a boy who loves the night like you do. I've watched you sit and watch the Lightning God and listen to the Thunder Spirit with fascination. On pleasant nights you search the skies for new stars. I have put those things on your shield.

"And see this," he pointed to the bottom corner, and there White Fox saw a painting of a white fox. Panther Man then pointed to the other corner, which was empty. "In this corner, I have left a place for you to paint something for yourself. Someday, when you have your warrior's vision, the Great Mystery of the White Fox may show you what image to put there."

Little Wolf and some of White Fox's other friends had gathered to watch the exchange. This made White Fox feel very proud, for no other boy his age had anything like this war shield. White Fox handed the shield to his father as he said, "I have made something for you too, Uncle." He took his medicine bag from his waist and opened it, pulling out two small obsidian arrowheads. "I chipped these for you because I know how much you dislike the job." He handed them to Panther Man.

Panther Man turned them over in his hand and felt the edges for sharpness. "You have taught him well, Running Elk. These are fine points." Running Elk nodded, and the pride he felt for his son was evident. Panther Man mounted his pony and motioned to White Fox. "Come get on behind me and ride along to the little creek."

White Fox jumped up behind his uncle. They rode to the edge of the camp, where Panther Man turned his pony and looked back at his sister and her husband. He put his arm toward the sky in a farewell salute. Then he turned his pony and rode away.

As uncle and nephew rode along the Great River, White Fox held tight to his uncle. He liked the feeling of closeness. They rode in silence until they reached the small creek. Panther Man reined the pony to a stop, and White Fox slid to the ground. Panther Man looked down at the boy. "This is a sad farewell for both of us, but I feel that we will be together again. We must both be as happy as we can be in the time between. Do you remember the day we met when you fell into this very creek?" Panther Man laughed his loud laugh, and White Fox couldn't help but laugh too.

With a final, fond nod to White Fox, the uncle turned his pony and followed the creek into the woods. The boy stood watching until he was out of sight.

PART TWO

CHAPTER ONE

1851

The pot bubbled over the midday fire, and good smells began to fill the lodge. White Fox and his father sat near the fire. Running Elk had found a large obsidian stone on one of his hunting trips, and now the pair were chipping new arrow points. White Fox was always fascinated by how quickly his father could make the points, only rarely ruining one. He watched as his father finished a point, using the tip of an antler horn for the final shaping. White Fox continued to chip on his point, hoping he would not break it before it was finished.

When he finished his tip, he handed it to his father to be inspected. Running Elk ran his thumb over the edge and then held the rawhide to be cut. The point easily cut the hide. Running Elk grunted his approval and patted the boy on the back. As they worked by the fire, Running Elk became warm and removed his deerskin shirt. White Fox looked at his father closely. The scars on his chest stood out in the firelight. The boy knew that the scars had come from the Sun Dance, which was part of his father's vision quest.

White fox leaned close to his father, watching him tie the arrowhead to the ash shaft. "Father," he said, "how will I know when I am old enough to seek my vision?"

Running Elk looked at his only child, and his face was very serious. "Do not worry about the time. The Great Mystery will decide for you when the time is right. I was five winter seasons older than you are now when I had mine."

White Fox watched his father quietly. "You said someday, when I was old enough to understand, you would tell me about your vision quest. Am I old enough now?"

Running Elk was thoughtful as he tied the final knot holding the point to the shaft. Then he looked at his son. "I think you are old enough to understand my vision. And maybe the time is right for you to hear it."

Running Elk laid the arrow and the feathers aside to be finished later. He settled his back against his backrest and began to speak. "I was seventeen winter seasons old when I first started to have dreams of taking part in a Sun Dance ceremony. After my third dream, I went to talk to our shaman, Rain Man. He told me that two other young men in the camp had the desire to take part in a Sun Dance but the Sun God had said there should be three. I was the third one. He said he would make the plans.

"The shaman called together the elders of the village, and they all agreed that it was the perfect time for a Sun Dance, for it was the Moon of Making Fat when the sun is directly overhead. The elders prepared for the ceremony. We were required to fast for three days, and during that time the elders built a new sweat lodge and erected the poles with the rawhide strips fastened to the top. The poles were in the exact center of the village. We each chose a helper. Only a warrior who had taken part in a Sun Dance could be a helper. I asked my father to be my helper.

"The day of the Sun Dance dawned clear and warm," Running

Elk continued. "We were taken to the sweat lodge for the purification ceremony. I will not tell you all the details of these ceremonies, for someday you may experience them for yourself.

"After the purification ceremony, we took part in the pipe-smoking ceremony. We smoked to the Four Directions, to Mother Earth and the Great Mystery. By this time, we were in a very relaxed condition. We went to the poles in the center of the village. I remember my father cutting the skin of my chest and threading the rawhide strips through the muscles. I do not remember feeling much pain.

"The sun was directly overhead when we started to dance. The drumming started slowly at first and gradually became faster and faster. I remember my father dancing and chanting behind me."

Running Elk paused in his story and closed his eyes as though to rest. Then he spoke again. "As I danced and watched the sun, it began to change. It became a large red blur. The singing and drumming began to fade. It was as though I was hearing it from a long distance.

"I don't know how much time passed before I had my vision. I remember feeling as though I was leaving my body behind. I was floating up into the bright, blue sky. I saw a large hawk glide by me, and he turned his head and looked at me. Then I remember my feet coming to rest on the edge of a bluff, very much like the one above this village. I saw the Great River below me. To the east, I saw black clouds coming. The black clouds were swirling and rolling, and suddenly out of the clouds came a large herd of elk, as many as one thousand animals. They were running with fear in their eyes.

"Behind the elk came men on ponies. Their long hair was flying in the wind. Some had hair growing on their faces, and I realized that they were not our people. I had only seen a few white traders before this time, but I knew what they looked like and how they dressed. These were white men, and they had the long guns that kill at a distance. They were shooting at the elk, and some of the elk were falling."

White Fox watched his father's face as he told the story. There seemed to be a glow about his features, as though he were seeing the vision again as he recounted it.

"I saw a huge bull swerve from the herd and come toward me. I could not move. He scooped me up onto his back with his antlers and carried me into the middle of the herd. We ran with the herd for a long time, until we left Suland behind and I could see the prairie ahead. The animals spread out and disappeared across the prairie. The big bull stopped running, and I jumped to the ground.

"The bull spoke to me in my own tongue. 'Listen to me, my son,' he said. 'The white men are coming to your land. Do not take their gifts. Beware of their poison water. It will kill your people. Some of your people will fight them, but they will not win. The white man and his promises will turn your people against one another. I have been sent to tell you to stay away from these people for as long as you can.'

"Then the bull turned and ran away across the prairie. I was left standing alone. When I awoke from my vision, I had been cut down from the pole and was lying in my father's arms. Later, I described my vision to my father and the shaman, Rain Man. The shaman was the one who gave me the name Running Elk."

White Fox sat very still and waited for his father to share more. His father looked very tired and sad. The boy decided not to ask any more questions. But Running Elk looked at him and said, "I want you to remember my vision as I have told it to you. Stone Man, our chief, also had a vision that day, and he too was warned about the white man. That is why we have chosen to remain in Suland, away from the main villages of our people."

Running Elk sat in silent thought. Just then, White Fox heard the little boys yahooing outside, signaling the return of the hunters. All of the people came from their lodges to see which of the hunters had brought home some game. Long Legs was the first hunter to enter the camp, followed by the others. None of the men carried any game.

Long Legs looked upset and walked directly to Chief Stone Man's lodge. The two men stood in full view, but they talked in low tones so no one else could hear. Then Stone Man beckoned to some young men. Soon they were moving about the camp calling all the warriors to a meeting at the council lodge.

White Fox joined his friend Little Wolf. "Did you hear what your father told our chief?"

Little Wolf shook his head. "Maybe we can crawl up behind the council lodge and listen, like we did the last time they had a meeting," he suggested.

Their village was not big. It consisted of about 50 warriors and 125 women, children, and old men. Not all the warriors would fit inside the lodge, so some would stand outside the doorway listening. The boys heard the chief speak first, in a loud voice. "Long Legs has something to tell you. I will let him explain to you what he and the other hunters saw today."

It got very quiet inside the lodge, and the boys heard Long Legs begin to speak. "We left the village this morning and crossed the little river, heading north to hunt. Most of you know where the oak woods end and the grove of birch trees stands. We were just a short distance up the trail from there when we heard people on the trail ahead of us. We scouted off the trail to the high ground where we could see the trail ahead. We saw a Chippewa village on the move. There must have been six or seven hundred people. They were coming in our direction."

A murmur went through the lodge like a spreading fire. Everyone knew what this meant. Stone Man spoke again, "You all know what we must do. We have been living closer to Chippewa territory than any other Dakota band, and now our time has run out."

White Fox felt a coldness spread through his chest. Little Wolf looked as though he was feeling sick. Stone Man spoke again. "Does anyone have a suggestion where we should go?"

White Fox heard his father's voice. "My brother Little Crow is now the chief of our main village, Kaposia. This is the place where Stone Man and I were raised to young manhood, and most of the people of this band have relatives still living there. We could move there for now and hope that some of those warriors will join us to return here and push the Chippewa from this area. I would not want to live in the large village permanently."

The boys could hear the murmurs from the other warriors, but they did not hear any objections to the suggestion. Finally Stone Man spoke again. "I agree that this would be the wise move to make at this time. Are there any objections or other ideas?"

There were none, and the meeting was over. The warriors poured from the lodge. Word spread quickly through the camp. The women wasted no time. The tepees started to come down, and White Fox ran to his lodge to help Spotted Fawn. There were food caches to be dug up, and the ponies had to be brought in from the meadow. Spotted Fawn looked at her son with sadness in her eyes. "Sit and eat this bowl of venison stew," she said. "It may be the last warm meal you will have for a while."

White Fox ate as quickly as he could and watched the activity around the camp. His mother was laying out bags of pemmican and gathering foods so she could collapse the tepee. Running Elk was carrying his bow, quiver, war shield, and hunting supplies out. As White Fox finished his stew, Spotted Fawn said, "Go to the meadow now and catch the ponies. We will be ready to load soon."

Little Warrior ran past the lodge yipping. He was caught up in the excitement of the move, as were many of the little children, who didn't realize the seriousness of it. As he neared the meadow, White Fox saw other boys gathering their animals. He saw his family's five ponies grazing together on the far side of the pasture and hurried to catch them. His father had stolen the old mare many seasons ago on a raid into Chippewa country. She was the mother of his own pony, Star, and two of the others. The fifth was his father's hunting pony, which Running Elk had won in a bet at a lacrosse game. He was very fast, and Running Elk often bragged about the pony's strength in the long run of a buffalo hunt.

One by one, White Fox caught three of their ponies, slipped ropes around their necks, and led them all back to the camp. He saw that the tepee was down and his father was cutting the long poles into shorter pieces to use as a travois. The whole village was beginning to look ready for the move. As White Fox neared his parents, Little Wolf ran up to Running Elk and said, "Father sent me to ask you if we could borrow the old mare to haul Little Sister."

Running Elk nodded his head, answering, "That would be a good job for the old mare."

The two boys ran back to the meadow and returned leading the old mare. They found Little Sister giggling and toddling around, excited by the activities. Walking Woman caught her and placed her in her cradleboard, tying her in tightly. The boys held the old mare while Walking Woman fastened the cradleboard on one side of the old mare. Walking Woman called to one of her sisters to bring a little cousin, who would ride on the opposite side of the mare to balance the weight. Each child would know the other was there, and they would coo back and forth as they rode.

Her task complete, Walking Woman turned her attention to the two boys. "If you boys walk the old mare around the camp, she will get used to carrying the little ones."

"Let's go to the burial grounds," Little Wolf suggested. "I want to say good-bye to grandmother."

The boys walked slowly, leading the old mare. She was a patient old pony and carried her burden as though she did it every day. The little ones enjoyed the ride and giggled and cooed to each other. The boys were thoughtful as they walked. "Do you think we will ever live here again?" Little Wolf asked his friend.

"I cannot imagine not seeing this place again," White Fox answered.

White Fox led the old mare between the gravesites until he found the graves of Moon Boy and Standing Calf. His chest tightened with sadness as he thought of leaving them behind. Little Wolf walked up beside him. "I always thought that if my life ended my body would rest here in this ground with our friends and relatives."

White Fox nodded. "I thought that way too."

The boys led the old mare back to Walking Woman. White Fox looked around the camp and said, "I think Straight Talker needs our help to load her things on the travois."

The two boys trotted over to the old medicine woman. White Fox and Little Wolf often helped the old woman gather her special medicinal herbs. They both enjoyed her company and her humorous nature. When Straight Talker saw the boys approaching, she called, "Go to the meadow to look for my pony. I could not catch him."

White Fox and Little Wolf ran to the pasture and found only the one pony left there. He was so excited that even the boys had a hard time catching him. Finally they got the rope around his neck and led him back to the camp.

"Look, White Fox,"—Little Wolf pointed—"Stone Man and his family are leaving."

White Fox looked to the far end of the camp and saw the chief and his family disappearing into the forest. Other were falling in behind. The boys led the pony to the medicine woman and helped her put the last of her things on the travois. Little Wolf hooked the travois rawhide straps to the pony, and Straight Talker was ready to join the others on the trail down the Great River. Straight Talker flashed her smile at the boys, and White Fox said, "We will be behind you. If you need our help, just wait for us. I will bring you one of our extra ponies later so you may ride when you get tired."

"I am strong walker, White Fox," she answered him.

White Fox watched the old woman move away, recalling a time when he had suffered a fever for many days. She had given him many of her potions. Finally, he remembered, she whispered in his ear, "Your time to leave is not here yet, little boy. You still have much work to do for me." She laughed gently, and from that time on he started to feel better.

He also remembered his mother telling him how Straight Talker had earned her name. She was always eager to help anyone she was asked to help. But if she felt that that person had used up his allotted time on Mother Earth, she would not pretend that she could help him. She would tell him the truth and continue to give her aid to the end. She was highly regarded throughout the camp and never suffered for want of fresh meat.

White Fox joined his parents as they started the trek through the woods. They followed Little Wolf's large family. The people moved as silently and quickly as they could. There was no time wasted looking back.

The people walked through the rest of the day and into the night. Finally they stopped, and Spotted Fawn unpacked a couple of buffalo robes to lay on the ground. She brought out some pemmican and tipsinna cakes. Little Wolf and White Fox sat on one of the buffalo robes. The moon was full, and the night was warm and humid. The night creatures filled the air with their calls. The people were silent, and their presence would not have been detectable except for the occasional yip of a camp dog. White Fox pulled Little Warrior close to his side, knowing that any dog that became too noisy this night might very well find himself in the cooking pot tomorrow night.

The longer they sat, the cooler the air felt. Finally the boys had their robes wrapped around themselves, leaving only their faces exposed. White Fox spoke to his father almost in a whisper. "Will you tell us about your brother Little Crow? I have not heard you speak of him before."

Running Elk looked at the two boys and said very softly, "I have not told you very much about my life as a young boy. This would be a good time to tell some of these things. You know that my father's name was Big Thunder and that he was the chief of our village, Kaposia, where I grew up. Your grandfather was one of the Mdewakanton chiefs who believed it was a good thing to trade goods with the white traders. And it was good in the beginning. But after a while, so much trading of skins took place that there was a shortage of game. As the people became more dependent on the white man for goods, the chiefs were encourage to trade land for supplies."

Running Elk paused and looked intently at White Fox. "I told you some of this when I shared the story of my vision quest." Then he continued. "My brother Little Crow was three winter seasons younger than me. As we grew into early manhood, he seemed to enjoy the company of the white traders more than I did.

"After I moved from Kaposia, your uncle grew to manhood, and he moved to an area to the south, married, and had children by two wives. Our paths did not cross again until many seasons later. I and some of our hunters visited a Sisseton village on one of our hunts. It was in the Lac Qui Parle area on the Minnesota River. This is where I met and married your mother. My brother Little Crow was living in this village and had married one of your mother's cousins. Your mother and I moved back into Suland, and I heard nothing of him for many seasons."

Running Elk took a bite of the pemmican he held in his hand and chewed it thoughtfully. The boys waited patiently. Running Elk spoke again in a low voice. "When our father died, Little Crow returned to Kaposia to claim the chiefhood from a young half brother. He had sent a messenger to me first to see if I intended to claim the right since I am older than he. I returned the messenger to tell him I was not interested.

"I learned later that there was trouble and my brother was shot. Little Crow survived the wounds, and some of the tribe killed the younger half brother. They made Little Crow the chief. He would made a good one, I think. He was natural leader."

Both boys sat with their eyes wide. They had not expected such a long story about the uncle. "It is time for us to sleep," said Running Elk. "Tomorrow will be a long day for all of us."

CHAPTER TWO

The band had been on the trail for five days. After the first night, they had felt it safe to build fires when they made camp. The women cooked and the men hunted. During the first days, the game was abundant. But now the band was only a short distance from the big village, and the game had virtually disappeared.

The men had met Dakota hunters from Kaposia, and Running Elk had sent ahead a message to his brother Little Crow, informing him of their impending arrival. On this morning, White Fox and Little Wolf had awakened early and had ridden from the camp. The sun was warm along the river bluff where they rode. Little Wolf stopped and slid from his pony's back. White Fox followed, and they made their way out to the edge of the bluff.

The boys sat in the grass, watching the river flow lazily below them. It was wider here, joined by several smaller rivers. An eagle soared overhead, making its screeching call. A soft breeze moved the grass gently. White Fox suddenly turned to his friend. "Little Wolf, I have been thinking about us since we have been on this journey."

Little Wolf looked at his friend. White Fox was not his little friend anymore. Now twelve winter seasons old, he had grown taller than Little Wolf and no longer looked like a little boy. "What have you been thinking?" Little Wolf asked, looking closely at his friend.

"We have always been the same as brothers. We have shared families," White Fox said. He reached to his belt and pulled out his knife. He looked into Little Wolf's eyes again. "Before we get to the big village, I want for us to be brothers. Blood brothers."

Little Wolf nodded solemnly. White Fox held out his hand and turned it palm upward. On his wrist was a tattoo. Spotted Fawn had put it there when he was a baby to mark him for the trail to the spirit world. White Fox slit the skin above his tattoo. Little Wolf then cut his own wrist, and the boys pressed their wrists together to let the blood mingle. Then they pulled their hands apart.

"From this time on, I will call you my brother," White Fox said reverently.

"You always have been my brother," Little Wolf answered with a smile.

The boys sat watching the river a while longer. Then Little Wolf stood. "We had better look for game, or we will soon be sleeping in the warm sun." They found their ponies grazing in the tall grasses, mounted them, and soon were back to the trail. They meandered along, eyes searching for game, when suddenly they emerged from the woods into an open meadow.

White Fox pulled his pony to a stop and whispered, "Look, what is that on the far side of the meadow?" Both boys sat with their necks stretched, straining to see across the meadow. Suddenly they heard whoops and the pounding hooves of ponies. Before they could move back into the protection of the trees, they saw three boys racing their ponies across the meadow, straight at them.

White Fox recognized the boys' clothing as Dakota and

relaxed a little. The boys saw Little Wolf and White Fox and reined their ponies to a halt. They eyed each other across the distance. Finally one of the strangers walked his pony forward and called, "Who are you?"

Little Wolf answered. "Little Wolf and White Fox, Mdewakanton Dakota, of Stone Man's band. We are on our way to Kaposia."

The three boys rode closer, and the biggest boy said, "I am Big Boy. This is Grey Wing and Red Bird. Where is the rest of your band?"

"They are back on the trail. We came ahead to hunt," answered Little Wolf.

The bigger boy spoke again. "We knew you were coming and came looking for your band."

"We will take you to our village," said the boy called Grey Wing.

"No, we must not enter the village ahead of our elders. It would not be right," replied White Fox.

The other boys nodded in agreement. "We will see you later then. We will tell our chief that you are near," responded Grey Wing. With this, they turned their ponies and rode off.

White Fox and Little Wolf watched as the other boys rode across the meadow and disappeared into the woods. "They seemed happy to see us," White Fox said. "I feel better about entering the village. I think we will be welcome there."

Little Wolf looked solemn. "I am worried about the lack of game in this area," he said. "We have a large family to feed."

The boys rode back to rejoin their band and found the procession not far away. They continued down the line until they saw Walking Woman leading the old mare with the children. Little Wolf slid off his pony to walk with her. White Fox continued until he found his mother. She was leading the pony hooked to the travois. The other pony followed behind.

"Where is Father?" White Fox asked. Not waiting for an answer, he continued. "Little Wolf and I met some of the boys from the village Kaposia. They seemed happy to see us."

Spotted Fawn looked at him and smiled. She too had had some

concerns about entering a village that would be strange to her. She silently scolded herself. When had a Dakota band ever turned away their own people, no matter what the circumstances?

"Your father was looking for you. We are not far from the place Where the Water Falls on the Great River. He wants to show you the Spirit Island where he prayed as a young man."

At that moment, Running Elk rode up and smiled at his son. "I am glad you are back. You can ride with me to a special place from my youth."

"I am ready, Father," White Fox answered.

Running Elk led the way, riding off the trail and into the woods. They hadn't gone far when they began to see buildings ahead. Running Elk turned to his son, his brow furrowed, and said, "I am confused about where we are. There are white man's buildings where there were none when I last visited this place."

They carefully picked their way through the woods, taking a wide berth around the buildings. Finally, Running Elk stopped and dismounted. "We will tie the ponies here and walk the rest of the way."

White Fox slid from Star's back and tied him next to his father's pony. He could hear the roar of falling water. He followed close behind his father, and soon they moved out of the trees to see the river. Running Elk sucked in his breath as they looked over the water. White froth tumbled over and down the rocks. On the far side, the white man had built a tall building, and some of the water was held back from that side of the drop. Running Elk watched in puzzled silence, as though he had never seen this place before.

"Father, where is the Spirit Island?" White Fox asked.

"It is there." His father pointed to a small piece of land made of rocks and a few trees that rose above the foaming, swirling water. "No one could get out to it now," he answered quietly. "There is almost nothing left of it."

Running Elk jerked White Fox to his chest and pulled him behind a large elm tree. Some white men had come out of a building not far from where they were standing. "We must leave now. This place is not the same as it was when I left here," Running

Elk said urgently. Moving from tree to tree, White Fox followed his father, and they kept out of sight of the white men. They did not exchange any words as they rode back to the trail and their people.

Spotted Fawn looked at them with curiosity, but Running Elk rode past her and up the trail. White Fox knew he was going to Stone Man and did not follow. He slid from his pony and walked beside his mother. "Did your father find the Spirit Island?" she asked.

"He found the place; but the white man lives there, and it is not the same."

The sun was dropping in the sky. It was the Moon When the Cherries Turn Black, and White Fox could tell that the sun was spending less of its time shining and warming them. The procession came to a gradual halt. People gathered in groups to talk. White Fox saw Little Wolf coming toward them, winding his pony among the groups. White Fox urged his pony forward to meet him. Little Wolf pointed to the group of men Running Elk had joined. "Some elders of the big village have come to meet us. They are talking to Stone Man and your father. I think one of them is your uncle."

White Fox looked at the group with interest and heard his uncle say, "Come and ride beside me. I will lead you back to the village." Running Elk and Stone Man moved up beside the chief and led the way, followed by the other two men. White Fox rode back to his mother and told her what he had witnessed.

"Your father and his brother will have much talking to do. We will have to be patient about meeting the family," Spotted Fawn told him.

The sun was low in the sky when they entered the village. Spotted Fawn left White Fox to take care of the ponies while she went to find Running Elk to decide where they would unload. She knew they would wait another day to find the long poles to put up their tepee. As she moved through the village, she smiled, thinking how much each village looked the same. This time of the year, most families were living in the elm-bark lodges. They varied in size according to the size of the family.

Spotted Fawn saw Running Elk walking toward her. "We will unload our supplies near my brother's lodge," he said, pointing to a group of lodges in the center of the village. "Tomorrow we will decide where to put our lodge."

The two of them walked back to White Fox and the ponies. At the same time, Little Wolf came running with the boy from the meadow called Grey Wing. Grey Wing did not appear to be very shy, and he looked Running Elk over carefully. "You look very much like our chief," he observed. "It will be good to have you here with us." Running Elk nodded, smiling at the boy. Grey Wing turned to White Fox and said, "Come, I will show you where my lodge is."

White Fox looked at his parents. Spotted Fawn nodded her consent. White Fox tied his pony to the travois so the pony would move with the supplies to the site where his family would unload. The three boys walked through the village until they came to a bark lodge built under a large elm tree not far from the Great River. The river was not so wide at his place, but the current looked strong. "You have a nice place for your lodge," White Fox said.

Grey Wing nodded, his chest puffing with pride. "My father is a shaman, and my old grandmother lives with us. My mother went to live in the Spirit World long before I had any memories."

Just then an old woman came to the dwelling carrying wood for the fire. Her face was deeply lined, and her hair was as white as snow. She moved close to the boys and looked at White Fox so intently that he felt she could see his spirit that lived inside his body.

"Grandmother, these are the boys we saw at the meadow today. They have come from the north, close to where the Chippewa live." Turning back to White Fox, Grey Wing said, "You must tell us stories of the enemy and the battles your warriors have fought." White Fox knew many battle stories, but he was not anxious to tell Grey Wing that they had fled a large Chippewa band without even a battle.

"Will you show us the rest of your village?" Little Wolf asked.

As the boys wandered through the village, they saw joyful families reuniting with relatives whom they hadn't seen for a very long time. White Fox saw his father standing with his uncle near a large bark lodge. His mother was there too, and women had surrounded her. Running Elk saw his son and called to him. White Fox walked slowly to the men. As he approached, his father said, "This is your uncle, Little Crow." Then he gestured to White Fox, "This is my only child, White Fox."

As his father introduced them, White Fox studied his uncle's features, and the boy's eyes slid down to his uncle's hands. Little Crow was holding his arms strangely, with his hands hanging at an odd angle. The hands were partially covered by the sleeves of his doeskin jacket. Little Crow spoke. "Your son is a handsome young man. I am sure he is already a good hunter for the family."

Running Elk nodded and smiled. "He is growing tall, and soon I will have a young warrior riding at my side. Perhaps I will take him along when we return to claim our village along the two rivers."

White Fox felt very proud at these words, but he saw his uncle give Running Elk a strange look. His father did not seem to notice and waved his hand to dismiss White Fox. The boy turned to go, glad that the introductions were over. Little Wolf and Grey Wing were waiting for him. As the boys wandered through the village, they saw women coming from the lodges carrying various foods. There would be a welcoming feast tonight with lots of good food and dancing. The boys moved to the center of the village to watch the fire that had been lit. The women had put ears of corn, still in their husks, in the river to soak. Now they stacked the corn near the fire to be roasted in the coals later.

"The roasted corn will be a special treat for us," White Fox said to Grey Wing. "My mother tried to raise it at the Two Rivers village, but the summer did not stay long enough to get the nice, big ears like the ones you have here."

"The white missionaries and traders have encouraged us to raise more corn and to stop our wandering into the forest for game and the gathered foods."

White Fox looked at his new friend in confusion. "What are missionaries?"

"The missionaries teach the white-man religion to our people," Grey Wing replied.

White Fox and Little Wolf both looked at Grey Wing with questions on their faces. "The white man does not believe in the Great Mystery?" White Fox asked.

"They pray to their God, 'Our Father, Who Art in Heaven.' I think this is the same as the Great Mystery in the Spirit World." Grey Wing faltered. "I am not sure of this; my father says I do not need the missionary lessons. He teaches me the way of our god and says I do not need any other religion. I think he is right."

"We will not be here long enough to worry about these lessons," White Fox commented.

Already the aroma of roasting meat was tickling their noses, and Little Wolf abruptly said, "I am going to find my bowl so I will be ready to eat when the food is done."

The boys went in separate directions to find their eating utensils. As White Fox approached the lodges of his uncle, he saw that his mother had unloaded the travois and was rummaging through their belongings. "Have you found my bowl?" he asked.

Spotted Fawn looked up and smiled. "You are smelling the roasting meat too, I see."

"I cannot let Little Wolf get started before me, or there will be nothing left," White Fox answered with a grin.

Spotted Fawn laughed and pulled his bowl and bone spoon from the supplies, and he quickly walked back to the fire. He found Little Wolf and Grey Wing already sampling the roasted venison, and each held a bowl of rabbit stew. One of the women offered them some bread made from corn.

All grew quiet as more of the people joined them at the fire to enjoy the food. Soon White Fox saw what he had been waiting for. The women pushed the ears of corn into the hot coals. White Fox knew the taste of the corn, but he had never seen such big ears. The boys scooted around the fire to be nearer the corn. Shortly, the women started rolling the ears out of the coals, and the boys each claimed an ear. The women had set bowls of deer tallow around the fire. They believed in using every part of the animals that gave up their lives for them. When they cut up the deer, they saved the fatty areas. It was a bitter white substance kind of like butter. So after the husks were pulled from the ears, everyone smeared the tallow on the hot cobs, enjoying the bitter of the tallow with the sweet of the corn.

Grey Wing handed White Fox a small bowl containing tiny white granules. "Try sprinkling this salt on the cob. We get this from the white trader." White Fox took a pinch and dribbled it over his corn as his new friend had suggested. It tasted good. The boys ate until their stomachs were full.

The drumming had started, and the dancing began. Everyone seemed to be enjoying the evening. It passed quickly, and soon all quieted down. The people started to drift back to their lodges. Suddenly Little Wolf poked White Fox in the ribs with his elbow. "Look." He tipped his head toward the place where the elders had been sitting. Only Running Elk and his brother remained, and they seemed to be having a heated discussion. Suddenly White Fox's father jumped to his feet, and the boys could hear him exclaim in a loud voice, "You cannot sell Mother Earth to the white man! The land doesn't belong to any man!"

Running Elk's eyes darted around the campfire, "Come!" he shouted to Spotted Fawn. His eyes connected with White Fox's, and the boy ran to his father's side. Running Elk's face was bright red with anger. He turned his back to Little Crow and started walking quickly to the place they had left the travois. Only one pony still was tied to a nearby tree, and Running Elk took its bridle and started to hook it to the travois.

Spotted Fawn started hurriedly to pack their robes and supplies, asking, "Where are we going, Running Elk?"

"We will find a place by the river," he answered shortly.

Spotted Fawn and White Fox followed the travois as Running Elk led the pony to the water's edge. Running Elk stopped under a cottonwood tree. "We will spend the night here."

Running Elk leaned against the tree as Spotted Fawn began to spread their robes under it. "Do you know what they have done?" he asked in an anguished whisper. White Fox stopped and looked at his father. Never had he seen such anger in his father's face. "My brother says he has signed papers selling Suland to the Great White Father."

White Fox felt a pain in his chest, and he saw the misery in his father's face. When his father did not say more, he slowly asked, "Who is the Great White Father?"

Running Elk waved his hand toward the river. "He lives far to the east. He is the chief of all the white people. My brother and a few other chiefs cannot sell Mother Earth. I will talk to Stone Man in the morning. We will return to Suland."

With this, Running Elk moved onto the robes and lay down. Spotted Fawn curled up next to him. White Fox lay down on his robes, but he could not make himself close his eyes. Never could he remember feeling the confusion he felt at this time. Suddenly White Fox jerked awake. He realized that he must have slept because it was getting light. He could hear voices, so he kept his head under his covers and listened. The voices belonged to his father and Stone Man.

His father was speaking. "How can a few chiefs of our people sign a paper and then tell us we can no longer live in Suland? I don't understand. I did not want to live here. I brought my family here only for a visit. I cannot stay."

Stone Man grunted in agreement. Running Elk continued. "Little Crow says now the land belongs to the Great White Father. His white children will come in great numbers to cut the trees and plow the land. We have seen these people in our woods for years. Can there be so many more of them?"

White Fox slowly peeked out from his robes and saw the two men looking out over the Great River. They did not see him.

Stone Man began to speak. "I once knew a warrior who had taken a Chippewa woman captive on a raid into the northern woods. She later became his wife and told him the story of her youth. Her tribe had lived far to the east along the Great Lakes. She remembered when the white man first came into their land and traded goods with her people. They gave her people the poison water and fooled and cheated some of the chiefs into signing papers they called treaties. Then they brought in the white soldiers and drove the Chippewa from their lands. That is why the Chippewa came into our northern lakes area and fought us for our land."

The two men were quiet again. Finally White Fox could stand it no longer and crawled from his bed. He crept close to his father and asked, "Father, are we going to leave this village today?"

Running Elk looked at him as though he were surprised to see his son. His father looked as though he hadn't slept at all. There were dark circles under his eyes, and his face looked weary. Stone Man spoke before Running Elk had a chance to answer. "We will talk to all the warriors of our band today and make a decision together. We will stay here for now." Running Elk nodded his assent.

White Fox moved away from the two men and saw his mother walking toward them with an armload of wood. "Are you hungry?" she asked him.

"I still have a full stomach from the feast last night," White Fox answered. "I am going to look for Little Wolf."

Spotted Fawn looked into her son's eyes. "Do not tell your friends of the things you have heard here. It is best to let the men discuss these matters."

White Fox nodded his understanding and walked off with his bow and quiver over his shoulder. As he walked through the camp, he observed it closely. There was very little meat on the drying racks outside the bark lodges. He noticed many canoes along the river in the upper part of the village. Across the river there were buildings that looked like a white man's trading post. He heard a shout and turned to see Little Wolf.

"Where are you going?" Little Wolf called.

"I came looking for you. Have you found some relatives to stay with?"

"My mother found another sister who still lives here. We camped next to their lodge last night. Little Sister is happy. Now she has more little cousins to play with." Little Wolf could see that he had lost White Fox's attention. His friend was staring off across the river. "What do you see over there?" he asked.

"I think it must be a trading post. I see some men moving

around it. I wish I could see better," White Fox answered. "I am curious to see if all the white men look alike. Do you remember the one we met in Suland who scared us?"

"I remember!" Little Wolf laughed.

Just then Grey Wing came toward them with a fishing spear in his hand. "Where are you going?" White Fox asked him.

"Down the river there is a creek that enters the Great River, and sometimes there are fish to spear. Do you want to come with me?"

The two boys fell in beside him. After they had walked for a while, White Fox asked, "The trader across the river—have you ever seen him up close?"

Grey Wing nodded his head. "I have seen him. My people call him Pig's Eye because he has funny-looking eyes. He has hair on his face, and he is scary looking."

White Fox and Little Wolf looked at each other and grinned. "Maybe all white men do look alike," White Fox replied. "Could you borrow a canoe and take us over there?"

"I am not allowed to go to the trading post alone," Grey Wing replied.

They came to a small creek entering the Great River where there was very little current. The water was clear and no more than a foot deep. The bottom was sandy. "Come stand in the water with me and do not move," Grey Wing instructed.

Soon many little fish were swimming around their feet. "They are too little to spear," Little Wolf said softly.

"Something bigger will come," Grey Wing replied. Suddenly they heard a cry overhead. They all looked up. There, flying overhead, was an eagle. "Now I know the big fish will come. The eagle is my friend," whispered Grey Wing with a smile.

White Fox looked intently into the water. Suddenly, something big swirled past his foot. Grey Wing lunged with his spear. White Fox could not step back quickly enough. He felt a flash of pain in his foot and saw Grey Wing bring up the spear with the fish wriggling on the end of it. Grey Wing stepped quickly out of the water so the fish would not wiggle off the spear and fall back into the stream.

White Fox stepped from the water, leaving a bloody swirl behind him. "Is that your blood in the water?" asked Little Wolf, looking at White Fox's feet.

Grey Wing laid the spear and fish down and bent to look at White Fox's foot. "Did I do that to you when I speared the fish?" he asked with concern.

"I think I got in your way. It was my own fault," White Fox answered.

"No, no, it is my fault. I should not have had you both stand in the water with me. That was foolish."

The boys examined the wound. A hunk of flesh was missing from the side of White Fox's right foot, and blood flowed from the open wound. Little Wolf gathered some leaves and soaked them in the water. He pressed them tightly to the wound to stop the bleeding. Grey Wing took his spear and began to unwind the rawhide binding from the handle. He sat down beside White Fox and carefully bound the leaves to his foot, winding the rawhide around and around until all the leaves were covered. Then Grey Wing took White Fox's moccasin and pulled it over the bandage.

"Does it hurt much?" Grey Wing asked.

"The tighter you wrapped it, the better it felt. It will be fine until my mother can put her medicine herbs on it," White Fox answered. "Bring your big fish over so I can look at it."

Grey Wing held up the fish and smiled. "Grandmother will be happy with this. She brags to the other women that I am a good fisherman."

As the boys walked back to the village, White Fox's foot felt better, and soon he forgot his injury. Grey Wing turned to walk toward his lodge but suddenly turned back. "If your foot is feeling better later, come to my lodge before dark. I will take you to see the trading post. But do not tell anyone where you are going."

White Fox turned to Little Wolf, his eyes sparkling. "I will meet you near Grey Wing's lodge when it starts to get dark. No matter what happens, I want to see that trading post."

White Fox walked back to the place by the river where they had slept the night before. Everything had been packed and moved again. He walked back through the village to Little Crow's lodge. There he saw his family's skin lodge set up next to the bark lodge of his uncle. He bent to enter the flap doorway. Inside, his mother was busy arranging her supplies. "Where have you been?" she asked.

"I went fishing with Little Wolf and our new friend, Grey Wing," answered White Fox. Spotted Fawn did not question him any further. White Fox was not her little boy anymore, and she must give him his freedom to grow into manhood. "Where is Father?" asked White Fox.

Spotted Fawn pulled the flap aside and pointed to a bark lodge not far away. "Go to that lodge, and you will find your father and another uncle who returned from a deer hunt today. It is because of this uncle that we are camped near the family again."

White Fox walked to the lodge. Two women were outside cutting up a deer. They looked up as White Fox walked to the doorway. "Come in," someone called as he peered inside. It took a few minutes for White Fox's eyes to adjust to the inside light. He saw his father and a strange man sitting together, smoking a pipe. "Come sit by us," Running Elk said. "This is another uncle, White Spider."

This man looked younger than Running Elk or Little Crow. He was a warrior in his prime. The uncle surveyed his nephew's appearance and said, "Welcome to our family, White Fox. Sit down and listen to the story I was about to tell your father."

White Fox sat beside his father. White Spider looked at White Fox and started his story. "I was not much older than you are now when our father died. One of the older half brothers claimed the position of chief that our father had held. I did not like this brother very much. He was a drunkard and visited the white man's post too much.

"Several full moons passed, and one day a group of warriors entered our village. I did not know my brother Little Crow at that time but soon was told who he was. He had come to claim his place as chief." White Spider nodded his head toward Running Elk. "He said that he had already talked to you, the eldest, and you had given your permission for him as second eldest to claim the position of chief."

Running Elk nodded in agreement, and White Spider continued. "That is when the trouble started. My half-brother stepped forward and said he had already claimed the position and that there was no place for Little Crow in this village. He told Little Crow to go back to Lac Qui Parle, where he belonged. He threatened Little Crow with a gun from the white man.

"By this time, most of the warriors of the village had gathered to watch the confrontation. Little Crow folded his arms across his chest and said, 'Shoot me then, where all can see.' My half brother did shoot, hitting him in the chest. The ball passed through both of Little Crow's forearms, breaking the bones. But it did not do much damage to his chest or face.

"The people took him to the white surgeon at Fort Snelling. The surgeon wanted to remove his hands. He said that it was the only way to save our brother's life. Little Crow refused. He said he could not be the chief without the use of his hands. He insisted that they bring him back to the shaman. He said if the shaman could not save him it was not the will of the Great Mystery for him to be their chief."

White Spider looked at Running Elk. "As you can see, he did recover. Our people took this as the sign that Little Crow was meant to be our chief, and they destroyed the other half brother. I did not see it, but I heard that someone shot him as he lay in drunkenness."

White Spider leaned close to Running Elk and his face took on an imploring look. "Running Elk, you must forgive your brother for signing treaties with the white man. You have not been here to see the pressures put on him. It was our father who started the practice of trading with the white man and taking annuities in exchange for land.

"But the more we traded and depleted the game, the more dependent we became. Most of the people here are so dependent on the annuities, which come as cash and food, they can't imagine life away from the trading post. There has been too little rain for the crops over the past two warm seasons, and we have not been able to harvest any food from them. There is not enough game to feed us. We need the government food and the trader's goods.

"Yet, things have happened that we do not understand. At first the annuities came, but we receive less and less as time goes on. And the traders do things with their records that we do not understand. When the cash does come, the people never get any. The traders get it all. We do not know the white man's way of doing things on paper."

Running Elk had listened quietly and thoughtfully to his brother's words. Finally he said, "I must return to my lodge and think about these things."

Running Elk and White Fox left the lodge and began walking back to their tepee. The sun had disappeared behind a ridge of clouds, and darkness was spreading through the camp. White Fox turned to his father. "Little Wolf and I have something we want to do before dark."

Running Elk waved his hand to dismiss him, and the boy ran off to find his friend. Now more than ever he wanted to see the trading post. White Fox walked to the lodges where Little Wolf's family was living. He saw Woodchuck emerge from one of the tepees. "Is Little Wolf here?" he asked the brother.

"I think he left to look for you," Woodchuck answered.

"Then I think I know where he went," White Fox replied. As he turned to leave, he saw Little Wolf come from the other direction. "I must have passed you on my way to your lodge," White Fox laughed.

"How is your foot?" Little Wolf asked.

"It doesn't hurt anymore ... well, maybe it hurts a little. But I want to see the trading post if Grey Wing will take us," he replied.

"It is getting dark fast. If Grey Wing is eating, maybe he will not notice," Little Wolf whispered.

The boys were leaning against a tree near Grey Wing's bark lodge. White Fox was not anxious to encounter the old gray-haired grandmother, but he was getting impatient. Finally he brought his hand to his mouth and hooted like the night owl.

He waited for a short time, then repeated the call. The flap was pulled aside, and Grey Wing emerged, smiling. "My father sent me out to chase away the sick owl that was hooting out here."

White Fox was glad for the darkness, for he could feel his face grow hot. Little Wolf snickered. "Someday, White Fox will want to court one of the young maidens, so he thought he had better practice the call."

White Fox slapped at Little Wolf but missed as he tripped over a drying-rack stake. He felt a sharp pain shoot through his foot. He stifled his grimace so the other boys would not notice. "I want to see the trading post," he blurted. "Can you take us there now?"

"Let's wait until it's a little darker. Then we can borrow my father's canoe, and no one will see us," Grey Wing replied.

The boys waited along the river. It was a strange evening. The moon was coming up bright in the east, but in the west there was lightning flashing in the dark cloudbank. Finally Grey Wing whispered, "It is dark enough." He moved to the edge of the river and looked at the designs on each of the canoes until he found the one he was looking for. The three boys quietly pushed the canoe into the water, climbed in, and started to paddle. The current grew very strong in the middle of the river, and all three paddled hard to stay on course.

As they left the strongest current behind, Grey Wing whispered, "Stop, let us drift." He ruddered the canoe to a place downstream from the trading post, then directed them to shore. "I didn't want anyone at the post to see us," he explained as they pulled the canoe up onto the sand and then into the bushes.

"Sneaking around like this makes me feel like I am on the first raid into the Chippewa country as a warrior," whispered White Fox.

"We had better not take any scalps, or we will be in big trouble when we return." Grey Wing chuckled, leading the two boys through the brush toward the trading post. The moon was bright and lit their way as they approached. It was not long before they saw the trading post through the bushes. Light flowed from the openings in the building, and they could hear laughter and singing coming from inside.

He saw that the openings were covered with a material that they could see through but would still keep out the wind. He could not help himself and reached out to touch the smooth, transparent covering over the opening. It was just as smooth as the obsidian arrowheads he and his father made. Grey Wing slowly reached out and pulled White Fox's hand back. "They can see you if you get too close," he whispered.

Just then another man came from a back room. He had small, squinting eyes. "Pig's Eye," Grey Wing whispered. He carried a jug, and the boys heard him say, "Here's a full one, boys. Drink up! We don't want to let the Indians have all the fun."

One of the men drank from the jug and passed it on to the next man. White Fox leaned back from the window. "What's in the jug?" he whispered.

"Our people call it the 'fire water.' It burns the throat on the way down and makes the person drinking it act strange and sometimes silly. If our people drink too much of it, they often get into fights and even hurt each other."

The boys continued to watch the men. One reached down and picked up a wooden box that had strings stretched across it. Next he picked up a stick, which had a string that stretched the length of the stick. He lifted his arm and brought the stick's string down and across the strings on the box. A high-pitched, scratchy sound pierced the air, and Little Wolf jumped back from the opening, bumping against some barrels stacked against the outside wall.

The boys watched in horror as the barrels started to move and then to roll and fall. The three sprinted for the bushes. They crouched in the shrubbery and watched as the men rushed from the cabin. "What the hell was that?" one of the men said loudly.

Pig's Eye looked around the corner of the building. "I had barrels stacked up against that outside wall. They must have rolled down, but they're empty, so no harm done." The three men started to laugh and talk and returned to the building. Pig's Eye remained outside for a while and looked around. He looked directly at the bushes where the boys were hiding. White fox felt a chill shoot through his body as the strange eyes looked in his direction.

Then the trader turned and entered the building. Soon the boys again heard the high, scratchy sound from the stringed box. Grey Wing spoke softly. "These people do not use drums to dance by. They have other kinds of music makers. I have seen one so small that you can hold it in the palm of your hand. They blow into it as we do our flutes. It sounds nice once you get used to it."

"Did you understand what the white man said when he saw that the barrels had rolled down?" asked White Fox.

Grey Wing nodded. "I forgot that you do not understand the white man's language. They thought the barrels had rolled down by themselves."

"How did you learn the language of the white man?" asked Little Wolf.

"I went to the mission school last year. Your uncle Little Crow insisted that some of us boys go. He sent his son, One Who Appeareth. I hated it at first, but now I am glad I went. As least now I know what the white man is saying. I think I will go again to learn the writing language. Maybe I can figure out what the trader writes in the trading book at the post."

"I think that would be a good thing," Little Wolf agreed.

"We must go back to the village now," Grey Wing said, turning to lead the way back to the canoe. As the boys paddled across the river, the dark clouds covered the moon, and the lightning was coming closer. Grey Wing skillfully directed their canoe to the place where marks in the sand told them it belonged. The boys pulled the canoe up into its place among the others. They covered any telltale marks in the sand and knew the rain would finish the job before morning.

With a wave, the boys split up and headed back to their own lodges. White Fox saw no light in his family's lodge. He edged quietly through the flap doorway, removed his clothes, and crawled into his sleeping robes. As his eyes adjusted to the darkness, he looked over to his parents. In the lightning flashes, he saw his mother looking back at him. She said nothing and neither did he. He could hear his father breathing evenly in sleep.

White Fox felt an ache in his injured foot. He would ask his mother to treat it in the morning. He relaxed and soon felt the heaviness of sleep begin to invade his body.

CHAPTER THREE

White Fox awoke in the early morning light. He did not feel well. He stretched himself slightly and felt a pain in his leg. He lay still for a moment and then slowly moved the leg again. The pain spread up his leg like fire. He heard himself moan. He turned his head toward his parents and called, "Mother."

Spotted Fawn heard him and sat up to look to her son's bed. She saw the look on his face. "What is wrong? Are you dreaming?"

"My leg, help me. It hurts so much." The words came out in an agonized whisper.

Spotted Fawn crawled from her bed to his side. "Where does it hurt?"

"I think it is my foot."

She pulled back the robes, asking "What have you done to your foot?" As she unwrapped the rawhide bindings and pulled some of the leaves from the wound, she gasped. By then Running Elk was kneeling by her side.

"Tell us what has happened to you," he demanded.

White Fox explained as best he could about the fish and the spear. He had never felt such pain as this. Moans escaped from his lips as his mother cleaned the leaves from the wound. "Mother, get Straight Talker. Tell her I need her." Spotted Fawn did not hesitate and hurried from the lodge to find the old medicine woman.

Word quickly spread through the camp that someone was in trouble, and when Running Elk stepped from the lodge he found his brother Little Crow waiting outside. Little Crow immediately saw the concern on Running Elk's face and said, "I will go to get the shaman, Wise Owl. He was the one who helped me when I was shot."

White Fox was alone in the tepee. He closed his eyes, his body filled with pain and advancing fever. He heard the flap pulled aside and someone enter. The person came close and knelt beside him. White Fox opened his eyes, but no matter how hard he blinked, he could not make out who it was. Then he heard the voice.

"It is I, Little Wolf. I will be here, close by. Do not worry."

Straight Talker entered, carrying her medicine bag. Little Wolf moved to the far side of the tepee and sat down. The lodge began to fill with people. Wise Owl came and the old grandmother. White Fox's parents entered and the chief, Little Crow. Grey Wing sneaked in among the adults and found Little Wolf. "He will get better," Grey Wing whispered. "My father is a good shaman."

"Straight Talker is a good medicine woman too," Little Wolf replied, "but even she knows that if a person's time on Mother Earth is used up nothing can stop the spirit from taking the walk on the Spirit Trail."

"Then we must ask the Great Mystery to give White Fox more time on Mother Earth," replied Grey Wing.

Little Wolf closed his eyes in quiet prayer. Grey Wing felt that he should leave the lodge to do his praying. He slipped out and walked to the Great River. White Fox had slipped into unconsciousness. Straight Talker knew by the looks of the wound that it might have gone too far. The foot was swollen and the wound was black and oozing. Streaks of red ran up the leg from the wound. Straight Talker applied hot packs of mud containing special herbs and medicines. Little Crow's wives brought her more hot wraps to keep the mudpack hot. Straight Talker spoke and sang to the Great Mystery.

Wise Owl sang and danced, shaking a dried gourd and sprinkling tobacco leaves over White Fox. The old grandmother sat close by, humming her song to the spirits. White Fox's parents sat nearby and watched, their hands clasped. They added their own fervent prayers to those being offered up.

Suddenly White Fox woke up. He was confused. He felt himself rising up from the mat. He saw all the people in the lodge. Straight Talker was working over someone. Wise Owl was dancing and chanting. His parents sat nearby, looking very sad and worried. He saw Little Wolf sitting near the doorway. "Little Wolf, what is happening?"

Little Wolf's eyes were closed, and he did not seem to hear White Fox. White Fox floated over to Straight Talker to see whom she was working on. Straight Talker continued to murmur a prayer, and he looked more carefully at the body on the sleeping mat. Suddenly he realized that it was his own body on the sleeping mat. He knew he should feel fearful, but he didn't. He began to understand. Death had taken his body, and now he must move on.

He floated up and out of the tepee. He knew his wrist was tattooed for the Spirit Trail. He looked down and could only see a faint image of himself, but he could see clearly the tattoo on his wrist. He felt so happy and free. He moved down the river trail, hoping something would show him the way to the Spirit Trail. His thoughts were of the people he would see in the Spirit Land. He remembered his mother telling him that even though he did not know his grandparents on Mother Earth, they would know each other in the Spirit Land. *I will see Moon Boy and Standing Calf,* he thought to himself.

Just then, he saw Grey Wing sitting under a tree beside the trail. Tears were running down his face. White Fox knelt in front of Grey Wing. "Why are you crying, Grey Wing?" His friend did not respond. *No one can see me anymore,* he thought.

White Fox seemed to move with no effort. He did not need his legs to carry him down the trail. He saw something white flash across the trail ahead, and then saw the white fox crouched at the edge of the trail. He saw the animal's mouth open as though to yawn. He heard a voice from the fox. "Come, young warrior, follow me."

The fox ran down the trail, and White Fox followed. They stopped by the creek where he had been injured. It was a beautiful, quiet place. He hadn't noticed that the first time. The animal lay down at the water's edge, and White Fox sat near him in silence. He listened to the gentle sound of the water running over the rocks and felt happy and drowsy.

The fox began to speak in a soft voice. "Young warrior, I am not here to take you into the Spirit Land as you think. I am here to speak to you of your people's future." The drowsiness vanished as White Fox listened to the fox. "As the next winter seasons pass, you will see many hardships come upon the people. They will have much confusion about their future. Because of the vision your father received from the Mighty Elk, you have been spared the life you would have lived in the village you are visiting now. You will always have the good memories of your childhood. But things will change for you. From this time on, you will have to put your childhood behind you and live as a young warrior.

"You will grow into manhood before the big trouble comes to your people. You must grow strong in order to survive this time, for many of your people will not survive, and the rest will be scattered to the winds." The fox stopped speaking for a moment. Then he turned his head and looked directly into White Fox's eyes. "The Great Mystery wants his children to live in peace. The Great Mystery did not make the land so people would fight over it. There are not many people living on Mother Earth who truly understand what the Great Mystery wants of them."

White Fox's mind filled with confusion as he listened. The fox had stopped speaking but continued to look into the boy's eyes. Finally White Fox spoke. "I do not understand these things you are telling me."

"You do not need to understand at this time. The words will stay with you, and you will remember them. Your time on Mother Earth is not over. Your mother named you White Fox because of me. Now I am telling you that even as you grow into manhood I will always watch over you."

White Fox did not take his eyes off the animal; but suddenly he realized that its image was fading, and he heard its words fade also: "There are difficult times ahead for your people." White Fox tried to stand, but he felt heavy and slow. Blackness enveloped him. The sound of the running water faded, and in its place he heard a gentle voice. The voice was that of Straight Talker. "Are you still with us, Little Warrior? Come back and put the joy back into our lives."

White Fox felt strange. He felt heavy, and he struggled to open his eyes. With great effort, he opened them little by little. The form before him slowly took shape. He realized he was looking into the face of Straight Talker and was lying on his sleeping mat in his own lodge. A smile flickered across the medicine woman's face. The boy turned his head and saw Grey Wing's father, Wise Owl, and his parents, all looking at him with concern.

"Do you feel any pain?" Straight Talker asked.

White Fox shook his head. He felt weak and tired, but he felt no real pain. He felt someone move close to him from behind and turned his head to look into Little Wolf's eyes. "I am glad you are back with us. The Great Mystery has honored our prayers."

"I am glad too," White Fox whispered weakly. Suddenly White Fox's eyes grew large, and he called, "Mother." Spotted Fawn and Running Elk moved to his side. "Mother, I saw the white fox. He talked to me. Father, I think I have had my vision."

Running Elk looked at his son with surprise. "You are too young to have had a vision, my son."

The adults stared at him. Wise Owl shook his head sagely. "Let us not speak of such things now. We do not know what has happened here today. We will hear what he has to say when he is well."

Little Wolf gently touched his brother's shoulder. "Grey Wing and I will be waiting for you when you grow stronger." Then he left the lodge to find Grey Wing. As he walked toward the river trail, he saw Grey Wing coming toward him. Before he could say anything, Grey Wing spoke. "Is he gone?"

"No," Little Wolf answered.

"Were you there the whole time? Did he ever leave the lodge?" Grey Wing asked.

"I was there the whole time. He never left."

Grey Wing looked confused. "But I saw him down by the river, just as I see you now. I was sitting against a tree, and I got a strange feeling, as though someone was near. I looked down the river path, and I saw him walking away from me. I wanted to call out to him, but I saw that he was following a white fox. Then he was gone, and I thought it might have been a dream because I was so worried that he would die."

Spotted Fawn was alone in the lodge with her son. She gently spooned small spoonfuls of broth into his mouth. She leaned close to his face and whispered, "Tell me, Son, did the white fox have beautiful, sky-colored eyes?" He nodded, and she smiled at him. He took only a few more spoonfuls and then started to doze off. She pulled the robe up under his chin. He slept for a long time, but she did not leave his side.

In a week's time, White Fox's foot was only slightly swollen. He could step on it lightly, and his father had cut a forked stick for him to use as a crutch. One day, Running Elk entered the lodge and looked at his son. "Wise Owl wants to talk to you now."

White Fox felt dread spread through his body. He had spent a lot of time pondering what the fox had told him, and he was not sure he understood any of it. They walked across the village in silence. When they neared the lodge, Running Elk cleared his throat loudly.

"Come into my lodge," Wise Owl called. "I have been waiting."

As White Fox entered the lodge, he smelled the pungent odor of burning sage. Grey Wing was inside, but when White Fox stepped toward him, Grey Wing moved away, saying, "Father said I must leave." Grey Wing pushed open the flap and went out, looking as though he wanted to stay.

Wise Owl motioned White Fox forward. "Come sit by the fire. The days are getting cooler." Running Elk guided his son closer to the fire, and they sat down, facing the shaman. No one spoke as Wise Owl prepared a pipe for himself and Running Elk to share.

White Fox's mind was racing. He knew that the shaman would ask him about his vision. He turned his head to look at his father. Running Elk had not asked him anything about that day, but the boy knew the questions were about to come. He looked into the shaman's eyes as the healer held out the pipe to Running Elk. "I think you know why I have called you here today, Little Warrior. I would like to hear what happened to you when you left us."

White Fox looked from the shaman to his father. Both were watching him expectantly. He sucked in a ragged breath and began. "I will tell you everything I can remember." The two men watched the boy as he stared into the fire and slowly began to speak. "I remember sinking into the darkness and then waking up. I was floating up above all of you. I saw Straight Talker and you praying over my body. She was putting mudpacks on my foot. I remember how ugly the wound looked. It was black and smelled bad. There were red streaks running up my leg from the wound." Running Elk and Wise Owl looked at each other.

"I saw Little Wolf sitting near the lodge door. He looked like he was in a trance. I spoke to him, but he did not answer me. I felt light and happy and did not feel any concern about the things that were happening to me. I went out of the lodge and saw Grey Wing sitting under a tree near the river. I talked to him, but he seemed to look right through me and did not answer."

White Fox looked at the two men. "This part confuses me," he

continued. "I think I realized that my body was dead, but I felt no sadness or concern about myself or any of you. I knew then that it was my time to go on to the next life. I walked downstream on the river trail as though I knew that was the way to go. That's when I saw the white fox. It was crouched beside the trail, and he opened his mouth wide and spoke to me in our own tongue."

White Fox's body trembled, and he sucked in his breath. The memories were coming back. His face grew pale, and the men leaned forward in anticipation of what he would say next. White Fox stared at them. He could not tell them what his memory had revealed to him.

"You are not completely well. Maybe we should talk about this at another time," Wise Owl suggested.

"No, I want to tell you now," White Fox whispered. "The fox told me many things that I do not understand. He said we cannot escape the advance of the white man." Again White Fox paused and glanced uneasily at Running Elk. "Father, I know you will not want to hear these things. He said we must pray to the Great Mystery for guidance and wisdom. He said that he, the white fox, would always be my protector as long as I remain on Mother Earth. That's all I can remember."

Wise Owl looked at White Fox with a puzzled expression. "I believe this was your vision quest. You did not have to seek it. The Great Mystery brought it to you early in your life. Maybe you will remember more about it as you grow older."

"Can I go now?"

Wise Owl watched him leave. He knew that they had not heard all of this boy's vision. He had a very uneasy feeling.

CHAPTER FOUR

Running Elk sat under an old oak tree working on an arrow point. He gently ran his thumb over the edge to feel the sharpness. He felt pride in his ability to make a point sharp to perfection. He sat on a bluff overlooking the Kaposia village, and he let his eyes wander over the scene below him. He saw White Fox, Little Wolf, and Grey Wing leaving the village on the river trail. The three boys were inseparable now. Grey Wing spent a lot of time at their lodge, and Running Elk had grown very fond of him. As he watched the boys move down the trail, he observed that White Fox still walked with a slight limp. His wound had healed nicely, however, and the limp soon would be gone.

The leaves on the oak tree were still a dark green, but Running Elk could see that the maples were changing to the bright red and orange of this changing season. His thoughts shifted to the reality of his people's situation, and the contented feeling seeped from his body. They had stayed too long in this village, and now it was too late to leave. They had no winter provisions to sustain them in a move back to the old village in Suland.

His brother Little Crow had taken him to the trading post to see all the white man's wares. There were blankets, axes, hats, hoes, knives with steel blades, and calico cloth. Many of the women in the village wore clothing made from this cloth. Running Elk did not like the look of it and thought it did not seem very sturdy. Little Crow had insisted on getting him a gun. He told Running Elk that it would be paid for with the annuity money, when it came. Little Crow had explained that this was the money the Great White Father in Washington would send to pay for the land.

This made Running Elk feel very uncomfortable. Since he had not sold the land, he told the trader that he would bring some of the skins and furs he had in his lodge to pay for the weapon. Running Elk brought him the furs the next day and hoped the debt had been marked off in the trader's book.

Again Running Elk let his eyes wander over the village. He could see Spotted Fawn working alongside Little Crow's wives. They were slicing pumpkins and putting them on racks to dry. Running Elk felt his heart swell with pride and affection. His wife was as beautiful and nimble as the day he met her in the Lac Qui Parle village. He knew he was a lucky man to have her.

Just then, he saw Little Crow walking up the incline toward him. They had planned to go hunting, even though there usually was no game to be found. Running Elk was beginning to understand how the game had been depleted. It had taken many furs to pay for the rifle he had gotten from the trader. As Little Crow approached, he said, "Come with me, Brother. I am going to the fort on the White Cliff to talk to the agent. I would like you to see the fort."

Running Elk got to his feet and picked up his bow. "I am not busy. I will go with you." He glanced at his brother and noticed that he carried no weapon. They walked up the trail parallel to the Great River and soon reached the place of the meeting of waters. They would have to cross the Minnesota River to get to the fort.

Little Crow pulled a canoe from the bushes and pushed it into the river. Running Elk climbed in, and they paddled across the river. Heavy summer rains had made the current strong, and they had to paddle hard to stay on course. When they had pulled their canoe up onto the sand of the opposite shore, Running Elk paused to take in the view. The White Cliff had always been a landmark for the people. Now, however, the landscape looked much different. The sun, still in the eastern sky, illuminated the cliff, emphasizing its white color. The fort, built upon the bluff, looked imposing from the river bottom.

Running Elk felt himself grow apprehensive as he followed his brother up the path to the fort. He kept glancing up at the white limestone walls. As they neared the front of the fort, Running Elk studied the structure. Towers rose above the walls in each corner, with a huge gun situated on each tower. He could see narrow openings built into the fort's stone walls. Little Crow saw his brother's expression. "The openings are for the soldiers to put their guns through to shoot any intruders."

Ahead of them was a great door made of logs. It stood open, and Little Crow walked through, looking poised and confident. Running Elk followed. Once inside the walls, the men stopped and looked around. On the far side of the enclosure, some men were walking in a line, side by side. Each held a gun propped against his right shoulder. One man, who must have been a chief, was shouting at the rest. They walked in a straight line, then turned sharply to make a square corner. Running Elk thought this looked very odd.

"Have you seen the white soldiers before this?" Little Crow asked his brother.

Running Elk nodded. "Only from a distance. Two winter seasons ago, a big boat with a large paddle on the back came up the Great River. We could see men on the boat with clothes that looked like these."

"Do you want to come inside to meet the agent?" Little Crow asked.

"I will stay here and watch the soldiers," Running Elk answered. He saw that the soldier who seemed to be the chief was watching him, and he decided not to move too far from the gate opening.

There were many doors on the buildings facing the square. Some of the doors stood open, and Running Elk would have liked to look inside. Instead he stood and watched the soldiers march. Every step was perfectly matched to the next man. Running Elk wondered why men would ever walk like that in battle; it looked very tiring.

Little Crow and a tall, bearded man finally emerged from one of the doorways and walked toward Running Elk. "I want you to meet this man. His name is Nathaniel McLean." Little Crow turned back to the white man and said in English, this is my brother Running Elk."

The white man stuck out his hand to Running Elk. Running Elk looked at him, not quite sure what to do about the hand. Little Crow laughed. He took his brother's hand and put it into the other's hand so the man could shake it. To Running Elk this seemed a strange thing to do to someone he had just met. "The agent says he is glad to meet you," Little Crow said.

"Tell this man I am glad to meet him too." Running Elk was not sure he was glad to know any of these men, but it seemed the right thing to say. With Little Crow's business completed, they left the fort through the big gate and crossed back over the Minnesota River. Each seemed deep in his own thoughts as they walked back to the village. Finally Little Crow spoke. "The agent told me that in the next Moon of the Grass Appearing, our band will have to move to the new home along the Minnesota River. We agreed to that at the treaty signing."

Running Elk turned to look at his brother. "You signed the treaty. I did not sign away any part of Mother Earth. I am returning to the land of the two rivers when the warm moons come, even if we must fight the Chippewa to live there."

"They won't be there," Little Crow replied. "That land now belongs to the white man."

Running Elk said no more. He wished he had not gone to the fort with his brother. He wished he had not seen the big gun.

PART THREE

CHAPTER ONE

1854

White Fox looked over the two rivers, and an ache spread through his chest. Three winter seasons had passed since they had left this place. So many times he had carried water up this path to the village. So often he and Little Wolf had played here at the water's edge where the little river entered the Great River. The landscape was so familiar and yet so strange without the village and its people. He saw his father walking up the old trail to the top of the bluff. Long Legs followed. White Fox knew they were going to the burial grounds overlooking the Great River. He watched them thoughtfully.

When he turned back to his friends, his face had changed. He looked serious, almost sad. "Come sit near me," he said. "There is something I must tell you." Little Wolf and Grey Wing moved close to White Fox and sat. "You remember three winter seasons ago when I walked near the Spirit World?" The boys nodded. "I did not tell my father and your father all that the white fox revealed to me that day."

White Fox sat in quiet thought for some time, looking out over the river. The white fox's message had troubled him greatly, but even after so long he had spoken of it to no one; yet now, fifteen winter seasons old, White Fox was beginning to sense the gravity of the fox's words.

"Tell us what he told you," Little Wolf urged.

White Fox turned back to his friends, his face troubled and confused. "He told me that many white men will enter our land. The white fox told me that not many of our people will survive this, and the ones who do will be scattered to the winds."

"Are you saying our people will die because of the many white men who are coming?" Grey Wing asked, his concern showing plainly.

"I'm telling you what I was told. I don't know what it means," White Fox said. "My heart has been heavy from not sharing this with anyone. At times I feel very afraid. Little Wolf and I have seen many new things since our life in this place. We have seen some of the young warriors drink the burning water of the white trader and lose all interest in our old ways of life. We have seen some of the women forget how to find the good foods of Mother Earth. You do not know the old ways, Grey Wing, and so you do not see the changes as we do." Little Wolf nodded in agreement as White Fox spoke.

Just then they saw Running Elk and Long Legs coming down from the bluff, and the boys grew quiet. The sun had disappeared behind the bluff, and the men took their sleeping robes from the ponies and made ready for the night. Running Elk had told all of them that he wanted to sleep one more time on this ground, where he had spent the happiest day of this life.

White Fox watched his mother. She was using her special stone to work one of the new skins they had brought back from the hunt into Suland. The hide was getting the soft, white look that hours and hours of work produced. She looked happy doing the work she enjoyed so much. Since their return, White Fox thought his father seemed happier too. He had begun talking about going to the plains for a fall buffalo hunt. The skins of the winter tepee needed to be replaced.

White Fox had heard his father and his uncle Little Crow talking the night they had returned from the hunt. His uncle was angry that Running Elk had taken a hunting party so deep into Suland. "The white agent will be angry and cause trouble for the whole band if he finds out," Little Crow had explained heatedly.

White Fox had watched his uncle try to live the way the agent wanted. He had even seen him try to turn the sod with a plow pulled by the strange, long-eared pony. "If we are to farm as the white men do, we will need very large corn fields," Little Crow had told him. His uncle seemed to enjoy White Fox's company, and White Fox liked his uncle, in spite of all his foolish ideas that the Dakota people could live as the white man did.

Little Wolf and Grey Wing rode to White Fox's lodge on their ponies. "Come, White Fox," shouted Little Wolf. "Big Boy and Red Bird want to go down the river to hunt. We have brought your pony."

White Fox grabbed his bow and quiver. He touched his mother lightly on the shoulder. "Leave the pot in the warm coals for me tonight," he said to her. She smiled in answer.

White Fox jumped on his pony's back, and the boys rode out of the village. They soon caught up to Big Boy and Red Bird. "Where are we going?" White Fox asked.

"To the mouth of the Cottonwood River. We can usually find some deer there," Red Bird answered.

"Let's watch the bushes for rabbit or squirrel to roast along the trail," Little Wolf said.

White Fox laughed. "You are always thinking of food, Little Wolf, and already you have grown as tall as your father."

"I'm not as wide as he is yet, so I must eat often."

"We will have to change your name to Big Wolf if you keep eating so much," Gray Wing grinned.

"My name cannot be changed until I am made a warrior," Little Wolf said solemnly. "This is hard to do when the chief will not let us go on raids into Chippewa country."

"Haven't you noticed that some of the young men disappear for a moon and when they return they have extra ponies and decorate themselves as warriors?" Big Boy replied. "Little Crow does not question them. I think that is the only way for us to become warriors, the way things are now."

Big Boy reined his pony to a stop. "Come look at this," he said, sliding from his pony's back. As the others came closer, they saw Big boy pull a red-tipped stick from the ground.

"What is it?" Red Bird asked.

"The white man calls it a surveyor's stake," answered Big Boy. "They use it to measure the land. It means a white man soon will build his cabin here."

"But this is our land, all the way to the Cottonwood River," protested Red Bird. "I heard Chief Little Crow say that."

"Always the white man takes more land." Big Boy grunted as he threw the stick into the weeds. "Let's flush those bushes and see if we can find a rabbit. I do not want to spoil the day by thinking about the white man."

The three boys stood ready as White Fox crawled into the brush and thrashed around. Suddenly he heard the hoots that told him rabbits had come out to the hunters. He emerged from the brush to see Red Bird and Little Wolf each holding up a rabbit. The boys put the rabbits into their rawhide game bags and moved down the trail.

Big Boy stopped his pony. "We are not far from the Cottonwood River," he said. "See the red bluff ahead? The old warriors call it Old Redstone. It is on an island. The river branches off and flows behind it too." The sun was high in the sky, and its bright light emphasized the red color of the hill. "From here, the woods on this side of the river grow thicker. We can watch for signs of deer. Red Bird and I are used to hunting together. We will move down the river. You three can hunt here. We will meet later," he called over his shoulder.

Little Wolf pointed to a thick stand of willow along the low river bottom. "That looks like a place where the deer might bed down during the heat of the day. Let's split up and move into the willows. One of us should chase up something." The others agreed and moved into the thicket.

White Fox tramped deep into the willow until the ground underfoot got too spongy. Then he changed course, moving back toward the trail they had left. He moved slowly and stopped often to listen. He stood perfectly still and saw a slight movement in the leaves ahead. As his eyes focused on the point of movement, he realized he was looking at a set of antlers that blended closely with the leaves. He knew he could not get a good shot through the heavy underbrush, so he moved to the side, circling, hoping to force the animal out into the opening he knew was nearby.

Suddenly the buck reacted and jumped toward the opening. White Fox lunged for the clearing and broke out at the same time as the buck. He had his bow up and ready. The buck was in full flight as he aimed. His arrow flew true, and he heard the thud as it hit. The animal did not slow and disappeared into the trees. White Fox knew he had made a good shot and found blood speckling the meadow grasses. He could see the blood trail easily and started to follow it toward the trees.

Just then, a doe broke from the willows and came toward him at a full run. White Fox had his bow up and another arrow in place. As she passed him broadside, he let the arrow fly. He saw the doe stumble, but she too kept running. White Fox heard a shout and turned back toward the willows. "Did you see a doe come out?" Grey Wing called as he emerged.

"I shot her, Grey Wing. She went that way," White Fox answered, pointing the direction. "You will have to follow her. I wounded a buck that I must find."

Grey Wing found the doe's trail and disappeared into the woods as White Fox continued following the buck's trail. He soon found more blood and knew the deer could not go very far. The hoof prints were closer and closer together and finally disappeared into some chokecherry bushes. There he found the buck, dead. The arrow had punctured its lungs.

"I am sorry that my shot was not better and you had to run," White Fox whispered solemnly. "Thank you for your life so we may live." Then he cut the animal's throat and started the job of dressing it out.

He was almost finished when Little Wolf rode up, bringing White Fox's pony. "You and the buck left an easy trail to follow," he said.

Star, White Fox's pony, snorted and pranced, complaining as he usually did at the smell of fresh blood. White Fox spoke to the pony in a low voice. "It is your job to carry the buck back to camp, so stop complaining."

Little Wolf heard and smiled. He liked to tease White Fox about how attached he became to his animals. White Fox's dog, Little Warrior, still sneaked under the tepee flap at night to sleep nestled against White Fox, even though he was now an old dog and smelled like one. Little Warrior should have been eaten at a dog feast a long time ago, Little Wolf thought. Now he was too old and stringy.

Little Wolf helped White Fox sling the buck across Star's back. The boys started back to find Grey Wing. The three boys had a fire burning and the rabbits ready to roast when they heard a shout. They looked up to see Big Boy and Red Bird coming down the trail. Red Bird's pony had a deer across its back, and the boys rode together on the other pony. Big Boy and Red Bird exclaimed when they saw the other two deer, and White Fox smiled, knowing that he had shot them both. His medicine must be strong this day.

Before long, the fire had burned down to a bed of glowing coals, and the boys surrounded it, each holding a green stick with a chuck of meat speared on the end. The air filled with the succulent smell of roasting meat. The boys all were as hungry as Little Wolf now, and they ate ravenously until the pile of meat chunks had disappeared. White Fox threw his stick aside with a groan and lay back in the grass. The others followed suit, and soon all the boys were lying on their backs watching the clouds float across the sky.

"Do you see those clouds there?" White Fox said, pointing. "My uncle Panther Man once lived in the Canada Country, and he told me that on a hunting trip he had traveled so far in the direction of the Going-Down Sun that he saw the tall rock hills that reach up to the sun. He said they had snow on their tops, even in the Moon When the Cherries Turn Ripe. He said they looked like those clouds."

"If they reached up toward the sun, why would they have snow on their tops?" Red Bird asked.

"My uncle said the higher they rode into these hills, the cooler the wind blew," White Fox replied. "I would like to see the tall hills sometime. Then I would know about these things."

All grew quiet around the fire until only the singing birds and rustling leaves were heard. Suddenly Little Wolf jumped up. "If we lie here any longer, I am going to sleep, and we are still far from the village." He gathered up the rabbit skins. "My mother will make warm winter mittens for the family with these."

The boys rode double on the ponies not carrying deer. Suddenly Big Boy pulled his pony to a halt and raised his hand so the other would stop. The boys sat still and listened. They could hear a thudding sound. They tethered the ponies carrying the deer and followed Big Boy as he nudged his pony from the trail and into the deep woods. They soon reached a clearing and looked across it without leaving the shadows of the trees.

Across the clearing, they could see a white man cutting up a tree with an axe. A small log lodge stood nearby. Not far from the lodge were two large animals grazing as far as their tether ropes would allow them.

"What kind of animal is that?" Little Wolf whispered.

"They are called oxen," Big Boy said authoritatively. "They are strong and can pull the plow easily."

Red Bird interrupted. "This man is on our side of the Cottonwood River."

"My father always tells me to stay away from the white man.

But if he comes onto our reservation, how can we stay away from him?" White Fox said softly.

"I think we should teach this white farmer a lesson," whispered Big Boy. "I think we should kill his oxen."

"How could we do that?" asked Red Bird.

"We will have to wait until he goes back into his lodge," Big Boy answered, still watching the farmer. A woman came from the lodge and walked over to where the man was working. They talked for a short time and then both walked back into the building. The boys looked at each other and Big Boy started to smile. "Our medicine is good this day. The Great Mystery must approve of my plan."

They watched for a while to be sure that the man was not coming back out immediately. Finally Big Boy said, "It would be best if one of us stays with the ponies. We could draw lots."

Red Bird picked five long stems of grass. He broke them all, leaving one a little shorter than the rest. Then he held them with the uneven ends concealed and let the others each choose a straw. Little Wolf snorted in disappointment as he pulled the short straw from Red Bird's hand.

White Fox felt excitement run through him as they moved, staying in the shadows of the trees, to the far side of the clearing. When they got near the animals, Big Boy used his hands to signal that Grey Wing and White Fox should kill the one animal, and he and Red Bird would shoot the other.

White Fox knew that the arrow would have to be driven deep into the chest to kill such a large animal. It would be like killing a buffalo. He pulled his bow from his shoulder and fitted an arrow into the string. He nodded to Grey Wing and pulled the bowstring as far as he could. He waited until he heard his friend release his arrow, and then did the same. The big animal jerked as the arrows struck.

The ox turned his head, and he seemed to look at the boys. Slowly his front legs gave way, and he sank into a kneeling position. Then his back legs collapsed, leaving the animal resting on his belly. Finally, he grunted loudly, and his head fell forward to the ground. White Fox hadn't heard the other boys shoot, but he saw the other beast fall on its side. He felt a sudden wave of sadness.

"Hurry, the farmer may have heard," Big Boy whispered urgently. The boys moved stealthily back to where Little Wolf waited. They leaped onto the ponies and took one last look across the clearing. No one had come from the cabin. The boys turned and headed back to the trail as quickly as the ponies could move through the heavy woods.

When they were near the village, Big Boy stopped and turned his pony to face the rest. "We will not tell anyone about the white man's work beasts. Our chief, Little Crow, would get angry." The boys agreed.

As they entered the village, the little boys whooped loudly to announce that the young hunters had returned with fresh meat. But White Fox had lost the pride he had felt about the hunt. He still could see the big work animals fall. Why did the white man always have to push farther into their land?

Running Elk had been in better spirits since he had led the hunting party back to the old village in Suland. He was busy organizing a Moon of the Changing Season buffalo hunt, urging even Little Crow to come with them. The young warriors were excited. They hadn't been on a buffalo hunt for many seasons, and some of them had never gone. Spotted Fawn and Walking Woman would go along to process the buffalo meat and hides on the site of the kill, as they always had in the past.

White Fox sat outside their lodge, braiding a new rawhide bridle for Star. He had found a red feather that morning and carefully attached it to the bridle. White Fox looked up suddenly, surprised to see Little Wolf watching him. "You move as quietly as the little wolf you have been named for." He grinned.

"That may be true, but I think you were deep in your thoughts," Little Wolf answered. "When do you think we will be ready to leave on the hunt?"

"I think my father is planning to leave after two more sleeps. He wants to lead the hunting party up the river to the Sisseton villages to find my uncle Panther Man. We are hoping that he will join us on this hunt."

"I remember when he came to our village on the two rivers," commented Little Wolf. "I did not like it when you spent so much time with him."

White Fox looked at his friend, surprised. "I did not realize you were unhappy at that time."

"We were little boys, and I was used to being with you almost all the time," Little Wolf explained. "It would be fun to meet him again. I remember him to have many interesting stories."

CHAPTER TWO

The sun hadn't yet broken over the horizon when the women finished packing the travoises for the buffalo hunt. Excitement was running high, and several of the young men were racing their ponies at the edge of the camp to wear off some of their tensions. Running Elk, leader of the hunt, was full of anticipation and anxious to leave, as were many others. Even Little Crow and two of his six wives had decided to go along.

Little Wolf and Grey Wing came riding through the camp to find White Fox. As they looked for their friend, bantering with each other, they did not notice Little Warrior, who came ambling up from the river. Now bereft of the sharp hearing and vision he had had as a younger dog, he walked directly into the horses' path. In an instant, he was under their hooves.

White Fox recognized the piercing yip of pain and ran to his old friend in alarm. He saw his old dog lying in the dust and knelt beside him. The dog's aged, pale eyes looked up at him, and the dog strained upward, trying to touch White Fox's chin with his nose. White Fox saw that the animal's rib cage was crushed and the dog's breath was coming in short gasps. He leaned down, gently wrapped his arms around Little Warrior, and pressed his face against the dog's wet nose, waiting as the labored breathing slowed and finally stopped.

White Fox felt a hand on his shoulder. Little Wolf knelt beside him, an anguished look on his face. "Do not worry, Little Wolf," White Fox said softly. "Little Warrior was old, and I was not certain he would be able to keep up with us on the trail. His spirit will wait for me in the next world."

He gathered the dog in his arms and struggled to his feet. His eyes traveled over the landscape, searching for the right place to bury his old friend. He started to walk slowly to the west, to the prairie. "I will put you where you spent so much of your time chasing the rabbits and the prairie dogs," he whispered.

As White Fox buried the dog, Running Elk gave the signal to move out and started riding up the river trail. The hunting party began to move, gradually falling in line. By the end of the second day on the trail, the hunting party was nearing a Sisseton village on another reservation along the Lac Qui Parle lake. Running Elk had spoken to some young Sisseton hunters earlier in the day and learned that Panther Man lived in the village ahead.

White Fox was anxious to see his uncle again and rode at the lead with his father. Running Elk turned to his son. "I have asked Long Legs to lead the party into the village. Come along with me. I am going to ride ahead to find your uncle."

White Fox felt excitement stir in him as they rode out in front. They could see the smoke and haze from the village as they rode down into a small valley. Soon they could see women and children walking toward them on their way to welcome the women of the hunting party. As they rode past, Running Elk heard tittering among the young women and, to his surprise, saw that they were looking a White Fox. He turned and looked intently at his son. He was surprised to see how tall and mature he looked sitting astride his pony. This boy riding at his side, now fifteen winter seasons old, was growing into a handsome young man.

Running Elk could see his resemblance to Spotted Fawn, but the boy's features had taken on the strong look of a warrior. He felt pride in the boy's strong chin and the hairline that came to a peak on the forehead, like his own. His son's complexion was lighter than his own, and the eyes had remained the same sky color as when he was a little boy. *Someday this young man will have the pick of the maidens,* thought his father, a smile spreading across his face.

From the village, a rider came toward them, his hand raised in greeting. Running Elk pulled his pony to a stop as Panther Man did the same, and they sat looking at each other. Running Elk spoke first. "It has been many moons since last we saw each other. You look strong and healthy, my wife's brother."

"I am glad to see you, Running Elk. And is this the boy who fell in the creek so many times?" Panther Man laughed, looking at White Fox. "I think the warrior has broken out of the little-boy cocoon."

Running Elk smiled and nodded his agreement. White Fox looked embarrassed by the attention. "I will go back to get Spotted Fawn. Tell me where to find your lodge," Running Elk said.

Panther Man gave the directions, and then turned to White Fox. "Ride back to my lodge with me so we can talk." White Fox turned his pony toward the village and fell into step beside his uncle. "How has your life been since we last enjoyed each other's company?" Panther Man asked. "I understand that you have been living on the reservation down river from us for three winter seasons."

A frown line appeared between White Fox's brows. "You know what our life was like in Suland," he said. "We have had a difficult time adjusting to this new life. But none of us as difficult a time as my father. He took some of us on a hunting trip back to the two rivers in the Moon of Making Fat. I saw him look at that place as if it was the last time he would ever see it. We found places throughout the woods where the white man had cut the trees and plowed the land. We even find them on the reservation where we hunt." Once he started to speak, White Fox couldn't seem to stop. He felt a need to tell his uncle all of the things he had seen. Panther Man listened solemnly.

By this time, they had entered the village. Panther Man stopped his pony in front of a lodge. As they dismounted and tied their ponies, a woman came from the lodge, followed by two girls. Panther Man turned to the woman. "This woman is my wife, Sunflower," he said to White Fox. "And this is my stepdaughter, Chickadee, and her good friend, Falling Star. And this," he said to Sunflower, "is my nephew, White Fox."

Sunflower stepped forward and said warmly, "Welcome to our lodge. You will be my nephew too."

White Fox knew that this was the woman his mother had spoken of when Panther Man left Suland—the woman he had wanted to make his wife. White Fox could see the goodness in her eyes, and the affection Panther Man felt for her showed in his.

The two girls looked White Fox over. He guessed that they were near his age, about twelve or thirteen winters old. Chickadee was a chubby girl with a round, smiling face. The other girl was taller, willowy and pretty. "I am happy to meet all of you," White Fox said. "I am always happy to have more family."

At that moment, Running Elk and Spotted Fawn arrived on their ponies. As Panther Man began the introductions again, Chickadee edged up to White Fox and said softly, "Come with us, Cousin, and we will show you the village."

White Fox was about to decline the invitation when his father said, "Go with your little cousin, White Fox. Your uncle and I will share a pipe. We have some talking to do."

Already his mother and Sunflower were walking away, talking among themselves, but White Fox would rather have stayed and listened to the men. However, Chickadee latched onto his arm and pulled him along. She kept up a chatter that reminded him of the little bird for which she was named. White Fox noticed the other girl following a few steps behind and glanced over his shoulder at her. He decided that she was probably a little older than his cousin. She had a slim body and a pretty face. That he took notice of her looks surprised White Fox. While his friends were always eyeing the girls and making remarks about their looks, he had never had any interest in the young maidens. But he thought this girl was almost as pretty as his mother.

Chickadee led him to the Lake That Speaks (Lac Qui Parle), and the three walked along the shoreline. Shouts and laughter caught their ears, and they headed toward the sounds. They soon found some young men playing a game, shooting arrows through a hoop made of grapevine. The three watched as the hoop was thrown into the air and one of the young men shot his arrows at a remarkable speed. He shot three arrows through the hoop before it hit the ground.

Seeing the threesome, the young man shouted, "Did you see that, Falling Star? I always get three arrows through the hoop before it falls back to Mother Earth."

White Fox looked at Chickadee's friend. Her face was lit with a shy smile. Her teeth were even and white, and her dark eyes sparkled with amusement. Chickadee moved close to White Fox and whispered, "Yellow Feather is always trying to impress Falling Star."

White Fox felt an odd feeling spread through him, and he suddenly stepped forward. He brought his own bow forward and said, "I would like to try to shoot my arrows through the hoop."

"Who are you?" one of the boys asked.

"This is my cousin White Fox," Chickadee answered. "He is a visitor to our village."

The same boy picked up the hoop once more. "I will throw the hoop for you. Tell me when."

White Fox faced the boy with the hoop. He reached back and pulled four arrows from his quiver. He carefully arranged the arrows in his left hand so they extended below the point where he held the bow. He and his friends had practiced this technique when they realized they were going on a buffalo hunt, but he had never tried to hold four arrows before. He looked at the boy and stood quietly for a short time, gauging the distance. Then he called, "Throw!"

The hoop shot straight upward, high into the air, and one arrow flew through it even before it reached the highest point. As it came down, two more arrows flew through the target. Then, just before it hit the ground, the fourth flew through, kicking up the dirt as it hit the ground beyond the hoop. A cheer went up from the onlookers.

Chickadee screeched and jumped up and down, grabbing at White Fox as though to give him a hug. White Fox did his best to stay out of her reach. The rest of the young men laughed, and White Fox could see from the corner of his eye that Falling Star was standing nearby with a smile on her face. Yellow Feather walked close to White Fox and looked at Chickadee sternly. She stopped jumping and returned his look. "I see nothing on your cousin's decorations to show he is a warrior. I have been to the Chippewa country on a raiding party. *I* am a warrior." Yellow Feather strutted away, a few of the other young men following.

Most of the young men had stayed, however, and were smiling and snickering. They didn't seem to mind that White Fox had beaten one of their own band. White Fox was glad when he saw the group dispersing. He could not believe how quickly he had shot his arrows, and he was glad that no one challenged him to do it again. Chickadee grabbed his arm. "Come. We will show you the mission school where Falling Star and I go to learn to read from the white man's books. Have you ever attended a white man's school?"

"After we moved onto the reservation, I attended a school at the Redwood Agency for three winter seasons," White Fox answered. "I can speak the white man's tongue and write some of his written words."

"Our teacher is a Black Robe," Chickadee said. "We have given him the name Soaring Eagle. He is a good teacher and tries to help our people in many ways." They walked along the lake until they came to small log lodge that looked the same as all the other white man's buildings White Fox had seen. Chickadee pushed the door open. She walked in, followed by White Fox and Falling Star.

The row of tables and chairs brought White Fox memories of the school at Redwood. "My father did not want me to go to the school," he said. "My uncle Chief Little Crow insisted that I go.

Finally my father gave in." White Fox moved among the tables, touching the smooth tops. "At first I hated the school and having to sit for so long a time; but finally the bad feeling left, and I enjoyed learning new things. Our teacher was wise and only kept us for short periods of time, because most of us could not stay inside for very long."

Suddenly White Fox sensed another presence in the room. He spun around. The girls looked toward the door too. There stood a Black Robe. A smile came across the Black Robe's face, and the girls smiled back at him. "Have you brought a new student here to our school?" he asked.

"We are just showing my cousin our school, Father Soaring Eagle," answered Chickadee. "He is traveling through our area and stopped to visit."

"Where are you going?" the Black Robe asked him.

"We are here just to visit," White Fox answered. He knew it was better not to mention the buffalo hunt to a white man. It could cause trouble because the hunt would take them off the reservation.

"Where do you live, young man, and what is your name?"

"My name is White Fox, and I live at Little Crow's village near the Redwood Agency," he answered. "But I wish we could go back to live in Suland," he blurted without meaning to. He looked at the Black Robe to see how he would react to this.

The Black Robe smiled. "I wish this were possible for all your people," he said gently. The Black Robe was thoughtful for a moment. "I have many things to do," he said. "You young people look around as long as you like." Then he left them.

"Your Black Robe teacher seems like a good person," White Fox said.

"We like him very much," Falling Star replied. "He treats us with respect, unlike some of the other white men we have come to know in this place."

These were the first words White Fox had heard the girl speak, and he liked the sound of her soft, low-pitched voice. She had the maturing body of a young maiden but possessed the serene look of an older woman. He almost smiled as he wondered where she found the patience to be friends with his little cousin. He wished he could talk to her without his cousin's company, but he could not think of a way to accomplish this gracefully.

By then, Chickadee had stood still long enough. "Come, Cousin. We will show you the big honking birds in the wild rice part of the lake. The young birds are learning to fly now. It can be funny to watch."

White Fox and Falling Star nearly had to run to keep up with Chickadee. *This cousin of mine certainly has a lot of energy,* he thought to himself.

Chickadee continued her chatter. "The Wahpetons from down the river are coming here tonight to join us in a Midsummer Feast and games. Maybe my father will invite your people to stay and celebrate with us. There will be many games and much food." Chickadee spoke rapidly as though she had so much to tell and not enough time to tell it all.

White Fox hoped they would stay. In Suland, they had celebrated many feasts, but there had not been any friendly bands nearby to share the good times.

Chickadee took a deep breath and continued. "There will be a big lacrosse game. Our medicine man has already carved the balls. I have seen them—one is black, one red, and one yellow. Our tribe will challenge the Wahpetons."

Chickadee stopped talking as they neared the lake. Through the wild rice grass they could see the big birds feeding. The young birds had their adult feathers but still were not fully grown.

The three sat down on the ground to watch. Soon they saw one of the young birds start to paddle its feet, gathering some speed. Then it began to flap its wings. Slowly it began to lift from the water, only to lose its momentum and splash back down. This did look funny, and soon White Fox and the girls were chuckling. The older birds took off and landed elegantly as though to show the young birds how to do it. The young birds continued their clumsy attempts.

White Fox got to his feet and looked at Chickadee. "Let's walk back to your father's lodge." The girls fell into step beside him. As they passed each lodge, Chickadee told him something about the family living there. She would make a good village crier, White Fox thought with a smile. When they reached the lodge of Panther Man, they found the adults sitting under a nearby tree. White Fox heard Panther Man telling his father about the Midsummer Feast.

"I cannot leave to go on a hunt until the feast is over," Panther Man said. "We would all enjoy having the company of our relatives at this celebration."

"I will talk to my brother Little Crow," answered Running Elk. "I saw him visiting with some of the people of your village. He once lived in this area, and all of his wives are Sissetons. I am sure he would enjoy staying here for a few days."

As Running Elk left the group to find his brother, Panther Man touched White Fox lightly on the shoulder. "We will be challenging the Wahpeton band to a lacrosse game," he said. "Because your mother is of the Sisseton band, I invite you to play on our team."

White Fox nodded enthusiastically. "I would like that."

Panther Man returned his smile. "Good."

White Fox suddenly realized he hadn't seen Little Wolf or Grey Wing since they had entered the village. He walked back to where he had left his pony, looking around the camp. He untied Star, Running Elk's buffalo pony, and Spotted Fawn's pony and led them back through the camp toward the meadow where the village's animals grazed. As he walked the length of the village, he realized that most of their hunting party had integrated into the village, finding relatives to stay with.

At the edge of the camp, he saw Walking Woman and Robin's Nest tending a fire, and White Fox turned in their direction. The women had set up two wickiups. Robin's Nest and Bald Eagle had married when they lived at the Kaposia village, and now White Fox could see that she was with child. Little Wolf's family would be growing larger again.

"Where are Little Wolf and Grey Wing?" he called out to the women.

"They have gone to the lake for water," Robin's Nest answered.

"When they return, tell them I have taken our ponies to the meadow," White Fox requested.

He led the three ponies along the well-used trail until he came to the top of a rise. There he stopped and looked over the meadow where all the village's ponies peacefully grazed in the lush grasses. He wondered if he should pound stakes and tie the ponies until they got used to this place. If he did, he would have to walk them to the lake to water them. White Fox saw a young man coming toward him. "Hi ya!" the young man called. "Are you from the hunting party that came in today?"

"Yes," White Fox called back. "I am trying to decide if I should stake out our ponies."

"I am a pony tender. If you leave them free, I will keep a special watch until they get used to the others. I am not alone here," he added, gesturing toward the hillside to show White Fox that there were more tenders watching the herd. "We have more tenders watching the herd at night," the pony tender continued. "Last Moon of the Falling Leaves, we were raided by a Chippewa party and lost twenty good ponies." Then he grinned and added, "Of course, we have stolen some of them back since then." White Fox returned the smile.

The young man looked admiringly at Running Elk's buffalo pony. "That one looks to be a strong runner," he commented.

White Fox confirmed his assessment, then said, "I will check back later. Our three will stick together. I am sure they will be fine."

"Do not worry," the young man called as White Fox walked back up the rise.

When he reached the top, White Fox paused and looked out over the prairie. His two friends were coming up the trail from the camp. "Look," he said to them, "I don't see a single tree out there." Little Wolf and Grey Wing joined him at the top of the rise. "My father said that we will travel for as long as a week and not see any trees except those growing along the rivers and streams," White Fox added.

"It makes me feel lonely just looking out there," Grey Wing said softly.

"Did you find your uncle Panther Man in the village?" Little Wolf asked.

"We found my uncle and his family. We have all been invited to stay for a Midsummer Feast. My uncle asked me to play in the lacrosse game."

"We have already heard about the Midsummer Feast," Little Wolf answered. "It is more the time of harvest than midsummer," he commented.

"It doesn't matter what we call the celebrations. They are always fun." White Fox grinned.

Little Wolf turned back to the village. "Mother has a pot of stew on the fire for us. Let's go and eat." White Fox and Grey Wing grinned at each other and followed.

The meal was more than sufficient. White Fox groaned in satisfaction and laid aside his bowl. "I am full!" he announced. "The stew was good, as usual," he said, looking at Walking Woman. She knew that this was White Fox's way of thanking her and smiled at him.

He picked up the bowl again and ran his finger around the edges. Walking Woman still carved her bowls out of wood and the spoons were made of buffalo horn. His mother used the old utensils too, even though most of the other women now used the metal dishes that they got from the trader.

White Fox and his friends slumped by the fire as the sun disappeared. He had decided to spend the night with his friends. His mother would not worry. The quiet of the evening sounded good to him after listening to Chickadee's chattering for much of the day. He leaned back, allowing his thoughts to drift to Falling Star. It felt good to think of her.

He turned to Little Wolf. "Remember last spring when you had feelings for Bluebird?" he asked softly. "How did it feel?"

"I don't know how to explain it," Little Wolf said thoughtfully. "Why do you ask?"

"I have no reason to ask," said White Fox as he felt his face grow warm.

Grey Wing chuckled. "Who did you meet on your visit into the village?"

"Come on, White Fox, you can tell your friends anything, as I did when I told you about my feelings for Bluebird," Little Wolf cajoled. "As I see it, your friends have a right to know what is going on in your mind."

In the darkness, White Fox could imagine the silly grins that were sure to be on his friends' faces. He began to tell about meeting his cousin and her best friend, Falling Star. "I feel funny when I look at her. She is very nice to look at, and I have not noticed that in any girl before."

"Maybe it is time to carve a courting flute," Grey Wing teased. "You may need it soon."

Little Wolf interrupted. "I will give you the same advice my father gave me when I was spending too much time thinking about Bluebird. He said, 'You are too young to court a maiden. You are not a warrior yet; so ignore the feelings, and they will go away.' Now Bluebird is married to Man Who Talks Too Much, and I don't think about her at all anymore."

This did not make White Fox feel any better. He decided not to talk about it anymore. "I am going to make a bed under that tree over there," he said.

"You can sleep inside one of the wickiups. There will be room for all of us," Little Wolf offered.

"I feel like getting used to this big sky tonight," White Fox replied.

Little Wolf pulled some buffalo robes from one of the travoises. "We will all sleep outside then. But if you really want to get used to the sky, we should walk out onto the prairie."

White Fox laughed. "We will get used to it a little at a time."

Three days had passed on the trail to the buffalo country. White Fox rode ahead of Little Wolf and Grey Wing, his head still full of the good times they had had at the Midsummer Feast. "White Fox seems deep into his thoughts this morning," Grey Wing commented softly to Little Wolf.

"There is a lot of time to think on a long trail like this one," Little Wolf answered. "I have been wondering if the agent back at the reservation will be angry with us for leaving on this hunt." Grey Wing shook his head without answering. Little Wolf continued. "I have been thinking about the white man. When he gets a piece of paper to own the land and farm it, does that mean he cannot leave the land? Is he a prisoner like we are?"

Grey Wing laughed. "You have many questions for the white man this morning. Too bad we don't see one."

"I am glad there are no white men out here on the prairie," Little Wolf replied. "On the reservation, I feel like a little mouse sitting on a big buffalo robe with nowhere to hide."

White Fox turned on his pony and looked back along the trail. Their procession was long. Panther Man had brought his family, including Chickadee's friend Falling Star. Five other families from their village had decided to join the hunt as well. The sun was at the highest point when White Fox noticed that the buffalo chips had a fresher look to them, indicating that the buffalo had been in this area not too long ago. The land here was rolling, and the leaders of the hunt had ridden over a rise and out of sight. When he reached the top, White Fox found himself looking down into a valley with a river winding like a snake at the bottom.

Little Wolf and Grey Wing rode up beside him, and the three of them raced their ponies down the gentle slope to the river's edge. Their fathers already had dismounted. "What river is this?" White Fox called to the men.

"The James River," Panther Man answered.

"We will camp here the rest of the day," Running Elk said. "The women will have to make bull boats to cross the river."

"I see a big patch of willows," White Fox said to his friends, inclining his head downstream. "Let's go and cut some. They make good hoops for the bull boats."

Spotted Fawn was unloading the travois when the young men returned with the willow boughs. She had laid out a buffalo hide, rawhide strips, and a ball of heavy buffalo sinew. Sunflower, Walking Woman, and Milkweed joined them, each carrying a buffalo hide. Chickadee and Falling Star followed close behind. White Fox and Little Wolf knelt in the sand and began to fashion hoops from the willow sticks. As the hoops were finished, the women fitted the hides onto them, stretching and sewing the hides into place.

"Why don't you girls see if you can gather enough buffalo chips to make a hot fire for the stew pot," suggested Milkweed. "Yellow Feather brought in a nice buck last night, and I have the meat ready for the pot. There is enough meat for all the pots tonight," she added, smiling.

"I found a nice batch of turnips on the prairie this morning," Spotted Fawn offered. "They will taste good in the stew."

As the sun lowered to the horizon, the women finished the bull boats, and the men had found the easiest place to cross the river. The fires had burned down into hot coals, and the cooking pots filled the air with mouth-watering smells. Everyone settled down around their campfires, and the soft sounds of conversation floated over the camp.

Running Elk had to select some of the young men to serve as wolves. White Fox and his two friends had been told they would take the second watch, so they used this time to rest by the fire. White Fox watched Yellow Feather and several other young men move up the hillside to take the first watch. Spotted Fawn saw White Fox watching him. "Yellow Feather's father died of sickness last winter," she told White Fox. "He is now the main provider for his mother and sister."

White Fox just nodded his head. He could not help feeling dislike for him, especially when he was around the girls.

The sunrise found White Fox sitting on the hillside overlooking the river. He watched as the sun's pink glow spread over the flat plains, down the hill, and into the valley below. He could see the camp coming to life below him. Swinging his bow onto his shoulder, he started down to the camp. Already the women were loading their supplies into the bull boats. Some were hooking up their ponies to pull the boats across; others had made boats large enough to sit inside and paddle across.

Spotted Fawn was riding one of their ponies into the water when White Fox saw her. She pulled their bull boat behind. His father was already halfway across the river. Star was tethered nearby. White Fox mounted his pony and followed his mother to watch for any trouble. When she reached the far side, White Fox turned Star back into the current to watch for Panther Man's family. He spotted a large bull boat coming across with Chickadee and Falling Star paddling and laughing. White Fox pulled Star to a stop on the sandbar in the middle of the river and waited for the girls to pass. "Is everything going well?" he called out to them.

"We are having a good time," Falling Star called back, smiling at him. As they passed near him, Chickadee raised her paddle and struck the water, sending a sheet of water over his head. His pony shifted to the left just as another plume of water came from Falling Star's paddle, drenching him again.

With a hoot, White Fox slipped from Star's back into the shallow water. He began splashing the water with a cupped hand, sending sprays over the girls until they were out of reach. Falling Star looked back at him, wiping water from her face and laughing.

Late on the sixth day, White Fox saw two riders coming in fast from the west. He recognized them as Yellow Feather and Burnt by Fire, and he could see that they were excited about something. White Fox spurred his pony forward and heard Burnt by Fire tell Running Elk, "We have seen the buffalo. They are three valleys to the west."

The exciting news spread quickly through the group. Soon all the men had gathered around Running Elk. He raised his hand for silence. "Since we have not seen any sign of an enemy on the prairie, I will take all the hunters ahead to see the herd. The rest of you will follow. We will set up camp in the next valley to spend the night. We will plan the hunt around our campfires tonight and be ready to proceed in the morning."

White Fox, Little Wolf, and Grey Wing rode together as the hunters kicked their ponies into a gallop. Yellow Feather, Burnt by Fire, and Running Elk were in the lead. No one spoke, but each felt the thrill of knowing the animals they hunted were just ahead. As they rode up the third rise, White Fox saw his father slow his pony to a walk. Near the crest of the hill, he dismounted and motioned for the rest to do the same.

Running Elk and the other men lay on their stomachs and inched up to the crest of the hill. The boys did the same. The scene below them was beyond anything White Fox had imagined. The valley floor seemed carpeted in black. The animals spread through the entire valley. The buffalo closest to them looked huge and powerful, inspiring a thrilling awe.

All of White Fox's life, he had lived in a tepee made from the buffalo's skin and slept under buffalo robes. He had used its bones for spoons and, in the winter, slid on a sled made from its ribs. But this was the first time he had seen a live buffalo.

Little Wolf let the air escape from his lungs in a soft whistle. He spread his hands. "They are gigantic," he whispered. Grey Wing pointed at the nearer animals as though with an imaginary bow. He pretended to release an arrow.

The hunters lay on the hill enjoying the view below them for quite a long time. Finally Running Elk signaled to retreat over the rise. The men gathered back where they had left their ponies and began talking softly and excitedly about what they had seen. "I may be too excited to sleep tonight," Grey Wing whispered. White Fox and Little Wolf agreed.

The women had the camp almost set up by the time the men returned. Cooking smells soon filled the air. As the sun disappeared over the horizon, White Fox walked through the camp and let his eyes wander over the people. Little Wolf's family took up a large area of the camp, as usual. White Fox smiled, hearing the laughter that came from that place. Long Legs' children all seemed to have the good humor of their father.

As White Fox returned to their wickiup, he noticed that Panther Man and Little Crow were camped next to each other. They had become good friends on this trip. These men had something in common; both had tried to live in the way the white men had taught them. Each farmed small pieces of land at his own village.

White Fox knew his father was one who would never change his thinking about the white man's way. The thought made White Fox feel sad because he was not sure the people would ever be free to live as they had in the past. He recalled the vision he had experienced on his walk near the Spirit World, but he did not like to think about it. It was too confusing.

When the evening meal had been eaten, the men began to gather around Running Elk's campfire. When he thought all the hunters were present, he looked at the eager faces and said, "I know that many of you have not hunted the buffalo before. But also I see the faces of some of our best hunters, and I know we will do well."

The experienced hunters sat back to let the younger men crowd in close as Running Elk spoke. He used a stick to draw on the ground. "This is how we will approach the herd." Running Elk made many small marks in the dirt representing the buffalo. Then he drew the outline of the hill. "We will ride over the hill slowly and approach the herd at an angle. They will not pay attention to us at first because their eyesight is bad. At the first sign that they are about to run, we will attack.

"Those of us with buffalo ponies will have an advantage; our ponies know what to do. But the rest of you will have your hands full, directing your ponies and shooting your arrows or guns, whichever you have chosen to use. By the time the sun is high in the sky, our women will know how much work we have made for them."

The meeting concluded, the hunters returned to their own camps. White Fox looked at his father with pride. Even though he had aged in the time they had spent on the reservation, he was still a strong-looking warrior any young man would be proud to call father. White Fox moved close to him. "Are you going to use the rifle to hunt the buffalo?"

Running Elk brought up his head quickly as though surprised that anyone was so near. "I am going to use it," he answered, "even though I am not sure it will work as well as my bow. It is too hard to reload on a moving pony. I have tried it, and it is hard to get used to."

"Maybe it would be best to use your bow."

"I am planning on going on the buffalo hunt every Moon When the Calves Grow Hair from now on, so I think I will try the rifle this time. Maybe I will go back to the bow next time."

White Fox took out his bow and looked it over carefully as he had almost every night since they left the Lac Qui Parle village. "Checking your bow one more time?" Panther Man emerged from the shadows, chuckling at his nephew.

White Fox smiled. "Which of your weapons are you going to use tomorrow?" He knew that Panther Man had acquired a new gun and the new bullets with the powder already inside. His weapon could be reloaded simply by pulling a lever.

"I will use my new gun," Panther Man replied. "I will find out if it is powerful enough to bring down the big animals."

Panther Man and Running Elk talked for a while, and then the uncle moved back to his own fire. The camp became quiet. White Fox rolled himself tight in his buffalo robe.

"Thank you, Great Mystery," Running Elk's voice carried among the hunters as they sat mounted on their ponies. "You have brought us to a great herd. Now we ask for your help and guidance to bring down as many as we need for our use."

As White Fox raised his head to look at his father, he felt a sudden wave of fear. He realized he felt the fear for his father, not for himself. He turned his head to look for his mother and saw that she was busy packing the wickiup onto the travois. The women would move to the hunt site as quickly as they could to be ready to do the butchering.

"What is wrong, White Fox? Your face has gone pale," asked Grey Wing.

"I do not know. I feel a sudden fear for my father. He has been on many hunts in his lifetime. I'm sure he will be fine." White Fox tried to brush away the feeling.

The older hunters rode out, and the younger ones followed. They moved through the first valley quickly and soon approached the rise that would show them the herd. Everyone moved in complete silence. Even the ponies seemed to understand and made no noise.

White Fox stopped Star and pulled three arrows from his quiver. He could easily hold two and fit one into the string of the bow. He had practiced long to become proficient at this, and now the time had come to use this skill. As White Fox rode over the rise, he could see his father's pony angling toward the herd. A few of the big bulls were watching them, and he saw one start and grunt loudly. Suddenly, all of the nearest animals started to move, and the hunters kicked their ponies into a gallop, riding parallel to the running herd.

White Fox heard the first shot and felt Star spring forward. White Fox pressed lightly with his right knee, directing Star into the herd. He targeted a fat cow. Star seemed to know which one he had picked and kept pace with her. White Fox pulled bowstring as far back as he could, leaned toward the animal, and shot. The arrow hit behind the buffalo's shoulder blade and buried itself up to the feathers. He saw the animal falter and quickly shot another arrow. It buried itself right behind the first. The cow fell, plowing up dirt and dust that came back into his face.

White Fox spurred Star ahead at full speed until he saw a huge bull. He pursued it, already imagining a war bonnet with a fine set of horns for decoration. Suddenly he caught sight of his father deep in the middle of the herd. Just as quickly, the thick dust obscured the scene.

Star came alongside the bull. White Fox shot two arrows into the animal and saw it stumble. Just then, his father's buffalo pony shot in front of him, moving to the outside of the herd. His father was not on the pony's back. Cold fear gripped White Fox as he steered Star out of the herd. The dust was thick as the herd continued to thunder past, a few hunters mingled with the hunted. Finally the last of the animals passed. The dust slowly cleared, and White Fox could see the black lumps spread across the valley.

White Fox frantically swept his eyes over the area, hoping to see his father standing beside one of the dead animals. He had heard stories of hunters falling from their ponies only to find refuge against a downed buffalo. He saw one animal trying to get back up onto its feet and rode close enough to shoot another arrow into it. As he turned away, he saw a small shadow among the larger ones. With dread in his heart, he steered Star toward it. Moving closer, he saw that it was a hunter lying facedown in the dirt. His father.

White Fox jumped from his pony and knelt beside his father. Gently he turned the body to its back. Running Elk's face looked peaceful, and White Fox could not see where he had been stepped on. As he looked into his father's face, Running Elk's eyes opened. White Fox felt his heart jump with joy as his father looked into his eyes. Running Elk let out a ragged breath and began to speak softly and with effort. "Listen, my son. I have shot a big bull this day. Find it and cut off its head. Place it on the scaffold with me, with the head facing the setting sun."

"You are not dying, Father," White Fox replied.

"I have already seen my father and mother. They are waiting for me." White Fox grasped his father's hand, and he felt the fingers squeeze his hand gently. "You must be the head of our family now. I saw you shoot your first buffalo today. Do not let it be your last. Tell your mother that we had a good life together and I will be waiting for her in the Spirit World." Running Elk's hand grew limp, and he expelled a slow, final breath.

White Fox heard a hideous wail and realized it was his own. Little Wolf rode up and knelt beside his friend. Gently he passed his hand over Running Elk's eyes to close them and began singing the song of death.

The hunters gathered around the lonely scene, the eerie sound of the death song rising into the air. As the women came over the rise, they could hear the song and came quickly to the place. Spotted Fawn's anguished cry joined the song of death.

Spotted Fawn woke to the darkness of the small wickiup. She could hear her son's soft, even breathing. Rolling to her back, she allowed her mind to drift back over the last two days. The horror filled her body again as she remembered that her husband was dead. She visualized cleaning the buffalo skin and stitching it tightly around Running Elk's body.

Little Crow and Panther Man had built the scaffold, and she watched as they lifted her husband onto it. White Fox had prepared a bundle with Running Elk's pipe and medicine bag. This he put beside his father on the scaffold, along with his war shield and favorite bow and arrows. Then he had added the bull buffalo's head, facing it toward the setting sun.

After they watched the sun set, she had returned to the wickiup and slashed her arms and cut off her hair. She stayed in the small lodge for two days. She felt weak and useless.

Suddenly White Fox thrashed in his sleep and moaned softly. Then he was awake, lying still and listening. "Mother, are you awake?"

"I am awake," she answered.

White Fox spoke softly. "I had a dream. I saw Father." He paused. "I cannot leave him out here on the prairie. I saw him standing in the trees of Suland. He was looking out over the two rivers. I must take him home, Mother, and bury him on the bluff."

"Yes," she said.

Chapter Three

1856

Dawn was breaking in the eastern sky as the five young men rode down the trail toward the north woods and the land of the many lakes. The travelers had a serious purpose. White Fox, Little Wolf, Grey Wing, Big Boy, and Red Bird had decided that the only way they would be recognized as warriors was to trek into the Chippewa Country and bring back horses and scalps. It was the Moon When the Ponies Shed. All the snow was gone, and the landscape looked fresh and new.

"Are you sure you know the country well enough so we will be able to find our way?" Red Bird asked.

White Fox gave a brisk nod yes. "All we have to do is move to the north until we see signs of the Chippewa. There are always trails to follow." Now seventeen winter seasons old, he remembered well the ways his father had taught him.

"We have been living on the reservation too long, Red Bird," Big Boy muttered. "If we still lived in the wild, you would not think these worried thoughts." White Fox grunted his agreement.

The boys followed the hunting trails for four days, careful always to continue moving north. Near the end of the fourth day, Little Wolf slid from his pony's back and crouched to the ground. He pointed to a track in the soft earth. All the boys crowded around. Little Wolf ran his finger around the toes of the imprint and said softly, "See how these moccasins have more rounded toes than the ones our mothers make? We are now in enemy territory."

The boys studied the tracks for several moments. Then White Fox spoke, "It is time for us to move off the trail. If we keep to the brush but move parallel to the trails, we will come to a village eventually."

The sun had moved close to the horizon when White Fox thought he heard a dog yipping. At the same time, Little Wolf stopped abruptly and motioned to White Fox to come up beside him. White Fox pushed through the thick brush to join his friend. Then he saw the clearing ahead. White Fox and Little Wolf stood at the top of a ridge, looking down into a valley. Nestled at the bottom was a village. The air hung blue with the campfire smoke, and they could see a river winding past the lodges on the far side of the village. People moved about finishing the day's tasks and preparing for the evening meal.

The others soon were beside the pair, and White Fox heard one blow a low whistle of surprise. They stood for some time, absorbing the scene below. Running Elk once had drawn pictures in the sand to show White Fox how the Chippewa built their lodges out of bark. The lodges had rounded tops and were called wigwams. They did not look at all like the bark lodges that the Dakota used for their summer homes.

"I do not see their ponies," Big Boy whispered.

"My father told me they always have them pastured to the

north of the village, just as we try to keep ours to the south, away from a raiding party," White Fox answered softly.

"I would like to get closer to the village to watch the activity," Red Bird whispered.

"We will move back and tether the ponies in the heavy brush," Little Wolf said. "Then we can watch the village and try to see where their ponies are pastured."

After tethering the ponies, the young men moved stealthily through the brush along the ridge until they had a good view of the village. From this vantage point, they could see the pony herd farther down the valley in a meadow, as White Fox had predicted. They watched the activities of the village for some time. They could just as easily have been watching one of their own camps, White Fox thought. He leaned back against a tree, closing his eyes and listening to the sounds around him. The evening cooking smells were reaching his nose, and he heard his stomach complain loudly. Suddenly White Fox jerked upright and opened his eyes. "Are there young men leaving the camp?" he asked.

Little Wolf turned his eyes back to the village below and saw two men walking from the camp toward the meadow. He nodded and held up fingers indicating that there were two of them. White Fox got to his feet and whispered, "It is time to get our ponies and move around the ridge to the north. Then we can see where the guards position themselves."

It did not take long for the young men to skirt the ridge and find a point with a view of the meadow. They exchanged smiles at the great number of ponies grazing peacefully below them.

"Are we going to kill the guards?" Grey Wing whispered. "We will have to decide how we are going to do this."

White Fox spoke thoughtfully. "I do not like the idea of killing these people just to steal their ponies. I know it was the way of our fathers, but there was much warring between our tribes back then. I do not feel any animosity toward these people."

"I agree with White Fox," Little Wolf said, unsurprisingly in support of his brother.

"The honor would be even greater if we could capture these

warriors and tie them up and count coup on them," White Fox added.

Grey Wing grunted his approval, and the other two nodded their agreement. "We will have to decide who is going to take care of the guards," Grey Wing said. "They will be the ones who will get the honor of counting coup."

Little Wolf bent to the ground and picked up five small sticks. He carefully broke them into short pieces, leaving two slightly longer. He arranged them in his hand with only the ends exposed. He reached out to each of his friends to let each choose one. The last stick was his.

They crowded together to compare sticks. Little Wolf smiled as he held up one of the longer ones. Big Boy chuckled deep in his throat as he held up the other. "Are you sure I should not cut the guard's throat and take his scalp?" he whispered.

"It will be harder for you to spare his life and bring him back to where we leave the ponies," White Fox answered. "But don't worry. I will steal a fine pony for you."

The plans were made. Darkness was settling quickly. The young men found vantage points at the top of the ridge and watched the guards move about so they would know where to find them when the time was right. The plan was to wait until later into the night to make sure no one wandered to the meadow on a romantic escapade.

The friends waited quietly and patiently as the full moon came up and cast its soft glow over the meadow. As time passed, they heard fewer and fewer sounds coming from the village. Finally only the sounds of the forest remained. Little Wolf looked at White Fox and nodded his decision that the time was right. The five young men gathered close, each cuffing the other's shoulder in encouragement. Then Little Wolf and Big Boy stole down the ridge to find the guards they were to eliminate. The other three waited a short time; then they too moved down the incline.

White Fox, Grey Wing, and Red Bird crouched in the tall weeds until Little Wolf emerged from the shadows carrying a bundle over his shoulder. The guard was knocked unconscious and tied securely. "Big Boy has the other one. He is tying him," he whispered as he passed.

The three young men entered the meadow and moved as quietly as they could among the ponies. The ponies moved around but did not seem alarmed. White Fox stepped up to a pinto with a white face. The pony did not seem frightened, and White Fox easily slipped the rawhide lead over its head. Next he saw a tall, dark animal and stretched his hand toward it. The pony extended its nose to him in response, and he gently looped the rawhide lead over its neck.

In the moonlight White Fox saw that his friends each had taken two ponies and were quietly leading them from the herd. He turned back to find the pinto but couldn't spot it at first.

The ponies were milling about, becoming nervous. White Fox saw the pinto and led the second pony in pursuit. He was reaching to grasp the rawhide lead on the pinto when something hit him in the back with such force that he flew forward into the dirt.

Reacting naturally, he twisted and rolled as he hit the ground. He had his hands up in time to receive the body that was descending on top of him. He saw the flash of the knife and felt it slash his face. Blood spurted into his eyes, blinding him, but he held the enemy's wrist. He pushed the weapon away from himself with all the strength his fear produced. He felt the other's strength overpowering him and knew that the knife was coming close to his throat.

Suddenly his vision cleared. White Fox blinked the blood from his eyes, and he looked directly into the brave's face. Instantly the face changed into the face of the white fox. "Your time on Mother Earth is not over. You have more strength. Use it!"

White Fox felt a calmness spread through his body, and a new strength flowed into his arm. He slowly pushed the brave's wrist upward. With a quick twist, he heard the bone snap, and the brave's hand turned in his grip. White Fox let the brave's body fall down on top of him and heard the man groan as the knife entered his own chest. With a new rush of fear, he pushed the enemy off himself.

Grey Wing was kneeling at his side. The look on his face was that of surprise and shock. "Are you all right, White Fox?"

"I think so. I didn't see him. He hit me from behind." White Fox sat up and brought his hand up to touch his cheek.

Grey Wing pulled his hand away. "Do not touch your face. We can take care of that later. We have to get out of here."

"I have two ponies with lead ropes on them. Find them for me."

Grey Wing moved to the enemy's side, took his knife, and slashed at the top of the brave's head. He thrust the bloody scalp into White Fox's hand, then moved quickly to the milling ponies. He was back a short moment later, leading the two ponies with the lead ropes on them. He helped White Fox onto the pinto's back and led them from the meadow through the tall weeds to the top of the ridge.

Little Wolf, Red Bird, and Big Boy met them coming up the ridge. They looked shocked when they saw White Fox's face in the moonlight. "What happened?" Little Wolf asked Grey Wing.

"I am not sure, but there is a dead enemy down there, so we had better move on as quickly as we can," Grey Wing answered.

They soon reached the meeting place. Little Wolf helped White Fox from the pony. Grey Wing's old grandmother always sent a medicine bag with him, even on the shortest hunting trip. Now he was glad that she had done so and also that she and his father had insisted he learn which of the medicines to use on wounds. He sat beside his friend and, in the moonlight, looked closely at the ugly slash on White Fox's cheek, gently working the skin back into place. He added a little water to two of the powders and smeared the salve over the wound. Then he covered the gash with several green leaves and wound a wide strip of softened rawhide around White Fox's head. Finally, he tied some narrow rawhide strips around it to fasten the dressing in place. "This will have to stay in place until we reach home," he said softly to White Fox.

There was no time to waste. Little Wolf helped White Fox onto Star's back. From his mount he looked down at his friends.

"It is up to you if you want us to kill the two guards," Little Wolf volunteered softly. The two young guards were tied and leaning against a tree.

White Fox shook his head no. "Leave them where they are. Their people will track us up here in the morning and find them. Let's go home."

CHAPTER FOUR

1857

"Pull! You're not pulling!"

White Fox was trying to hoist a large doe up into a tree as Little Wolf pulled on a rope tied around its neck. "I've got it. Come and help me pull," Little Wolf grunted. White Fox jumped to Little Wolf's side and added his weight. Slowly the animal started to rise, when suddenly the branch broke and the doe dropped to the ground. The young men tumbled back, falling one on top of the other.

White Fox sat up with a moan. The air filled with gleeful giggles from the audience of boys gathered around the scene. Little Wolf jumped to his feet, grabbing a stick and raising it menacingly over his head. As he gave chase, the boys scattered like prairie chickens, laughing and yelling as they ran.

He stood and brushed the dust from his clothing. Out of the corner of his eye, he noticed his mother approaching them, leading her pony with the travois behind. Spring had come early to the river valley, and she and several other women and children had gone to the sugar camp. "Mother, you are home. Did you have a good harvest?"

She nodded her response, smiling. "It looks like you two have been entertaining the whole village this morning."

White Fox's cheeks burned as he glanced around the camp and saw many eyes and smiles turned in their direction. Shrugging off his embarrassment, he said, "I am glad you are back. I did not look forward to cutting up the doe alone."

As Spotted Fawn turned toward their lodge, one of Little Wolf's nephews approached and stood in front of her. "There are visitors entering the camp from the north," he said to her. "It is your brother and his family."

"Go with your mother, White Fox. I will get Grey Wing to help me with the doe," Little Wolf urged.

Spotted Fawn's excitement showed in her face as she handed the pony's rope to her son and walked quickly ahead. White Fox knew how much she had missed Panther Man after Running Elk's death. Panther Man had invited them to live in the Lac Qui Parle village, but at the time White Fox could not bring himself to live away from his friend Little Wolf and his family.

The visitors had already reached the lodge as White Fox approached. Panther Man slipped from his pony's back and reach out to Spotted Fawn. With him were three women riding separately, and another pony pulled a heavily laden travois. White Fox could see that they had packed for an extended visit, and he felt joy in his heart.

Panther Man looked no different than when they had been together on the buffalo hunt three winter seasons ago. Spotted Fawn looked at her brother with such affection that White Fox stood back for their reunion.

"How has life been for you, little sister?" Panther Man asked.

"My son has proven to be a good provider," she replied, her smile glowing.

Panther Man glanced at White Fox. "I can see that you both look healthy."

"Your family looks well too," Spotted Fawn answered.

As the exchange took place, White Fox observed the women still seated on the ponies. He recognized Sunflower immediately and flashed her a smile. A very pretty young maiden sat astride the pony next to Sunflower's, and as his eyes rested on her, a smile brought up the corners of her mouth. "How are you White Fox?" she asked as she slid from the pony.

"Is that you, Chickadee?" White Fox stammered in surprise. "What has happened to my chubby little cousin?" He stared at the tall, pretty maiden standing in front of him.

She reached forward and gently touched the scar on his cheek. "Who has put the scar on your face, Cousin? It makes you look like a warrior."

White Fox's eye caught movement as the third woman dismounted her pony. She turned and looked into his eyes, and he realized that this was Chickadee's friend, Falling Star. She was even prettier than he remembered. White Fox had not allowed himself to think about this young maiden, assuming that she had married the warrior Yellow Feather by this time. White Fox found his voice and said, "I am glad to see you again, Falling Star."

"I am glad to see you, too," she answered softly.

"Come, come with me," Spotted Fawn said to the women. "We have much unpacking to do. I had just returned from the sugar camp, and White Fox has a beautiful doe hung on the other side of the camp. We will have a great feast tonight." She emanated happiness.

White Fox turned to Panther Man. "We will take the ponies down to the meadow. I am glad to see you again, Uncle."

As they walked side by side to the meadow, Panther Man asked, "How has life been for you without your father?"

White Fox was quiet for a time, brooding on the question before answering. "By the time I had taken my father back to the two rivers and buried him there, I was at peace with what had happened. You know how my father felt about reservation life.

That thought made it easier for me." White Fox paused. "I know my mother still misses him terribly at times, but she tries to hide it from me. She is still a beautiful woman, and some of the men have shown an interest in her. She is not interested in them."

Panther Man smiled at his last remark. "There are many changes in three winter seasons. Did you see how Chickadee has grown up?"

White Fox laughed. "She hardly looks like the same person. Why is Falling Star traveling with you? I thought she would be married by this time."

Panther Man smiled. "It is not the fault of the young men of our village. Many have tried to court her. Her mother died the last warm season, and you remember that her father has been gone since she was a little girl. Now she lives with us, and she is a very useful member of our family. She will make some young man a good wife someday, when she is ready. With two young maidens in our lodge, there been no shortage of flute music in the evenings."

The men found a place with good grass for the ponies and tethered them to the ground. As the men walked back to the camp, Panther Man spoke thoughtfully. "I noticed the war shield I made for you when I visited your Two Rivers camp. It was hanging over the doorway of your lodge with a scalp lock hanging with it. It looks like you have been to the Chippewa country to the north."

"I did not go looking for a scalp, only to steal ponies," White Fox replied.

"I can see the change in your eyes. You are a warrior now."

The new tepee was set up and ready when the men returned. The young women were cutting the fresh venison into roasting pieces. A fire was burning hot, and a pot was hung over it. Panther Man had gone into the new tepee to look for his pipe when Chief Little Crow walked up to the campsite with a pipe in his hand. "Where is your other uncle, White Fox? I have come to smoke with the two of you."

"He had the same idea and is finding his pipe and tobacco."

Panther Man emerged from the doorway, smiling. "Little

Crow, I thought I heard your voice. I am glad to see you looking so well."

"I have only a little time," Little Crow answered. "The agent is coming to my lodge soon. But I wanted to catch up on the news from Lac Qui Parle. Do you have your corn planted yet?"

A short laugh burst from Panther Man's lips. "You sound like a white-man farmer!" He grinned. "The ground is too cold now, but Sunflower's sisters will plant ours if we are not back in time."

"Are you planning a long visit?" Little Crow seemed in a hurry with his questions.

"We are not here just to visit," Panther Man answered. "We are on our way to the quarries to dig some of the sacred red stone. I have not had the chance yet to mention it to White Fox and his mother, but we want them to travel with us and make this a family journey." Panther Man looked at White Fox as he spoke. "We will see what your mother has to say about this later."

"That sounds like a good thing to do," Little Crow answered. "I see my son One Who Appeareth coming. I think the agent has arrived. I will come back to talk and smoke with you tomorrow." With this, Little Crow hurried off.

White Fox chuckled. "My uncle likes to play cards with the trader and agent. They play for white-man money or supplies. He is good at their games and often wins, I am told."

Darkness came into the camp as White Fox and his uncle sat smoking the pipe and talking. A figure emerged from the darkness, and Little Wolf dropped down beside White Fox. He leaned toward his blood brother. "I have decided to visit your fire this evening. I suspect you will have much good food to share."

Panther Man tried unsuccessfully to stifle a laugh. He saw Little Wolf's embarrassed look and said, "I see by the feathers you wear that you too have become a warrior since I last saw you on the buffalo hunt."

"I have counted coup on an enemy and have an extra pony," Little Wolf answered.

Panther Man leaned forward, offering his pipe to Little

Wolf. "I would enjoy sharing my pipe with another new, young warrior."

The three sat and passed the pipe in contented silence. Mouthwatering smells from the pot were filling the air, and the soft chattering of the women was relaxing to their ears. White Fox noticed that Chickadee repeatedly glanced over her shoulder and seemed to be watching Little Wolf. Little Wolf did not seem to notice.

Two days later, a small party rode down the trail toward the pipestone quarries. White Fox, Spotted Fawn, and Little Wolf had decided to travel with Panther Man and his family. The group moved at a slow, relaxed pace, surrounded by an air of tranquil contentment. White Fox was thoughtful as he rode. Their friend Grey Wing had been invited to go with them, but he was busy helping his old grandmother collect her medicine plants. White Fox recalled that Grey Wing's father wanted him to take part in his religious ceremonies and learn to be a shaman, but Grey Wing had said he was not called to be shaman and instead preferred to learn about the medicine plants with his grandmother.

Panther Man rode up beside White Fox and Little Wolf. "Sunflower would like to make a short side trip to visit a sister. She is married to a Wahpekute man, and they live at a lake called Shetek. It is not far from the quarry and would be a pleasant stop."

White Fox nodded his agreement. He was happy to make this trip last as long as possible, he thought, looking back at Falling Star. She and Chickadee rode side by side, and he could hear the soft murmur of their conversation. White Fox had to admit that he had a special feeling for this young maiden. He shook his head hard and blew out a sharp breath.

Little Wolf looked at him questioningly. "What is wrong?" he asked.

"I was shaking some silly thoughts from my head."

Little Wolf laughed quietly. "Did you get rid of them?"

"Maybe for a little while," White Fox answered.

Little Wolf twisted on his pony and looked back, speaking softly. "I think you have finally met a maiden worth thinking about. Am I right?" Little Wolf saw the quick smile flash across White Fox's face, but his blood brother did not answer him.

The sun was low in the sky on the third day when the group topped a rise and saw, in the valley below them, a village situated on the shore of a lake. The lakeshore was heavily wooded, and they could see only a small part of the lake through the trees. A blue haze hung over the valley, and the budding leaves added a lush, deep green. The group paused to enjoy the lovely, peaceful scene. Sunflower eagerly moved out in front, and they began the descent toward the village. The view of the lake opened to them, and the setting sun glittered on the small waves across the surface of the water.

"I had always thought that only the prairie lands existed in this direction," Little Wolf commented. "I am surprised to see this beautiful place."

The people of the village gathered around the travelers as they entered the village. With a squeal of delight, one of the women pushed her way through the crowd and clasped Sunflower in her arms. White Fox watched Sunflower and her sister, wondering how many daughters their father had been blessed with. He could remember meeting three more at the Lac Qui Parle village.

Before the darkness came, the women had their tepee set up. The women of the village brought special treats to add to the travelers' meal. After the meal, the group sat around the campfire, contentedly watching the flames lick at the wood. Then Walking Crane, Sunflower's sister's husband, spoke. "Have you young people ever been to the Sacred Quarry?" He looked around the fire and saw them shake their heads.

From a rawhide case, he pulled the most beautiful calumet White Fox had ever seen. Walking Crane held up the pipe so all could see it. "I know all of you have heard the story of the beautiful maiden, Buffalo Calf, dressed in white buckskin, who first brought the sacred pipe to our people. This pipe is made exactly as the first pipe was described."

White Fox remembered the story of the first calumet and saw that Walking Crane's pipe indeed matched its description. Carefully taking some tobacco from a pouch, Walking Crane spoke again. "Tonight, all the warriors around this fire will smoke of this pipe while I explain the sacred pipe once again." He lit the pipe and sent two puffs of smoke floating skyward. Then he handed the pipe to Panther Man.

"With this sacred pipe, you will send your voices to Wakantanka, your father and grandfather," Walking Crane said. "With this pipe, you will walk upon the earth, which is your mother and grandmother. All your steps should be holy.

"The bowl of the pipe is red stone, which represents the earth. A buffalo calf is carved into the stone facing the center, symbolizing the four-legged creatures who live as brothers among you. The stem is wood and represents all growing things. Twelve feathers from the spotted eagle hang from the place where the stem fits into the bowl, and these represent the winged brothers who live among you.

"All these things are joined to you who will smoke the pipe and send voices to Wakantanka. When you use this pipe to pray, you will pray for and with all things on Mother Earth. The sacred pipe binds you to all your relatives, your grandfather and father, your grandmother and mother."

Walking Crane paused, letting his words sink in as the pipe was passed, one man to the next. The warrior took another deep breath and continued, the flames of the campfire lighting his eyes with the passion of his speech. "The red stone represents the Mother Earth on which you live. The earth is red, and the two-legged creatures who live upon it also are red. Wakantanka has given you a red road, good and straight, to travel. You must remember that all people who stand on this earth are sacred. From this day, the sacred pipe will stand on this red Earth, and you will send your voices to Wakantanka.

"There are seven circles on the stone, representing the seven rites in which you will use the pipe." Walking Crane swept his gaze over the young people around the fire. "Now that you young men are warriors, you will all take part in these rites at one time or another, so I will not explain all of that to you." Turning his attention to the young women, he said, "Do not forget, young maidens, that it was the Buffalo Calf maiden who brought the sacred pipe to our people. And it was an Omaha woman who discovered the quarry while trailing a sacred buffalo and found where his hooves had uncovered the red stone."

The men passed the pipe around several times and enjoyed the fine tobacco that Walking Crane had packed into the bowl. Panther Man finally broke the silence. "Do you have a trading post nearby?"

Walking Crane blew a puff of smoke upward and nodded. "Just a short distance through the trees." He waved toward the south. "The Des Moines River begins its journey to the south at that end of the lake. A trader has built his cabin on the other side of the stream. He has started to build a dam to hold back the water as the beavers do. We have such a beautiful lake here now I do not know why he does this." Walking Crane furrowed his brow. "He talks about building a sawmill to cut up the trees. I do not understand."

"Are there more white men in the area?" Panther Man asked.

"One lives at the far end of the lake," Walking Crane pointed over the trees to the north, indicating that the lake lay much farther in that direction than they could see from this point. "He is a friendly farmer and always welcomes us when we stop to talk or trade for his chicken eggs. There is another along the east shore who is not friendly and has chased us away with his gun."

Walking Crane carefully packed his pipe back into its case. "It is beautiful on the lake in the morning," he said. "We will borrow enough canoes so you all can paddle around the lake tomorrow." Then he stood and nodded his good night to the group.

Sunflower's sister patted her hand, saying, "You and I will have time tomorrow to visit. We will leave you now to rest." She joined Walking Crane, and they departed to their own lodge.

The morning dawned clear and calm. The lake was indeed beautiful. As promised, Walking Crane had borrowed enough canoes to fill their needs. This morning, the women did not start a fire but rather gave each person a piece of pemmican and a tipsinna cake to start the day. Thus sustained, the adults climbed into the canoes and paddled out into the tranquil water.

The four young people watched as the others paddled away and then waited awhile on the shore, preferring to go by themselves. Sunflower's sister's young son Running Rabbit had stayed behind, hoping the young people would invite him to join them. He looked crestfallen when White Fox pushed a canoe into the water and invited Falling Star to paddle in the front of his canoe. The boy could not hide his disappointment as the pair pushed off from the shore.

Then Chickadee called, "Running Rabbit, do you want to ride with us?" The little boy nodded eagerly and hurried to follow Chickadee into the canoe. She moved to the front, and he sat in the middle with Little Wolf in the rear. As the threesome paddled out onto the lake, the pink hues of the dawning sky reflected on the water. Little Wolf steered their canoe in a circle so they could enjoy the beauty of their surroundings. Then he paddled with more strength to catch up with White Fox and Falling Star.

White Fox could hear the chattering from the other canoe as it approached, and he could tell that Little Wolf and Chickadee were having a good time together. They were nearing an island, and White Fox guided his canoe around it. The others followed. They watched the pelicans flying overhead and landing in the trees on the island, making their noises of approval or disapproval as to who chose to perch next to whom. White Fox could hear the little boy telling his companions about the behavior of the birds.

White Fox continued paddling around a tip of the island, and unexpectedly he and Falling Star were alone. He laid his paddle at his feet and let the canoe drift in the soft breeze. Falling Star did not seem to notice and gently continued to paddle. The young warrior took a deep breath. "Falling Star, let the canoe drift for a little bit. I want to talk to you."

Falling Star twisted in her seat and, seeing that White Fox

had laid down his paddle, did the same. She turned and faced him with a curious expression on her face. He was filled with shyness, just as he had sometimes felt as a little boy when one of the elders spoke to him. He had never before had this feeling about speaking to a maiden, but he had never looked upon a maiden he thought as beautiful as Falling Star. She looked at him with her dark eyes questioning. Finally the words spilled from his mouth. "I thought you would have been married to Yellow Feather by this time."

Falling Star shook her head. "I had no special feelings for him. I enjoyed him as a friend."

"Did he ask you?"

"Yes. I told him I was not interested in marriage at that time. He found a young maiden who was interested, and they are very happy. They have a little son now. I am happy for him."

White Fox spoke softly. "I am glad you did not marry him." A shadow of a smile crossed her face. They both turned as the other canoe came around the point, laughter echoing across the water.

"There they are," Running Rabbit yelled.

As the other canoe approached, White Fox turned their canoe and paddled up beside the other. Chickadee was convulsed with laughter, and the two males were smiling broadly. "What's so funny?" he asked.

"We thought we had lost you. Running Rabbit said we must be careful when the big birds fly overhead because they can almost fill a canoe with their droppings. We thought you two had been swamped," Chickadee said, wiping the tears from her eyes. "Now we can see you are safe."

"We are all right," White Fox answered, flashing a smile at Falling Star.

The young people spent the entire day exploring the lake. Two days later, the travelers were back on the prairie. Walking Crane had suggested they take a route south and then west to see a rock cliff that looked blue in the distance. Now, however, as they approached it, the afternoon sun bathed the rocks in warm orange light. Panther Man held up his hand to signal a halt. "We will set up the tepee here," he said. "It will be fun to stop here to explore."

It didn't take the women long to unload the travois and set up the tepee. They placed it near the bluff on a patch of soft, green grass. White Fox watched until Falling Star had finished helping Sunflower. Then he moved up behind her and grabbed her hand. "Come with me to explore the rock ridge," he whispered in her ear.

White Fox and Falling Star picked their way along the side of the bluff. They worked their way up until they stood at the top, looking across the land to the south. White Fox spoke softly. "The land looks much bigger when it is bare of trees."

Falling Star nodded in agreement. "I would not want to live out here all the time. I do not feel as safe here."

White Fox lowered himself to the rocks and tugged at Falling Star's hand. She sat beside him. They watched the prairie grasses below wave in the gentle breeze. Quickly a striped gopher poked his head out of a hole along the edge of the rocks. He looked directly at them, then scurried from the hole and past their feet into the tall grass. Falling Star turned her head and smiled at White Fox. His eyes locked with hers and he moved closer to her. He had seen his parents touch lips in moments of affection and leaned forward. She did not turn her face away as he brushed his lips against hers.

Falling Star reached up to his face and gently traced her finger along the scar on his cheek. She gazed into his sky-colored eyes, he into her dark ones. Voices from below snapped them back to reality. White Fox dropped to his knees, crawled forward, and peeked over the edge of the bluff. He turned back to Falling Star and waved her forward, putting a finger to his lips to indicate silence.

Falling Star crawled to his side and slowly peered over the edge. Below them, Chickadee and Little Wolf were seated on a rock, apparently involved in a serious discussion. White Fox moved back, gently pulling Falling Star with him. He picked up handful of small pebbles and tossed them over the edge. They heard the pebbles bouncing their way to the ground below. Then all was quiet.

Falling Star lay motionless, waiting to see what White Fox would do next. Still there was no sound from below. Finally, White Fox stole forward to look again. He saw nothing below them and leaned farther. Suddenly White Fox jerked back and a spray of pebbles flew over his head and landed all around them. They heard muffled laughter from below.

"There must be a ledge below. I could not see them," White Fox whispered, helping Falling Star to her feet. He tugged her hand, and they ran along the top of the ridge, finally slowing to a walk. White Fox felt so at peace he wished he could stay out there forever with Falling Star at his side. The young people returned to the campsite to find the air full of good smells.

Spotted Fawn handed each a bowl. "Eat some of the good turtle soup we have prepared."

"We will all sleep in the tepee tonight," Sunflower said. "Your father just came down from the bluff and said the sky to the north and west is very black, and already I have heard the Thunder God giving his warnings."

Panther Man looked at his wife. "I am fortunate to have such wise women on this journey. You have chosen a campsite with the protection of the bluff when we will need it the most."

"It is the spirits who brought us to this place at the right time," Sunflower replied.

White Fox smiled as he waited for sleep to come. They were crowded into the tepee with their feet to the middle. On one side, he could feel the warmth of his mother's back. From the other side, he could already hear Little Wolf's soft snoring.

No one had lain very close to the flap door, for as the wind blew, the flap would be gently sucked in and out, keeping anyone near it awake. The smoke flap on the top was closed to keep out the rain. White Fox could hear the soft pelting on the roof. He also could hear the heavy winds; but the bluff protected them, and the tepee barely moved. He felt sleep enveloping him.

White Fox awoke with a start. Already the sun was shining, sending a glow through the pale buffalo skin of the tepee. White

Fox slipped outside and walked away from the camp into the long grasses of the prairie. Here he stopped and raised his arms to the Great Mystery. "See me, Father. Be kind to us this day, Mother Earth. We are here to take some of your sacred red rock, and each of us will fashion ourselves a pipe. We will use these pipes to speak to you, Father. We will use them every time there is an important decision to make or a ceremony to perform. Be with us, Father, as we enter the sacred grounds of the red rock." White Fox dropped to his knees, clutching his medicine bundle close. He closed his eyes, visualizing the items he carried in the bundle: the tiny turtle pouch that held his dried umbilical cord; the small polished stones from the Two Rivers village; the tuft of white fur from a white fox, his spirit helper; a perfect obsidian arrowhead that his father had made for him. When White Fox turned back to the camp, he could see his family packing up the tepee and preparing to move.

By midday the travelers could see a rock ridge in the distance. "There it is," Panther Man said. "Remember what I have told you," he continued. "No matter who is camped at the site, they will give us no trouble. The Sacred Quarry is neutral ground to all the nations."

Panther Man selected a campsite, and immediately the women began setting up the lodge. They would stay here for a longer time, so the young men set up a wickiup for themselves and put their supplies inside. "I can see that this area is used by many for a campsite. We may have to look far for enough burning wood," Sunflower said to the girls. Falling Star and Chickadee needed no prodding. They found their wood slings and set off to scour the area for dry wood.

The girls gathered any dry wood they could find along the little creek that flowed from the quarry. Falling Star hummed a song and scanned the landscape. She stopped short when she saw Chickadee sitting on a large rock, tears running freely down her cheeks. "What is wrong, Chickadee? Did you hurt yourself?"

Chickadee sniffled loudly and looked at her friend. "My hurt is on the inside, right here," she pointed to her heart. "I had my life all planned. I wanted to be a teacher like our Black Robe, Soaring

Eagle. I wanted to teach our little children to read and write the white man's way. Together he and I were going to develop an alphabet for our language so we could put our thoughts and history down on paper as the white men do."

"Those are good things to do, Chickadee. Why does this make you sad?"

"On this trip I have grown deep feelings for Little Wolf, and he shares these feelings I think. I have a great ache right here, and I don't think I can live without him. This is so terrible. What will I do?" The words rushed from Chickadee like a flood.

Falling Star was not surprised to hear her friend speak so of Little Wolf. The surprise was that Chickadee was so upset about it. "I don't know what to tell you. I have always wanted to find a special man to spend my life with."

"What is wrong with me, Falling Star? I have never cried over a young warrior before. I do not like these feelings."

Falling Star stood up. "Let's get this wood back to the campsite."

"Is my face red?" Chickadee asked.

"A little. It will look normal by the time we walk back."

As the girls walked back to the campsite, they saw Panther Man talking to a stranger a short distance from their camp. The girls walked quickly to the tepee and joined the women, who were working but also keeping a sharp eye on the two men. Panther Man broke away and walked back to their tepee. When he saw Sunflower's inquiring eyes, he said, "The warrior I was talking to is an Apache from the south country. He would be willing to trade some of his silver metal and blue stones for maple sugar and porcupine quills."

Sunflower looked surprised. "Is this the reason you told me to bring along such a large bag of sugar?"

Panther Man nodded with a smile. "Everyone knows that if the Apache are here they will be eager to trade silver and turquoise for our maple sugar. It is a special treat for them."

Sunflower pulled out the bag of maple sugar and gave it to him. "Make it a good trade, my husband."

"I have a second bag of quills, Brother," Spotted Fawn said, handing it to him.

Panther Man was negotiating with the Apache when White Fox and Little Wolf returned to the campsite from the direction of the quarry. As White Fox slid from Star's back, he pointed toward the Apache camp. "Is that my uncle I see over in the other camp?"

Spotted Fawn answered. "Your uncle is trading with a brave from the Apache nation. We are a little nervous about it."

After a short time, however, they saw Panther Man leave the other camp carrying an armful of trade goods. The women did not run to meet him, but White Fox could see the excitement in their eyes. Spotted Fawn laid out a square-cut piece of hide and indicated to Panther Man to place the goods on it. As he did so, even the young men squatted down to see what he had brought back.

He emptied a small bag, and a treasure of shiny silver circles spilled onto the hide. They had been pounded into different sizes. Some had designs scratched into them, and some did not. A smaller bag tumbled onto the hide, and Sunflower picked it up and opened the drawstring top. She shook out the contents. The women gasped in surprise. There lay a small pile of beautiful blue stones. They were polished to perfection and reflected the sunlight.

White Fox's eyes connected with his uncle's, and Panther Man motioned him aside. They walked some distance from the others and stopped. Panther Man had another bag slung over his shoulder. "The Apache had something I knew I had to have for you," he said, reaching into the bag. "I remember that when I visited the Two Rivers village when you were only twelve winters old you already had your pony, Star. I thought you would like this for him." He pulled a plaited bridle from the bag and handed it to White Fox. The nephew gasped in surprise as he took the bridle and turned it in his hand. Star stood only a short distance away, and White Fox walked swiftly to his side. He gently tugged the old bridle over the pony's head and replaced it with the new one.

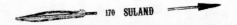

The rawhide straps that fit down each side of Star's face were decorated with three silver circles each, the middle circles etched with the tiny figure of the buffalo. The small plaited strip that ran across the bridge of Star's nose was embedded with the tiny blue stones. The wider strip across Star's forehead also was trimmed with the stones, and in the middle was a perfect silver star. Star stood perfectly still looking at White Fox with his ears pricked forward. White Fox touched the pony's nose and whispered, "A perfect silver star that fits right over the star on your forehead. You are the best pony a warrior could have." The animal brought his nose down and nudged White Fox's chest, snorting softly.

When White Fox returned to their campsite, he saw his uncle emerge from the lodge carrying a tool unlike anything White Fox had seen before. "What is that you carry?" he asked.

Little Wolf joined them as Panther Man handed the tool to White Fox. It had a long wooden handle and a long, arched, pointed metal end. "When our white trader heard I was coming here to the quarry, he traded me this tool for some of my muskrat pelts from the early spring hunt. It is called a pickax. He said that the white miners use it when they search for the gold. I think it will work well to break loose the hard stone of the quarry. We will try it now before the sun disappears from the sky."

"Little Wolf and I have brought our stone axes along," White Fox said.

"They will work well too. That was all we had to work with the other times I came here."

As the men entered the quarry, they saw the Blackfeet men already at work. They could hear soft clinking sounds as the Blackfeet men chipped at the stone. They had accumulated a small pile of rock, and one man was putting it into bags to carry it back to their camp. "I have not been here for a long time. I do not remember where we worked last," Panther Man said, looking around him as he walked. Finally he stopped and looked up, raising his arms to the sky. "Great Mystery, help us this day to find the sacred stone. Help us to make it into pipes that will be pleasing to you." Then he cast his eyes downward. "Mother Earth, we thank you for the gift of the red stone."

The three stood silent as all the sounds of the quarry grew quiet. Panther Man took several steps forward and raised the pickax over his head. He brought it down with all his might. They saw the chips fly. "We will start a new trench here. It is the wrong time of the year to try to use the old trenches, for they are still filled with water."

Both of the young men moved close to see what Panther Man had uncovered. He knelt down and examined the pink rock. "This is not the rock we are looking for," he said. "The soft sacred stone is below this, and this pale rock is what will make it difficult to get to."

The three men took turns using the new sharp pickax until the sun dipped low in the sky. Finally Panther Man examined a piece of dark red rock and shouted triumphantly. "This is the sacred stone. See, I can make marks in it even with my fingernail."

As the young men continued to chip the hard rock away, Panther Man used a sharpened antler to gently tap and pry loose long slabs of the soft stone. By the time darkness came, the three had several fine slabs of stone. They wrapped each piece in rawhide and marked their place with a decorated ring that claimed this site as their place to work.

As the three men carried their treasure from the quarry, White Fox saw that the moon was coming over the horizon, bathing the site in a pale glow. He wondered how many of his ancestors had felt the same peaceful feeling that he now experienced at this place.

White Fox awoke with a start. Little Wolf already was gone. He pulled on his shirt, leggings, and moccasins and was out the door almost in one movement. Everyone else was out already. Panther Man and Little Wolf had unwrapped the sacred stone and were examining it. His uncle had broken a slab into smaller pieces. He had laid a small rawhide square on the ground and had arranged on it several sizes of sharp flint stones for carving the soft, red rock.

White Fox and Little Wolf watched over Panther Man's shoulder as the older man drew an outline of a pipe bowl on one stone piece. The he picked up one of the flint stones and gently began to follow the outline over and over in a sawing motion. "I have broken the slab into the proper sizes for you," Panther Man said. "You can start your pipe as I make mine, and I will instruct you. You have seen many pipes as you've grown up. You can design yours any way you like."

Panther Man brought a piece of the hard, pink-colored rock back from the quarry, and he showed the young men how to hold the pipestone bowl in their hands and scrape it against the harder rock to round the corners. "We will not spend too much of our time smoothing the bowls just yet," he said. "We will drill the holes through the middle first, because if the bowl is going to crack, this is the time it will happen." Panther Man pulled a sharpened stick from his tools. "Chickadee," he called, "could you bring me a small amount of water?"

Chickadee eagerly jumped from her seat and dipped a buffalo horn into the large pot of water near the fire. She brought the hornful of water over to her father. Finally she had an excuse to watch the men work. Panther Man took the horn from her and handed it to White Fox. "Now would you bring us a handful of the coarse sand from around the anthills?" Chickadee returned quickly with her hands cupped together and filled with the sand, pouring it in a pile on the ground where her father indicated.

Panther Man took the small, sharpened stick and held it between the palms of his hands. He looked up at Chickadee and smiled. "You can hold the pipe bowl for me. Little Wolf, as I twirl the stick between my fingers, you drop pinches of sand onto the bowl. As soon as you see a little hole start to form, then you, White Fox, can add a drip of water. This will help the stick to drill through the red stone more quickly." Soon the procedure was going smoothly.

Chickadee was aware of Little Wolf brushing her shoulder every time he reached forward to drop a pinch of sand into the tiny smoke hole. This sent a pleasant, warm sensation through her body, but she kept her head down and did not look at him.

The pounding of hooves broke the peaceful silence. "Someone is coming," Chickadee whispered to Panther Man.

The three men turned at the same time. They saw many ponies and riders approaching and watched as they passed by. The leader raised his arm in greeting, and Panther Man did the same. "They are Dakota," he said. "I wonder from which band they come."

After the riders had passed, Sunflower walked over to the men. "I know who that man is. His son married Little Leaf from our village. This man's name is Inkpaduta."

"The renegade?" Panther Man responded, looking surprised.

Sunflower nodded. "He became chief of his band by killing the chief before him. The rest of the Dakota did not approve of this and will not let his band settle near any of our villages. They travel around the country and seem to cause trouble everywhere they go. I do not like it that they are here."

"They are keeping their distance," White Fox observed. "It looks like they have chosen a campsite beyond the creek." They watched as the group of riders dismounted. The man they believed to be Inkpaduta pulled a robe off a woman still mounted on her pony. Sunflower sucked in her breath as she realized the woman was dressed in white woman's clothes. The man reached up and pulled her from the pony. Almost at the same time, one of the other braves reached up and pulled another blanket-clad figure down to the ground.

Panther Man kept himself busy, but White Fox could see that his uncle was watching the other Dakota camp. They were not close enough to see all the activity, but it was plain that there were two women captives in the camp. White Fox was grateful when the sky darkened. It was a relief not to be able to see what was going on in the other camp.

The air filled with the good smells of the rabbit meat as they held pieces over the fire and watched them sizzle and drip fat into the flames. Reaching into the boiling pot with a long, sharpened stick, Spotted Fawn speared a plump turnip for each of them. The women ate quickly and then returned to their projects. White Fox and Little Wolf could not rest until they were sure they had found all the turnips in the boiling pot and had eaten the last of the rabbit meat. With a moan, White Fox finally leaned back against the travois. "I think we have found all the turnips." He laughed when he looked over at Little Wolf.

"There is one more in there, but I can't seem to catch it," Little Wolf mumbled, looking into the steaming pot.

Panther Man went into the tepee and came back to the fire, carrying his old pipe and his bag of tobacco. "I feel that this is truly holy ground. It is not right to bring captives to this place."

White Fox looked at this uncle and could see the troubled expression on his face in the firelight. "You cannot change what is happening, Uncle."

Chickadee emerged from the tepee. "Look," she said, "the other Dakota camp is gone."

Both of the young men looked toward the creek. "They are gone," Little Wolf agreed. "It is a relief."

As the day progressed, the Blackfeet also departed. Panther Man, White Fox, and Little Wolf continued their work on the pipe bowls. They drilled the smoke holes and buffed the red stone to a soft gloss. Panther Man brought out several branches of the ash tree. He handed a branch to each of the boys and sat down with one for himself. "This will be the stem of your pipe," he explained. Panther Man began gently scraping the bark from the wood. White Fox watched for a while and then started the process on his own small branch.

The boys leaned close to the uncle as he used his sharpest knife to split the skinned branch the full length. Then he scraped the soft pit from the center of the two shafts to create a smoke hole. Panther Man spoke softly as he worked. "We will look along the creek for a tree to provide some sap to glue the two pieces back together. Then we will bind them tight with sinew. Finally, the women will trim the stems with porcupine quills, dyes, and beads."

As the sun lowered in the sky on the third day, the men made one final trip to the trench. White Fox had promised Grey Wing that he would bring him some of the sacred stone. Little Wolf wanted to bring some back for his older brothers. As they chipped the stone from the trench, Panther Man carefully wrapped the pieces in damp rawhide to preserve the softness as best they could.

Late on the third day, Falling Star laid out the completed doe-skin dress that she had been working on since they had arrived at the quarry site. The other women moved close to admire her work. She had sewed a fringed yoke across the front and had trimmed above it with porcupine quills that she had dyed in cranberry juice and cottonwood bark. She had fashioned the quills into arrowheads that faced the center and came down to a point, following the line of the fringe. Above this design, she had used quills to design small seagulls, which she positioned at random. She also had made a belt trimmed with beads that Panther Man had brought from the trading post. She had arranged the beads to create a blue background with white stars. The skirt of the dress was simple with three rows of fringe. As the women looked at her fine handiwork, they murmured their approval.

White Fox noticed that the women were admiring something and moved close to take a look. Sunflower reacted. "Shoo, go away. Young men are not to see a young maiden's new dress until the next feast occasion." White Fox quickly moved away, looking sheepish.

He had finished his pipe. He had decorated the bowl stem with the fox on one side and the running elk on the other, honoring his father's spirit helper. He had left room under the bowl for a lead inlay. His uncle had said that he had some small pieces of lead back at the village that could be melted down and used for this purpose. White Fox also would have to wait for his mother to find the time to do her beautiful quill and beadwork on the pipestem. He would not smoke the pipe until all the work was completed.

The morning passed quickly as the small group packed the travois for the trip home. White Fox watched Panther Man walk back into the quarry carrying a bundle of food and tobacco. Panther Man laid his gift at the foot of a rock formation he had called The Three Maidens and bowed his head. White Fox knew he was saying a prayer of gratitude to Mother Earth for the gift of the sacred stone.

As Panther Man turned around, White Fox leaped onto Star's back. His gaze traveled over the scene one last time, the cliff and the waterfall cascading down the rocks. An ache touched his heart as they turned their ponies and started the trip back to the Redwood Agency and Little Crow's village. He wondered if the others were feeling this sense of sadness as he was.

White Fox urged his pony ahead to Panther Man's side, saying, "See the ravine and brush over there? Little Wolf and I are going to check it for game."

Panther Man nodded and watched as the two young men rode off to hunt. He kept moving, knowing that they would catch up later.

Little Wolf rode up beside White Fox. "There is something I want to ask you." White Fox turned to look at his friend and saw a serious look on his face. "We are warriors now and old enough to take a wife. Are you thinking of doing this soon?"

"Why do you ask?" White Fox returned the question with a chuckle.

Little Wolf took a deep breath. "You know I have never had much interest in the young maidens before. But I have spent this time with your cousin, and I think she is different from the others. She makes me laugh and feel good. But I am not sure she is a very good worker. I have not seen her do much of that on this trip."

White Fox was quiet for a time and then answered. "I have seen some of the clothes she has made, and they looked very nice. She did seem to be deep in her own thoughts while we were at the quarry. Maybe she was thinking about you." Little Wolf glanced at his friend to see if he was teasing, but White Fox's expression was serious. "I too have been having serious thoughts about Falling Star, and I might court her when we get back. Maybe instead of hunting for rabbits we should be looking for willow branches to make courting flutes for ourselves."

"No. First things first. By the time we camp tonight I will be hungry. I would not be very good at courting if my stomach were empty, and we must prove to the women that we are good providers."

As the sun slipped from the sky that evening, the two young men sat together watching as Falling Star stood by the fire turning the spit that held the three large jackrabbits. Chickadee had pushed some prairie turnips into the coals, and they could smell them roasting as well. The two older women had cut out the pieces for new moccasins and sat nearby stitching them together.

When Panther Man finished eating, he rested his back against the travois and watched the others finish. Finally he cleared his throat to get their attention. "Sunflower and I have been discussing something that we would like to share with you before we return to your village." The others looked at him expectantly. He cleared his throat again. "We would like it very much if you, Spotted Fawn, and White Fox would come to live with us at Standing Buffalo's village upriver. We would like to be one family with you there to share our lives. I know you will want to think carefully about this, which is why I am speaking of it tonight."

Everyone exchanged quick glances, and then all looked at Spotted Fawn. She looked at White Fox and spoke softly to him. "I would like to live next to my brother and his family, but it is up to you as the provider to make such a decision." She then turned her attention back to Panther Man. "Almost all of our friends from the Two Rivers village are living in Little Crow's village. White Fox has many friends there whom he has known since childhood."

White Fox turned and looked into Little Wolf's eyes. Then his gaze shifted to Falling Star and finally back to the fire. "I will have to think about this," he said softly.

When they resumed their journey, Spotted Fawn rode her pony in thoughtful silence. The terrain had changed from the open, flat country of the prairie to the more hilly, partially wooded countryside that told them they were nearing the river area. As she scanned the hillsides, she realized how much she missed the heavy forest of Suland. Every tree held a life of its own, and that life seemed to add to one's own life power. She did not understand these powers as the medicine people did, but she knew it was true. She started in surprise, realizing that White Fox was riding close beside her. "You are deep in thought," he said, smiling.

"Yes, I was enjoying the hillsides and the trees," she answered thoughtfully.

"I have made a decision about the move to Standing Buffalo's village. I think this would be a good thing for both of us. We will do it."

Spotted Fawn's face lit with a wide smile. She watched as White Fox kicked his pony into a trot and rode up to talk to Panther Man. The party entered Little Crow's village with the sun low to their backs. Spotted Fawn saw that Little Crow already stood by their lodge waiting to welcome them back. Sunflower moved close to Spotted Fawn. "Panther Man said we should unload only enough of our supplies to stay the night. We will move on in the morning." She flashed Spotted Fawn a smile. "He told me of White Fox's decision. I am very happy about this. I will help you pack your things in the morning."

As they drew nearer to Little Crow, Spotted Fawn noticed that he had an excited look about him, and he started speaking even before they had dismounted their ponies. "I am glad you are back," the chief said quickly. "There has been some trouble since you left. I think you should all hear what I have to say." Chickadee and Falling Star slid from their ponies and moved closer to hear. "There has been trouble to the south at a place called Spirit Lake. A chief called Inkpaduta has killed many white people in that area. Since Inkpaduta and his followers are of the Dakota Nation, the white leaders are holding us responsible for their actions."

Little Crow studied their faces as though looking for a reaction to his words. "I do not understand this, for I do not know this chief," he continued. "I don't even know what he looks like. The white agent said that the government will not send us our annuities this summer unless we take out a war party and catch the renegades."

White Fox and Panther Man exchanged looks. Then White Fox said, "We saw this chief at the place of the sacred stone.

Sunflower recognized him. They had two white women with them."

Little Crow looked surprised. "I have called a council meeting here tonight. I have called together the chiefs from the surrounding villages." He put a hand on White Fox's arm. "You will come to the council?"

White Fox nodded and squeezed his uncle's arm in assurance. "I will be there."

As darkness settled over the village, leaders from the different bands began to arrive and gathered around the large council fire in the center of the village. White Fox recognized some of the chiefs, Wabasha, Mankato, Big Eagle, and Traveling Hail. Each took his place at the fire. Little Crow beckoned to White Fox and Panther Man and made a place for them beside himself. When everyone was in place, Little Crow stood and pointed his pipe to each of the four directions then down to Mother Earth and up to the Great Spirit. He took a deep draw and then passed it around the circle to all chiefs. When it was returned to him, he handed it to White Fox to hold as he spoke.

"I have called you here to discuss the trouble with Inkpaduta. All of you have heard of this trouble, and now I have been told by the white agent that the annuities will be held back from us until we take out a war party to find him and bring him back for justice."

Whispers spread among the chiefs like the movement of dry leaves. Chief Wabasha from the southeast area of Minnesota spoke. "I do not see that it is our responsibility to bring this group of warriors to justice. We do not know both sides of this. We do not know if a past incident may have led them to retaliate against the white man. You all know from past experiences that the white man only sees the bad that our people do to them. They are blind to their own indiscretions."

Just then a young man stepped from the shadows and looked at the gathered men as though to determine who was in charge. Little Crow quickly stood. "Who are you, and what do you want?"

"I have a message from Cloud Man," the young man answered.

"There has been trouble at Yellow Medicine." The messenger paused, looking at the faces turned toward him.

"Tell us what has happened," Little Crow urged.

"The white soldiers had heard that Inkpaduta's son was back visiting his wife, Little Leaf, near Cloud Man's village," the young man continued. "The soldiers took Little Leaf captive. Some of her relatives from Cloud Man's village attacked the soldiers and have taken her back." The young man looked at Little Crow. "Cloud Man wants you to come and help with this terrible situation."

Again the whispers spread around the fire ring. Finally Wabasha stood. "I wash my hands of this incident. It has nothing to do with my people." With this, he turned from the fire and walked to where the ponies were tied. One by one, the other chiefs stood and followed him.

The council was over, and Little Crow looked at his nephew with trouble in his eyes. "I will think about this tonight and will have an answer for this young man in the morning." Then he turned to the young messenger. "Come, you will sleep and eat at my lodge tonight."

White Fox and Panther Man walked back to the lodge and entered to the smell of fish. White Fox leaned over the cooking pot and sniffed. "Your cousin One Who Appeareth brought us a fine fish to put into the soup," Spotted Fawn remarked. She looked at her son with questions in her eyes.

"I don't know what this trouble means to us, Mother. But I think that no matter what my uncle Little Crow decides it is still the right time for us to move on to a new life."

Sunflower leaned over and hugged Spotted Fawn. Panther Man looked at White Fox and nodded his approval. White Fox filled a bowl from the cooking pot and handed it to his uncle. After all the bowls were filled, White Fox looked across the fire into Falling Star's eyes. He could see the pleased look on her face. He looked at Chickadee. She flashed him a quick smile. White Fox finished his bowl and laid it aside, rising to his feet. "Have more of the good fish soup," Spotted Fawn urged.

"I have eaten enough for now," White Fox answered. "There

is something that I must do." He pushed aside the blanket over the doorway and disappeared into the darkness.

Fires flickered throughout the camp, and dogs ran about sniffing the air and looking for handouts. White Fox walked to the lodges that held Little Wolf's large family. As he approached, he coughed loudly. He heard Long Legs' voice invite him inside. Little Wolf was sitting at the fire with his father, mother, and the three younger children, Weasel, Red Squirrel, and Little Sister.

"Little Wolf was telling us about your trip to the Sacred Quarry," Long Legs said. "It sounds like you had an enjoyable time there."

White Fox nodded, seating himself next to Little Wolf. All eyes turned to him, and he studied their faces in return. "You all have been my second family since I was a small child, and I am going to miss seeing you every day of my life."

Walking Women spoke softly. "Are you leaving us, White Fox?"

"My mother and I are going to move upriver with my uncle Panther Man and his family. I realized on this trip that I have deep feelings for the young maiden Falling Star, and I will whittle a flute to court her soon."

Long Legs studied White Fox thoughtfully. "Our adopted boy has grown up. We wish him the best of times and always an abundant harvest." He then turned to the children. "Call the rest of the family from the other lodges. They will want to say their good-byes to White Fox too."

Weasel, the littlest, ran from the tent to take the news to the others. Soon the lodge of the parents was full to bursting. White Fox looked from one face to the next as though to imprint the images into his mind so he would never forget them. "Moving away from all of you will be the hardest thing I have ever done," he said. "I have never left family behind before." He paused, fighting the overwhelming emotions he felt.

Long Legs spoke up. "No matter what happens in this life, you will always be welcome in our lodge as a son."

"Enough of this serious talk." Little Wolf laughed. "It is time to tell some of the stories that each of us remembers about White

Fox from the time he was a little boy." There were many stories to tell, and they talked and laughed together until late in the evening.

There was a soft, red glow on the tepee wall facing the east when White Fox crawled from his sleeping robes. His mother still slept soundly as he pulled on his clothes and quietly left the lodge. He walked quickly to Little Crow's lodge and was about to announce his arrival when a voice came from behind him. "I am here."

White Fox turned to see his uncle approaching. "You look as though you have not slept at all."

"Another messenger has arrived. The news is that both the white women captives have been ransomed," Little Crow answered. "Two more who were taken captive were killed. Forty-two whites have been killed in the Spirit Lake area where the trouble began."

Little Crow leaned heavily against a tree. He looked exhausted. "I have been up all night. The agent told me that the government will stand firm, that if our people do not bring in Inkpaduta there will be no annuities this summer. I have sent a message to Cloud Man that I will lead a mission to capture the renegade and bring him back to the soldier's fort." Little Crow sighed deeply and crouched down on his haunches. He picked up a stick and started to draw marks in the loose dirt. Then he looked at White Fox. "I have gathered enough young warriors willing to go on this mission, but I would like to have my nephew at my side."

White Fox felt a sadness spread through him. He studied his uncle's tired face and slowly answered. "I know how much the people of this village depend on the annuities, but I do not like the idea of fighting our own people for the sake of the white man. I will travel with you as a tracker, but I will not take part in any hostilities toward a Dakota," he said firmly. "I know where they camped at the Sacred Quarry. We could pick up their trail there." White Fox also picked up a stick and started to draw marks in the dirt as he continued. "I came here this morning to tell you that my mother and I have decided to move upriver to live with Panther Man's family. They are leaving today. I will send my mother with them and join them later."

The young warrior stood, dusting off his hands, and left in search of Spotted Fawn. White Fox found his mother and Walking Woman packing the travois. He watched discreetly from behind a tree, knowing that they were saying their good-byes. The two women hugged each other tightly, and then Walking Woman took her leave, wiping her eyes as she went. White Fox moved from the tree to his mother's side. He lifted a heavy bundle of skins onto the travois, then stopped as Panther Man arrived with ponies. "I won't be leaving with you today," White Fox said to his uncle.

Spotted Fawn and Panther Man stared at him, waiting for an explanation. "Little Crow has decided to take an expedition after Inkpaduta. He has asked me to go with him. I cannot refuse." White Fox turned from his mother's concerned look to face Panther Man. "You will take my mother with you until I have finished this mission with Little Crow?"

Panther Man measured his nephew with his eyes, weighing the young brave before him before replying. "We will be waiting for you at our camp. I will smoke a pipe to the Great Mystery for your safe return. From what I hear, this renegade will not be taken without a fight." The two men clasped hands tightly.

Over his uncle's shoulder, White Fox saw Falling Star standing nearby, waiting for him. Without a word, they turned together and walked to the meadow where the ponies grazed. Falling Star turned to White Fox, a tangle of emotion in her eyes. "I was at the lodge of the shaman and overheard your uncle Little Crow tell the shaman that you are going with him to find the renegade Inkpaduta. I want you to carry this stone with you on this journey. I found it in the creek at the Sacred Quarry."

White Fox took the stone from her outstretched hand and turned it, carefully examining the surface. In the stone's striations and colors, he could make out an image. "I have shown it to the shaman, and he says it is mine to do with as I please, for the

Great Mystery chose me to find it. I want you to have it to put into your medicine bundle, if you think it belongs there." Falling Star's gaze anxiously traveled over White Fox's face as he examined the strange stone.

"I see the face of a warrior," White Fox said. "But his hair is cut differently from ours; it is cut in a strip from back to front. I can see one eagle feather tied into his hair at the back." The colors in the rock made it appear that the warrior wore a red scarf around his neck, and below that appeared to be a cut in his chest, with a trickle of blood flowing from the wound.

Falling Star eagerly volunteered more information about the stone, still anxious to see if White Fox would accept the gift. "The shaman says the hair looks like that of a tribe that used to live far to the east. No paint has been used to make the image, so only the Great Mystery could have put it there. The shaman said our Creator would only have put this man's image on the stone if he had been a great warrior or holy man, and anyone carrying the stone will share in the warrior's strength and wisdom."

"I will put the stone in my medicine bundle," White Fox said, looking tenderly at Falling Star. "You will be in my thoughts every day I am gone." He reached out and lightly brushed his fingertips across her forehead and down her cheek. Then he turned and walked away. She watched him go, but he did not look back.

CHAPTER FIVE

1858

White Fox's love for Falling Star was no secret to anyone in Standing Buffalo's village. Only days after White Fox returned from the expedition to capture Inkpaduta, the flute was heard outside Panther Man's lodge in the evenings. Each evening, after a short serenade, Falling Star would emerge from the lodge, and the two would walk to the lakeshore or the meadow to talk and share their time together.

One especially warm evening, they walked side-by-side, quietly enjoying the serenity. Falling Star broke the comfortable quiet. "What happened on the expedition that you just came home from?"

White Fox looked at her with sadness in his eyes. "We tracked Inkpaduta to a lake where he had joined a village with women and children. I did not want to capture him any longer, so I stayed back in the trees. Little Crow and his men went in and attacked the village. They killed four of his warriors, but Inkpaduta somehow escaped. When they attacked the village, some of the women and children got scared and tried to escape by jumping in the lake, and several of them drowned. It was terrible." White Fox and Falling Star continued walking in silence. He felt better just having shared the experience with her.

Finally after many evenings of serenading, White Fox brought gifts to Panther Man, and the wedding arrangements were made. Word was sent downstream to Little Crow's village that a wedding was to take place in the Moon When the Calves Grow Hair. As soon as the guests arrived, the ceremony would take place.

The sun had disappeared from the sky, and White Fox and his mother had finished eating.

White Fox's thought roamed through memories of his past life. He leaned back against the backrest of his willow mat, closed his eyes, and relaxed. The coolness of the evening began to seep into the lodge, and Spotted Fawn laid down her beading and started a small fire. Warmth soon filled the tepee, and White Fox found himself growing drowsy. He was content to sit and think about his future.

His thoughts drifted to Falling Star. His body tingled with warmth as he thought of the pleasures that would soon be theirs. The old shaman Wise Owl had told the young people that the Spirit of Love would allow more pleasures to those who waited until their wedding night to enjoy each other's bodies. White Fox thought this was probably true, for the young maidens who gave themselves to a man early were often humiliated at the maiden's feast by the very same young man who had begged her for the pleasures. Also, the young man often found himself in trouble with the maiden's family in the end, bringing honor to no one.

White Fox and Falling Star had spent much time together over the passing seasons. They were already as one in their thoughts. They had discussed their religious beliefs. She had accepted the teachings of the Black Robe, Soaring Eagle. Falling Star prayed to the Great Mystery through his son, Jesus. She also had a string of beads she used for praying, but White Fox understood this, for he had his medicine bundle with his own religious items tucked inside. He knew she would hang her crucifix in their lodge, but he also knew that the scalp of his first battle would hang from the pole holding his war shield. She would attend the religious ceremonies that the Black Robe held every seventh day, and he would travel into the hills to have his vision quests to seek the advice of the white fox. They would do these things after their marriage, just as before. All this they had discussed and agreed upon.

White Fox was about to doze off when the camp dogs began barking wildly. He pulled the tepee flap aside to look out at the camp. He could hear the talking and laughter of many and knew that it was a friendly group entering the village. White Fox reached back into the lodge to grab his shirt. "I am going to finish these moccasins, so if it is our relatives, send the women to my lodge," his mother said as he left.

White Fox walked quickly through the village. The voices were coming from near Standing Buffalo's lodge. As he drew near, he saw Little Crow and all of his family with a travois loaded with supplies. Little Crow had many relatives in these bands on the upper Minnesota River. This would be a good visit for them. "Here comes the bridegroom," Little Crow said loudly when he saw White Fox.

The crowd parted to allow White Fox to walk to the center. He realized with resignation that he would be the center of attention until this occasion was over. Just then, someone stepped from the shadows and grabbed him in a familiar bear hug. "Little Wolf, my friend," was all White Fox could utter as the wind was squeezed from his lungs.

Then someone else stepped from the shadows. White Fox grabbed him in a hug, speaking softly. "Grey Wing! Now the celebration will be complete."

There was much giggling from the women, and White Fox stepped aside to show Little Crow's wives where they could find his mother's lodge. They went, taking with them the travois that held at least one lodge to shelter the large family. Standing

Buffalo and Panther Man, acting as hosts, had brought out their pipes and bags of tobacco. The older men soon were seated around the fire.

White Fox pulled his two friends aside. "Are your parents not coming to my wedding?" White Fox asked Little Wolf.

"They will be here," Little Wolf replied. "Robin's Nest and Bald Eagle had a baby girl two days ago, and they stayed for the ceremony of commitment to the Great Mystery. I am sure they will be here by the time the sun is at its highest tomorrow."

"That pleases me," White Fox answered. "I could not imagine being married without my second family." White Fox turned back to the fire. "Let's join my uncles and smoke with them."

"I am going to see Chickadee first," Little Wolf said, starting toward Panther Man's lodge at the far end of the camp.

Grey Wing chuckled. "Were you surprised at how many times Little Wolf came up the river to visit over the passing seasons?"

White Fox shook his head. "No, our feelings for the maidens grew on the journey to the Sacred Quarry. Little Wolf and I have been friends since we were little boys. It only seems right that we should someday marry two maidens who are close friends."

The two young men heard Standing Buffalo ask Little Crow, "Tell us about your trip to the house of the Great White Father."

White Fox lowered himself next to Little Crow and saw his face change as though a cloud had passed over the sun. "We will not talk about that until after we have celebrated this wedding," Little Crow replied. White Fox glanced at his friend Grey Wing and was surprised to see him staring at the chief with a look that approached hatred.

The silence grew long until finally Panther Man asked Little Crow how the crops had turned out at the Redwood Village. Soon the older men were talking again. White Fox was glad the subject had been changed. If there was bad news from the white government, he did not want to hear it this night.

Thankfully, Little Wolf returned and White Fox's two friends sat by the fire talking until late, or the night would have seemed much longer. Back at his lodge once more, White Fox thought of his uncle Panther Man and the deal they had struck for the hand of his adopted daughter. White Fox had given him in exchange two ponies and a fine bow and six arrows that he carefully had made. He knew that not all young men would have dealt so easily for such a fine-looking maiden. His uncle had made it easy on him, he reflected and smiled.

White Fox jumped from his sleeping mat and grabbed his clothes. This would be his last chance to spend a little time with his friends. When he stepped from the lodge, he saw two figures under the old cottonwood tree waiting for him. "Go back and get your bow," Little Wolf said. "We have time for a short hunt this morning."

White Fox stepped back into the lodge and lifted his bow and quiver from their place on the pole. Then he joined his friends in the early morning light. The young men walked quickly from the camp on the trail leading toward the Big Woods. The swamps and small lakes spread before them as they walked. They did not put much effort into looking for game, for their real purpose was enjoying each other's company. "Grey Wing," White Fox asked, "is there any chance that you someday will take a young maiden to be your wife?"

His friend answered with a chuckle. "It seems that my friends have chosen the only maidens with any good qualities."

Little Wolf hooted. "Don't blame us if you are not willing to give up even one of your fine spotted ponies in trade for a wife." Little Wolf turned to White Fox. "He has been sneaking off to the Chippewa Country every now and then and returns with the finest looking ponies I have ever seen. I am beginning to think that one of these times he will return with a fine-looking Chippewa maiden."

White Fox laughed and then glanced back at Grey Wing. "I thought that by this time you would be a medicine man, taking the place of your old grandmother."

"I am still interested in the medicines. But sometimes I feel the need to live wild and free, as you did when you were little boys. When I go into the enemy's land, sometimes I travel far to the north. I like to see new things."

The young men sat under a tree at the edge of a quiet pond talking and laughing until the sun was high in the sky. Then, with a hint of regret in his voice, White Fox said, "We must head back. My uncles are probably already constructing the sweat lodge for my purification rites. If they can't find me, they will wonder if the bridegroom has run off."

His friends laughed. "You have been playing the flute for Falling Star for so long I don't think anyone is going to wonder about that." Grey Wing grinned.

When the friends returned to the village, they found that indeed the sweat lodge was under construction. By the edge of the lake, Little Crow and Panther Man were making a circle of tender saplings, bending the tops to push the ends into the soft ground. Sunflower brought them a hide with which to cover the saplings and form the sweat lodge. Already a fire had been started to heat the rocks, and little boys were filling birch-bark buckets with water.

When the friends reached White Fox's lodge, he turned to them and said, "I want the two of you beside me through this ceremony. I want to know that you are nearby when I am in the sweat lodge, and I want you on each side of me when I take Falling Star to be my wife." Little Wolf and Grey Wing nodded, looking pleased. Then they turned away as White Fox entered his lodge.

Inside the lodge, White Fox found that his mother had bundled up all of his possessions, and he knew that after the wedding ceremony he would find his belongings in the new lodge. He sat down on his willow mat and leaned against the backrest. There was no need to hurry, for it would take some time for the rocks to heat at the sweat lodge. He allowed himself to slip into sleep, enjoying the solitude of his mother's lodge for the last time. He wondered what Falling Star was doing now. He would give anything to see her and talk to her.

Little Wolf's voice awakened him. "Your uncles are calling for you." White Fox stepped from his lodge, and immediately his two friends stepped to his side. White Fox smiled at them.

The elders of the village had gathered around the little hut, and their faces turned toward White Fox as he approached. His two uncles were waiting for him at the entrance of the sweat lodge. They helped him quickly to shed his clothes and enter. Inside, the small area was thick with steam. The intense heat took his breath away for an instant. Through the steam, he could make out the naked figure of Wise Owl, the old shaman.

White Fox moved opposite the shaman and sat on the floor in his usual cross-legged position. He could hear the old man chanting softly. White Fox tipped his head back and breathed, filling his lungs with the hot, damp air. Wise Owl got up and began to shuffle around the young bridegroom, circling clock-wise. He continued the chant and rattled a gourd over the young man's head, summoning the good spirits. Then the old man set-tled back into his own place.

As White Fox tipped his head back again, breathing deeply. He wondered what Falling Star was doing at this time. Wise Owl had explained the purification rites to him a few days before and also had explained why the women never took part in a sweat purification. He had said that every moon when a woman sheds her blood she passes through a natural purification. Because of this, it would be a dishonor to the Creator for a woman to take part in this type of ceremony.

He let his body relax and felt the sweat trickle down his skin. He slipped into a dreamy state and was unsure how much time had passed. He heard the uncles pour water over the stones at dif-ferent times. Someone must have handed some burning sage into the hut, for the small area filled with its sweet smell. Gradually he became aware that the steam was thinning and the old sha-man's chanting had ceased.

White Fox was startled awake as the old man stood and moved to the flap doorway. Wise Owl pulled the flap aside saying, "Run, young warrior, run to the lake. You are now purified. Wash your-self clean for your wedding."

He did not hesitate. In one move he bolted through the door and ran as fast as he could into the lake, diving into the deep water. He did not feel the extreme cold, only the cleansing of the water. He swam far out into the lake, then turned and swam back to the shore. There stood his uncle Little Crow, holding out a clean blanket for the walk back to his mother's lodge. After Little Crow wrapped the blanket around him, Little Wolf and Grey Wing stepped to his side to escort him back. The boys of the village were piling dry sticks and wood chunks high for the ceremonial fire. White Fox recalled the times he and his friends had been in charge of building the woodpile as high as they could reach.

As White Fox entered the lodge, he was shocked at how empty it was. All of his belongings were gone. But on his mother's sleeping mat lay the most exquisite set of clothes he had ever seen. He fingered the soft doeskin, bleached almost as white as the winter snows. The shirt was trimmed with fringe, dyed quills, and colored beads. Tiny weasel tails were stitched along the shoulders and across the back. The pants had fringe down the sides with matching beadwork decorating the seams. Beside the clothing was a newly decorated headband with his notched eagle feather already attached. White Fox turned as his mother came through the doorway and moved to his side. "How do you like the wedding garments I have made for you?" she asked.

White Fox studied her face as his emotions came to the surface. "Since I was a little boy, I have noticed that the clothes you made for me and Father were special. Your love shows in the work you do."

She smiled affectionately at him. "Sit. I will comb your hair and braid it for you," she said, reaching for her porcupine brush. White Fox sat quietly and enjoyed her touch. She ran her fingers through his hair and gently massaged his head, just as she had done when he was little. She traced the hairline that peaked on his forehead like his father's. Then she parted the strands and made two thick braids to hang forward over his shoulders.

When this was done, she took the blanket from his shoulders and handed him the pants she had sewn. Next he put on the breechcloth, which served only as a decoration. (With the summer leggings, the breechcloth was a necessity.) Finally, she held the tunic shirt for him to slip over his head. Spotted Fawn stepped back to admire her son. The tunic fringes hung long and would swing gracefully as he walked. She handed him a beaded belt that would gently gather the tunic around his waist. The headband with the eagle feather was the final touch. She enfolded White Fox's hand in both of hers, saying, "I hope you are as happy this day as I was the day I married your father." White Fox smiled and touched her cheek.

The young bridegroom sat on his mother's willow mat to wait. He knew the ceremonial fire had been lit for he could hear it crackling. The light in the tepee had gradually dimmed, and he knew the time should be near. He had been waiting for this day for so long, and now he was growing impatient. Then, from outside, he heard Little Wolf's voice. "We have come for you." White Fox took a quick, last look around the tepee. Then he pushed aside the skin door and stepped out into the cool evening air.

Little Wolf and Grey Wing walked on either side of White Fox, escorting him to the fire. As they approached, a hush spread through the crowd gathered around the fire. White Fox's eyes traveled around the gathering. To his right, he saw Little Crow's family, Little Wolf's family, and some of his new friends from the village. On the other side were the families of Panther Man and Sunflower. This was a wedding party where the relatives were shared by the bride and groom. White Fox seated himself, Little Wolf sat to his right, and his mother sat next to Little Wolf. Grey Wing sat on his left.

No sooner had he settled into his place when he heard the gasps and oohs of appreciation that announced the arrival of the bride-to-be. Falling Star was seated directly across the fire from White Fox, and there was no way for him to see her. He knew that Chickadee would be seated next to her as an attendant, but the rest was left to his imagination.

When the crowd quieted again, food was brought to the groom on one side of the fire and to the bride on the other. Little Crow's son One Who Appeareth brought roasted meat to White Fox faster than he could eat it. Soon a mound of tipsinna cakes and corn bread was piled beside him. Sunflower brought him a bowl of mashed raspberries sweetened with maple syrup into which to dunk the corn bread and tipsinna cakes. Walking Woman brought him a bowl of cooked wild onions and prairie turnips. As she set down the bowl, he grabbed her hand, saying, "I am so glad you are here."

She squeezed his hand then nodded toward the food. "Eat, a bridegroom needs to eat."

Though White Fox could not remember having eaten at all that day, he was not very hungry. But he ate as much as he could to please the women who had cooked these good foods. The women concentrated on feeding the bride and groom, for the guests would eat again later and celebrate late into the night. Some of the drummers had started drumming a slow beat. One by one, the young warriors in their finery got up from the fire and started the tapping dance around the drummers.

At this point of the ceremony, the bride and groom got knowing looks from the older people. Most had not forgotten how impatient they felt before their own weddings took place, but now they thought it very funny to see these young lovers wait.

The camp grew quite dark before Standing Buffalo finally stood to make his announcement. He stood silent for a few moments until everyone noticed and all grew quiet. "You have been invited here at this time and place to witness the marriage of White Fox, son of Spotted Fawn and Running Elk, members of the Mdewakanton Tribe of the Dakota Nation, and Falling Star, adopted daughter of Panther Man and Sunflower, members of the Sisseton Tribe of the Dakota Nation." He gestured for the bride and groom to stand. Their eyes sparkled in anticipation, but still neither could see the other.

Standing Buffalo stepped back, and the shaman, Wise Owl, took his place. He walked to Falling Star, stood in front of her and then, taking her hand, led her around the fire to White Fox.

White Fox inhaled sharply, dazzled by the beauty of his bride. He did not take his eyes off her face even long enough to admire the beautifully trimmed, white doeskin dress she wore. Her thick, black hair hung loose around her small, oval face and flowed past her shoulders. She wore a white headband decorated with small silver stars, which White Fox knew had been gotten in trade at the Pipestone Quarry. A white mink tail was attached to the headband on each side of her face, hanging over the dark hair. Her lips were tinted pink from the juice of some secret berry that the women used on special occasions.

Wise Owl grasped White Fox's right hand and Falling Star's left hand and laced their fingers together. Then he spoke. "White Fox takes Falling Star to be his wife to gather the wood for his fire, to dress the animals he hunts, to take care of his lodge and care for any children the Creator may bestow on them. Falling Star takes White Fox to be her husband to provide meat for their household and to protect her from the enemies of our people." Wise Owl stepped back, and Little Wolf, Grey Wing, and several other young warriors stepped forward. They lifted their bows and discharged their arrows over the heads of the young couple.

White Fox turned his back to Falling Star and lowered himself slightly. She crawled onto his back and he trotted off in the direction of their new tepee, carrying his bride on his back. A wild array of hoots and hollers went up from the crowd around the fire, and the din continued until the newlyweds disappeared into their lodge.

White Fox and Falling Star fell laughing through the flap doorway. They both lay on the floor looking around the inside of the tepee. White Fox saw all of his belongings set about for him to straighten and arrange. He saw the bundles that must contain his new wife's things. The only items that had been arranged for them were their two sleeping mats. The mats were on the far end of the tepee and were pushed tight together. As they both noticed this, they looked at each other and smiled. Abruptly, Falling Star jumped up and started to put things in order.

White Fox moved over to sit on the sleeping mats and watched her work. Finally he could not keep from smiling and said, "Falling Star, we have been together a long time sharing our dreams. Why are you fussing over our home when you should be near me, becoming my wife?"

Falling Star turned to face him, and he saw that her cheeks had reddened. She came to him and knelt at his side. "I know nothing about what I should do," she whispered. "I have heard the sounds of love in the darkness of the night, but I do not know what to do."

White Fox moved over on the mat and said softly, "Come, sit by me. We will talk as we have always done." Falling Star moved onto the sleeping mat and sat close beside White Fox, as she did when they talked by the lake or in the meadow. He looked down into her face. "Do you know how beautiful you look today? There was not a young man at the ceremony who would not have traded places with me, except maybe Little Wolf."

Falling Star turned her face up to look at her husband, a sparkle in her eye. "There was not a young maiden in the camp today who would not have traded places with me, except Chickadee." She laughed. "If these words we speak are true, we are two lucky people to have each other."

They both started to laugh and giggle as the tension of the day began to leave their bodies. Then White Fox hugged his wife tightly. "I am glad this day is over," he whispered in her ear, and he started to nuzzle her pink lips with his own.

Some time later, White Fox awoke to feel his wife's soft breath on his cheek. He smiled in the darkness as he thought of the ways they had enjoyed becoming husband and wife. Now he knew that the old shaman was right when he had told them about waiting to enjoy bodily pleasures. He was sure no two people had ever experienced all the feelings they had felt. Then he whispered into the night, "Thank you, spirit helpers, for leading me to this woman so that I may spend the rest of my life with her." He reached out and shook Falling Star. "Wake up, sleepy wife. We have no more time to waste."

Falling Star moaned and stretched. She could see White Fox digging through one of his bundles and realized that the longer she was awake, the brighter it seemed in the tepee. The moon was at its fullest, and apparently no clouds were covering it. "What are you doing?" Falling Star whispered loudly.

"Come on, get up. We are going to escape from this camp while everyone is asleep. Is your pony easy to catch?"

"Where are we going?" she asked with a yawn.

"I want you to see Suland. I want you to see my boyhood home on the two rivers."

Falling Star sat up, instantly wide awake. "Isn't that a long way from here?" White Fox grunted a positive answer and started to pull his clothes from one of his bundles. "I need to find my clothes too," Falling Star said softly. She reached into her bundles until she found her skirt, tunic, and moccasins and quickly slipped into them. Then she searched some more until she found her new blanket coat. Glancing at her husband, she saw that he too was dressed and was fastening his sheathed knife around his waist.

Falling Star searched through more bundles and finally drew out a rawhide bag. "I made a garment bag to store our wedding clothes in," she said. She carefully folded their wedding clothes and slipped them into the bag. Then she quickly gathered a few items she would need for a journey. She looked around the tepee. Even in the moonlight, she could see that their searches had made a terrible mess of their first home. "I should clean up this mess before we leave," she whispered and hurriedly began picking up.

White Fox surveyed the chaos. Then he laid the items he wanted near the door and started pushing everything else back into the bundles. Falling Star stopped and watched him for a moment. Then, laughing, she followed his lead. Housekeeping could wait until they returned.

The moon was bright enough to cast shadows as they emerged from their doorway. "We must tell your mother where we are going, or she will worry."

"It was her idea that we go away on a trip," White Fox answered. "She already knows where we are going. She prepared these provisions for us to take with us."

They left the camp like two children sneaking away and walked quietly to the meadow where the ponies grazed. White Fox knew that Red Wing, a young man from the village, was on guard duty. White Fox could see his outline up on the hillside, sitting at the base of an oak tree. "You stay here," he whispered to Falling Star. "I am going to see if I can sneak up on a future warrior."

White Fox skirted back and around the hillside and soon was standing just behind the tree against which Red Wing leaned. This seemed almost too easy, and when he peered around the tree, he saw the reason why. Red Wing was sleeping at his post.

White Fox unsheathed his knife and reached around the tree. He put his left arm around the young man's neck and grabbed him, pulling him to his feet. Red Wing stiffened and started to struggle until he felt the point of the knife in his back.

"You would be a dead man now if I were a Chippewa," White Fox whispered in his ear. He felt the young man's body go limp with relief. White Fox released his grip and spun him around. Red Wing looked back at him through his now wide-awake eyes.

"Do not tell the elders that I was asleep. I will do anything for you," Red Wing begged.

"I am in a good mood tonight, but you must be more careful. If you want to become a warrior, you must take your responsibilities seriously. Sometimes it is when we least expect trouble that it comes." White Fox studied the young man's face in the moonlight and could see how upset he was. "Help me find our ponies, and we will forget all about this."

As they walked into the meadow, Falling Star stepped from the shadows. "I have found Flash over here," she said in a hushed voice, moving into the herd.

White Fox turned back to Red Wing. "We are going on a trip into Suland. I will not mention what happened here tonight, but promise me that you will never let this happen again, for the people of the village depend on you."

"It will not happen again, White Fox. You have my word," Red Wing replied.

As their low voices drifted over the herd of ponies, White Fox saw one of the animals moving toward them. He knew it was Star, for Star always came to the sound of his master's voice. White Fox and Falling Star mounted their ponies at the edge of the meadow. "How did your pony get the name Flash?" White Fox asked his new wife as they started to ride.

"My father gave him to me when I was eight winters old," she answered. "One day I was riding along the edge of a swamp when a black bear burst out of the underbrush just beside us. Flash almost jumped out from under me, and he outran the bear. I was so busy hanging on, I did not realize how close the bear had gotten. But after we got back to camp, I saw she had deep, bloody claw marks on her rump. You can still see the scars," Falling Star said, patting the pony on the right side of her rump.

"My father said that because she ran like a flash she saved both of us. After that, we called her Flash."

White Fox reached out and patted the pony. "Because you are a fast pony, I now have a beautiful wife. I will make sure we always take good care of you."

Falling Star watched her husband. "That is one of the things I noticed about you," she said. "Even as a young man, you always took time to pet or talk to the animals of the village."

"I know, but I only did this because I knew it impressed the young maidens," he answered with a grin.

She pulled a pinecone from an evergreen tree and threw it at him. It sailed over his head, and he kicked Star in the ribs, spurring him into a canter. Falling Star's pony soon loped up beside him. "You forgot"—she laughed—"I ride a pony named Flash."

The pair rode through the remaining night and all the next day. As evening drew near, White Fox chose a campsite beside a small stream. "I will go and find us a rabbit to cook," he said after he unloaded the ponies.

Falling Star watched him walk away then started to gather dry twigs and branches, wandering away from the creek to find some birch bark. She was pulling a dry branch from under a tangle of plum trees when swiftly a grouse burst from the limbs over her head. Startled, she dropped to her knees but blew out a deep breath when she realized what it was. She smiled at her reaction to the bird; a warrior would have had his bow up quickly enough to send an arrow after the potential meal.

As Falling Star continued to gather wood, she heard the drumming of the grouse and followed the sound into a cluster of cedar trees. She studied the ground under the trees and the branches above, then smiled knowingly. She hurried from the place and picked up the wood she left along the way. Back at the campsite, she arranged the twigs around the birch bark and pulled a handful of dry grass to tuck into the middle. Then she found her flint in her pack and soon had a crackling fire blazing.

When she was sure the fire would continue to burn on its own, she hurried from the camp with a special mission in mind. The woods were growing dim as the daylight faded, and she would have to be quick. She needed a sapling, one strong for its size but long enough to reach into the cedar trees. Finally she found just the right little red oak sapling. It had grown tall reaching for the light through the shade of the big trees. She felt a pang of guilt as she whittled off the small trunk and said softly, "I need you, little tree, but I will bury an acorn here for your spirit to enter into. You will grow again." She found an acorn that the squirrels had missed and pushed it into the soft ground. Then, with the sapling in hand, she hurried back to the campsite.

She heard White Fox before she saw him. "Where have you been?"

"I am here. I had wood to gather," she answered him. As she came nearer, she could see the concern in his eyes.

"You must have traveled far into the woods. There could be bears around here. We have entered the Big Woods now and must be more careful."

Falling Star smiled at him. "We must not live our lives trying to protect each other from the unknown. It would take away the little freedom we now enjoy."

White Fox looked at his wife. "You are very wise. The spirits already know the days that are allotted for each of us. We should not worry." He looked curiously at the long, thin tree she carried. This did not look like dry firewood.

She answered him before he asked. "The sky will be clear again tonight and the moon bright. I am going to take you on an adventure."

Then she saw what White Fox had been doing. Two fine rabbits, already skinned and gutted, lay near the running water. She knelt down and washed the animals in the cool water. White Fox had found some rocks and was building a spit. By the time the rabbits were cleaned, he was ready to hang them over the fire.

While the rabbits cooked, Falling Star spread out the buffalo robe and arranged two blankets over the top. A short while later, they sat on the bed watching the moon rise and enjoying the succulent meat. A big owl hooted occasionally to let them know that they were not alone in the woods. When they had finished eating, White Fox walked some distance downstream to bury the bones and the roasting stick flavored by the meat. They did not want any unexpected company overnight.

When he returned to camp, he found Falling Star bent over the buffalo robe, carefully cutting a narrow strip off the edge. She pulled off any hair that still remained on the strip and formed it into a loop. Then she tied the loop to the long sapling. White Fox watched her, looking puzzled. She looked up at him and patted the robe beside her. He sat next to her and pulled one of the blankets up around their shoulders.

White Fox slid his arm around her waist and cupped her breast in his hand. He pulled her tight, and she could tell that he was working up to some of the pleasures they had enjoyed the night before. Falling Star threw the blanket aside, saying, "The time is right. We must go on the adventure now." She grabbed the sapling and stood up.

"What are you planning to do?" White Fox asked, disappointment showing on his young, handsome face.

"Come, follow me, and I will show you how a truly skilled hunter gets her prey." She walked softly into the darkness of the woods.

The farther they got from the campfire, the more their eyes adjusted to the moonlit darkness. Falling Star led her new husband through the trees until she saw the dark outline of the cedars. She stopped abruptly and turned to White Fox, motioning to him to stay where he was. She took several steps forward, then glanced back to see him following her again. She shook her head sharply and motioned for him to stay. He could see that she meant it and watched as she disappeared into the dark evergreens.

White Fox stood alone in the darkness, impatiently moving from on foot to the other. He was tempted to disobey and follow her but thought better of it. After what seemed like a long time, he saw the small figure come out of the evergreens and back to his side. She carried something in her hands and held it out to him.

He took the small object from her and examined it in the moonlight. It was a dead brush grouse. As he turned back to her, he realized she had disappeared again. It wasn't long before she returned with another bird. This time he whispered to her, "I want to see how you get them."

"No," she answered. "You men have big feet. You make too much noise."

White Fox could not help but chuckle at this comment, but he did not argue. She seemed to be enjoying showing him her talent, and he enjoyed watching her do it. He waited patiently for her until she had brought him four birds. The she said, "There are many more, but these will be enough to feed us for another day." White Fox nodded, and they quietly walked through the moonlit trees to their camp. He had heard of women hunting the grouse this way in the old days, but this had been a new experience for him.

Falling Star sat on the edge of a bluff overlooking the large lake below her. In her lap she held a small sketchbook that the Black Robe Soaring Eagle had given her. He had encouraged her to draw after seeing some of her sketches of the people of her village. She had brought the book and sketch pencils along so she could record this trip as she saw it.

Two days earlier, White Fox had led them to the mouth of a small river that emerged from a small lake. They had followed that stream until it emptied into this large lake. White Fox had told her that the stream would emerge again farther down the lakeshore and flow toward its meeting place with the Great

River. That would be the place he most wanted her to see. White Fox was sure that he could still find some of the caches of rice that were left there. Normally the people would have returned to retrieve all of it, but the village had moved so unexpectedly that he was sure there was still some buried at the gathering site.

Falling Star lost herself in sketching the lake. Suddenly she jumped, realizing that someone was behind her. She twisted her body to see and sighed in relief as she saw White Fox standing there, watching her work. "You are careless when you work. I could have been an enemy," he chided softly. "We are not far from their land."

"Your uncle Little Crow claims that they have moved to reservations far to the north. Do you not believe him?"

"He only repeats what the white agent tells him," White Fox answered tartly, sitting down beside her. "It still is beautiful up here," he added.

Falling Star continued to draw, and White Fox grew quiet. After a time, she glanced over to see that he had fallen asleep. She flipped the page and started to sketch her husband looking so peaceful. She was beginning to understand why he missed his life in this area and talked about his childhood so much. The beauty of the woods and lakes was something that she had never before experienced.

When her drawing was finished, she snuggled up against White Fox and closed her eyes. She listened to the calls of the white gulls sailing over the lake. She must have drifted off, for she heard no more until White Fox woke her with his stretching and yawning.

"It is time for us to move on. I would like to travel around the east side of the lake and find a trail that I remember going in the direction of our sugar camp." White Fox pointed to the east. "The rice lake is over there. We will come past it on the way back and try to find the rice caches. It would make my mother very happy to once again hold in her hands the same rice that we gathered so long ago."

"Do you think it has kept well for such a long time?" Falling Star asked.

White Fox shrugged. "Mother always said that if we dried it properly and packed it tight in the rawhide cases it would last for many seasons. We will find out if she was right."

White Fox and Falling Star walked their ponies through the sandy outlet of the river and skirted the edge of the lake before they found the trail leading to the east. Falling Star could see the excitement of her husband's face. He was back in his home country.

As they traveled through the countryside, they saw more of the sugar maple trees. The cool evening had told the trees that the season was changing, and the leaves were turning to bright reds, oranges, and yellows. Falling Star was so engrossed in her surroundings, the colorful display of leaves against the clear blue sky, that she was surprised when Flash stopped. She saw White Fox leaning forward, studying something through the trees. She gently nudged Flash up to his side.

There before them was an area that a white homesteader must have cleared. The big trees had been cut and burned. The black dirt had been turned and laid in even rows. Brown stalks of the harvested corn still stood in the rows. Falling Star turned to White Fox. His face looked as though it were chiseled in stone. Abruptly, he turned his pony back to the trail, and they rode on. Twice more they saw areas of cut trees and carefully skirted the locations. They both knew that their people were not allowed to travel this country anymore, and it would be better if no one saw them.

It was late in the day when they entered a heavily wooded area of sharp little hills and valleys. Some of the leaves had fallen, and the ponies made swishing sounds with every step. The sun shining through the leaves gave the world around them a golden glow. They rode into a small clearing, and there between the hills stood an old lodge. It had been made as a summer lodge with elm framing and covered with elm bark. One side had collapsed, and the rest of the lodge tilted in that direction. White Fox walked around the structure, reaching out to touch it. "This is it, Falling Star, the sugar camp lodge. We can clean out the good side and get out of the weather tonight."

Falling Star studied the old structure. She really preferred sleeping out under the stars, but if one night under this roof made her husband happy, it would make her happy too. "Where is the Silver Lake that you told me about?" she asked.

"It is over there, beyond those trees," White Fox answered, pointing the direction. "It is not many steps from here. We will clean the old, damp leaves out of the lodge and replace them with dry ones. Then we will walk down to the lake for water. I know I can find some rabbits in a stand of cedars near the lake. We will not have to eat pemmican tonight."

A short time later, they stood atop a rise, looking out over the small, sparkling lake. Falling Star could see how well the name Silver Lake fit this body of water. It reminded her of the color of the stars on her wedding headband. She stood at her husband's side and imagined him there as a little boy. She could visualize him terrorizing the chipmunks and squirrels with his little bow and arrows. The thought made her smile. "I understand now why you wanted me to see this country before any more of the white men move here," she said. "You must have had a wonderful life here as a child."

White Fox nodded absently. He seemed lost in his own thoughts. Falling Star started to climb through the brush down the bank to the lakeshore. She bent over the water and filled the water bag she carried. Soon she was back beside her husband. He looked at her as though surprised at her presence. "The sun is low in the sky," he said. "We can do more exploring tomorrow. You can find your way back while I go to find a rabbit for our meal." With a firm grip on his bow, he turned and walked toward the stand of cedars.

As Falling Star walked back to the camp, she thought about the way she and White Fox already were falling into a pattern of partnership. They worked well together, and she often knew before he spoke what he was thinking. They would share a good life together she thought, even if within the confines of the res- ervation. She also knew that someday soon White Fox would have to decide if he would live the life of a farmer as the white agent insisted they all must do. If he chose not to follow the agent's advice, she knew she would go anywhere with him without question.

As these thoughts kept her mind busy, she kept her hands busy gathering wood and starting the fire. She put a few stones at the edge of the fire to heat. Later she would put these into a small wooden bowl she had carved to make the tea they had found packed with the pemmican. She resolved to go with her mother-in-law on more of her gathering trips when they returned. Spotted Fawn could teacher her much about the uses of Mother Earth's plants and herbs.

The rustling of leaves shook her from her thoughts. Even her husband could not move soundlessly in the dry leaves. White Fox appeared from the shadows and held up a huge jackrabbit. "He may be a little tough, but we will have meat tonight," he said, the cheer back in his voice.

Falling Star skinned the rabbit and cut up the meat. She handed the soft fur to White fox. "Can you put the skin up in a tree so the animals will not steal it?"

"I will take it into the woods away from the camp, but if there are cats in the area, we will lose it anyway," he answered.

"We have only heard the wolves the last few nights."

"That may be because the wolves tend to brag more loudly about where they are."

They sat by the fire, quietly chewing their tough but tasty meat and sipping their tea until the total darkness had settled around them. The wind was picking up, and Falling Star looked at the lodge, glad they had a snug place to sleep this night. White Fox took one of the blankets and wrapped it around them as they watched the fire burn down. After a time, he said softly, "You have never told me about your parents. Will you tell me about them tonight?" He felt her shiver as she took a deep breath.

"I was nine winter seasons old when it happened," she started. "My father and Chickadee's father were best friends. One day in the Moon when the Cherries Are Ripe, they went with about ten other warriors of the village into Chippewa Country. The Chippewa had raided our ponies one moon before and had killed the young man who was guarding them. My mother was nervous and upset the whole time they were gone." Falling Star paused, and sadness filled her eyes. "I think she knew before the war party returned that she would never see my father again in this life."

White Fox moved closer to her and pulled the blanket tighter around them. "When the war party returned," she continued, "they brought back many ponies, but two warriors were lost, Chickadee's father and mine. The warriors said that my father saw Chickadee's father in the midst of many enemies and went back to help him. There were too many, and they were killed quickly. The rest of our warriors fought their way back into the camp and retrieved the bodies. But they buried them along the trail rather than carry the bodies such a long distance. We didn't even have a body to take care of and grieve over."

"I feel bad that you suffered so," White Fox said softly beside her ear.

Falling Star continued as though she needed to get all the story told. "Chickadee and I grieved together, and our mothers became inseparable. We lived as one family. Two winter seasons went by, and we existed on the generous gifts of our young hunters. Of course, our mothers were good at collecting the harvests of Mother Earth, and we girls helped with the corn and pumpkins we raised near the village.

"Then one day, your uncle came to our village. Soon he was courting Chickadee's mother. When they married, it left my mother very lonely. She finally agreed to marry a warrior who had been pursuing her for a long time." Falling Star took a deep breath. "At first we were happy, but as time passed my stepfather grew mean. He hit my mother for no reason and was always angry at both of us.

"One day, my mother told me she wanted me to move my things to Chickadee's lodge. I had been spending most of my time there anyway and was always accepted the same as a daughter. Two days later, my stepfather came to your uncle's tepee and asked me where my mother was." White Fox felt Falling Star's hand squeeze his tightly. "It frightened me very much, and I started to cry. After he left, I told Panther Man about a special place where my mother went when she needed to be alone. He told me to stay in the lodge with Chickadee and Sunflower, and he went to look for her. He found her at that special place, hanging from a bent basswood tree. She did not want to live in this world anymore."

Falling Star stared into the fire with tears streaming down her cheeks. White Fox said nothing, raising her hand to press it tenderly against his cheek. When the cleansing tears had dried, he asked, "What happened to this stepfather?"

Falling Star pulled herself up straight. "He came to your uncle's tepee after the burial and demanded that I come back to his lodge. Panther Man stepped between us and said he would fight until one of them was dead before he would give me up. Many of the people of the village heard the commotion and came to stand around our lodge. Wise Owl came through the crowd, and our chief Standing Buffalo followed. Wise Owl spoke in a loud voice, saying that my mother had come to him and had told him that if anything happened to her I was to become the daughter of Panther Man and Sunflower. Because this man was not a good father, he should have no claim to me.

"Most of the people there had witnessed his meanness toward us and knew I would not be safe with him. They agreed with Wise Owl, some with loud voices. A few days later, this stepfather left the village. Some said they saw him at Scarlet Plume's village the next hunting season. I have not seen him since that time."

A sharp, cold wind had come up while Falling Star spoke. White Fox got up from the fire and took a spare buffalo robe from their pack. He hung it over the open end of the old lodge. "Come, Falling Star. It is time to crawl into our cozy shelter. I will hold you in my arms until all these sad thoughts leave you." She smiled at him, and together they crawled into the shelter.

Falling Star watched her husband's back as they rode up the narrow, wooded path. Sometimes the trail wandered along the creek and sometimes through the trees that were, every day, showing their colors more intensely. She had enjoyed this morning at the old sugar camp very much. White Fox had shown her the very trees that his mother and the other women had tapped. Then they had walked around the small lake, and he showed her the many burial mounds of the ancient ones. She loved to see his excitement at being in this place.

They were riding along a small creek, which White Fox had told would lead them to the Great River. He said they should be there by the time the sun was at its highest. The day turned warm as they rode, a light breeze from the river keeping the travelers comfortable. Eventually, the trail moved inland from the river and gradually climbed. Finally White Fox and Falling Star crested a hill, and the country unfolded before them in glorious beauty. It was heavily wooded, and the river wound through it like a glittering ribbon.

Pointing upriver, White Fox said, "You see the course of the river ahead?" He swung his hand in a curve, indicating the area he meant. She nodded. "We called that part of the river The Big Bend."

Both were startled by a loud noise from down river. They turned to look toward the sound, and, after a time, a large boat came into view. They watched in awe. "Look how big it is," Falling Star exclaimed softly. "Soaring Eagle showed us pictures of such boats, but I didn't realize they were so big."

"I have seen this type of boat at the Kaposia village," White Fox commented, "but I remember them as being smaller than this one."

Again the loud noise came from the boat, like a blast from a giant horn, and they saw steam shoot into the air from a pipe on the top. "I wonder why everything the white man does must be so noisy?" Falling Star whispered. "They will make Mother Earth angry."

"I think Mother Earth already is angry with the white man for cutting her trees and tearing up the land with their plows."

Abruptly White Fox got to his feet and began walking back to the top of the bluff where their ponies grazed in the long grasses.

They soon were back on the trail. A few minutes into their ride, White Fox pulled Star to a swift halt. The land ahead of them had been cleared, and there stood a white man's lodge. Falling Star nudged her pony up beside her husband's for a closer look. The outside of the building was built of wood slabs. They had been cut narrow and laid one on top of the other then painted white.

Falling Star studied the structure in amazement. "Never have I seen a white man's lodge like this one," she whispered.

White Fox also was studying the structure. The big building was not square but had eight sides, and each side had two windows, one toward the top of the wall and one toward the bottom. The house had a porch that extended all around it. Another building had been added on one side. "I wonder how many families live in this lodge?" Falling Star said softly.

This comment seemed to bring White Fox out of his thoughts. He glanced around nervously. "Come quickly into these trees. We are not welcome here. We will hide the ponies and walk the rest of the way." He quickly found a ravine and tethered the ponies where they were hidden by heavy brush. Turning to Falling Star, he pointed. "See over there, toward the Great River, where the haze hangs over the trees? That is where our village stood. We will go through the brush until we can see over the bluff."

White Fox was the first to see the view below them. Falling Star heard him gasp. She stepped up to see what he was seeing. There, spread below them, stood a small white man's town. As White Fox's eyes took in the scene, she heard his breathing become irregular.

Falling Star saw a ferry crossing the Great River. She recognized it because one similar crossed the Minnesota River at the Redwood Agency. As it got nearer she could see a horse and buggy on it and four people standing along the wooden railing. She could hear their voices drifting across the water. Just beyond the point where the ferry would come onto the sand stood the large paddleboat they had seen earlier that day. It appeared to be empty now.

To the left, Falling Star could see where the small river moved toward the Great One. *This must be the one White Fox called the Clearwater.* The white men had built a dam to hold its water back. She could see that a paddle was being turned by the water. Another large building stood along the small river, nearer the point where it entered into the Great River. To their right, along the hillside, were the white man's homes. She could see that one was very big. The arrangement of the windows told her that it had three levels.

Finally White Fox said, "See that building where the big boat is anchored? They sell the firewater there."

"How do you know that?" she asked softly.

"See all the barrels leaning against the back of the building? The firewater comes in those barrels. I saw a place like it at Kaposia. The trader Pig's Eye ran such a place along with his trading post." The words poured from White Fox as though a dam had burst. "They have ruined the beauty of the little river. It used to twist its way to the big river. They have changed the way it flows, and now the water covers where some of our lodges once stood." Falling Star heard the pain in his voice.

White Fox pointed. "See where the trail runs down between their lodges? They have cut many of the big trees that used to live there." Then he turned to the left. "See where they hold the Clearwater back? The water looks deep. We used to cross the river there. It was shallow then."

White Fox grabbed Falling Star's arm. She had heard the sound too and stood completely still. Slowly they looked back to the trail. A small boy came walking quickly along the trail. As he came even with their hiding place, he stopped. He looked into the brush as though he could see them. They stood so still that Falling Star could not even hear her husband breathe.

They watched as the boy left the trail and stepped into the brush. He pulled his manhood from his pants and made a stream of water that barely missed White Fox's moccasins. The stream dwindled, and he tucked his private part back into his pants and started to back away. White Fox stepped from his hiding place and grabbed him, clamping his hand over the startled boy's mouth. White Fox pulled him deeper into the brush and turned the boy face to face with Falling Star. He held the little body tightly until he gradually felt the boy stop struggling.

Falling Star spoke to the little boy in his own tongue, "Do not be afraid, little boy. We will not hurt you." The little body relaxed in White Fox's arms. "Will you be quiet if my husband takes his hand from your mouth?" Falling Star asked.

The little head nodded sharply, and White Fox slowly took his hand away. The little fellow lay back in White Fox's arms and looked up at him, then turned his eyes back to Falling Star. His eyes were a deep blue and his hair the color of dry prairie grasses. She spoke to him again, "We are not here to hurt anyone. We are here looking over your town because my husband once lived here as a little boy."

The child turned back to White Fox. "You lived here?" he queried softly.

White Fox nodded. "I lived down there by the little river when I was about your age."

The boy sat up. "Was that a long time ago?" he asked.

White Fox nodded again. "It seems like a long time ago."

"Where did your house stand?" The little boy was losing his fear, and his curiosity showed on his face.

"I am not sure anymore. Things look so different. They have changed the way the river runs," White Fox answered. Then he pointed. "I think our lodge stood there. Do you see the cherry trees? We were between those trees and the river."

The boy looked hard at the place where White Fox pointed, as though trying to imagine a tepee on that spot. Then he looked back at the two faces watching him and smiled. "They built the dam last summer to run the sawmill. They held back the water for a day. Then they opened it, and the water made a new path for the river. See the big building? That is the new flour mill."

"They grind the grain seed into flour inside that big building?" White Fox asked, looking at it. Then he looked back to the boy. "What is your name?"

"Eddie," he answered. "What is your name?"

"My name is White Fox, and this is my wife, Falling Star."

The boy turned to Falling Star. "Did you live here too?"

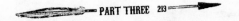

"I did not live here," she answered. "This is the first time I have seen this place."

The boy named Eddie stared at the two of them with a very serious expression. Then he said slowly, "You must not come down into the town unless you wait until after dark. The people who live here do not want your people around this area anymore."

"We know it is not safe to go among your people," White Fox said, equally solemn.

Their attention was pulled back to the town below. A group of men had come out of the firewater building and walked down the wide trail to a three-story brick building. "That is the hotel," Eddie said.

"What is a hotel?" White Fox asked.

Eddie eagerly explained. "It is a building where the traveling people stay overnight. It has many rooms upstairs, and each has a bed. Downstairs the woman who runs the place feeds the travelers. The people who come on the paddleboat stay there." Eddie looked back at White Fox. Seeing that he still held the young warrior's attention, he continued. "That little building down there is the blacksmith shop. Farther down the street is the store."

White Fox interrupted. "Is that like a trading post?"

"No, the storekeeper only takes paper money for his goods; although my mother sells him eggs, and he gives her the things she needs in exchange." Again Eddie pointed. "That house is where our doctor lives. Do you have a doctor where you live?"

"We have a shaman and also medicine people. They work together to heal our sick or wounded," White Fox answered. "Who lives in that big lodge up on the hill?"

"Simon Stevens. He started this town and is the postmaster now." With a glance at White Fox, he explained. "He takes care of the written letters that come by paddleboat. He keeps them until the people come to collect them."

"Who writes these written papers?" White Fox asked.

"My mother got one once. It was from her sister who lives back East."

Again their attention was drawn to the brick hotel. A large

group emerged from the building and walked down to the Great River. They were led by a man dressed in black and carrying a book. A man and woman followed close behind him, and the rest followed them. When they reached the riverbank, they stopped, and the man in black turned to face the couple. He opened the book and began to read from it while the people stood and listened. "A wedding!" Eddie whispered excitedly.

White Fox and Falling Star glanced at each other, then looked back to the event taking place by the river. They could hear the man in black say some words; then the other man repeated them. The man in black spoke again, and the woman repeated the words. Then the man in black raised his hands in the air as though to speak to the Great Mystery. Finally the man in black brought down his hands and said a few more words to the couple. This ended the ceremony, for all those watching cheered and clapped their hands. They gathered around the couple, hugging them and shaking their hands.

White Fox and Falling Star looked at each other, then back to their new friend. The little boy looked back at them for a moment and then said, "I must go now, or my mother will come looking for me."

White Fox nodded to him. "You can go."

The boy's face grew serious. "Will you remember me when you return to your home?"

"We will always remember that we have a friend at this place and that his name is Eddie," White Fox answered, smiling.

"I have something to tell you, if you will not laugh at me," the little boy said seriously. White Fox and Falling Star looked at Eddie expectantly. He started to speak slowly. "I have seen two little Indian boys playing in the woods. There is a puppy with them. I have tried to talk to them, but they disappear. I have not told anyone about this. Do you know who they are?"

White Fox looked into Eddie's eyes. He could see that this was a serious matter to the little boy. "I know the boys you are speaking of," he answered. "Their names are Standing Calf and Moon Boy. They are both buried at the top of this bluff. Standing

Calf's puppy was buried at his side. They were always together in this life."

The little boy did not look surprised. White Fox continued, "The next time you see them, call out their names and they may not disappear. Tell them that White Fox sends his greetings and looks forward to the time when he will see them again in the Spirit World."

"I will," Eddie said, smiling. "I did not think you would believe me."

"Why would we not believe you?" White Fox asked. Eddie shrugged and did not say any more. He looked back toward the river.

"You had better go now, Eddie, or your mother will be looking for you," Falling Star reminded him.

The little boy looked intently into their faces. "Good-bye. I will ask God to take care of you and see you safely home again." With this, he left the hideaway on the hillside and headed back up the trail. He turned once to wave before he disappeared.

White Fox took Falling Star's hand, and they moved through the brush to a sheltered place nearer the river. There they settled back against a large elm tree. Falling Star snuggled against her husband, and soon they were both asleep in their hiding place.

Falling Star awoke to her husband's nudges. It had grown dark. She could see the lights twinkling from the windows in the town. "Come," White Fox whispered, "now we can explore the town, and no one will see us."

They moved from the bushes and walked quickly down to the dam. The moon was nearly full, and it cast a soft glow over the landscape. The water dropping over the dam was noisy and frothy white in the soft light. White Fox watched it fall, remembering the soft gurgling sounds of the river so long ago. He turned his back on the water, wondering where all the earth had come from to hold the water back at this place. The land did not look right to him. "I wonder why the white man feels the need to change the designs of Mother Earth?" he whispered.

"It must be important to them to cut the wood into slabs and to grind big amounts of grain into flour," Falling Star volunteered.

The pair walked beside the moving water until they came to the point where the two rivers merged. White Fox stood quietly and studied the way the water of the small river became one with the big river. "Looking out over the water, everything looks the same," he said softly. Then he turned to face the land. He looked up the small river, studying the outline of the big flourmill. Then he turned to look down the trail into the town. Finally his eyes slid up the hillside.

White Fox walked along the small river, and Falling Star could see him studying the hillside. She followed. He stopped and pointed. "See those cherry trees? Our lodge must have stood about right here." He swung around, facing the river. "I am glad they built the flour mill on the other side. I would not want that ugly building standing here on this place."

He stood silent, as though sharing his thoughts with Mother Earth. Then he turned and walked back toward the Great River, the Mississippi. He walked near the firewater building; but there were no lights, and all was quiet. He walked up the trail into the town site until they were almost directly in front of the brick hotel.

Falling Star grew nervous. The lights were on, and they could hear music and laughter coming from the building. Apparently the white men also celebrated their weddings well into the night. White Fox grabbed Falling Star's arm and pulled her around the back of the building.

She had noticed that as they walked into the town, the land gradually rose above the river. The town site was on this flat plateau. Beyond it, the land rose into a second bluff. White Fox led her to the riverbank. There the ground dropped sharply to the river. White Fox motioned for her to stay at the top, and he climbed over the edge, looking for something.

"I have found it," he called finally. Falling Star carefully climbed down to join him. White Fox was studying a large rock in the moonlight. He ran his fingers over a design scratched in the stone. Falling Star knelt beside it, and she too ran her fingers over the design. She could see that it was a running animal with antlers.

She looked up at White Fox. "A running elk, like your father's name?"

White Fox nodded and pointed to the right side of the stone. "My father is buried here." He patted the ground. "Come, sit here beside me." Before they had come down from their hiding place on the bluff, White Fox had returned to the ponies and retrieved his pipe and tobacco bags. Now he carefully took the pipe from its bag and laid it where he believed the grave to be.

He reached around him, pulling handfuls of dry grass and leaves from the hillside, and made a place to light a small fire. He drew his flint from his medicine bag and picked up another small stone to make a strike. A few clicks of the stones and the spark caught. He gently pushed leaves and twigs into the small flame then sprinkled a few leaves of sage over the top to make a purifying smudge. They watched the smoke spread over the gravesite, then drift over the riverbank and skyward.

White Fox picked up the pipe and packed it with his kinnikinnick tobacco. Then he held a twig in the small fire and used it to light the pipe. He took a few drags on the pipe, watching the smoke curl upward. He tipped his head to the sky and said, "Father, I call your spirit back to earth."

Falling Star sat perfectly still, realizing the holiness of this time for her husband. The sudden rustling of leaves drew her attention to the riverbank below. Several small trees grew at the edge of the riverbank, and their leaves were moving wildly. Then Falling Star felt a soft, cool breeze touch her cheeks. She heard White Fox say, "Father, we are honored that you have come to join us."

White Fox smoked in silence for a while. Then he said, "I was not yet a warrior when I buried you at this place, so I never had the honor of smoking the pipe with you. I want to share this smoke with you." He continued to smoke quietly until he seemed to remember Falling Star's presence. "I have brought my wife to this place. I wanted her to see its beauty. I know you have been with us many times, Father. I have felt your presence."

Falling Star realized that the celebratory sound from the hotel had ceased and the area had grown unusually quiet. Even the animals and birds of the forest were listening to the conversation White Fox was having with the spirit of his father. "I will probably never return to this place again, Father," White Fox spoke softly, his face tipped upward. "When I first saw the town built on this place, I thought that I would move your bones to rest somewhere else. I am not going to do that. This was our home first, and this is where you belong. The white man has changed the flow of the small river, but so far they have only crossed the Great River with a ferry. Maybe you can protect it from further destruction."

White Fox paused thoughtfully. "We met a small boy at this place, and we could tell that he had a good heart. Maybe after the white men live here for a while, they will become more respectful of the land and try to preserve its natural beauty. We will pray to the great Spirit for this to happen."

The leaves of the small trees began to rustle and swirl as cool air moved over them again. Then, as quickly as it had come, it disappeared, and all grew quiet. White Fox spoke softly. "Good-bye, Father. We will leave this place now, but I will always remember our life here. Everywhere I go, I will carry with me the wisdom and goodness of the things you taught me here." White Fox had finished his pipe. He tapped the ashes out of the bowl onto the grave.

They traveled the trail back to Big Stone Lake for four sunrises before Falling Star knew they were getting close to the village. White Fox had been quiet on the trip home, and Falling Star did not break into his thoughts. She knew he was feeling the sadness of knowing that he would never again visit his boyhood home or his father's grave. Finally she spoke. "It seems that we would have met some of our young hunters on this trail by now."

White Fox turned to look at her, puzzled. "I have been lost in my thoughts, but you are right. We will see the pony herd as soon as we get to the top of the next hill."

Falling Star rode up beside White Fox as the trail grew wider. She was anxious to see the valley of the Big Stone Lake. As they crested the last hill, they stopped their ponies and gazed over the valley. "Where are the pony herds, White Fox?" Falling Star exclaimed.

White Fox kicked Star in the ribs and took off at a gallop toward the village. Falling Star followed. They passed through a small stand of trees and out into the open. To their surprise, the land was empty except for the three tepees of their families. White Fox did not slow his pony until he reached the tepee and then pulled Star to a stop and jumped from his back.

The pounding hoofs brought Spotted Fawn from her lodge, and she found herself being swung into the air by her son. She saw the fear in his face. "I am so glad to see you," he said. "I was worried when I saw the village had moved. Where have they gone?"

Spotted Fawn caught her breath. "They have moved, my son. They have moved to a new place, but I will let your uncle tell you about it."

"We have much to tell you about our trip," White Fox began. "But that can wait until later."

As Sunflower and Chickadee emerged from their tepee to hug the returning newlyweds, Panther Man came from the lake with a string of fish. He handed the fish to his wife. "Here are some fish for the soup. I want to smoke and talk to my nephew."

The women disappeared into Spotted Fawn's tepee, and the two men stepped into Sunflower's lodge. Panther Man brought out his pipe and tobacco bag. He carefully filled the pipe and sat cross legged, facing his nephew. After the pipe was lit and each had taken a few puffs, Panther Man looked into White Fox's eyes. "What has happened here, Uncle? Where have the people of our village gone?"

Panther Man laid his pipe aside. "The day after your wedding ceremony, your uncle Little Crow called a council with Standing Buffalo and the elders of our village. He told us about his trip to Washington. This place Washington is where the Great White Chief lives, far to the east.

"Little Crow told us that he had gone to this council to try to get some answers about the failure of the white government to live up to the promises and treaties of the past. He wanted to know why the annuities were held back during the Inkpaduta trouble. He wanted to know what happened to the money that was due under the 1837 and 1851 treaties. He wanted answers as to why the traders received so much money when only a few of our people had debts with these men."

Panther Man picked up the pipe and took a few puffs then handed it to White Fox. He continued. "Next he mentioned the border line of the Cottonwood River that had been agreed upon in the Treaty of 1851 and how the farmers have been settling on our side of this border ever since that time. It was at this time in the council that a man named Mix brought out the old treaties. Your uncle saw his own signature on these papers, but when the papers were read, they were not the same as he had remembered the agreements to be. Your uncle believes that because our chiefs could not read the written words on the treaties, they were changed later or were read to the chiefs differently than they were actually written.

"He was told at the council that we do not really own the lands we are living on now but are allowed to live here only through the good nature of the Great White Chief."

White Fox shook his head. "None of this makes any sense to me."

Panther Man had become very agitated as he told the story. He continued in a loud voice. "You will understand better when I tell you what the chiefs have done now. Little Crow and the others have signed a new treaty. Even though these government people in Washington say we did not own the reservation land we have been living on, they have agreed to buy the part of it that is north and east of the river. Then they will give us the part that is south and west of the river for a reservation. I think the chiefs have been tricked again, for if we didn't own the land, how could they buy it from us?"

"Do you know where the village has moved?" White Fox asked.

Panther Man shook his head in disgust. "Standing Buffalo was very angry and only said they would move to the west side of the lake. We can follow their trail."

White Fox spoke softly, soothingly. "It is easy for us to see the wrong in what my uncle and the other chiefs have done, but I am sure none of us would do any better against the white man's government."

Panther Man agreed. "There is a new fort north of here," he added. "It is called Abercrombie. They have put soldiers there to watch our people. Your uncle Little Crow said he was going home to his village and would now start to live the white man's way. He would plant more corn and build a white man's house to live in. He told me that on their journey to Washington they saw more white men than the locusts in the field on a dry summer day. He said that they will force our people to live the white man's way. There are too many of them and too few of us."

White Fox nodded. "We saw much the same thing on our trip back to my boyhood home. They have built a town on our village site. It is not the same." Both of the men grew silent and smoked until Sunflower entered the tepee with a bowl of fish soup for each of them.

CHAPTER SIX

1861

The sun was warm against White Fox's back as he leaned forward to stretch. His eyes stayed fixed on the door of the women's lodge. He hoped that someone would come out soon. This waiting was hard on a young warrior. Falling Star had moved from their tepee during the night without waking him, and now he waited for someone to tell him what was happening inside.

Panther Man sat down beside him. "It is a good day for a little one to make his entrance onto Mother Earth," he said, smiling. "It must have been the journey to the lower villages that shook the little one loose."

White Fox chuckled. "I enjoyed that trip. It was good to see Little Wolf and Chickadee finally become husband and wife.

They will have a good life with Little Wolf's big family around them."

Panther Man was quiet for a while, then said softly, "Do you wish that you had stayed in their village?"

"I have been happy here, Uncle. Living near you and Sunflower has been good for Falling Star and me and has made my mother as happy as she could have been after losing my father." White Fox paused, brooding on the information he had to share. "Little Wolf told me that since the farmers have moved in across the river from their village the game is disappearing. Life in the lower villages is becoming more difficult for them."

Panther Man nodded. "I heard some grumbling too while we visited there."

The sun already had reached the highest point of the day and was now on its way down to the place where Mother Earth would hide it for the night. White Fox heard a soft noise and then excitement coming from the women's lodge, and then his mother came through the doorway with a bundle in her arms. She walked quickly to him as he scrambled to his feet. A radiant smile lit Spotted Fawn's face. "I have a new little son who is waiting to be held by his father." She handed the bundle to White Fox. He carefully pulled the soft, rabbit-skin wrap back from the baby's face. Could this tiny face be that of a future warrior? He gazed at the little one in amazement.

Panther Man crowded close to look and reached out to touch one of the small hands. "This is a small child, but he looks perfect to me."

White Fox looked into his uncle's eyes and remembered Panther Man's story of his first wife and little boy whom he had lost in the Canada Country. "I am going to dedicate this child to the Great Spirit now, and I want you to hold him for me." White Fox pulled the child free from the rabbit fur wrap and handed the tiny, naked body to his uncle. Panther Man lifted the baby high in his outstretched hands. White Fox stepped close, laying his right hand on the wriggling baby and extending his left toward the sky. "Great Spirit, take this child as one of your own. Give him a clear mind so he will learn the patience and wisdom of our people. Send him a spirit helper to protect him through the trials of life."

Then White Fox stood silent. Panther Man waited, knowing that this would be the time for the father to give his child a name. Then White Fox spoke the name in deliberate, slow tones. "I give this child the name Sparrow Hawk."

Panther Man slowly lowered the baby and looked at White Fox in surprise. "You remembered."

"I remembered," White Fox answered, nodding his head slightly, taking the child from his arms.

Panther Man looked up. "Look! White Fox!" From the sky, a bird dropped in a steep, fast dive. Just as the two men ducked, it pulled out, swooped upward, and came to rest in a tall oak tree. There it sat in all its colorful glory, staring at the two men, a fine sparrow hawk.

"Where did he come from?" White Fox asked in wonder.

"I don't know," Panther Man answered. "When I named my son for this bird, he had been around the camp all day and had spent most of that time perched in the tree under which I sat. He seemed to be waiting with me for the little one to be born. During the years that my son lived, the hawk was often seen around our camps. All the people of the village got used to seeing him."

Panther Man helped White Fox to wrap the baby in the soft fur. Then he said, "I am honored that you have given your son the same name as my son. His spirit helper has already come to him, and I am sure some of my son's spirit will live on in him. If that happens, this child will be a great joy to all of us, as the first Sparrow Hawk was to me and my first wife, Girl Who Walks with a Limp."

Spotted Fawn came to get the baby and looked into White Fox's eyes. "Have you given your son a name?"

White Fox nodded and smiled. "Come, we will take him back to Falling Star. Then the grandmother will hear this name as I tell it to his mother."

Falling Star was cuddling the newborn and rocking him gently. White Fox was finishing the cradleboard, attaching the skin sack that Falling Star had decorated so beautifully with beads and dyed porcupine quills. Falling Star watched her husband work. "The cradleboard is turning out nicely," she said. "It will hold your son out of the way of trouble until he finds out what his little legs are for."

White Fox looked fondly at his wife. He noticed that her face held a thoughtful look and waited for what was to come next. "The men have been preparing for the fall buffalo hunt, and I want you to go too. We need new robes for the approaching cold season. I have asked your mother to move into our lodge now, and we can do that while you are gone." White Fox flashed his wife a smile. She knew that he would want to go on the hunt, and this made it easier for him.

Spotted Fawn sat upright and added, "Sunflower had mentioned to me that she is going with Panther Man on the hunt. The three of you will be able to dress out the hides and take care of the meat."

White Fox looked at his wife and son and realized that he was not as anxious to go as he had been before the baby had arrived. He also knew, however, that the buffalo hunt had become more important to their survival than it had ever been. He would go.

PART FOUR

CHAPTER ONE

1862

One winter season had passed since the birth of Spotted Fawn's grandson, and she smiled as she thought about how their lives had changed. She was following White Fox as they returned to the village from the summer buffalo hunt. They had been away for one moon, and now they were nearing home. Spotted Fawn had enjoyed the time she had spent with her son and Panther Man, but she was growing anxious to see her grandson. Falling Star had decided not to come on the hunt. Her mother, Sunflower, had not been feeling well for quite some time, and Falling Star had stayed behind to care for her.

Spotted Fawn thought about the hunt and felt a wave of sadness and concern. They had not found nearly as many buffalo as they needed. Half of the men, including their chief, Standing

Buffalo, had decided to go farther out onto the prairie to continue the hunt. It was the Moon When the Cherries Turn Black, late in the summer, and they knew it was necessary to prepare for the cold season ahead.

White Fox twisted on his pony to look back at her. "Mother, I am going to ride on ahead to the village."

Spotted Fawn nodded her approval, then turned to Panther Man. "You go on ahead too, Brother. I will take care of your pack pony." She knew that he had been feeling anxious for his wife all the while they were away. Panther Man smiled his thanks and rode out of the line to catch up with White Fox. Spotted Fawn and the rest of the group rode on in silence until they saw the village smoke hanging over the horizon ahead. Then the pace quickened, each member anxious to see the loved ones left behind.

Spotted Fawn rode directly to their summer bark lodge. White Fox stood beside it holding Sparrow Hawk. "Look, Sparrow Hawk. Here comes your grandmother."

Spotted Fawn smiled, thinking that it still sounded strange to her to be called grandmother. Now as she saw the little boy, she realized how deeply she loved him. She knew she would make any sacrifice to keep him safe and happy. Falling Star and Sunflower leaned close, watching Spotted Fawn unwrap her harvest of prairie turnips, seeds, and beans. "You had better luck with your gathering than the men did with the hunt," Falling Star said thoughtfully. "This will add to our winter cache."

Spotted Fawn looked into the faces of the other two women. She knew what they were thinking. They had suffered terrible hardships during the past winter season. The cold had been the worst in years, and the previous summer's corn had perished in the drought. Most of the people of the village had not had enough to eat, and some of the old people had died because they gave their rations to the little ones.

"Put a kettle of water on the fire, Falling Star," Spotted Fawn suggested. "I dried some of the buffalo's lung and liver so you could have some of it when we returned." She turned to

Sunflower. "You look much better than when we left. Have you recovered from your illness?"

"My daughter has taken good care of me. Little by little, I began to feel good again. Sometimes I worry about what will happen to us; maybe I was worrying too much."

Spotted Fawn nodded. "We are a wandering people by nature. I don't think it is good for us to live the way we are living here. I could see this on the hunt. Even though the game was scarce, the people seemed happy to be able to move around as they pleased."

"I was not idle while you were gone," Falling Star announced. "I left Sparrow Hawk with Mother, and I gathered the river onions and turnips and even used your techniques to steal from the mice. I gathered quite a store of foods myself."

Spotted Fawn smiled at her. Falling Star had been an apt pupil. She had become an expert at gathering because she paid attention when Spotted Fawn showed her how to do a job. "I am proud of you, Falling Star. You have learned well."

The women busied themselves cutting turnips into the water that already contained the liver and lung. Soon the lodge was filled with a delicious aroma. White Fox entered shortly and sat by the fire. Only Panther Man still was missing, but after a time he too came through the doorway and settled beside his nephew.

Spotted Fawn and Falling Star dished up the stew, and soon all was quiet except for the gentle noises of eating. Even Sparrow Hawk was quiet as he ate from his bowl. Panther Man finished eating first and sat back. When the rest had finished, he cleared his throat and said, "There was some trouble at the Yellow Medicine Agency while we were gone."

White Fox looked at him questioningly. "What kind of trouble?"

"The agency has not paid out the annuities that were due two moons ago. The food from the government was in the warehouses, but the agent would not give it to the people until the gold payment arrived from Washington." Panther Man paused thoughtfully. "Many of our people think that with the white men fighting a war among themselves they will not send the gold at all.

"Some of our young men broke into the warehouses and took some of the flour," he continued. "The agent's men shot at them and called in the soldiers to help. The head soldier had one of the big guns pointed at our people, but he did somehow convince the agent to give the people some pork and flour. It seems the agent would rather have the meat spoil in the warehouses while our people starve a few feet away. I do not understand him."

"What is happening now at the agency?" White Fox asked.

"From what I understand, most of the people have moved back to their camps to wait. But some of the young men are getting tired of the way we are being paid for the land the white man took from us, and they are talking of making war." Panther Man slowly got to his feet. "I am going up to the Yellow Medicine Agency in the morning. You can come with me if you want to. Come, Sunflower, I have become very tired."

White Fox watched his uncle and aunt leave the lodge. Then he picked up Sparrow Hawk and squeezed him so tightly the little boy began to wiggle and whimper. The father gently sat his son down next to the toy he had been playing with and laid his hand lightly on the little boy's head. The boy looked up at his father with round, dark eyes. The two women watched. White Fox spoke to them softly. "You both must promise me that if anything happens to me you will take this boy out onto the prairie, then far to the north where the country is still wild. I will tell Panther Man of my wishes, but you must promise me."

"What are you talking about, my son? You will be here to make those decisions for us and to look out for your own son." Spotted Fawn stared at him, shocked at his words. White Fox did not answer her. She saw a look in his eyes that she did not recognize.

White Fox awoke to the patter of raindrops on the lodge's bark roof. He could tell it was morning even though almost no light filtered through the old blanket that covered the doorway. He knew that the rain would not stop Panther Man from traveling to the Yellow Medicine Agency, so he reached for his clothes.

Moving quietly so as not to wake the women, he reached up to remove his bow and quiver from the hook over his bed. He frowned, realizing that he was probably the only warrior in their whole village who still carried a bow instead of a rifle. He blamed his father's death on the long gun his father had carried on the buffalo hunt. He had seen his father practicing to reload the gun on his moving pony and was sure he had lost his hold and slipped to his death while trying to reload. The rifles for which the warriors now traded were shorter and reloaded with a lever. The powder was contained inside the bullet. These guns were much easier to use. Maybe the time was right for him to get one of these new guns.

White Fox heard his uncle's sharp cough outside the doorway. He slipped the bow and quiver over his shoulder and stepped through the opening into the rain. He fell into step beside his uncle as they skirted the lake and followed the path to the meadow where the ponies grazed. "The sky is clear in the west. We will not have to ride in the rain for long," Panther Man observed. "I am not sure the rain will help the corn. Think it is beyond help," he added.

White Fox grunted an affirmative response as they topped the rise and saw the pony herd below. One of the young men from the village was coming up the trail toward them. White Fox recognized him as Red Wing. "I am hurrying home to sleep," Red Wing volunteered. "It has been a long night to be awake." He put extra emphasis on the word *awake* and looked at White Fox. White Fox chuckled softly and gave him a gentle shove as he passed. Panther Man looked at his nephew, then turned to watch the young man walk away. White Fox continued on his way, and Panther Man shrugged and followed him.

The sun had moved to its highest point and started its downward swing when they saw the agency buildings ahead. As they drew nearer, they could see that there were many of their people still camped close to the agency buildings. Panther Man rode directly to the agent's headquarters. He turned to White Fox.

"Are you coming inside with me to hear what the agent has to say?"

"I will come with you. I have not met this man before."

As they entered the agency building, a man came from the back room. He smiled when he saw Panther Man. "Greetings, my friend," he said. "I have not seen you around here for a long time."

"I have been gone on a hunting trip onto the prairie to the west," Panther Man answered. "I have heard of the trouble you have had here."

The agent, Galbraith, got a strange look on his face. "What did you hear?"

"I heard that you would not give our people the supplies that are here in the warehouses and belong to them."

Galbraith shifted nervously from one foot to the other. "I would not give out the supplies because the gold has not arrived. It is too hard to keep the records straight unless we can give out both at the same time."

"Is it better to have the trouble and have the people go hungry than to figure out a way to keep the records?" Panther Man asked. "It is already two moons past the time they should have been handed out." His uncle stared hard at the agent, and White Fox could tell that the man felt uncomfortable by the way he tugged at the high collar of his shirt and the small beads of sweat that appeared on his forehead.

"We have given out some of the supplies, and I expect the gold to arrive any day," Galbraith defended himself.

Panther Man spoke softly, but his voice held anger. "I think you are making a mistake. The young men are getting agitated more every day, and soon the elders will not be able to hold them back from bigger trouble than you have ever seen here."

"I have to do my job the best way I know how. I have not been at it long, you know."

"I know," Panther Man said in a low voice. "Be careful, my friend, and pray to your God for wisdom in this situation."

As though noticing him for the first time, Galbraith asked, "Who is this young man?"

Panther Man turned to White Fox. "This is my nephew, White Fox, my sister's son. He is the same as my own son." White Fox felt honored by these words. Since his father's death, he often had depended upon his uncle for the advice of a father. White Fox's feelings had grown for his uncle, and now it pleased him to hear that his uncle's feelings mirrored his.

"I cannot persuade you to give out all of the supplies?" Panther Man persisted.

"Not at this time," the agent answered, "not until the gold comes in."

"Then we have nothing else to talk about here," Panther Man said, turning toward the door.

"Please, stay to eat a meal at my house," the agent blurted. "I will send someone to tell my wife we are coming."

"We must be on our way. We have been hunting for one moon and need to spend the time with our families."

Galbraith spoke again. "You know the white government does not approve of you going off the reservation to hunt. You should not do that."

"Would it be better to stay here and starve sitting next to your full warehouses?" Panther Man's voice rose.

The agent looked at the floor. He did not meet Panther Man's eyes. "I am only telling you what I must."

Panther Man turned to his nephew. "We are leaving now." The two men strode from the agency building and mounted their ponies. They had prodded the ponies into a trot when they heard a voice calling them. "Wait, wait, I want to talk to you." Panther Man and White Fox reined their ponies and turned toward the voice. A Black Robe was riding from the trail to the south.

"It looks like Soaring Eagle," Panther Man said. "Greetings, Soaring Eagle," he called out to the Black Robe.

"Greetings to you, Panther Man."

"You are coming from the south. Were you visiting the Redwood Agency?" Panther Man asked.

"Yes, I am just returning, and I already know your next question." Soaring Eagle laughed. "I did visit your daughter. She is well, and Little Wolf and his large family are all fine too. I think I met all of them this time."

White Fox chuckled at this and then asked, "Are they having any of the problems that we have experienced at this agency?"

"Yes," he replied. "The annuities are usually handed out even sooner down there than they are here. But the people there have received neither money nor supplies. Their warehouses are full, just as they are here." Soaring Eagle shook his head slowly. "It is even worse there because quite a few of the families have become farmers and have stopped hunting altogether. They have been in bad way since last fall, when the corn crops failed. A few days before I came to the agency, one of the traders had told some of the young men that if they were so hungry they should eat grass." Soaring Eagle looked at Panther Man. "You can imagine how the young men reacted to that statement. I am afraid that the Redwood Agency is a powder keg that is ready to go off at any time."

Soaring Eagle stopped, realizing that he was upsetting the two men. He knew there was nothing they could do to change what was taking place. Then he smiled, saying, "I am so glad I saw you. Chickadee made me promise to tell you that she is well and happy. Now I won't have to make a special trip to Standing Buffalo's village to do that."

"We are going back to our village now," Panther Man said. "It has been good to get some word of Chickadee. I will tell her mother that she is well."

"God be with your family. It was good to see you." Soaring Eagle held up his hand in farewell.

As they rode back to their village White Fox felt the old familiar ache that filled his chest every time that he thought of his friends. Little Wolf, Chickadee, and Grey Wing had come up river to visit the summer that Sparrow Hawk was born. Now two winter seasons had passed since that time, and he missed his friends.

CHAPTER TWO

White Fox sat under a tree watching Sparrow Hawk as the little boy tried to hold the small bow and arrow his father had made for him. White Fox took his son's hands and placed them in the right places; but the small fingers could not hold the arrow in place, and it dropped to the ground. "I see that the father is learning the art of patience this morning," said a voice from behind them.

White Fox laughed as he turned to face his uncle. "I think it would be better if the grandfather took over this job so the father could go off on a hunting trip."

Panther Man settled down next to White Fox, using the old cottonwood tree as a backrest. He picked up Sparrow Hawk and sat the little boy on his lap, cuddling him close. The little fellow did not protest and snuggled against his grandfather's chest. All three sat quietly enjoying the warmth of the late-summer sun. White Fox too leaned back against the tree and relaxed.

He had almost dozed off when he heard a commotion coming from the other end of the camp. He saw that Sparrow Hawk was sound asleep on his grandfather's lap, and Panther Man was blinking as though he too had been dozing. Across the camp, they could see a small group of men walking in their direction. "Let me take Sparrow Hawk. I will put him on his sleeping mat inside the lodge," White Fox said, lifting the small boy from Panther Man's arms. "Falling Star and my mother have gone to one of their gathering places."

When White Fox stepped from the lodge again, he saw that the men were gathered around the cottonwood tree and seemed to be waiting for him. They appeared agitated. Rainman, one of the elders spoke first. "We have some bad news. Standing Buffalo is not yet back from the hunt, and we have just gotten word that there is trouble down the river at the Redwood Agency. Some of the warriors there have attacked the agency and have killed the white traders." Rainman looked at White Fox. "They say that your uncle Little Crow is leading the war party."

"I do not believe that!" White Fox exclaimed. "My uncle has been living the way the white agent has encouraged, and I know that he has had a good relationship with this man."

"We are only telling you the news as we have heard it, White Fox," Rainman explained. "We do not know if it is true."

"I think this is just a rumor," said Man Who Laughs. "What do you think, Panther Man?"

Panther Man spoke slowly and thoughtfully. "I think we have seen this coming for a long time. I don't think this is a rumor."

Rainman looked to Panther Man for leadership. "What do you think we should do? Our chief is not here to lead us."

"Go back to your lodges," Panther Man suggested. "Each of us must decide what is right for our own families." The group dispersed.

White Fox began to pace under the cottonwood tree. Finally he said, "I am going to ride downriver and see what is going on. I am the young warrior of this family, and it is my responsibility to scout out this situation." Panther Man nodded his approval to this. "I ask you, Uncle, to take care of my family while I am gone."

"I will watch over them," Panther Man replied. "I think you will indeed find the trouble we have heard about," he added.

"I will not worry about my family here. I know you will take good care of them. But I have a fear, right here, for Little Wolf, Chickadee, Grey Wing, and all of Long Legs' family," White Fox said, laying his hand on his chest.

Panther Man grasped White Fox's shoulders and looked deeply into his nephew's eyes. "Make sure my daughter is safe."

White Fox entered his lodge and knelt next to the sleeping form of little Sparrow Hawk, now one winters old. The father gazed at the little face, so peaceful in sleep. "I am glad that you are little, my son, and do not know what is happening," he whispered. White Fox stepped toward the doorway then went back and lightly touched his sleeping son's hair. As he moved out the door, he saw his mother and Falling Star returning to their campsite.

Spotted Fawn did not wait for him to speak. "We have talked to Panther Man and already know what has happened," she said quickly. "I will pack you some food."

"I have already taken some of the pemmican," he answered.

"I will get you a bag full of tipsinna cakes," she said, disappearing into the lodge.

White Fox put his arm around his wife and gently led her under the cottonwood tree. "It looks like you had a good day of gathering," he said, softly.

"We found more than we could bring back. We will go back tomorrow," Falling Star replied, but he could see that the joy was gone from her eyes.

"Your father will stay here and look after all of you while I am gone. We must find out what is happening before we can decide what is best for us to do. I hope that I will not be away for long."

Falling Star nodded and pressed her face into his chest. He heard her mumble into his shirt, "I think we all knew this time would come." Then she pushed herself away from him. "Are you ready to go? Do you need for me to do anything for you? Where is Sparrow Hawk?" The questions came like the arrows from a warrior's bow.

"I am ready," White Fox answered. White Fox looked back at the village from the top of the rise. He wondered if he would ever again see it look as peaceful as it did at that moment. Then he turned Star and urged his pony into a trot down the trail to the south.

Time passed quickly on the trail, and soon the buildings of the Yellow Medicine Agency came into view. He recalled the meeting he and Panther Man had had with the agent only a short time ago and rode directly to the main building.

White fox slid from Star's back and opened the door into the brick building. He was surprised to see the building full of white people and mixed bloods.

He heard a voice say, "He is a friend," and scanned the faces until he saw one of Panther man's friends, John Otherday. Otherday was making his way through the people to get to White Fox.

"Is you uncle with you?" Otherday asked.

White Fox shook his head. "I am alone. Is the news we have heard true?"

"It depends on what you have heard," Otherday answered. "There is killing going on farther down the river. I think it will come this way, so I am going to take these people to the east to safety. What are you going to do?"

White Fox looked at the faces of the people gathered there and saw their fear. "I am riding down the river to Little Crow's village. Some of my family lives there."

Otherday looked at him, concern in his eyes. "I have heard that Little Crow is leading the warring people."

"I have heard that too. But he is my uncle. I must speak to him."

"Each of us must decide what is right for ourselves," Otherday replied. "May the spirits travel with you and keep you safe. Maybe you can convince your uncle that this is not the way to handle our problems."

White Fox studied Otherday's face. He knew this man had a white wife and mixed-blood children. Otherday had been living as a white farmer and had been very successful at it. White Fox nodded at his statement and bid him goodbye.

White Fox turned toward the meadow where the ponies grazed. When he reached the top of the rise, White Fox looked back at the village. He wondered if he would ever again see it look as peaceful as it did at this moment. Then he turned Star and urged his pony into a trot down the trail to the south.

White Fox rode south through the day and most of the night, determined to reach Little Crow as quickly as possible. He was engulfed in his worry and thoughts as Star plodded on and on and was startled when he felt Star stumble. He stopped his pony and realized that the animal was wet with sweat. He slid from Star's back and rubbed the animal's neck. "I have been so deep in my own thoughts that I have forgotten about you," he said. "We have stopped only a few times to rest and drink from the creek. We both need to rest."

White Fox grasped Star's halter and led the pony down the riverbank to drink. Then they walked down the moonlit trail until he found a path leading off into the woods. He followed the path and found that it led to a farmstead. White Fox cautiously led Star behind the barn and carefully peered through a window. There was complete darkness inside. He listened and, hearing no sounds, decided it was empty. He led Star quietly to the front, and they slipped inside.

White Fox stood still until his vision adjusted. In the bit of moonlight that filtered through the windows, he saw that they had found exactly what both needed. Loose hay was piled in the corner, and straw was spread out in another. Immediately, Star began nuzzling the meadow grass while White Fox took some of the pemmican and tipsinna cakes from his bag. He retreated to the straw in the corner and settled into it.

As White Fox chewed his food, he remembered another barn and another time when he and Little Wolf had let their curiosity get the best of them. The thought made him smile. He recalled the giant of a man who had chased them. It had been his first encounter with a white man. The smile faded from his face as he wished it had been his last.

White Fox awoke and, eyes still closed, reached out to touch his wife. He fingers touched only straw, and he opened his eyes, realizing where he was. Star whinnied softly, and White Fox propped himself up on his elbow to look around in the dim morning light. Star was standing near him, looking toward the barn door. White Fox followed the horse's gaze and saw the shape of a wolf in the doorway.

He froze, waiting to see what the animal would do. As his vision adjusted, however, he realized that it was not a wolf but a dog. The animal looked at him for a time, then let out a deep whimper and ran away. White Fox scrambled to his feet, not sure what to expect next. He moved to the door and carefully peered out into the yard. The dog was nowhere to be seen, and the area was unusually quiet. Even the morning birds were silent.

White Fox stepped back into the barn and gathered his things. Taking the pony's reins, he walked cautiously into the farmyard. In the early morning light, he could see that the door of the house stood open and a form lay on the porch. The sight puzzled him, for no one would let their door stand open at night, even in the hottest weather. Star snorted softly and nudged him in the back. White Fox stepped quietly toward the house, pulling his knife from its sheath.

As he drew closer, he could see that the form on the porch was that of a man. He climbed the two steps onto the porch, his knife ready. The body lay face down in a pool of blood and the man's scalp had been ripped from his head. White Fox crouched down beside the body and gently turned it over. He pulled back, clenching his teeth as he saw the man's face. The man's eyes were wide open, and fear was still etched in his features. White Fox turned the body face down again and stood up.

He turned toward the yard and listened. The woods around the farmyard were perfectly quiet. He turned guardedly back to the house and looked in through the open door. The house seemed deserted. He stepped in. The little one-room house had been torn apart.

Cooking utensils were scattered everywhere. A curtain, which had secluded the bed from the rest of the room, now lay on the floor. The lifeless body of a dark-haired woman lay on top of the curtain, killed where she had tried desperately to hide.

White Fox saw something glittering on the floor in the early light and bent down to pick up a picture. The glass was shattered as though it had been thrown across the room. He realized it was the photograph of a wedding featuring a young man with light-colored hair and a dark-haired young woman. He looked back to the bodies, suspecting that they were the people in the photograph.

The table was strewn with papers. White Fox stepped closer. On top lay what looked like a government paper with a gold stamp in the form of an eagle. White Fox had not tried to read the white man's written word for a long time, but as he looked at this paper, the words began to make sense. The names on the paper were James and Anna Muller. From the numbers and directions printed on the page, he suspected that the paper was a deed to the very land he was standing upon. For some reason, this angered him, and he dropped the paper back on the table. He would never understand how these papers could say that any person owned a piece of Mother Earth. It made no sense.

White Fox heard a sharp howl and glanced out the doorway. There, standing over the man's body, was the dog. He howled again, and the sound sent a chill through White Fox. He stepped into the doorway and locked eyes with the animal. The dog stood as though transfixed as White Fox walked to his side. The young warrior put the knife to the animal's throat and made the quick move. The dog made no sound and dropped onto his master's body.

"Go now," White Fox whispered. "Go to be with your master where you belong."

White Fox watched the animal's blood mingling with its master's. Then he turned and stepped back into the house. He had an odd feeling about this room and was not quite ready to leave it. His eyes traveled over the room until something high up on the fireplace caught his attention. It was a small bow, and above it were arranged two tiny arrows with the shafts crossed. White Fox moved the only unbroken chair to the fireplace and soon held the bow in his hands. He turned it slowly and gaped when he saw the fox design etched on the one end. On the opposite end was the serpent. Again he reached up, removing the two arrows. His knees felt weak. He had never expected to find this link to long ago.

Carefully climbing down, he turned to the table and picked up the picture one more time. He studied the face of the young man and then glanced again at the body lying on the porch. White Fox closed his eyes and let himself drift back in time. He could see the white farmer's children. He remembered the light-haired boy chasing his sister around a log house and stealing her doll away from her. He also vividly remembered dropping his special bow and arrows as the farmer chased him and Little Wolf.

White Fox opened his eyes. He laid the small bow and arrows on top of the papers and carefully wrapped them. Then he walked quickly from the building and found Star patiently waiting for him. He tucked the package into his rawhide bag, mounted his pony, and turned from the yard and back to the path that would lead back to the river trail.

The sun was midway to the highest point of the day when White Fox entered Little Crow's village. He urged Star to the place where Long Legs' family lodges stood. He wanted to talk to Little Wolf first. White Fox heard a yell and turned to see Chickadee coming from the river with a string of fish in her hand. "White Fox," she called joyfully, "I am so glad to see you."

White Fox slid from his pony's back and walked to meet her, smiling. "I am glad to see you too. Is Little Wolf in the camp?"

Just then Little Wolf emerged from one of the lodges and called out to his friend. "I am here. Come to my father's lodge. We need to talk to you."

Chickadee reached out and took the pony's reins from his hand. "I will take care of Star. Go and talk to the men."

White Fox followed Little Wolf into the bark summer lodge and was surprised to see that they had a small fire burning on such a warm day. The sweet aroma of sage hung in the air. Long

Legs looked up as the two young men entered. "We are glad you have come," he said. "Little Wolf and I were just about to smoke some of the good tobacco that Walking Woman raised this summer." Long Legs packed the fresh tobacco into the bowl and lit it. He took two long drags then handed the pipe to White Fox, who in turn puffed on the pipe and handed it to Little Wolf.

White Fox broke the silence. "Tell me, Father. What has happened here?"

Long Legs took a deep breath. "Two nights ago, long after I had gone to sleep, I was awakened by a young warrior and told to come to Little Crow's house. They were having an emergency council." Long Legs took another puff on the pipe. "It was a large council. Many chiefs from downriver were present. They had been talking before I arrived. Little Crow explained to those of us who came late that four young warriors from Red Middle Voice's village had gotten into trouble with the white men. They had been hunting in Suland and came home to admit to their chief that they had killed some people, including several white women." Long Legs looked at White Fox. "How much of this do you already know?" he asked.

White Fox shook his head. "I have heard only that there has been killing going on down here and that my uncle is leading the war parties. Is this true?"

Long Legs nodded. "It is true. I will tell you exactly what was said and how your uncle became involved in this.

"Everyone at the council that night knew the seriousness of the situation. These young men would be hunted down by the white soldiers and taken from their families. There was much arguing. Some of the chiefs thought the young warriors should be turned over to the soldiers. Many of the young warriors said this was the time to make war and take the land back from the whites. The soldier's lodge asked your uncle to lead them in this war," Long Legs continued, speaking of the group of Dakota who enforced discipline over the tribe. "That made Little Crow angry. He told them that they should be asking the person they had chosen to be their new spokesman, Traveling Hail. But now that there was serious trouble, they asked Little Crow to be their leader again."

Again Long Legs took a drag from the pipe, and the tobacco glowed brightly in the bowl. "I will tell you the exact words that your uncle spoke that night, and you know that I have a good memory." Long Legs sat up straight and stared into the fire. "'I am not a coward nor a fool, braves. You are like little children. You know not what you are doing. You are full of the white man's devil water, whiskey. You are like dogs in the hot moon when they run mad and snap at their own shadows. We are only little herds of buffalo left scattered. The great herds that once covered the prairies are no more. See! The white men are like locusts when they fly so thick that the whole sky is a snowstorm. You may kill one, two, ten, yes, as many as the leaves in the forest yonder, and their brothers will not miss them. Kill one, two, ten, and ten times ten will come to kill you. Count your fingers all day long, and white men with guns in their hands will come faster than you can count.'" As Long Legs finished speaking, his body drooped as though all his energy was spent.

White Fox spoke. "It sounds like my uncle refused to lead them."

"I am not finished, my son. At this time, many of the young men of the soldier's lodge started saying that Little Crow was a coward if he would not lead them. Your uncle stood up and said in a sad voice, 'You will die like the rabbits when the hungry wolves hunt them in the Hard Moon. Little Crow is not a coward. He will die with you.'"

White Fox studied Long Legs' face. "Do you know where my uncle is now?" he asked.

Little Wolf spoke up. "He rode out this morning with the soldier's lodge and most of the young warriors from the villages. Our friend Grey Wing rode out with them, as well as my brother Woodchuck and my sister's husband, Bald Eagle. I did not go because I do not know if it is the right thing to do."

"Do you know where they went?" White Fox asked.

"They were going to attack the soldier's fort, called Fort Ridgely," Little Wolf replied.

"I am going to the fort," White Fox said, getting to his feet. "I must see what is happening and talk to my uncle."

"I will go with you," Little Wolf said, glancing at his father.

White Fox grabbed his friend's arm. "I do not want to be the one to take you from your family. I can do this alone."

"I had made a decision even before you rode into the village. We must fight the white man now if we ever want our children to have a life like we once had. Everything that has happened this summer has proved to me that the white government will not honor the treaties. And even if it would, this is not the kind of life I want to live."

White Fox stared at his friend. He could see that Little Wolf truly believed the words he spoke. "This is what I have decided too, my brother," he said. "We will have to fight to regain the life we once lived."

"I will talk to Chickadee and be ready to ride shortly," Little Wolf said, and he left the lodge.

White Fox turned to Long Legs. "What do you think of our decision, my father?"

Long Legs looked piercingly at White Fox. "I know what your father would have done, but I think I will stay out of it for now. If your uncle is right, we do not have much chance of winning, and it will be a waste of lives. I wish he had not agreed to lead the young warriors. But I think that when the young hunters took the first lives, there was no changing what is to come."

A short time later, Long Legs watched the two young men ride from the village. White Fox and Little Wolf rode directly to the Redwood Agency. As they neared the agency, they saw the bodies. The wooden buildings were reduced to piles of smoldering ashes.

The young braves rode slowly through the grounds and looked at each of the bodies, searching for familiar faces. Along the edge of the grounds, they came to a body lying on its back. Little Wolf stopped. He motioned to White Fox to come over for a look. "Andrew Myrick," Little Wolf said. "He was the trader who told our people to eat grass if they were so hungry. I was here the day he said it." White Fox looked down at the corpse. The mouth had been stuffed with grass.

The young men rode quickly from the agency and prodded their ponies down the embankment to the ferry. White Fox was glad to see the ferry on their side of the river. The river was deep, and now they would be able to keep their feet dry in the crossing. As they pulled the ferry rope to cross the river, they noticed bodies scattered along the riverbank and into the brush on each side of the trail. "This is the battle that our warriors were celebrating last night. They said they had killed many soldiers," Little Wolf whispered. Neither spent any time looking at the bodies here and rode quickly from the ferry.

"I remember Crooked Arrow from the time we were boys. If he hasn't changed, he will enjoy the killing too much to spare anyone," White Fox replied.

The two young men urged their ponies into a trot, ignoring the bodies that lay along the trail. After a time, they came to a narrow place on the trail and found they were blocking the path of a lone warrior. "It is Owl Man," Little Wolf said, recognizing the warrior.

The warrior rode up to them and stopped his pony. "Where are you going?" Little Wolf asked him.

"I am on my way back to the village."

"Tell us what has happened at the fort."

"Nothing. Little Crow and the other chiefs wanted to attack the fort this morning, but the chiefs don't have enough control over the younger warriors. Most of the braves wanted to attack New Ulm instead, so that is where they went," Owl Man replied. "My woman was sick when I left, and we have a small baby. I did not want to go that far to make war."

White Fox and Little Wolf moved their ponies out of his way. "I hope your wife is well when you return," Little Wolf said as the other passed by. Owl Man nodded and continued down the trail. White Fox and Little Wolf did not discuss the news that Owl Man had given them but rode on.

White Fox took the lead as they rounded a bend. Suddenly the quiet was shattered by a gunshot. Before White Fox could react, a second shot was fired, and he saw a white man fall on the trail ahead of him.

Little Wolf rode past White Fox and slid from his pony to examine the fallen man. He looked at White Fox. "Are you all right?"

White Fox felt a sensation in his arm and pulled at his sleeve. There was a bullet hole through the doeskin. He pulled up the sleeve and saw a bloody crease below the elbow. His head whipped back up, and his large eyes met Little Wolf's. "I did not even see him. How did you shoot so fast?"

"As I came around the bend, I saw him standing almost in the bushes with his rifle aimed at you. I thought he had you. Good thing he was not such a good shot."

"You are good with that rifle, Little Wolf," White Fox said, studying the man on the ground.

Little Wolf pressed his lips firmly into a grimace. "Now I guess we, too, are in the war. I have killed one of the farmers."

"Let's go on to the fort. I want to see how many soldiers are there," White Fox said. "I will watch more carefully," he added.

White Fox rode on past the road that led to the fort. He reined Star to a stop at the bottom of a ravine. "We can hide the ponies here and follow the ravine almost up to the edge of the fort," he suggested, recalling the terrain from happier days hunting the area.

It did not take them long to move up the hill, through the heavy brush. Soon they lay on their stomachs watching the activities at the stockadeless fort.

Two men pushed one of the big guns from inside one of the buildings and turned the barrel in their direction. "My father once saw one of those guns fired at the fort at White Cliff," White Fox whispered. "He said it threw a big ball and made a loud noise." He cocked his head and turned his attention to Little Wolf. "I wonder why the warriors did not want to attack here this morning. It doesn't look like there are many soldiers here now."

Little Wolf shook his head slightly without answering.

"We had better move on," White Fox whispered. They moved quickly back down the ravine.

Little Wolf looked thoughtful. "Do you think it is true that the young warriors would not listen to their leaders?"

White Fox shrugged. "I have been thinking about what Owl Man said, too. The young warriors who are now of fighting age have been raised on the reservation. They do not know the old ways. Back at the Two Rivers village, even as children in our war games, we picked a war chief and followed him into battle. It was the way our fathers had taught us."

"Let's cross the river and follow the trail on the other side. I do not want to see any more of the farmer's bodies," suggested Little Wolf. "I think if we could drive the soldiers from the fort, the farmers would leave on their own."

"I think you are right," White Fox agreed.

They had been on the trail only a short time when they heard the shots from down the river valley. "They must have attacked the town of New Ulm," White Fox muttered. "I wonder if there were many people there."

"We will know soon." Little Wolf pointed. "See the smoke up ahead."

White Fox had seen the little town only once before. He remembered it being built on a long hillside above the river. The white people built their homes in straight lines, and it had looked like steps going down the hill.

As the two topped the hill, they saw a group of warriors just below them. One of the group called out to them, and Grey Wing rode toward them, waving his rifle in the air. "Hi ya, I am glad you are here," he called.

"What is happening?" White Fox asked.

"We have attacked the town. So far, the whites have fought back bravely," Grey Wing answered seriously. "We have set some of the buildings on fire, at least the ones we could get close to. I think we could have taken this town already, but our young warriors run off in all directions and don't listen to anyone but themselves."

"Where is my uncle? He is your war chief, isn't he?" White Fox asked.

"The chiefs grew angry and returned to their homes." Grey

Wing turned to Little Wolf. "Your brother Woodchuck and sister's husband, Bald Eagle, are here, and now White Fox, the nephew of our chosen war chief, has arrived. Maybe we can pull the warriors together and make a successful attack on the town." His excitement growing, Grey Wing did not wait for an answer. "I will send out runners to call all of our warriors together." Abruptly, he turned his pony and rode away.

White Fox and Little Wolf looked at each other. "Let's move down the hillside and see how many buildings are left and, if we can, see how many white people are gathered here," White Fox suggested.

The two located a point where they had a good overview of the town. All of the buildings on the upper level were either on fire or lay in ashes. They could see that the people had gathered together in the buildings at the bottom of the hill. "It looks like they have built barricades around the lower part of the town," Little Wolf said.

"The town is much bigger than I remembered it," White Fox commented.

"The area has filled with the farmers, and the town has grown just as quickly," Little Wolf replied.

"Look!" White Fox pointed to one end of the town. A small band of warriors pursued a wagon loaded with a white family. The men of the town quickly opened a place in the barricade and the wagon entered. Some shots rang from behind the barricade, and the warriors turned and rode away. White Fox and Little Wolf watched as the people below were helped from the wagon. The driver had been hurt and was laid on the ground.

The young men heard a call and turned to see Grey Wing waving to them to return to the top of the bluff. They arrived to find Woodchuck and Bald Eagle and many additional warriors gathered together. Grey Wing called out to the others, "Come close around. Someone is here who can lead us." White Fox did not like the sound of this and glanced at Little Wolf.

Woodchuck stepped close to White Fox and cuffed his arm. "We are glad to see you here, White Fox. Has your uncle sent you here to lead us in the fight?"

"I am not here to lead anyone in a fight. I'm not sure why I am here."

"It was time to hold council anyway and talk over our plans," Woodchuck responded. "It has not gone well today."

During this time, the sky had grown steadily darker with storm clouds. A sudden flash of lightning signaled the start of the storm. The sky opened, and the rain fell in sheets. The warriors scattered and ran for cover. Little Wolf spoke to his brother and brother-in-law over the roar of the rain. "White Fox only came here to talk to his uncle, and I came along to see what is happening. I think it is time to return to the village and talk to our war chief."

Even Grey Wing agreed. "The Thunder God is telling us the time for fighting is over. I am ready to return to the village."

Woodchuck shouted to the warriors gathered under the trees. "We are going back to the village. The fighting is done for this day." White Fox looked back as the five urged their ponies into a gallop. Many of the other warriors were catching their ponies and soon would follow.

Darkness came on quickly with the heavy rain. The trip home was a cold, wet one. As they entered the village, Little Wolf leaned close to White Fox. "Come to our lodge to dry your clothes before you go to your uncle's house." White Fox nodded and followed. Grey Wing joined them.

A short time later, Chickadee filled bowls of hot stew and placed them into the young braves' outstretched hands. They hid their nakedness under the blankets she had thrown over them. Their wet clothes dried by the fire. Grey Wing tasted the stew and uttered his approval, saying, "I am too often a guest at your fire."

Chickadee smiled. "You are always a welcome guest in our lodge." Grey Wing smiled at her. He knew he was welcome, for he and Chickadee got along very well. He often felt a tinge of jealousy toward his friend for winning her as his wife. Chickadee was a tall, handsome woman whose intelligent eyes told of many secrets she kept. Grey Wing admired her very much.

Little Wolf broke into his thoughts. "Tell us how the battle went today before we arrived."

Grey Wing sipped on his hot stew, then looked up at his friends. "Your uncle Little Crow had planned to attack the fort this morning. We could tell that there weren't many soldiers there. But the soldier's lodge and the younger warriors started arguing. Some wanted to go attack New Ulm instead. And some were being governed by something other than their intelligence. They thought there would be more young women to capture in New Ulm. In short," Grey Wing said dryly, "your uncle finally agreed, and we all moved on to New Ulm. But once we got there, he could not get the warriors to work together. Finally, he got angry and left us. You saw the rest: a few people were killed, some buildings burned. Maybe it will be enough to scare these people from our land," he concluded hopefully.

White Fox watched as Little Wolf donned some dry clothes. "I did not bring any extra clothes," he said, looking at Chickadee. "Do you think you could find me something to wear tonight while my clothes are drying? I would like to go to my uncle's lodge and see what he has to say about this war."

"I will find you something of Little Wolf's to wear," Chickadee answered, going to a far corner of the bark lodge. The next moment, she held up an outfit, laughing. "Do you remember this one, Little Wolf? You were wearing it when you fell from your pony last summer." She held up a pair of pants with holes torn in the knees and a shirt with most of the arm fringes ripped off.

Little Wolf chuckled. "If it weren't for those pants, my knees would have looked like that."

"I am afraid this is the only outfit I have for you, White Fox," Chickadee said apologetically. "I can quickly stitch the holes shut for you."

"They will cover me up. That is all I care about," he answered.

"I will put on my wet clothes for the run back to my lodge," Grey Wing Said. "I have dry clothes there."

"You will meet us at my uncle's lodge shortly?" White Fox asked. "I want you there."

"I will be there," Grey Wing mumbled through his wet shirt as he pulled it over his head.

Before long, White Fox stood in his repaired pants. He looked at his feet, grinning. "You are a tall man, Little Wolf. I have enough pants left over to sweep the ground as I walk."

"Here, let me cut them off for you," Little Wolf said, leaning over and swishing his knife close to White Fox's feet.

White Fox jumped out of his reach, growling, "I need shorter pants, not shorter legs."

Chickadee smiled at the two men. Then she changed the subject. "Your uncle lives in a frame house now, like the white men live in. I don't think you have seen it."

"He lived in a tepee the last time I visited him," White Fox concurred.

Little Wolf broke in. "Your uncle truly had decided to live the white man's way. He built himself the frame house and started to seriously raise corn and wheat. That is why it is hard to understand why he allowed himself to be talked into leading this war. I am not sure what he was thinking. The young men who first started the trouble were not even from our village."

White Fox took his knife and hacked off the bottoms of the pants. Then he stood up. "It is time to have him explain this to me himself."

As White Fox and Little Wolf walked toward Little Crow's house, Grey Wing came out of the darkness to join them. When the structure came into view, White Fox stopped short and stared at it. He could not imagine his uncle living in this building.

Many people were coming and going from the dwelling. Some of the young warriors they had seen at New Ulm were gathered around the doorway and around the fire that blazed outside. White Fox saw a young man he recognized from his youth. Crooked Arrow saw White Fox at the same time, and the two stared at each other. What White Fox remembered most about this man was how he had harassed him about his sky-colored eyes.

Another young warrior stepped forward and called White Fox's name. White Fox could not remember this man's name, but he looked familiar. "White Fox, you must talk to your uncle," the young man demanded. "He is protecting the cut-hairs in his lodge. Tell him to let us have these people so we can kill them. We cannot rid the country of the white man if these traitors are spared."

White Fox had heard this name "cut-hair" before and knew it was given to the people who had gone the white-man way by joining the churches, cutting their hair, and farming. Some of the people who had chosen the old ways considered these people traitors. "I have not had the chance to talk to my uncle yet. I am here to do that now," White Fox replied. "I will talk to you later and tell you what I think."

White Fox and his companions pushed through the doorway and into the house. Little Wolf shut the wooden door behind them as White Fox scanned the room for his uncle. Little Crow's son One Who Appeareth came from a back room and stopped abruptly when he saw White Fox. He quickly stepped back into the room behind him, and they heard him say, "Father, White Fox is here."

White Fox walked past his cousin, saying, "You have grown into a young warrior since I saw you last."

One Who Appeareth smiled. "Just in time to take part in a war."

There were a few chairs scattered around the room, but Little Crow had been sitting on the floor. He came toward White Fox with his arms outstretched. Little Crow was not usually such an affectionate man, but now he pulled his nephew close. "I am glad to see you, White Fox," he said softly. "I need someone from the outside to talk to." Then he pushed White Fox away and looked at him. "Where did you get these clothes?" he asked, looking amused.

"Mine are drying over Chickadee's fire," White Fox replied. "I was out in the rain at New Ulm late this day."

"You were at New Ulm?" Little Crow looked surprised. "Tell me how this came to be."

White Fox glanced at the fire blazing in the fireplace. "Let's move close to the fire. I am still chilled." Little Crow, White Fox, and Little Wolf moved to the fireplace and sat cross-legged near the fire. Grey Wing paced nervously, glancing out the windows to watch the crowd. White Fox recounted his day. "I came to the village this morning and found that you had left to go and attack the fort. Little Wolf and I rode out to the fort but found none of you there. We hid in a ravine and watched the fort for some time. We thought it would have been a good idea to attack it today, for there were not many soldiers there."

Little Crow grunted loudly and shook his head. White Fox continued. "We met a young warrior on his way back to the village. He told us the war party had gone to New Ulm instead."

"What did you see at New Ulm?" Little Crow asked.

"The warriors we talked to said that there were too many white men protecting the little town." White Fox turned to Grey Wing. "Grey Wing was there. Come and tell my uncle what you saw."

Grey Wing walked to the fire and settled himself beside the three men. He cleared his throat and looked uncomfortable. "The soldier's lodge could not seem to organize the young warriors from all the different villages. They ran in different directions and attacked in small groups here and there. Some of the buildings on the west end of the town were burned."

Little Crow sat silent and waited as though expecting to hear more. White Fox turned to his uncle. "There are warriors outside who say you are protecting the cut-hairs, that you are hiding them here in your house." He hesitated, then continued. "Tell me, Uncle, how did you get involved in this trouble?"

The fire crackled and filled the room with flickering glimmers of light. Little Crow kept his eyes on the fire as he spoke. "Do you remember when your small band of people came out of Suland and joined our village at Kaposia? Your father and I had many long talks about your life in the Big Woods. I had almost forgotten how good life could be in the wild, but those talks reminded me." Little Crow turned and looked into his nephew's eyes. "I saw the differences between you and the children who had been raised in the big villages. Your eyes held the pride of being a true Dakota."

Little Crow turned back to the fire. "Your father was very unhappy with the life we lived on the reservation. Because I was one of the chiefs who had signed the agreements and treaties, he blamed me. The longer we lived on the reservation and watched annuities disappear, the more of our land the white man took, and the more I knew in my heart that your father was right."

Wisps of smoke curled from the pipe, which lay beside the fire. White Fox picked it up and handed it to his uncle. Little Crow slowly inhaled the smoke and handed it back to his nephew. "You remember the buffalo hunt, but you do not remember it with as much pleasure as I do. It was one of the most enjoyable times of my life. To spend so much time on the prairie with your father hunting for the buffalo was like the old times. Then your father was killed. I was so sad to lose him and to see you and your mother suffer. But I also envied him. He died beneath the hooves of our sacred buffalo. He died with honor, as a Dakota warrior should." White Fox stared into his uncle's face, surprised to hear these words. He could feel the sadness emanate from Little Crow.

"Now I see the excitement of the young men. They have killed the farmers for many miles around. They think this is our chance to take back the land. They are probably right. We shouldn't let anyone live." Little Crow stood up. "Come upstairs. I think you will know someone up there."

White Fox followed his uncle up the steps to a second story. At the top was one big room, and it was filled with people. White Fox heard his name whispered by someone in a back corner. He strained his eyes in the dim candlelight. "It is I, Mrs. Brown." White Fox saw a woman struggle to her feet and come toward him. He recognized her as the wife of Joseph Brown. White Fox had met the lady at many of the upriver festivals. She was a relative of Sunflower's, and her husband was a white trader whom most of the people respected.

"It is good to see you, Mrs. Brown," White Fox said, feeling a bit odd about greeting her this way at such a time.

"Have you come to join in this war, White Fox?" she asked.

"I have come here to find out what has happened."

"Is your uncle Panther Man here?" He could hear the hope in her voice.

"No," he answered. "Little Crow also is my uncle. He is my father's brother."

"I did not know that," she replied. "If you go back upriver, will you tell my relatives that I am here?"

"I will tell them," he answered.

"Do you know if Standing Buffalo or any of the other chiefs from the Upper Agency are joining in the war?"

"Standing Buffalo was away on a buffalo hunt when we heard the news. I don't know what the other chiefs will do." White Fox paused, then asked, "How did you end up here?"

"My husband was away on a hunting trip when we received the news, so I took my children and tried to get to the fort. We met many people on the trail and ended up in a group. Then we were all captured and brought here."

One of the men spoke up. "If it weren't for Mrs. Brown, I think they would have killed all of us." White Fox saw many heads nodding in agreement.

White Fox turned to find that his uncle had gone. He descended the steps and found Little Crow standing by one of the windows. He turned as White Fox reached the bottom of the stairs and walked back to stand in front of the fireplace. White Fox stood beside his uncle, studying his face. Little Crow looked weary, and the age lines on his face had grown deep. "Uncle, you look tired. I think it is time for you to sleep and rest your mind a bit."

"While you were upstairs some of the warriors for the soldier's lodge came to speak to me," Little Crow responded. "They want me to lead them in an attack on the fort in the morning. This time they have promised to listen to my plans and to follow them. But now I am concerned that the white soldiers may have received reinforcements since this morning." Little Crow touched White Fox's arm. "Will you stay here tonight?" he asked.

"My clothes are drying at Little Wolf's lodge. I will spend the night there."

"I would like to have you at my side tomorrow."

"I have much to think about tonight and much to discuss with my friends," White Fox answered. "Whatever I decide, I will talk to you in the morning."

White Fox lay in the bed Chickadee had made for him. He could tell by the others' breathing that no one in the lodge was sleeping peacefully. He, Little Wolf, and Grey Wing had talked late into the night and finally had decided that since the war was a reality, they had better join in if they ever wanted to live the life they had once enjoyed.

He had watched Chickadee's face for disapproval during their long conversation, but he had not seen any. Finally, driven by his curiosity, he had asked for her opinion. She had spoken bluntly about how she had tried to help some of the families who had run out of food the previous winter. Even Little Wolf looked surprised when she described holding an infant while it died from lack of nourishment. She admitted that she did not know if a war was the answer to their problems but said she had no other answers.

Troubling thoughts filling his mind, White Fox drifted into fitful sleep. Early the next morning, he slipped from the lodge and walked upstream. He faced the east with the river at his feet and raised his hands to the sky. "Great Mystery, hear my prayers this day. We are your people, and you have taught us how to live on Mother Earth. You have taken care of us and given us the spirit helpers to be near us at all times. Look down on me this day and show me how to fight the battles that are sure to come. Help us to win back our old life."

He dropped his arms, and his head fell to his chest. He stood silent, and all the land around him grew silent. His eyes were closed, and his body completely relaxed when his senses told him there was another presence nearby. Slowly he opened his eyes and turned his head to the left. There, a short distance from him, was a white fox. The intense blue of its eyes reached out to his own. He stood perfectly still and felt a calmness settle over his heart. Then the fox vanished.

White Fox returned to the lodge just as Little Wolf emerged. Little Wolf carried a war shield and his new lever-action rifle. He propped them against the outside of the lodge and went back inside. White Fox waited outside. He did not want to interrupt any good-byes between Chickadee and Little Wolf.

As he waited, he sat down beneath an oak tree and closed his eyes. He visualized Falling Star and little Sparrow Hawk. Falling Star would have no idea that her husband was going into war this day, and he was glad for that. "I am doing this for you, my little son," he whispered into the wind. "I promise that I will earn for you the right to live free of the white man. I will give you and your mother the chance to live as our people have always lived."

"There you are, White Fox. Are you ready to go?" Grey Wing came from behind, startling him.

"I am ready. But I think we should paint our faces for battle, and I have not brought any paints. I did not intend to go into battle. I did not even bring my war shield. But I have my medicines," he said, touching the medicine bag that hung against his chest. "I have all the protection I need right here."

"My father is making medicine for our safe return," Grey Wing replied. "I think he would like to paint our faces for war. I will get Little Wolf."

A short time later, Grey Wing and Little Wolf, faces vividly painted, sat watching as the shaman smeared paints on White Fox's face. The shaman sang his songs as he worked. The lodge was filled with the sweet smell of the sage that had been sprinkled into the fire. Other herbs simmered in a small pot of water over the fire. Finally the religious man finished with the painting and served each of the young warriors a cup of the herbal tea.

White Fox could only imagine how he looked. He knew the shaman had shadowed white around his eyes with shafts of yellow streaking away like rays. The shaman had made slashes of black across his cheeks and had painted two blue stripes across his fore head. White Fox smiled as he looked at his friends in their war paint. He remembered the paint jobs they had done on each other as boys when they played at war. Now they would experience it in its chilling reality.

The three young warriors walked through the camp, noting the excitement as they went. The village had grown considerably overnight. White Fox saw new scalps hanging from the poles nearest the lodge doorways, and many more captives were huddled in small groups. The captives were being watched by the women of the camp and sometimes even by the children.

As Little Crow's house came into view, they saw that a cluster of tepees had been set up almost on the chief's doorstep. Little Crow emerged from the house and came directly to White Fox. "I am glad to see you are still here today," he said, sounding relieved. "One Who Appeareth has gone to get my pony; then I will be ready to ride. I think we will be able to make it to the fort almost before the sun rises on this new day."

Little Crow looked carefully around the camp then turned back to his nephew. "I am not happy about all the captives. They will be a nuisance if we should have to move the village." Then he flashed a smile at White Fox. "I am glad to see that you painted yourselves. It will make me feel like I am leading a real war party."

"We noticed that very few of the warriors have decorated themselves for battle," White Fox commented. "Apparently this is another tradition that they have lost on the reservation."

The three young friends left the camp ahead of the main war party. They rode to the Redwood Agency and quickly continued through it. The bodies still lay as they had seen them the day before, and the stench was worse. The ferry stood in the middle of the river, and the young men did not waste the time to pull it in. Their ponies plunged into the water and swam the deepest part.

The blue-uniformed soldiers lay along the riverbank and seemed to have grown larger in death. White Fox remembered, as a boy, watching the body of a weasel deteriorate. First it had grown large with air, and then it had shrunk small until most of it sank into the ground, leaving only the fur behind. His father had explained that all living things return to the land to make it rich to support more life.

They rode on, silent and serious. When they came to the division of the trails to the fort, they bypassed the one that led up the bluff to the fort and continued down to the ravine. White Fox turned to Little Wolf and Grey Wing. "We can hide our ponies here. I would like to go to the top of the ravine, as we did yesterday, and observe the fort."

The others agreed. They tethered their ponies and started up the ravine, White Fox leading the way. The rain of the previous night made the ground muddy and slippery, and the ravine was much more difficult to climb than it had been the day before. It took some time to reach the top, but finally White Fox peered over the edge of the ravine and looked toward the fort. Little Wolf and Grey Wing heard his gasp.

White Fox ducked down and motioned for them to look. Little Wolf moved up beside White Fox to see. "They must have gotten reinforcements since yesterday," he said.

Grey Wing joined them. "Did you see the big guns they have pointed out over the prairie to the north?" he asked. "It will be much harder to capture the fort today than it would have been yesterday."

Little Wolf answered determinedly. "There are more soldiers here today, but since there is no enclosure around the fort, we will be able to shoot into their midst. We can still win a battle here. We are Dakota warriors. We can fight a battle to the finish, just as our fathers did in the past."

White Fox grunted his approval. "Let's go back down to the river bottom and follow the other ravine that leads to the northeast side of the fort," he suggested. "I think we will be able to see more from over there."

The three started back down the gully, sliding their way down. They followed the river farther downstream and found the ravine they were looking for. Then they began working their way back up the bluff.

White Fox stopped abruptly. He turned his head slightly and

cupped his hand behind his ear. The three stood motionless, listening. Faint voices came from the ravine ahead.

White Fox moved ahead slowly and stealthily, stopping at intervals to listen. Little Wolf and Grey Wing followed closely. Finally White Fox stopped and peered through the underbrush. Then he stepped aside so the other two could see.

Two soldiers were standing in the ravine, filling buckets from a spring. A short distance up the ravine, another man holding a rifle stood by a mule that had barrels strapped on either side of it. The men took their filled buckets and emptied them into the barrels. They were laughing and talking, unaware of any danger.

White Fox quickly stepped back down the ravine and waved his friends to follow. "We have the chance to stop them from getting their water supply for this day," he whispered. "See the ridge of brush along the edge of the ravine?" He pointed. "We can use it for cover to position ourselves above them."

Little Wolf pulled the war club from his belt. "We cannot use our rifles or the soldiers at the fort will hear the shots. We can hide them here."

White Fox watched his two friends hide their rifles in the brush. Then the trio quietly climbed the side of the ravine and crept along on their bellies until they were above the white soldiers. They heard the men talking the whole time.

"How should we take the three soldiers? What do you think, Little Wolf?" White Fox studied his friend's face. Even as children, his blood brother had always had a plan, and it usually worked.

Little Wolf motioned toward White Fox. "You, White Fox, are the smallest and the lightest on your feet. You lead out and use your knife to take out the guard. Grey Wing and I will get the other two before they can reach their weapons."

White Fox nodded his understanding and extended his hand to his friends. Each laid his hand on top, forming the alliance. Then White Fox moved down the slope. He pulled his knife from its sheath and held it in his right hand. He moved quietly. White Fox remembered his father's words as he walked. *My son, even the mountain cat could not teach you anything about moving silently through the forest. You are the best.*

The soldier and the mule stood ahead of him. They were looking down the ravine, watching the other soldiers. White Fox did not breathe as he traversed the last distance to within reach of the soldier. Suddenly, the man started to turn and White Fox made the lunge. He brought his left arm tightly around the soldier's shoulders and brought his knife up to the man's throat. A quick move finished the job and he saw the blood spurt. Just as the men down the ravine turned and looked up at him, two bodies shot past him, one on either side. They closed the distance in an instant.

Little Wolf's war club hit the soldier's head. White Fox heard the bone shatter under its weight. Grey Wing grabbed the other man as he reached for his rifle. Grey Wing's knife flashed as the two rolled together down the incline and out of White Fox's sight.

White Fox suddenly realized that the mule was braying loudly. He grabbed the animal's nose in both his hands and held its mouth shut. He laid his face against the mule's and whispered, "Stop, stop, or I will have to slit your throat." The animal snorted and quieted down. Slowly White Fox released his hold and rubbed the mule's neck.

He was relieved to see Grey Wing climb back up the incline, a scalp in his hand. Grey Wing waved it at his friends.

The three young warriors drank deeply from the fresh spring water. Then they looked over the dead bodies. White Fox stepped beside the man he had killed and cut the scalp from his head. He rubbed it on a small tree to remove the blood and attached it to his belt. He had braided his first scalp into Star's mane earlier that morning; already he had another to add to his honors.

The mule stood quietly as the three soldiers were laid over its back between the barrels. The warriors planned to move the bodies farther down the ravine and hide them in the thick brush.

Little Wolf took one of the soldiers' rifles and handed it to White Fox. "This is the same lever-action gun as mine. Now you have a gun of your own, and you know I have plenty of ammunition to fit it. There is a leather case of shells lying over there, too."

White Fox took the gun from his friend and looked at it, his brow furrowed. He was not sure he wanted a weapon unfamiliar to him at such a time.

Little Wolf read White Fox's thoughts. "You will do well with the gun. We will get to practice as soon as the others get here, when we attack the fort."

The three friends buried the soldiers under the heavy brush in a gully off the main ravine. They tethered the mule there. Then they continued to the river bottom and got their ponies just in time to be joined by the rest of the war party.

Little Crow guided his pony to White Fox's side and slid to the ground with ease for a man of his age. He did not waste time on greetings. "What have you seen up at the fort?" he asked his nephew.

"We saw many more soldiers today than we saw yesterday," White Fox told him. "I believe more soldiers must have arrived since that time. It would have been wise for the young warriors to have followed you into battle here yesterday."

Little Crow nodded grimly. "This means that the word has been spread to the other white settlements. We no longer have our advantage of surprise."

"We have been through both of the ravines and have discovered a spring in this one. They have been supplying water to the fort from it. We have killed three soldiers and have a mule and two barrels they were using to move the water."

Little Crow shot his nephew a look of surprise. "I am glad you came ahead, Nephew. I can see that you and your two friends will be wise ones to have at my side. No matter what happens here today, I will see this war through to the end," he vowed.

Little Crow's attention was caught by the scalp swinging from White Fox's belt. "I see you have already claimed your first scalp in this fight."

"I have committed myself to the fight for our land," White Fox answered. "But you must understand that I cannot take part in killing the farmers or their families."

"I do not want this either, White Fox. Some of our young warriors have gotten carried away with their newfound strength. But you must remember that some of these men have watched their own little ones suffer and even die because the white men have forced us onto the reservation and then have not honored the agreements. Now their bitterness has turned to revenge."

Little Wolf and Grey Wing approached, interrupting the conversation. "Do you have a plan for us to follow?" Little Wolf asked the war chief.

"You three have seen the situation at the fort. What do you think would be the best way to start this battle?" Little Crow returned the question.

White Fox turned to his blood brother. "My friend Little Wolf probably already has a plan worked out in his head. Tell my uncle what it is."

Little Wolf looked down at his feet in embarrassment. But after a moment of thought, he squared his shoulders and raised his eyes to his chief's. "I do have a plan. I suggest that you, our war chief, take half of our warriors up the west ravine and make a big show of attacking from the northwest side of the fort. We could take the rest of our warriors up the east ravine and do a sneak attack from that end. There are buildings near the ravine. We can probably get to them and use them for protection."

"I like the sound of your plan. I will split the warriors and make certain that the ones who go with you know that you three are in charge." Little Crow stepped close to White Fox and touched his arm in affection. "May the spirit of war be with you today," he said softly.

"And with you, Uncle," White Fox answered. "May we all enjoy a victory."

Little Crow turned and walked into the large body of men waiting to hear his words. Slowly, warriors began to drift over to the three waiting at the edge of the ravine. Woodchuck and Bald Eagle were the first. Woodchuck grabbed White Fox and Little Wolf, one in each arm. "It is good that we will fight with our brothers at our side," he said, grinning broadly.

The warriors turned as Little Crow shouted a war cry and

waved his gun in the air. The war chief turned his pony and led his group of warriors upriver. Woodchuck stepped up beside White Fox. "We have left our ponies upstream. Some of the women will be here soon to set up cooking at the river bottom. Little Crow did not think the battle would be a quick one."

White Fox glanced at the warriors surrounding them and realized that they were waiting for him to make a move. Little Wolf saw the look on his friend's face. "You are Little Crow's nephew. They are looking to you to be our leader."

"The plan is yours, Little Wolf. It is up to you to lead us."

"I will be at your side. But they are looking to you, not to me."

White Fox stood, unsure for a moment. Then he raised his new rifle over his head and let out a loud war cry. He heard their answering cries. White Fox moved into the brush that filled the ravine and started the climb to the top. He knew there was no hurry, for it would take Little Crow some time to travel upriver and then up the west ravine.

The warriors slowly climbed the incline until the spring came into view. White Fox turned to Little Wolf. "This is good. It looks like no one has been here looking for the water detail. Our attack should come as a complete surprise."

At the top of the ravine, the land leveled into prairie, and White Fox soon looked out over the flat land to the fort. He turned to the men below him and motioned to them to lie low and wait. They did not have to wait long.

From the distance, they heard shooting and the yells of an attack. White Fox saw several soldiers dash from the nearby buildings and run across the field to the inner part of the fort. White Fox whispered to the men close enough to hear, "Now is the time. We will use the three closest buildings for protection." He quickly climbed out of the ravine and dashed to the nearest building. Little Wolf followed close behind.

White Fox stopped at the first building and glanced back to make sure the rest of the warriors were following. Then he darted to the second and on to the third. This building had a doorway on the side, and he slid through it to the inside. He let out a sigh of relief when he saw three windows facing the fort.

Little Wolf and Grey Wing came through the doorway. White Fox moved to a window and used his rifle to break out a pane of glass. He poked his rifle carefully through the opening. He glanced back to see each of his friends choosing a place from which to shoot. White Fox knew that the rest of the warriors were waiting for him to take the first shot.

When he thought that most of them were positioned to shoot, he brought the new rifle to his shoulder. He looked down the sights as Little Wolf had shown him and trained the gun on a soldier who was crouched down on one knee and appeared to be shooting at Little Crow's warriors. White Fox lifted his rifle slightly to allow for distance and carefully pulled the trigger. The man jerked but did not fall. The soldier turned to look toward White Fox just in time for a volley of shots. Someone else had a better aim, and the soldier fell to the ground.

White Fox took aim again and shot one shot after another as chaos broke out in the fort. He saw one soldier make a break for a building doorway, took aim, and pulled the trigger. This time his aim was true. The man spun to one side and fell. A woman came from the doorway and dragged the soldier inside.

White Fox heard Little Wolf's voice close by him. "Look! They have more of the big guns." While others fired protective shots, two soldiers rolled out another cannon and turned it toward the warriors. The shooting slowly dwindled as though the warriors were pausing to watch the soldiers load the big gun. White Fox needed to initiate an attack before any more of the big guns were brought from the buildings. With a loud cry, he broke from the protection of the building and ran toward the inner fort.

Everything seemed to happen in slow motion. He heard the other warriors' screams and knew they were following him. He saw a soldier step back from the cannon and lift a fire stick to light it. White Fox brought his rifle up to his shoulder and fired as he ran. The soldier spun away from the big gun but not soon enough. The gun jumped backwards as the cannonball burst from the barrel.

The ball was coming at White Fox, but he could see that it was dropping. It hit the ground in front of him and broke apart like a rotten apple, flying into many pieces. White Fox was not aware of falling but found himself sitting on the ground. He looked down to his legs. He felt no pain, but saw a fountain of blood gushing from his right leg. His life was flowing from the wound, but he had no strength to reach down and try to stop it.

"I am here," he heard Little Wolf's voice and felt his hands. A fog came across his vision, and then everything went black. White Fox felt his body moving upward. Gradually his vision cleared. He could see the fort buildings and realized he was looking at the battlefield from above. He saw the rest of the warriors retreating back to the ravine and saw Little Wolf hurriedly carrying a body. Grey Wing was protecting him, shooting his rifle at the soldiers who were reloading the big gun.

White Fox floated above the warriors as they moved back down the ravine to the spring. He watched Little Wolf lay the body near the flowing water and bend over it. White Fox moved close and looked into the face of the wounded one. He was only mildly surprised to see his own face, the eyes closed.

He watched as Little Wolf cut the pant legs from the body. He saw that the one leg was gashed almost from top to bottom. White bone showed on the lower part of the leg, but the deep wound at the top must have been the one that had sent him on to the Spirit World. Little Wolf had tied his rawhide belt around the wound. He didn't seem to realize that his brother's spirit already had left its body.

White Fox came close to his blood brother and said gently, "Do not worry about this body, Little Wolf. I am sitting right here next to you, and I am feeling no pain." Little Wolf did not turn to look at him but continued to work quickly, fitting the torn meat and skin back over the exposed bone. Grey Wing came to his friend's side with a handful of rawhide strips, and they bound the wound shut.

"White Fox, come over here," a voice came from the bushes.

"White Fox, I am over here." White Fox did not feel he should leave the body or the brothers who were still working on it, but he allowed himself to move toward the bushes. Behind one thick bush, he saw a misty image. The image gradually cleared until before him stood the most handsome warrior he had ever seen. The warrior was dressed in white doeskin pants with a loincloth over the top. His upper body was bare and was decorated with paints. He wore a single eagle feather in his thick, black hair. As White Fox looked at the image, he began to recognize the man.

"Father. Is that you?"

"It is I, my son," came the reply. White Fox did not see the other's lips move, yet he heard the words clearly.

"Father, you look different."

The young warrior smiled. "You look different, too," he replied.

"Father, I don't know what I am supposed to do."

"For the second time in your life, you have come to the edge of the Spirit World," his father answered, "but you cannot enter yet."

"Father, please let me come now," White Fox begged.

"It is not up to me, my son. Do you remember your first walk to the edge of the Spirit World? Do you remember what the white fox told you? Not many of our people will survive the wars with the white man. You have more to do on Mother Earth. You will return to your body. You must go back to your family and take them away to the Canada Country." The warrior looked intensely at his son. "I watch my grandson Sparrow Hawk every day. Someday he will be a great leader of our people, but you must make sure he survives at this time. Go back, White Fox. Go back now."

White Fox was still, watching as the image of the warrior slowly dissolved into the background. Then he heard the voice again, only this time it sounded far away. "I am with you every day, my son. You have done well."

White Fox moved back to the body and saw that Little Wolf was cleansing it with the cool spring water. Unexpectedly he felt himself slipping back into the body, and a deep moan rose from his lips. "White Fox, talk to me," he heard his brother say. Slowly he opened his eyes and saw Little Wolf bending over him. Grey Wing stood behind him.

Little Wolf spoke gently. "I am glad you woke up. We weren't sure that you still lived."

White Fox forced a slight smile to his lips. "I am still here, my brothers."

"We will carry you the rest of the way down the ravine," Little Wolf offered. "The medicine man Willow Man is at the river bottom. He will have to sew you up with horse hair. You have lost much blood, but we have the bleeding stopped with matted leaves. We cannot find any bones broken."

White Fox felt an overpowering weakness overtaking him. The blackness began to cover his eyes again, but this time he would rest and not fight it.

White Fox awoke with a start. He felt a sharp pain in his leg, and a moan escaped from his lips. He opened his eyes and looked up into the eyes of his uncle Little Crow. "I must hear about the battle," White Fox whispered with effort.

"I will tell you later," Little Crow replied. He tucked the robe up around the young warrior's chin and watched as he dozed off again.

White Fox awoke some time later. He slowly opened his eyes to see a woman looking back at him. He blinked and recognized the familiar, mischievous smile. Chickadee bent near him and whispered, "Cousin, you sure do get yourself into a lot of trouble."

White Fox answered, "Cousin, do you realize that even though you are a grown woman you still have your little-girl smile?"

She laid her face upon his chest. "I am so glad you are alive. I cannot imagine life without you in it." White Fox lifted his arm and hugged her weakly. She sat up and took his hand, gently pressing it onto her stomach. "Inside of me, there is a little one growing. I want him—or her," she added with a chuckle, "to call you Uncle."

"I am happy for you and Little Wolf," White Fox said feebly.

"Do not tell anyone. Little Wolf thinks we are going to keep the good news to ourselves for a while," she said, smiling at him.

Just then, the flap was pulled aside, and Little Wolf and Grey Wing entered. They saw that White Fox was awake and stepped to his side. Little Wolf spoke first. "You are looking better. Is the pain lessening some?"

"I am better," White Fox answered. "I remember Willow Man helping me to drink the willow tea many times, even when I was too sleepy to be of much help to him. I think the women have been feeding me broth too. My memory is kind of hazy." He studied his two brothers' faces, then asked, "Was anyone else hurt or killed in the fighting?"

Little Wolf looked at him with sadness in his eyes. "No one you knew very well. We thought for a while that we had lost *you*."

"I did walk to the edge of the Spirit World again, Little Wolf."

"I know. This time it was I who saw the white fox. He was in the brush at the edge of the ravine while I attended you."

White Fox lay quietly for a time. Then he said softly, "I talked to my father. I saw him, and I talked to him."

"You look very tired, White Fox. Sleep some more, and we will come back to see you later," Little Wolf said, standing up.

Finally after many days he awoke, feeling that strength was returning to him. He slowly pulled himself up to rest on his elbows. At that moment, Robin's Nest peered through the doorway, a little one strapped to her back. "I am so glad to see you awake," she said in surprise, entering the tepee. "You look much better."

"How long have I been sleeping?"

"Many days," she replied.

Just then Little Wolf entered the lodge. "You are looking awake and alert," he said looking as surprised as his sister had.

"I finally feel like I can stay awake," answered White Fox. "Is my leg in good enough shape to stand on?"

"I will go and get Willow Man," Little Wolf replied. "He will tell you what you can do." He headed out the doorway only to come right back in, followed by the medicine man. "I did not have to go far," he chuckled.

Willow Man squatted down beside White Fox and looked at him closely. "Your eyes are clear, and your skin has regained its color," he observed. "Your leg is not broken, and I removed all the metal pieces I could find. The quicker you get back on your feet and move about, the better to regain your strength."

"I am grateful for your help and will repay you with skins and supplies," White Fox answered.

Willow Man shook his head. "I will not need any payment for the healings that have taken place here. We are not sure where we will be when this is over." The medicine man stood up and moved toward the door. Looking back, he said, "I am glad that you have survived. I don't think you will have any long-lasting effects from the wound."

As the medicine man departed, White Fox turned to his friend. "Tell me what has happened while I have been sleeping."

Little Wolf lowered himself beside White Fox and looked to the ground, gathering his thoughts. "I don't know where to start, let me think...The day after you were wounded, we attacked the fort again. We did well at first, but by then they had enough men to hold us off while the others loaded the big guns. The balls they shoot from these guns fall apart when they hit the ground, throwing metal pieces everywhere, like the one that hit you. Many of our men were injured. Even your uncle was injured slightly."

Little Wolf paused, recalling the chain of events. "Our warriors grew too frightened of the big guns, so the attack was called off again. We attacked New Ulm again the day after that. The people there fought back with spirit, and we could tell they had received some reinforcements too. We couldn't take the town that day either."

Again Little Wolf hesitated. "White Fox, I have seen things that don't make any sense. Some of our war parties go off in one direction and kill the farmers, men, women, and children. Then others go off and warn certain white people they consider to be their friends and tell them to flee to safety. Even our friend Grey

Wing went across the river to warn a family that he has been friendly with for a long time. He found them at their church and warned all the people there to flee. But they must not have thought it to be very urgent. Later we heard that Crooked Arrow and his friends caught most of the people as they walked home from the church and killed them all."

"Where is our brother Grey Wing now?"

"I am not sure. He was with me at the Birch Coulee battle." White Fox looked at Little Wolf with questions in his eyes. "We found a group of soldiers with wagons camped at the coulee," Little Wolf explained. "They were not very smart and had camped where we could sneak up the coulee to attack them. We would have wiped out all of them except that a large group of soldiers from the fort must have heard the shooting and came to help them. General Sibley led the soldiers. Some of our people recognized him."

White Fox interrupted. "I remember my uncle Little Crow talking about a General Sibley a long time ago. They had been friends at one time. They had even hunted together."

"He is the one who has led a great many soldiers here from the White Cliff fort," Little Wolf continued. "Even your uncle now knows that we will have to retreat up the river toward the Yellow Medicine Agency. We cannot fight such a great number of soldiers, especially with the big guns they pull behind their ponies."

Both young men grew silent, each thinking their own thoughts. Little Wolf asked, "Do you remember the village on Lake Shetek? The place we visited on our journey to the Sacred Quarry? The chief's name was Pawn."

White Fox nodded. "Chief Pawn has killed all the white farmers who had moved in around the lake. The war has spread far."

"What time of day is it?" White Fox asked, looking toward the doorway.

"It is dark," Little Wolf answered. "We will be moving in the morning," he added.

"I must try my legs," White Fox said, struggling to his feet slowly and with great effort. Little Wolf reached out to steady him as he weaved from side to side. "Go out and find a sturdy branch with a crotch for me to lean on," White Fox requested. "I must get my legs to work if I am to move on with you tomorrow."

Little Wolf laughed. "You have already moved with us twice on a travois. Star is getting used to being a pull pony."

White Fox looked at his brother in surprise. "Go find me a stick. I will ride on Star's back in the morning."

Early the next morning, White Fox moved clumsily through the tepee doorway and leaned heavily on the crutch, watching the people prepare for the move. He looked around, noting their surroundings and determining just where their camp had been located. He noticed the many captives now in the camp, and an ache swelled in his chest. Babies were crying and little children were clinging to their mother's skirts. He was glad none of the frightened faces looked familiar. A voice from behind him startled him. "Can you tell me where Chief Little Crow is? I need to talk to your chief."

Using his crutch, White Fox turned awkwardly and looked into a familiar face. He could not remember the man's name, but he saw recognition flash across the other's face as well. "You are Panther Man's nephew. I do not remember your name."

"White Fox."

"My name is Nazamani. I would like to talk to the chief about the release of these captives. Do you know where Little Crow is?"

"I have just come from my lodge, and I do not know where he was camped," White Fox replied.

Nazamani nodded and looked intently at White Fox. "I wish you quick healing of your wounds. May we meet again in better times." The warrior strode away, disappearing into the crowd of people.

A short time later, the procession began. White Fox rode astride Star. The pony seemed happy to have his master riding on his back and at intervals turned his head back toward his rider, snorting gently. "You did not like being a pull pony?" White Fox asked him with a chuckle. Star seemed to understand and snorted loudly.

As the day wore on, a gradually intensifying ache settled into White Fox's leg. As the pain grew worse and he became increasingly weary, he began to wonder if he could stay with the group. A rider came up beside him, and he heard the medicine man's voice. "I have brought you some willow tea." He handed the young man a small drinking pouch. "Sip on this as you ride. But be careful. The wounds you have are deep, and you would not want them to open up again."

White Fox took the small pouch and gave Willow Man a look of gratitude. However, the medicine man had already turned his pony and moved on, probably to deliver the pain-relieving willow tea to someone else.

The procession moved slowly until finally it reached the Yellow Medicine River. The river was not high this time of year, and those on foot waded across. Star put his head into the water and drank deeply before crossing. Soon after crossing the river, White Fox saw the agency buildings, or what was left of them. Most were lying in burnt ruins with curls of smoke still rising from the ashes. It was hard to believe that he had stopped here to ask about the war such a short time ago.

As they passed by the ruin, White Fox saw his uncle riding toward him alongside the long line of people. When Little Crow reached his nephew, he swung his pony around to ride beside him. "How is the traveling going for you?" he asked.

"Chickadee is keeping a protective eye on me. I think she would like it better if I were riding on a travois. But Willow Man brought me some of his special tea, and it helps the pain," White Fox answered.

"We will travel as far as the place where the Chippewa River enters the Minnesota. That is where we will set up camp and make another stand for the land," Little Crow informed him.

"I will not be fighting anymore, Uncle. Not only because of my wounds but when I was near death, I had a visit from my father. His message to me will not surprise you," White Fox said. "He said that we cannot win this war and I should take my family and escape to the north. I am going to follow that advice. I may never see you again."

Little Crow was silent for a time. Finally he looked intently at his nephew. "You are sure it was your father you spoke to?"

"I am sure."

"Then you must listen to him and save your family. You understand why I cannot go with you?" White Fox nodded as his uncle reached out and touched his arm. "This is our farewell then. May the Great Spirit always shower his wisdom on you and your son. May you live long lives on Mother Earth." These words said, Little Crow kicked his pony in the ribs, and White Fox watched as he rode up the long line of people and out of sight. White Fox felt a new sadness spread through him as he realized that another part of life had just ended. He had become close to this uncle, and he would miss him greatly.

The sun was dipping low in the sky when the Chippewa River came into view. White Fox could see that the people ahead were stopping and knew his uncle had chosen the place where they would set up camp. He was more than a little relieved and dismounted carefully. Leaning on his crutch, he hobbled to a tree and slid to the ground. Star followed him and moved a short distance away to nibble on the tall, dry grass. Chickadee came to her cousin with concern in her eyes. "Are you feeling all right?" she asked.

"Go and choose your campsite, Cousin. I am going to sit here with my eyes closed and rest. You can come for me later," White Fox answered.

When White Fox opened his eyes again, he was surprised by the darkness. He still sat in the same place but found he was covered by a wool blanket. He struggled to his feet and, crutch under one arm and blanket swinging from his shoulders, started toward the soft light to find his adopted family. He found the big family nearby, sitting around a large campfire.

"We are glad you have finally decided to join us," Long Legs called out as White Fox hobbled into the light of the fire.

"I am glad to get here too," White Fox answered. His eyes traveled around the campfire and spotted Little Wolf and Grey Wing, who were already making room for him. He could smell turnips baking at the edge of the coals and saw a pot over the edge of the fire that would surely have something good cooking in it. His stomach growled for the first time since he had been wounded.

There wasn't much conversation around the fire. The men seemed to be patiently waiting for the food to be done. Walking Woman came from the newly erected tepee with a basket of cornbread. The women started to serve from the pot near the fire and dig the turnips from the coals. While he waited to be served, White Fox turned his head away from the fire to look to the other camps. There was not much activity around the other camps, he noted. Maybe some of the other families were short of supplies to make a meal, he thought, and the realization sobered him.

When the eating was done, White Fox leaned close to Little Wolf and whispered, "I am going to talk to your father." Little Wolf watched his blood brother struggled to his feet and limp to the other side of the fire. He already knew what White Fox was going to discuss.

Long Legs saw White Fox coming toward him and moved to make room for him to sit. "I must talk to you," White Fox began, lowering himself carefully. He spoke to his adopted father in low tones. "Little Wolf has probably already told you that I had a vision of my father. Take all of your family and come with us to the north. I believe it is the only way for some of us to survive this war."

Long Legs looked into White Fox's eyes. "You are young, and much of your father lives on in you. He always thought that it was best to move out of the reach of the white man. But I believe the white man will always follow and take the land. I think we must make our stand at this place. We cannot go with you, White Fox."

Long Legs became quiet, and his eyes traveled around the fire. Then he turned back to his adopted son. "You may ask each of the warriors at this camp to go with you. They are all old enough to make their own choices. I will not condemn their decisions, whatever they might be." Then he reached out and grasped White Fox's arm tightly. "I will ask the spirits to protect you and your family, and I will never forget the good times your father and I shared, raising our families together back at the Two Rivers village."

White Fox saw the glitter of a tear traveling down the older man's cheek. He squeezed Long Legs's arm in return and then used his crutch to get to his feet. White Fox watched as the family started to leave the fire, going to their own lodges. He knew in his heart that he would not be able to convince any of this big family to go with him, except maybe Little Wolf and Chickadee. Chickadee was part of his own family, and she might want to be with her mother.

White Fox followed Little Wolf back to his tepee. Chickadee had stayed behind to clean the bowls and the big cooking pot. They entered the lodge, and Little Wolf turned to White Fox. "I already know what my father's answer was. The men of the family had already discussed their plans before you joined us at the fire. Woodchuck, Bald Eagle, and Burnt by Fire all feel that we must stay here and fight." He saw the look on White Fox's face and continued. "I must stay here and take part in this with my family. But there is something I want to ask of you. Will you take Chickadee when you leave? She should be with her mother at this time."

White Fox answered in a soft voice. "I will take her with me, but how will you find us later?"

"I will find you," Little Wolf answered with certainty.

"I will be leaving in the morning, but now I must find Willow Man," White Fox said. "I will need some of his special tea to make the rest of my ride tomorrow." Little Wolf nodded and watched his brother limp away.

White Fox hobbled down to the river and washed himself in the cool water. He could tell that the summer's heat was spent and the cool nights would soon come. A sudden thought entered his mind. He wondered how cold the nights would get in the north country.

White Fox's head jerked up from the water as he heard pounding hoofs entering the far end of the camp. He flicked the water from his face and used his crutch to get to his feet. He could hear excited voices and started his slow walk back to Little Wolf's lodge. As the tepee came into view, he saw Little Wolf and his brothers talking to a group of warriors still on their ponies. White Fox heard Grey Wing's voice call out to him, "I am glad to see you on your feet again." The young warrior slid from his pony's back and stood waiting for White Fox.

The two friends studied each other briefly until White Fox laughed. "It looks like you haven't been on your feet all the time either."

Grey Wing looked down at his doeskin pants and brushed off the dust and briers that had gathered on them. He grinned at White Fox but then turned serious. "We have found a group of soldiers camped by Wood Lake. Some of our warriors are lying in the weeds waiting for the sun to come up. I have come to camp to get more warriors to join us."

Little Wolf turned to White Fox. "I am going with Grey Wing to this fight. I am afraid that you will have to go without Chickadee. She will not leave me."

"Chickadee is a good wife to you. Maybe it is right that she stay here by your side," White Fox answered.

"I am going to catch my pony. I will be back," Little Wolf called as he followed his brothers toward the meadow.

Grey Wing studied White Fox's face. "Will you be here when we come back?"

"No. I am going back to the Big Stone village and am taking my family to the north, as my father told me to do," White Fox answered.

Grey Wing turned from his friend and leaped to his pony's back. He turned the pony to face White Fox. "I will miss you, but I will not say good-bye to you." Then the young warrior rode to the edge of the camp to wait for the rest.

White Fox looked toward the meadow and saw Long Legs racing his pony back toward the village, followed closely by his sons. As they approached him, they slowed their ponies to a walk, and each reached down to clasp the hand that White Fox extended up to them. His mind raced as he looked into each face.

He would miss them. He wanted desperately to go with them. Would he see any of them again?

Little Wolf came last. He leaned down and put his arms around White Fox. "You will be with me every day in my thoughts. I have no doubt that we will be together again someday."

White Fox's heart ached as he rode along the Lac Qui Parle lake. He had never before ridden away from his adopted family wondering if he would ever see them again. This was the hardest thing he had ever done. As the sun rose high in the sky, he turned his thoughts to reuniting with Falling Star, Sparrow Hawk, his mother and uncle. He was glad that he had passed beyond the constant reminders of war. He began to hear the birds singing and saw some wildlife scurry across the trail. These things lifted his spirits out of the blackness of the early morning, and the day began to seem normal.

Finally he reached the Big Stone Lake. His heart swelled as he saw the haze in the distance from the campfires of Standing Buffalo's village. He prodded Star into a canter to cover the ground a little faster. As the village came into view, White Fox realized that he felt as though he had been gone for a very long time. He pulled Star to a halt and looked over the quiet scene before him. He was not anxious to move his family to the unknown. Sobering thoughts mixed with the joyful ones. He nudged Star into a walk and entered the village.

He rode directly to his own lodge. Falling Star was on her knees working a large buffalo skin. She looked up as he approached and then jumped from her place and ran to meet him. As she drew nearer, she slowed to a walk, and he saw her eyes move to his torn pants leg. He saw the concern fill her face and all of a sudden he realized how beautiful she was. Her gentleness showed in her soft face and large, dark eyes. She put out her arms to him, and he gently slid to the ground and into them.

"I am glad you are home," she whispered in her ear.

"I am glad to be here," he answered her.

Spotted Fawn came from the tepee, a little, short-legged boy toddling close behind her. Sparrow Hawk dodged behind his grandmother's skirt and peeked out at his father with large, dark eyes. "You haven't forgotten me that quickly have you?" White Fox laughed at the little boy.

Sparrow Hawk squealed at the sound of his father's voice and tottered over to White Fox, his hands held out to him. White Fox was balancing on one foot, and, as the little boy ran into him, they both rolled onto the ground. White Fox hugged the little one tightly, enjoying the feel of the warm, cuddly little body.

Panther Man and Sunflower heard the voices and emerged from their lodge, hurrying to greet White Fox. "We are glad you are back," Panther Man called out, then hesitated as he noticed the bandaged leg. "You must have much to tell us," he added quietly.

White Fox had pushed himself back onto his feet and reached for the crutch that his mother had retrieved for him. Quickly he realized how weary and hungry he was. "We will have a family meeting as soon as my mother can make me a good bowl of soup. My stomach has been empty all day, and I am feeling weak. Then I will share my story with you all," he finished in a weak voice. With this, he turned to his lodge. He had been thinking of his own sleeping mat and now wasted no time getting to it.

Panther Man looked at his sister. "Call us when he is rested and the soup is ready."

White Fox slept into the darkness. When he finally stirred in his robes, the tepee was filled with the delicious aroma of the soup. He opened his eyes to look directly into the eyes of his little son, who was lying close beside him. The young warrior smiled and reached out to pull one of the little ears. A deep cough came from outside their doorway, and White Fox sat up. "Come in, Uncle," he called out.

The flap was pulled aside, and Panther Man and Sunflower stepped in. Sunflower carried cornbread in her hands. White Fox felt happy as he watched his family gathering around the fire. Spotted Fawn announced, "The soup is ready," and she started to fill the bowls. She handed White Fox the first bowl and her brother the second. The little boy got the next helping in his small bowl.

White Fox smiled, noticing that already the grandmother was

grooming the little one to be the next warrior of their lodge. Falling Star noticed his grin and smiled too. She felt no jealousy toward her mother-in-law and the closeness the grandmother and grandson shared.

When the meal was finished, Panther Man brought out his pipe and tobacco. He touched a small stick to the coals for a light. White Fox waited for his mother to finish cleaning the bowls and join them at the fire. As soon as she was seated, he cleared his throat and began. "First, I must tell Sunflower that Chickadee and Little Wolf are in good health. All was well with them when I left their camp this morning." He would not mention that Little Wolf had ridden off to battle just before he left the camp. "They are not so far away anymore. They are camped at the junction of the Chippewa River and the Minnesota." Sunflower gave White Fox a relieved smile.

White Fox continued. "I have participated in some of the fighting, as you might have guessed," he said, patting his leg. "I lost enough blood at my first battle that I slept through all of the others." He paused to take a small puff on the pipe his uncle handed him. Sparrow Hawk mimicked his father, "smoking" a little stick that he imagined to be a pipe.

"The battles have not gone well," White Fox continued. "Our young warriors have been raised on the reservation and do not know the old ways. In the beginning, they were hard to organize. By the time the chiefs gained control of the warriors, the advantage of surprise had been lost and reinforcements were arriving from other settlements. The white man has too many soldiers, and they have many of the big guns that shoot the rotten balls. The flying metal from one of those balls is what hit my leg."

Panther Man interrupted. "Standing Buffalo has returned to the village. He has already told us how the war got started and how your uncle got talked into leading the warriors into battle. He does not approve of the fighting and had tried to convince Little Crow to release the captives."

White Fox nodded in agreement. "I also talked to my uncle about the captives. He felt they might need the captives for bargaining purposes later. I could not argue with that. They cannot win the battles against the army unless more of our villages join in the fighting, and I don't think that is going to happen."

He looked into each of the faces around the campfire until his eyes settled on his mother. Looking at her, he said slowly, "I got my wounds when we attacked the soldier's fort. I lost so much of my blood that I traveled to the edge of the Spirit World, just as I did as a young boy. You remember that, Mother." Spotted Fawn nodded to this comment, her eyes gentle and full of emotion.

He did not take his eyes off her face as he continued. "I saw Father. He was a young warrior. But I knew him. He told me what I must do, and now I must follow his instructions. He told me to come back here and to take all of you to the north, all the way to the Canada Country. He said that not many of our people will survive the wars with the white man."

White Fox grew pale as he relayed the message from his father, and Falling Star moved close to him so he could lean against her. Everyone sat silent, digesting what they had just heard. Then White Fox sat upright again. "This is the second time I have been given this message. When I was a boy and walked to the edge of the Spirit World, I received the same message from the white fox. I did not tell the shaman Wise Owl or Father at the time because I was not certain of what it meant. I think the old shaman knew I was not telling him everything, but he did not ask me to tell him any more."

White Fox turned to Panther Man. "I know you once told me that you would never go back to the Canada Country because of the bad memories you have. But now I am asking you to lead all of us there so my son can have a childhood like the one I had in Suland. I need your help, Uncle."

All eyes rested on Panther Man. They could tell by the look on his face that this would not be an easy decision for him. Finally he said, "I will think about what you have said and smoke on it. I will give you an answer by the next sunrise."

"I have more to tell you, Uncle. The war has spread to the place you called Lake Shetek. Your friend Pawn is said to have massacred many of the whites in that area. I saw your friend

Mazamani too. He is against the war and has been trying to get Little Crow to release the captives."

Panther Man listened to White Fox without comment. Abruptly, he got to his feet, saying quietly, "If you have told us everything you know, I will return to my lodge to smoke and think." Panther Man and Sunflower exited, and the lodge grew quiet.

All of a sudden they heard the wind rise and begin to whistle around the lodge. A cloud of smoke was forced back down the smoke hole, and it filled the tepee, making the air blue and stinging their eyes and lungs. Falling Star scrambled to her feet to go out to change the smoke flap, but just as suddenly, the wind changed direction again and pulled the smoke back out, leaving the air clear. Falling Star looked at White Fox in alarm. "I have never seen the smoke act like that before."

"Perhaps we have just received a message from the Great Spirit," Spotted Fawn suggested. "He is telling us that our lives will be cloudy for a while but later things will change for the better again."

"I think you are right, Mother. The spirits are speaking to us this night," White Fox replied. Then he started to remove his clothes. Both the women could see the lines of fatigue etched into his face. "I must get my strength back for the long journey. Whether Panther Man is willing to lead us or not, I have decided that we will go the north for the sake of our little one." With this comment, White Fox burrowed into his sleeping robes until only the top of his head showed.

The sun was well up when White Fox finally came out of his deep sleep. He shifted up onto his elbow and was surprised to see that the women were still laying on their mats. The blanket on the other side of Falling Star started to wiggle, and he saw a small face peek over her. The little boy's face lit up with a smile, and he wriggled out of the robes that covered him.

White Fox lifted his blankets and crooked his finger at him, inviting the little boy to join him under his covers. Sparrow Hawk quickly crawled over to his father's sleeping mat and snuggled inside. The boy felt warm and soft against White Fox's skin as they quietly lay together. A moment later, White Fox heard his uncle cough loudly outside the lodge and knew he was asking to come in.

White Fox stretched his leg and felt only a slight stiffness. He pulled on his tattered pants, thinking that Falling Star could find him a better pair later. Slowly he lifted himself from the sleeping mat, reached for his crutch, and moved to the doorway. He pulled the flap aside and stepped out into the morning sunshine. "Good morning, Uncle," he said in greeting to Panther Man, whom he found pacing outside.

Panther Man did not take time for a greeting but immediately began. "A runner arrived this morning to bring us more bad news. There has been a battle at Wood Lake."

White Fox's attention instantly was riveted. His uncle was speaking about the battle Little Wolf and his father and brothers had left to fight just as White Fox departed from their camp. "What has happened, Uncle?" White Fox urged.

"The battle went poorly for our warriors. Some of the soldiers were sneaking away from their camp and discovered our warriors hidden in the grass. The battle started before all of our people were ready. Again the soldiers used the big guns. They must drag these guns along everywhere they go," Panther Man said in exasperation.

"Chief Mankato had too much pride to step aside when he saw a ball coming at him. He was killed. My friend Mazamani had come to find Chief Little Crow to try once more to convince him to release the captives and had his leg shot off by a big gun. He died up on Chokecherry Bluff, and his family buried him there overlooking the river valley." White Fox watched his uncle's face and could see the sadness and pain he felt. "The runner said he thinks even Little Crow now knows that this war is over for us. Little Crow talked about taking his family and fleeing out onto the prairie."

Panther Man studied his nephew's face thoughtfully. "You are right about our future here," he said. "Many of the people here think that because they weren't involved in this war, the white man will do them no harm. I do not believe that is true. I am ready to move to the north. I will lead the way for our family. I have already told Sunflower of my decision. She is very sad to leave not knowing where Chickadee is."

"I will explain to her," White Fox replied. "Little Wolf wanted Chickadee to return with me, but she chose to stay with him. She is part of a big family now, and they will take care of each other. If they know the war is over, they may be moving to the north as we speak."

Panther Man looked relieved to hear White Fox's words. "It is time to pack our belongings," he said soberly. "The runner also said that the soldiers are moving up the river valley now."

White Fox stepped inside the tepee and saw Falling Star pulling a shirt over Sparrow Hawk's head. Spotted Fawn was searching through some rawhide cases and pulled out White Fox's wedding outfit. She turned to him with a slight smile. "I don't think you will be wearing this clothing to any feasts soon, so you might as well use it now to replace what you have on."

White Fox took the garments from her and started to change. He looked at Falling Star and his mother and felt pride in them. They were busy packing for the move, not once questioning his judgment.

They spent many days on the trail to the north. At last, in the distance, they could see a dark outline of hills. While they traveled, Panther Man had described the country of the Turtle Mountains in Canada. Here they would find trees, rivers, and good hunting. Yet they would be close to the prairie to hunt the buffalo that still remained if they were willing to travel some distance to the west. White Fox's spirits lifted with the sight of the trees and waters of the new land. He would have to forget the Two Rivers country that the white man now had claimed.

CHAPTER THREE

DECEMBER 1862

It was a cold, clear day in early winter. White Fox and Panther Man had traveled some distance from their own camp to hunt. Now they lay on their bellies studying a village below them. "See the designs on the lodge in the center of the circle? They are a Dakota people," Panther Man whispered to his nephew.

"Then we have nothing to be afraid of. We will ride into the camp," White Fox whispered back.

The two men rode slowly into the camp to let the people see the designs and decorations on their own clothing. The little children of the village followed the two men, whooping and making noises to let the adults know visitors had arrived. From the center lodge emerged a tall man with a full eagle-feather bonnet. White Fox looked at his uncle to see if he recognized the man, who appeared to be the chief of the village. They turned their ponies in his direction and dismounted. Panther Man put up his right hand in a greeting to the chief.

The chief spoke in a clear Sisseton dialect, "Greetings, brothers. Where have you come from?" he asked, looking at Panther Man.

"We have come from our camp up the Pembina River," Panther Man answered. "Before that, we came from the south, where the war was taking place." White Fox saw a cloud pass over the chief's face at the mention of the war.

"Come into my lodge, to the fire," the chief said. "The wind is blowing cold this day." As they entered the lodge, the chief gave the children inside a stern nod, and immediately they scrambled out through the door flap. The chief then looked at the two men with keen eyes. "Did you take part in this war to the south?" he asked.

Panther Man looked at White Fox and replied, "My nephew took part in one battle. He was wounded by one of the big guns. We decided nothing could be gained and came to live here."

"My name is Red Feather," the chief said. "We have heard much about this war. There are soldiers all over the plains to the south. They hunt down our Dakota people and kill whole villages. None of our people is safe from them. We have staying here with us two warriors who had taken part in the war."

White Fox leaned forward, the curiosity showing on his face. "Who are these men?" he asked.

The chief looked at him suspiciously. "I have been told that sometimes the soldiers use some of our own warriors to scout out our villages."

"I am a nephew of Little Crow," White Fox offered, watching for the chief's reaction.

The chief studied White Fox's face, then slowly got to his feet. "I will bring the two men here. If you are who you say you are, they should recognize you. Wait here, and my woman will give you a bowl of stew from the pot on the fire."

The chief left the lodge, and a woman stepped forward and filled two bowls for them. White Fox's stomach had acknowledged the good smells, and his mouth started to water. They devoured the stew and were starting their second bowlful when the flap was pulled aside and the chief entered, followed closely by two men. The three men joined the two already at the fire and each stared into the other's faces.

White Fox spoke slowly. "Medicine Bottle? You were the chief of the village across the Redwood River from my uncle's village." Then he looked to the other. "Shakopee. I remember you well."

"This is White Fox, the nephew of Little Crow," Medicine Bottle confirmed.

White Fox grew excited and began to fire questions at the two men. "How is my uncle and his family? Where are they?"

"Your uncle Little Crow and his family are camped not far from the James River. They were all safe the last time we saw them," Medicine Bottle replied.

"Do you know Long Legs or any of his family? Did they flee to the prairie too?"

"I do remember this family. Long Legs has many sons, and they chose to stay and face the white man. It did not turn out well for them. I have heard that the sons of Long Legs were put on trial for what the white man calls 'war crimes.' One of the sons is in a prison in Mankato and has been sentenced to death. The white soldiers are going to hang thirty-eight of our warriors on the last day of this moon according to the white man's calendar."

White Fox's face turned white, and he clutched his chest, drawing in his breath in a long, ragged gasp. Then he jumped to his feet. "We must leave! Now!" he cried.

Medicine Bottle stood up too. "I do not like to be the giver of bad news. Do not go to the south to try to help your friend, or you may join him on the gallows. From what we have heard, the trials are not fair. The white man does what he wants."

Panther Man could see by the look on his nephew's face that he was not hearing what the older man was trying to tell him. White Fox burst from the lodge, leaving Panther Man to show their gratitude for the food and information. By the time the uncle emerged from the tepee, White Fox was mounted, and Star was prancing in confusion, feeling his master's urgency to be on his way. Panther Man mounted his pony, and the two men left the village in great haste. As soon as they were out of the village, White Fox prodded his pony into a full gallop in the direction of their campsite. Panther Man followed; but the snow was deep in places, and he soon slowed his pony to a walk, letting White Fox disappear in the distance.

Some time later, Panther Man found his nephew waiting for him on the trail ahead. As he approached, White Fox said soberly, "I must not kill Star because of the fear that is eating at my insides." Panther Man nodded his understanding and rode past White Fox. His nephew fell in behind and followed for the remaining distance back to their camp.

As the two men came over the rise and angled their ponies down through the trees to the riverside camp, White Fox thought again what a beautiful place they had found for their new home. The women were outside the lodge gathering wood, and Sparrow Hawk was playing in the snow with the toboggan that White Fox had made for him out of buffalo ribs. White Fox slid from his pony's back and watched his son at play. His heart swelled with emotion.

White Fox pushed Star hard as they traveled across the prairie to the south. The snow cover became less and less as they got farther south, making it easier to travel quickly. Twice they had detoured to avoid the white soldiers. Both times he had seen the soldiers before they saw him, and he felt grateful to his spirit protectors.

As the miles passed under Star's hoofs, White Fox stayed deep in his own thoughts. He kept seeing the faces of his family as they had looked at the time of his departure. Realizing that the blanket under him was damp with sweat, White Fox reined Star to a slow walk. The sun was low on the horizon, and he saw a ravine ahead with brush he could use for cover while he caught a little sleep. Star needed to rest and graze, and he needed some time to quiet his thoughts.

They did not rest long and continued to travel, entering the Minnesota River Valley under the cover of dusk. White Fox found himself turning his pony toward the place where Standing Buffalo's village had stood. He would have hardly recognized the place, for all the lodges were gone and it looked as though the whole band had left in a hurry. Pony and rider quickly moved on downriver toward Joseph Brown's house. He was sure the Browns could tell White Fox what he needed to know.

White Fox crossed the river as it narrowed. He wanted to avoid the Upper Agency and stayed inside the tree line as he passed the agency on the other side of the river. He knew he must be nearing the Brown house, and indeed soon the dwelling came into view in the soft moonlight of the early evening. He pulled Star to a stop and looked. The large stone house had been partially burned. Only the stone walls remained. A fabric tepee stood next to it.

He nudged Star back into the tree line, wanting to stay concealed until he was ready to be seen. He rode close to the damaged house then slid from the pony's back. He crouched down and watched as Mrs. Brown moved in and out of the tent. When he determined she was alone, White Fox secured Star to a small tree and stepped into the opening in front of the tepee. He waited for Mrs. Brown to emerge.

He did not have to wait long. When he saw her coming out, he called, "Mrs. Brown! Do not be afraid of me. Susan Brown! It is I, White Fox." He saw surprise and then fear flash across the woman's face at the sight of a man standing in front of her. Then her features relaxed in recognition.

"What are you doing here?"

White Fox answered quickly, still fearful that she might panic and run from him. "I have come to find out what has happened to my adopted family. My uncle Panther Man said I should come to you and ask for your help in his name."

She looked at him carefully. "I last saw you when I was a captive of your other uncle Little Crow."

White Fox nodded, answering, "I was there."

"Your uncle did us no harm. We were finally released near Red Iron's village. I am not angry at any of your people for what has happened," she added, sighing deeply. "From what I have been told by my husband," Susan Brown continued, "many of the warriors who actually took part in the uprising have escaped onto the prairie. The people who stayed behind have been moved to the White Cliff fort, called Fort Snelling, as prisoners. Eventually they will be moved out of the state of Minnesota." White Fox stood transfixed, listening to her words.

Susan Brown looked hard at him. "I do not want any more of our people to suffer, for I too am a Sisseton. I am married to a white man, but that does not make me white. My children have the blood of our people running in their veins. But my husband and sons have gone out onto the prairie with General Sibley, chasing our people who have escaped."

Quickly she grabbed White Fox's arm and pulled him inside the tent. "It is foolish to stand outside. Someone could ride up and see you." she said urgently. "You are in great danger coming here to look for your friends. You could be captured or murdered by the white soldiers."

"I cannot go back until I find my brother Little Wolf and his family. I have gotten word that one of his family is to be hanged within a few days at the town of Mankato."

Susan looked at White Fox, saying nothing. Then she turned and walked to the far corner of the tent, picking up a piece of paper. She handed it to him. "Can you read the white man's word?" she asked.

White Fox looked at the paper. "I can read it, but it is not easy for me. It has been a long time since those school days at the Kaposia village."

"I will read it to you. The white soldiers' court was held at the camp where I was released. They later finished the trials at the Lower Agency. My husband said that in the last days of the trials they tried as many as forty warriors a day. Some of the trials lasted only ten minutes. Three hundred and seven were sentenced to death. We can thank our Great White Chief Lincoln for not approving of all the sentences. Because of his decisions, only thirty-eight will be hanged. They say the evidence shows that these men killed civilians, which means the farmers."

Susan held up the paper. "This is a list of their names. I will read it to you." As she began to read the names, White Fox's breathing slowed until he seemed almost to be holding his breath. Some of the names were familiar to him, and some were not. "Baptiste Campbell, Makatanajin, White Dog, Red Leaf, Little Wolf." She stopped as she heard a moan escape from her listener's mouth. Susan knew she had found the name he had hoped he would not hear.

White Fox stood silent for some time. Finally he said softly, "I already knew his name would be there." He touched his fist to his chest. "I knew it in my heart." He looked at her. "How can I save him?"

"You cannot save him, White Fox," Susan Brown said softly.

"I must talk to him."

Susan studied the young man's face thoughtfully. "You have a lighter colored skin than most of our people, and you have the blue eyes. With the right clothes, you could pass for a farmer."

White Fox stared at her, shocked. Susan walked to the corner again and picked up a mirror. She handed it to him to look into, then gently took his hair into her hands and pulled it to the back of his head. White Fox studied his reflection and said slowly, "All my life, I have hated my blue eyes, even though I thought they were a gift from my spirit helper, the white fox. Now maybe I understand the gift."

"There are some clothes of my husband's in the shed," she said. "With a needle and thread, I can make them fit you."

As she hurried to the shed, White Fox stepped outside to check on his pony. His eyes settled on the rawhide bag tied to Star and an idea popped into his head. He removed the bag and carried it with him back into the tent. Susan had returned with pants and a shirt, and she held the clothes up against White Fox. With a chuckle she said, "You have grown tall enough to wear my husband's clothes, but you need more flesh on those bones."

A quick smile crossed the young man's face. Then the serious look returned as he handed her the papers he had removed from the bag. "I found these papers in a farmers house after the uprising had started. I think they have the Dutchman's name on them. He was dead and can't use them anymore. Maybe I can borrow his name. Then I would have papers to prove who I am if the need should arise."

Susan took the papers from his outstretched hand and studied them. "This is a homestead certificate," she said. "The names on it are James and Anna Muller. Were they both dead?"

"Yes."

"You could use this as you said," Susan affirmed. She handed the papers back to him and set about altering the pants and shirt. After some time had passed, she laid aside the clothes and looked at White Fox. "You must stay here with me tonight. I am here alone on the most holy night of the year in my Christian faith.

"It is the one we call Christmas Eve," she said. "On this night, we celebrate the eve before our Great Spirit chose to have his son born on Mother Earth."

White Fox nodded his understanding. "Falling Star also celebrates this time. I remember it from the last winter season."

"Will you stay here tonight and share a meal with me?" Susan Brown asked quietly.

"I will stay the night," White Fox answered. He knew he owed Susan Brown much for the help she was giving him, and it would feel good to share a warm lodge for the night and have all the food he could eat.

White Fox stirred from the warm bed before the sun was up and tried on the clothes that lay beside the cot. Susan had done a good job of tailoring, and they fit him quite well. White Fox did not like the feel of the wool against his skin, but he would have to tolerate it. He carefully folded his deerskin pants and shirt and put them into the rawhide bag with the homestead paper.

Just then Susan appeared from around the edge of the blanket that had been hung for privacy and looked at him carefully. "I will be back in a bit," she said, and she made another trip out to the shed that stood behind the tent. She returned with a wool coat over her arm. "Put this on," she directed. "And here are some old boots that may fit your feet and a pair of wool socks. These boots will hurt your feet, but you will have to bear that for a while."

Then she pulled a chair away from the table. "Sit," she commanded. "There is one thing left for me to do. Sit on the chair." White Fox sat without questioning her and watched as she picked up a pair of scissors. He was familiar with this item and knew that his long hair soon would be lying on the floor.

When the clipping ceased, she picked up the mirror and handed it to White Fox. He looked into the mirror and flinched noticeably. He didn't speak for some time, and Susan began to wonder if he was angry with her. Finally he said, "I am grateful for all you have done for me, and if I fail to find my friend, it will be my own fault, not yours." Then he stood up and began to gather his things.

"I wish you could have stayed longer," Susan said softly. White Fox smiled at her. He knew she was lonesome for her man and her sons. She continued. "I will pray to the Great Spirit for you. I will ask him to help you to find your friend."

White Fox nodded. "I am glad that you are married to a white man. It is good that some of our people can live on this land." Then he turned and walked out into the open air.

As White Fox rode, he tried to change his pattern of thinking. He did not have to hide from the white men anymore, but he did need to hide from people of his own blood. He began to worry about speaking the white man's tongue and wished he had practiced it on Susan Brown. She could have corrected his mistakes and told him if he sounded believable.

The trail on the east side of the river was not as good as the one on the west, but White Fox had seen soldiers on the other trail and preferred to stay where he was. The less he had to speak to anyone the better. Finally White Fox saw the town of Mankato ahead. The last time he had been near this place, where the Blue

Earth River entered the Minnesota, there had been no town at all. Now there were many buildings here.

The town seemed to be overflowing with people, and White Fox decided that he had better look for a place to leave Star, or the pony might be stolen. He had not ridden far into the town when he saw a fence with a few horses inside it and the building that the white men called a barn. He rode directly to the fence and dismounted. A man came from the barn and looked at him. "You need a place for the horse?" he asked then added, "Fifty cents a day, hay and rub included."

White Fox nodded and handed the man the pony's reins. "Where did you get the Indian pony?" the man asked.

"Found him on the prairie," White Fox answered, using as few words as he could. The man nodded and didn't seem to question this at all. This gave White Fox confidence, and he turned back to the man. "Where are they keeping the Indians who are to be hanged?"

The white man hooted and answered with a grin, "Hey, you're not the first farmer who has come to town to get your hands on the savages. You can forget about that. The soldiers are keeping a close watch on them until the hanging tomorrow. They are keeping the heathens in a couple of log buildings down by the river." The man paused and looked carefully at White Fox. "If you really want to see them, follow this street until you see the hanging platform. You won't be the only one down there trying to get a glimpse of the savages," he finished with a laugh.

White Fox turned from the man and started to walk down the street. His stomach began to churn as he made his way through the crowd. The white men pushed and shoved and seemed to have no patience as they walked to their destinations. Their talking was loud and brash and unpleasant to his ears.

Finally the gallows came into view. Some men were still working on it. White Fox stopped and studied the structure, a cold feeling growing within him. He pulled his attention away from the platform and turned slowly, trying to spot the log buildings that the liveryman had said were being used as a prison. As White Fox scanned the crowd of people, he saw a Black Robe emerge and walk in his direction. He watched the man come toward him, and making a quick decision, he stepped directly into the Black Robe's path. The religious man was about to step around him when White Fox blurted softly, "Will you talk to me?"

"What do you want?" the Black Robe asked gruffly.

White Fox was looking into the face of Soaring Eagle. At the same time, he saw recognition cross the Black Robe's face. "Do you know who I am?" White Fox asked quietly. The religious man nodded, not saying anything. "I have come here to talk to my brother Little Wolf." White Fox continued to speak, hoping the Black Robe would not call out to the soldiers who were nearly everywhere. "I must talk to him tonight."

Soaring Eagle looked around furtively and put his hand on White Fox's arm, whispering, "Come with me." Swiftly he guided the young man into the shadows between two buildings. "Now we can talk," he said. The priest's eyes traveled over White Fox from head to toe. "Someone has helped to disguise you and has done a good job of it."

White Fox did not completely understand the Black Robe's words and did not answer. "So now tell me. Why are you here?"

"I must talk to my brother before they take his life away from him."

"You must not take the chance to try to talk to him. It is too risky. But I will take a message to him for you. They are only allowing us religious leaders in to see the prisoners."

"I must see his face one more time," White Fox implored. "If you have any deep feelings for Chickadee and Falling Star, give me this one chance to see my brother and talk to him."

Soaring Eagle's face grew troubled, and White Fox could see the lines on his forehead grow deep in thought. After some time, he said, "I will help you, but we will need to think of a story to explain why you are here."

"I have already made up such a story," White Fox answered. "We know that many of our people warned the whites of the trouble and saved their lives. I will tell the soldiers that Little

Wolf had warned my family and myself of the danger and I must thank him before they take his life."

The white priest looked troubled and paused to think. Then he said, "This story will only work if I tell it. Your white tongue is not good enough. We will go now, but you must let me do the talking."

Soaring Eagle did not want to spend too much time thinking about what they were about to do, and their walk to the prison buildings was quick. The soldier at the entrance stepped aside for the priest but barred White Fox's way. Soaring Eagle stepped back and gently pushed the soldier's gun aside. "This man has come here to speak to one of the condemned Indians. His family was warned and saved by the one called Little Wolf." The priest spoke with quiet authority, as though he knew this statement to be true.

The soldier looked at White Fox suspiciously and replied, "Father, you know that we cannot allow any of these farmers near the Indians, no matter what kind of story they have to tell."

"I know this man. He has no weapon," Soaring Eagle answered. "I know he is only here to do good."

The white soldier thought for a moment, studying the priest's face. Then he turned to White Fox and roughly pushed him up against the log wall. He did a quick search of White Fox's body, patting the obvious hiding places. Then turned back to the priest. "I will hold you responsible for this man and for the Indian while you are here," the soldier growled. "Get this visit done quickly. It is getting late."

The priest and White Fox hurried past him and into the darkness of the building. White Fox cringed at the musky, unpleasant smells that met them in the dim light. His eyes started to adjust, and he could see the warriors sitting in small groups on the dirt floor. Some were wrapped in blankets. Others sat without any extra cover. The building had an eerie chill, and the silence hung heavy as though all were waiting for something. Abruptly, from a dark corner, White Fox heard a voice. A figure got up and moved toward him. The body was wrapped in a blanket with even the face concealed.

The figure moved past White Fox and to the priest. "I am glad to see you." White Fox heard his brother's voice. "Do you have any word from Chickadee?" Little Wolf questioned Soaring Eagle.

"I have spoken with her," the priest answered quietly. "But I have another surprise for you. Look who has come with me." Soaring Eagle reached for White Fox and pulled him in front of Little Wolf.

Little Wolf gasped, and the blanket fell away from his face. "The Great Spirit has answered my prayers," Little Wolf whispered. He reached out to White Fox and nearly collapsed into his arms.

White Fox held his brother tightly, feeling the eyes of the other prisoners on them. Then he gently pushed him away and looked into his face. The eyes that looked back at him were familiar. But the face was bruised purple and swollen, with a long, red slash across one cheek. "What has happened to you?" White Fox asked softly. "I want to know everything since we last saw each other."

At the far side of the room sat a table with two chairs and a lighted lamp in the middle. Soaring Eagle took the two young men by the arm and led them to it. "You two can talk here. I will share my news with the others." The priest moved away, leaving the two alone.

Little Wolf chuckled weakly. "You make a fine-looking farmer, my brother."

"You do not look much like yourself either, my brother. What has happened to you?"

"I have a long story to tell you, and I am not very strong. But I will tell it from the very beginning, because I have been asking the Great Spirit to send you before it was too late and I have much to ask of you."

White Fox saw that the familiar eyes held a great deal of sadness. "I will stay for as long as it takes you to tell me everything," he said.

"You left our camp the day we were leaving for the Wood Lake battle," Little Wolf began. "We didn't even get to the battlefield before we heard shooting. Some of the soldiers had discovered our warriors hiding in the grass. The battle did not go well, but you probably know about that. After the battle, even your uncle Little Crow knew that the war was over for us, and he fled with his family to the prairie. Most of the warriors who had taken part in the massacres of the white farmers ran away, like our childhood enemy Crooked Arrow. By leaving when they did, these warriors escaped any punishment at all."

Little Wolf paused. "My father felt that most of our family had not taken part in any of the fighting and those of us who had had only joined in the battle as we would in any war. The whites who were negotiating with our people said that if we would stay everything would return to normal."

White Fox could see how weak Little Wolf was. His brother's hands shook as he retold the story. "Take your time. I will not leave until you have told me all that is to be told," White Fox whispered.

Little Wolf began again. "When the white soldiers came, they gathered up all the people. There were no exceptions. All the men were brought before the soldier leaders to be looked over by the white captives and anyone else who was there at the time. Anyone who was recognized as taking part in the battles or doing harm to the white farmers was found guilty of a crime.

"At first, Woodchuck, Bald Eagle, and myself were found guilty and sentenced to death. We were convicted mostly by our own words because we admitted that we had been at some of the battles. Later, the Great White Chief in Washington pardoned all the men who had only fought soldiers. But he did not pardon the ones who had killed any of the farmers."

White Fox looked at Little Wolf in confusion. "You never did that," he protested.

Little Wolf looked sick. "Do you remember that first day when you and I followed the trail to the fort? When we came around the bend and the white man shot at you? I shot and killed him." White Fox nodded as the memory came back to him. "The man's family was hiding in the bushes, and they saw me shoot him. It didn't matter that he had shot at us first."

White Fox shook his head violently. "I should have been at the trial to tell them how it had happened."

"They would not have believed you or cared how it happened. This I know!" Little Wolf spoke with such force that White Fox believed what he said. Then Little Wolf said urgently, "You must listen to me. I have much to ask of you." White Fox leaned close to his friend. "I will die tomorrow, and I have accepted that," Little Wolf said.

"No! I will not let that happen. I will get you out of this place tonight," White Fox hissed.

Little Wolf reached out to his friend, shaking his head. "There is no way you can save me. There are more soldiers and white people than we can count who want us dead. I have accepted the religion of our wives. The Great Spirit's son Jesus has helped me to accept my faith. I will be with him tomorrow by the time the sun reaches its highest place in the sky." Little Wolf looked at White Fox and said, "The white man's religion is good. But from what I have seen, most of the people carry the book that tells of the son Jesus, but they do not follow his teachings. This I do not understand."

Just then the door opened, and the soldier entered. Soaring Eagle quickly walked over to him, and the friends heard the two men whisper. The soldier said something in a gruff tone and then left the building. The priest glanced at the two young men, and they knew their time was limited.

Little Wolf seemed to be drawing strength from somewhere beyond himself and began to speak quickly. "I want you to help Chickadee. She is at a prison camp near the White Cliff, at Fort Snelling. It is set up below the fort, next to the river. She is carrying our child, and I want her to be free. I have been praying to Jesus that you would save her, and now I know that my prayer has been answered. Will you do this for me?" Little Wolf looked at his friend pleadingly.

"I am here because I would do anything for you, as you would for me," White Fox answered.

Little Wolf glanced at the door and said, "I must hurry. Our time is growing short. Soaring Eagle told me that the people attacked again at the town of Henderson. Robin's Nest had her baby snatched from her arms and dashed against a tree. The baby was killed. They had to leave its body in the crotch of a tree. Robin's Nest is grieving for the baby and wants it to be buried so the white people cannot do the baby's body any more harm. She told Soaring Eagle that the tree was off the main trail near a small creek, but he has not been able to find it."

Little Wolf had spoken so quickly about these things that White Fox had become confused. He repeated to Little Wolf, "You want me to go up the trail to this Henderson town and try to find the baby's body and bury it? Then continue to the White Cliff to find your family and try to get Chickadee out of the camp?"

Little Wolf's look held desperation. "Do you think you can do these things I ask of you?"

"I will do as you ask," White Fox nodded. Then he added, "We now live in a wild place in the Canada Country, Little Wolf. You would like it there. It is much like Suland. We live by a river called the Pembina. My son will be raised as a free person, hunting, fishing, and playing as we did."

Little Wolf reached out and grasped White Fox's hand tightly. His hand felt cold, and the bones seemed close to the surface. "Now I am sure that you will save Chickadee and our child." White Fox looked into his friend's bruised face as Little Wolf continued, "I have had a dream. In the dream I saw two little boys playing at the edge of a river. They were not you and me but two other little boys. I think the dream was a vision into the future. White Fox, the two boys were our sons."

A smile pulled up the corners of Little Wolf's mouth. White Fox asked softly, "Do you want me to be here tomorrow?"

"No! I want you on your way to the prison. My time on Mother Earth is almost over, but I know now that I have a son who will have the chance to live the life that was cut short for me."

A shaft of light cut across the room as the door swung open, and the soldier entered. He looked at the two young men seated at the table. Little Wolf spoke softly, "Do not grieve, my brother.

We will be together again through our sons and later in the Spirit World. Go now and do not look back."

A light snow was falling as White Fox rode downriver. He had taken Star from the livery stable during the night. He smiled as he thought of the liveryman discovering the pony missing in the morning and fearing the return of the farmer who would be angry that his pony had been stolen.

White Fox tried to steer his thoughts from the awful event that he knew would take place sometime before the sun reached its highest point. The cloudy, dismal sky made it difficult to tell the time of day. Fortunately, there was only a thin cover of snow on the ground, and traveling was easy. Finally he saw the little town that he knew must be Henderson. He passed by it and hadn't ridden far when he saw where the trail crossed a small, swift stream. He stopped his pony and watched the water flow. He looked around him, searching. He had no idea where to look for the tree that held the baby's body.

White Fox sat quietly and let his thoughts drift back to the time he had been wounded and was cared for by Little Wolf's family. He remembered Robin's Nest coming to care for him with her little boy child toddling beside her and an infant in the cradleboard. He wondered which one of these little ones the tree held in its arms.

Unexpectedly, Star nearly bolted out from under him, snorting loudly. The pony reared up on its hind legs and almost sent its master to the ground. White Fox jumped off his steed, gripping his rifle tightly. Star pranced to the side of the trail and stood staring straight ahead. An animal stood on the trail, gazing back at them. White Fox realized that it was what his people called the brush wolf, or little wolf.

White Fox locked eyes with the animal. Star calmed down just as he himself felt a strange peace settle over him. He walked slowly toward the animal and followed as it moved off the trail and into the woods. The little wolf broke into a trot, and White Fox did the same to keep up. They had not gone far when the animal stopped under a tree, tipped its head back, and howled softly. White Fox's eyes were drawn upward, and there, tucked into the crotch of the tree, was the tiny bundle tightly bound in a deerskin wrap. The baby's body had been placed just out of reach, and he knew he would need Star to reach the tiny bundle. He felt something brush against him and turned to find the pony at his side.

"You have no fear of this little wolf, do you? He has brought us to the place where the baby was hidden." White Fox pulled the pony to the tree and leaped to his back. "Stand still," he instructed as he carefully stood up on Star's back and reached up to retrieve the bundle. He tugged it from the place it was wedged and hugged it close to his body as he slid back to the ground. The little bundle felt cold and stiff to his touch, and he laid it gently on the ground.

White Fox turned to see the wolf scratching at the frozen ground. He walked to the spot, and the animal moved away but stood watching him. White Fox picked up a sturdy stick and dug in the same place. He broke through the frozen layer of earth and found the ground soft underneath. Soon he had dug a hole deep enough to bury the little body. He knelt and laid the baby's body gently into the ground. He pushed the dirt back over the bundle then searched the small area until he found enough stones to cover the grave. Finally, he used leaves, sticks, and a scattering of snow to conceal it.

White Fox stepped back to look at the grave. "Rest here in Mother Earth's beautiful woods, little one. Your parents will come to you someday, and until that time you will have your uncle Little Wolf to look after you." At that moment, the sun broke through the heavy clouds and shone brightly on the place where he stood, warming him. The little wolf had disappeared.

Star nudged his master's arm and seemed to be reminding him that they must be on their way. "We have seen the spirit of my brother in that little wolf," White Fox whispered to the pony. "He is already on the other side." Star looked at his master as though he understood every word.

White Fox nudged Star into a trot, and the distance passed quickly. As he rode on, the heavy clouds covered the sun again, and darkness began to descend early. White Fox felt the wind pick up, and tiny needles of ice began to pelt his cheeks. He noticed a small trail leading away from the main one and followed it, thinking it might lead to a farmstead.

The sleet was coming down harder as White Fox rode into a clearing holding a small house and a barn. He rode Star into the barn without dismounting. There weren't any animals in the structure, but he could see a neat pile of hay. He led the pony to the corner and let him sink his nose into the sweet-smelling, dry grasses. "I am going to check the house. If I get chased away, at least you will have your stomach full," White Fox said to his pony. He made a dash from the barn doorway to the porch of the house and tapped lightly on the door, as he had seen his uncle do before entering a white man's house.

He heard nothing inside and gave the door a push. It swung open as though it hadn't been latched. He found the room just as someone had left it. There were blankets on the bed and jars of food on the shelf. He picked up a hard loaf of bread from the table and bit into it. It was only slightly stale. He put it back on the table and walked to the bed. He sat on it and touched the soft blanket that covered it. Colorful threads had been carefully stitched through the fabric to make a pretty design. White Fox thought that white women were not so different from the women of his people. They too spent extra time to make the everyday items in the home special to the eye.

White Fox eyed the fireplace and wondered if he dared light a fire. Then it occurred to him that even if someone caught him here, he could explain that he had been forced in by the weather. He was a "white man" himself now and had no one to fear. Soon a fire was burning brightly.

With the room warming and the food filling his stomach, White Fox realized how fatigued he was. He walked to the bed, yanked the blankets off in one pull, and spread them on the floor. Then he lay down on them, using one for a cover. As he began to doze, he heard the lonely howl of the little wolf. He replied to the call, "Go on to the Spirit Land, my brother. I can handle the things you have asked me to do here."

Some time later, White Fox woke with a start. He lay motionless for a bit, listening, then cautiously raised himself on one elbow. Something had awakened him, and a glance out the window at Star told him that the pony was nervous. White Fox quickly got up and dressed and went outside. "It is time for us to leave this place," he whispered to the pony. He quickly tied the rawhide bag back in place on the animal's back and touched the medicine bundle that hung around his neck. Then he slung the rifle over his shoulder and, picking up the pony's reins, started for the doorway.

He inched the door open and looked out into the yard as best he could. He saw nothing unusual in the dim, predawn light. The sleet had stopped falling during the night, and only a trace remained on the ground. White Fox made his move, quickly stepping out the door and across the porch. Star's hoofs clopped loudly, the sounds echoing through the yard. The pair sprinted for the cover of the trees. Once there, White Fox stood still and listened. Although he heard nothing, the uneasy feeling stayed with him. He waited.

Then he did hear a sound coming from the path leading to the main trail. He gently put his hand over Star's nose to let the pony know that he must be quiet. All of a sudden a silhouette of a man appeared at the edge of the clearing. The man tied his pony to a tree and moved along the edge of the tree line until he was even with the side of the house. White Fox could tell by the way he moved that he was not a white man.

As the man disappeared around the back of the house, White Fox made a dash for the little house that the white man used for his private needs. This brought him near the house, and as the stranger came around the corner, White Fox brought his rifle up and stepped in front of him. Their eyes connected, and White Fox gasped as he recognized his friend. "Grey Wing!"

Surprise flashed across Grey Wing's face. Abruptly he grabbed White Fox and pulled him against the wall. "There is smoke in the air. I think someone is inside," he whispered.

"There is no one inside. Star and I spent the night here. We had a fire."

Grey Wing stared into White Fox's face. "What are you doing

here? You are dressed as a white man. I would not have known you from a distance."

"Go inside the cabin and warm yourself. I will get your pony and Star and take them to the barn so they can fill up on the white man's hay."

Moments later White Fox entered the house to find his friend wrapped in one of the blankets and sitting cross legged in front of the fireplace. White Fox carefully stacked some pieces of wood over the still-glowing coals, blowing on the coals so the wood would begin to ignite. Then he sat down beside his friend and studied his face. "How did you end up here?" he asked.

"I was traveling to Mankato, but a wolf howled on the trail directly in front of me. My pony became so skittish that I could not get him settled down. I came up this small trail to circle around the wolf and ended up here."

White Fox chuckled. "I have had my own experiences with the wolf. But first I must know the whole story of what has happened to you since we last saw each other."

"I will tell you, my friend. But I think your story may be more interesting, by the looks of you."

White Fox nodded but encouraged Grey Wing. "Tell me. Were you put on trial for war crimes as our brother Little Wolf was? I must hear it all."

Grey Wing took a deep breath. "After the Wood Lake battle, the village split up. Many of the warriors who had taken part in the fighting took their families and fled to the plains. My father, being a holy man, felt he needed to go with the people. Long Legs and his family chose to stay."

White Fox put up his hand to stop his friend. "I know their part of the story," he interjected. "Were you put on trial, as Little Wolf and his brothers were?"

"I was tried and convicted. But I was pardoned in the letter from the Great White Chief. Do you know what is going to happen to Little Wolf?" Grey Wing asked in a subdued voice.

White Fox looked away from his friend's face. "It has already happened." An anguished moan rose from Grey Wing. "I was there. I did not see it happen, but there was no way to stop it."

White Fox looked at Grey Wing and saw that his face had turned a sickly pale color.

Grey Wing started to shake noticeably and pulled the blanket tighter around himself. "I finally figured out a way to escape from the prison camp at the White Cliff, stole a horse from a farmer's barn, and was on my way to try to help our blood brother. I cannot believe that he is gone." He then looked closely at White Fox. "You look like a white farmer. Is that how you found out what happened to Little Wolf?"

White Fox looked into the fire and began to tell his story. "We were living up in the Canada Country by Turtle Mountain when I got the word of what had happened to Little Wolf. I came back to the river valley and had some help in changing my appearance. I managed to get into the prison with the help of the Black Robe Soaring Eagle."

"You actually got the chance to talk to Little Wolf?" Grey Wing interrupted. "What did he tell you?"

"He was at peace about dying. He said he had always felt that his time on Mother Earth would not be long. This surprised me, for our brother never told me that he felt that way. I always thought we would grow old together. He asked me to do two things for him. One already is done. One is left to do." Grey Wing pulled the blanket still tighter around himself and seemed to slip deep into his own thoughts. He threw the blanket aside and emitted a horrific wail.

White Fox saw the flash of his knife and threw himself onto his friend, knocking Grey Wing backwards onto the floor. The knife sailed across the room. "Don't!" White Fox hissed into his ear. "I will not allow you to slash yourself and grieve. We do not have the time for this now!" Grey Wing stopped struggling and lay quietly under White Fox. "Do you think it has been easy to keep my thoughts away from the death scene in my imagination?" White Fox asked, his voice shaking. "I do not have time to grieve now, and Little Wolf's last words to me were, 'Do not grieve for me. I have not lived in fear, and I will not die in fear.' He asked me to do two things for him, and I will not waste my energy grieving for a spirit that has gone on to a better place."

A sob came from deep in Grey Wing's chest. White Fox felt the tears spring from his own eyes and flow freely down his face. The two lay entwined in each other's arms as the sun peered over the horizon.

White Fox heated the container of coffee over the fire and showed his friend how to dunk the dry bread into the liquid. They shared the last of the pemmican, neither saying a word as they ate. Finally Grey Wing leaned back. "What were the two things Little Wolf asked you to do?"

"Do you remember when Robin's Nest and Bald Eagle's baby was killed?" White Fox asked.

"I did not see it happen," Grey Wing replied. "The warriors were separated from the women at the time."

"Little Wolf asked me to find the body and bury it. I would not have found it if it weren't for a brush wolf that showed me the way." Grey Wing's head swung around and he looked at his friend. "That's when I knew for sure that our brother was on the other side," White Fox concluded.

"You found the baby's body and buried it?"

"Yes. That was the first thing he asked me to do. The second thing is this: I am going to take Chickadee from the prison at White Cliff and take her with me back to our camp in the north country."

Grey Wing nodded and slowly got to his feet. "The sun is up. Let's get started to the White Cliff."

As the two neared the main trail, Grey Wing turned to his friend. "It is not safe for me to travel here. To get here, I followed a game trail along the edge of the river. It takes longer, but it will be safer for me. I will find you when we reach the White Cliff."

"We will travel together," White Fox answered. "We have been apart long enough."

The two young men picked their way along the edge of the river, sometimes finding the trail overgrown with brush. Finally, as the sun passed its highest point and began its descent, they could see the bluff opening ahead. They were nearing the Mendota, "the meeting place of the two waters" where the Minnesota River added its strength to the Mississippi. "The river is wide and shallow at the bend ahead. We can cross there," Grey Wing said.

The trail on the north side of the river was easier to follow. Soon the White Cliff came into view, Fort Snelling looming menacingly at its top. They could not see the prison encampment below the fort, but they could see the heavy, smoky haze drifting over the valley. They rode on until they came to a meadow, and there, spread before them, was the prison encampment. White Fox stopped his pony and surveyed the scene before them. The camp was surrounded by an enclosure of logs standing on end. They could see the tops of some of the tepees inside the enclosure.

"It is not safe to take the ponies any closer." Grey Wing spoke slowly as he tied his pony to a small sapling. "We need to have a plan before we do anything else."

White Fox grunted his agreement. "You have been in the camp. Can you draw me a picture to show me how it is laid out and where Long Legs' family is situated?"

Grey Wing squatted on the ground, picked up a twig, and started to draw in the thin blanket of snow. He sketched a large square and showed the middle where the soldiers had put up a pole to fly the United States flag. "This is the gate." He pointed to the side facing the bluff and the fort. "It is the only way in or out of the camp. The soldiers guard it at all times." He looked up at his friend. "Do you have any idea of how you will get inside?"

White Fox studied the drawing, then asked, "Where is Long Legs' family?"

Grey Wing pointed to an area near the log fence on the west side of the camp. "They have two lodges about here."

White Fox swung his head up and looked at the camp. "They are on this side of the camp with only the log wall separating us?"

Grey Wing nodded. He leaned forward, again touching the diagram with the stick. "The soldiers guard the gate here, but there also is a patrol that marches around the outside of the log wall. We could even hear them march at night."

"We will leave the ponies here and move along the ridge to get closer to the camp. I want to watch the soldiers," White Fox said softly.

The two young men stayed within the protection of the brush, moving along the bluff until they could see the two soldiers guarding the gate. White Fox crouched on one knee and watched as four more soldiers marched in formation past the gate and on, circling the perimeter of the camp. They turned the corner in a square, snapping formation and continued down the west side. White Fox and Grey Wing stayed perfectly still until they saw the soldiers disappear around the corner to the back side of the camp.

"I would not like to walk all day and not get anywhere," Grey Wing whispered from behind his friend.

"There are many things the white people do that I would not like to do," White Fox replied. "We will go back to the place where we left the ponies and build a lean-to. I want to watch the guard and make sure they do not change the pattern of the watch during the night.

White Fox was wrapped tightly in his blanket. He could tell by Grey Wing's even breathing that he was asleep. They had moved closer to the prison camp after dark and had observed that nothing changed in the soldiers' duties. Now White Fox allowed his body to relax and felt the fatigue in his muscles. The pair had not taken the risk of building a fire, but the lean-to that Grey Wing had built sheltered them from the winter wind, and he felt warm enough.

His thoughts drifted back to the very first time he saw this place. The people of his village had marched along the river bottom and had crossed not far from the place where the prison camp now stood. They had been traveling to the Kaposia village on the Mississippi River not far from this place. White Fox could clearly recall how he felt at that time. He was twelve winter seasons old, and everything he saw was new to him. He remembered feeling fear and wonder at the same time. He remembered his father telling him later about the big gun at the fort, the same fort that he was camped so close to now.

He recalled sitting near the river's edge beside Little Wolf, watching the big steamboats pass by while Grey Wing tried to explain what made the big paddles go around—Grey Wing, the authority on all the new things they saw. He remembered the Pig's Eye trading post and the white missionary's school. It was there he had learned to speak and read the white man's tongue.

His hand slid to his medicine bundle, and he fingered the shapes of his sacred items. "Oh Great Spirit," he whispered into the darkness, "you knew I would need to know these things to get through the hard times. When I attended the white man's school, I did not yet even know my cousin Chickadee. Now I am here to save her and Little Wolf's child. Help me! Send the spirits to help me! I do not yet know how to get her out of the prison camp. My mind is weak and tired."

Grey Wing sighed in his sleep, and White Fox's thoughts turned to him. "Thank you, Great One, for this blood brother who is sharing this time with me," he whispered. "It still seems strange as I think back to the time when Little Wolf and I first met him: Why did he give up his childhood friends and become our companion? It was as though we had always known him. There are so many things I will never understand . . ."

White Fox awoke from his sleep and looked into Grey Wing's open eyes. He reached his arms over his head to stretch and could feel a new strength throughout his body. His stomach growled loudly, and Grey Wing chuckled and sat up. "We have not eaten since yesterday morning. I think we had better do that sometime today."

"I think you are right," White Fox answered. "The cold weather does not make it so easy to fast. The body needs some nourishment. You can go back upriver and find us some rabbits for a good meal."

"I cannot shoot my gun so close to the white man's fort," Grey Wing said thoughtfully.

White Fox reached for the extra blanket and unwrapped his bow and quiver of arrows, laying them at Grey Wing's feet. "I have come prepared with almost anything we could need. I am going down to the camp and try to talk my way into the enclosure," he added. "We will meet back here later."

White Fox watched as Grey Wing moved the ponies deeper into a patch of willows where they could eat more of the tender shoots. Then Grey Wing departed with a wave, and White Fox turned toward the meadow. "Now I must think as a white man," White Fox coached himself silently as he walked across the meadow and around to the front gate. He walked directly to the two soldiers standing on each side of the opening. They stepped forward and crossed their rifles ahead of him, barring the way into the camp.

"What do you want?" the biggest soldier barked. White Fox studied the soldier's face for a moment. The man had a mustache that curled up on each side. White Fox had never seen facial hair quite like this before. "Answer me! What is it you want?" he demanded again.

"I must see my friend," White Fox replied, carefully speaking the white man's language.

"What friend are you talking about?"

"There is an Indian in this camp who saved me and my family. His name is Woodchuck. I must find him and thank him before they send him away."

The soldier grunted and looked at White Fox carefully. "If it weren't for those blue eyes, I would say you are a savage yourself." White Fox felt a stab of fear. Had he not spoken the right words?

The two soldiers looked at each other and smirked. The biggest one spoke again, "You go to our officer. If he gives his permission for you to enter this camp, we will let you in."

White Fox turned and looked around the area. "Where does this officer live?" he asked.

"In the blockhouse over there. That is his office. You will find him there."

White Fox drew his rawhide bag tight to himself as he started his walk to the blockhouse. Another soldier stood in the doorway of this structure, his gun held angled across his chest. White Fox stepped onto the porch, saying, "I must talk to the officer who lives here."

"You mean General Taylor," the soldier said.

"If that is the man who lives here," White Fox replied.

"He does not live here. This building is his office. What is your name?"

White Fox caught his breath and felt the blood drain from his face. "My name is … my name is James Muller," he answered.

The soldier looked at him for what seemed an eternity. Then he stepped aside and turned the doorknob, opening the door only a little. He called out in a loud voice, "A mister James Muller to see you, sir!"

"Come in, come in," a voice called from inside.

The soldier stepped aside to allow White Fox to enter. White Fox stepped gingerly through the doorway. He felt as though he were entering a cave full of rattlesnakes. "James Muller is it?" the man said in a loud voice. "I was getting so bored sitting here I would have welcomed even a savage."

White Fox nodded, not understanding exactly what the general was saying. Then he stepped forward. "I am here to get your permission to speak to an Indian in the camp."

The general sat silently studying the young man in front of him. "You said your name is James Muller? Can you prove that to me?"

White Fox froze for a split second. Then he remembered Susan Brown stuffing the paper she called a homestead deed into his bag. Her words came back to him: "You may need this." White Fox looked at the general as though in thought. "I have my homestead deed in this bag." As he reached into the bag, he saw the general staring at it.

"Where did you get that bag?" the officer blurted.

"I found an Indian pony on the prairie during the uprising, and the bag was tied to him," White Fox answered as he pulled the paper out and laid it on the general's desk. He carefully smoothed out the wrinkles and turned it the right way so the general could read the writing.

The officer looked at the paper, his brow furrowed. "Why do you want to see this savage?" he asked.

White Fox paused, carefully choosing his words. Then he began to speak slowly and deliberately. The words did not come easily, and he did not want them to sound wrong. "Woodchuck, the son of Long Legs, was a friend of mine. He often stopped by our cabin when he was hunting in our area. When the trouble started, he came and warned us of the danger and saved our lives. I must thank him and see him one more time before they send him to another country."

The general muttered, "What do you mean, another country? They will send them to another territory."

White Fox stuttered, "That's, that's what I meant."

General Taylor looked at him thoughtfully. Then he said, "You are not the first white man to come here to see these people. Even I am beginning to doubt the wisdom of relocating all of them. After all, they did live on this land long before any of us came here." The officer dropped his head into his hands and rubbed his temples with his thumbs. "But I guess none of this is for us to decide," he mumbled under his breath. Then, louder, he said, "I will write you my permission."

As the general wrote on a paper, White Fox realized how sad and old the man looked. General Taylor stood up and handed the paper to White Fox. "I hope you find the man you are looking for." White Fox nodded and turned to the door. He could feel the officer staring at his back and was glad to escape into the daylight.

"Wait!" He heard the shout as the door closed behind him. White Fox stopped in his tracks and waited. The door opened, and the general stepped out. "You forgot your deed." He handed the paper to White Fox.

"Thank you. I will need that," White Fox said, hoping he had used the words properly.

The general smiled for the first time since they met. "Good luck!" he said, holding his hand out to the young man. White Fox extended his hand to the general, and the man gave it a firm shake.

White Fox turned and walked back to the gate where the two soldiers stood guarding the way. He handed the paper to the bigger one. The soldier looked toward the blockhouse and saw the general still standing on the porch watching them. The big soldier grumbled, "We will let you enter, but we will keep track of the time you spend here. Do not waste it!" He handed the paper back, and White Fox hurried past the two soldiers and through the gate into the prison enclosure.

He walked quickly through the camp, seeing many heads turn in his direction. He kept his own head down, not wanting anyone to recognize him until he found the lodges he was looking for. Visualizing the drawing Grey Wing had made for him, he walked to the flagpole in the middle of the camp, then turned right. He spied the lodge he was looking for, the paintings on the outside telling the life story of its occupant, Long Legs. He stopped and looked at it as though he were seeing it for the first time. Many of the events shown here also had been depicted on his father's lodge.

No one was outside the tepee, and he coughed loudly to announce his presence. The flap was pulled aside, and a small face peeked out at him. White Fox did not recognize the little face, and it quickly disappeared. He could hear the excited chatter inside as the little one told the others of the strange white man standing at their door. White Fox leaned close to the flap, saying softly, "Long Legs, let me come in. It is I, White Fox."

All grew quiet inside the lodge. A moment later, the flap was thrown open wide, and Chickadee's face appeared in the doorway. She stepped out of the lodge and looked hard into the visitor's face. With a squeal of joy, she grabbed White Fox and almost squeezed the air from his lungs. White Fox quickly unwrapped her arms and pushed her back into the lodge, following behind her.

Inside the tepee, White Fox looked around the fire into the eyes of all the women of Long Legs' family. He spotted Walking Woman and noticed her look of shock. White Fox realized then how strange he must look to them with his short hair and white man's clothes. He saw Robin's Nest and Burnt by Fire's wife, Pretty Bird. There was another young woman he did not know. Chickadee saw him look at her and explained. "This is Woodchuck's wife, White Lily. They married on the trail to this place. Did you recognize Big Eyes, Burnt by Fire's daughter?"

White Fox had not at first recognized the little girl who had peeked out at him, but he realized it was because her face was so thin. His eyes traveled again around the fire, and he saw that all of their faces were shallow, pale, and gaunt. "Where are the men?" White Fox asked Chickadee.

"They are in the other lodge," she answered, gesturing the direction. "But talk to us first. We have much to ask you. Do you know that Little Wolf has been condemned to death? Now that you are here, maybe you can help him."

"I cannot help him, Chickadee," White Fox replied softly, his eyes looking deeply into hers.

Chickadee grew still as stone. Then, from deep inside her, a wail rose to a high pitch. Walking Woman joined in, and the lodge soon was filled with the sounds of grief. White Fox crawled to Chickadee and took her into his arms, pressing his lips to her cheek. He whispered into her ear, "Do not hurt yourself, Chickadee. I need for you to be strong and healthy." He held her tightly as she wept deeply. Then, slowly, he felt her relax and grow limp in his arms.

She looked up at him and said in an anguished whisper, "I cannot live here without him."

"I have a message for you, and when you hear it you will change your mind."

Quickly the flap of the tepee was pulled open, and Long Legs peered in. "What is wrong in here?" he asked in a loud voice. His eyes fastened on White Fox. Long Legs let out a cry and he dived at the white man whose arms held Chickadee.

"Stop!" Walking Woman cried, throwing herself between the two men. Long Legs already had the young man in his grip. "Stop! It is White Fox."

Long Legs pushed the body back and looked into the young man's face. "White Fox?" he said in disbelief. "What is happening here?" Everything grew quiet, and Long Legs looked with confusion at the women and then back to White Fox.

White Fox turned to the women. "You must be quiet. I have only a little time to spend here with you, and I cannot waste it." Then he turned to Long Legs. "Go to the other lodge and bring all of your family here. I have much to tell you and not much time to do it."

Long Legs disappeared out the doorway and soon returned with all of the men of the family. They all squeezed into the tepee. Burnt by Fire was the first to speak. "You make a good-looking white man, White Fox," he said, grinning.

"You remember the trouble my sky-colored eyes gave me as a child? Now they have served me well," White Fox answered. His eyes traveled slowly around the circle as though he were memorizing each face. Then he began to speak softly, "I have been looking for you, and now I have brought bad news to you. You must listen to me carefully."

The men sat nearest the fire and they leaned forward in anticipation. The women huddled behind them, already knowing the bad tidings. White Fox continued. "I came back from the north country because Panther Man and I met Medicine Bottle and Shakopee on the prairie. They told us what had happened to all of you. I started back at once and went to Joseph Brown's house. Mrs. Brown told me more and helped me to look like a white man so I could come looking for you. She also knew about Little Wolf."

Long Legs cut in. "Have you seen my son?"

"I saw him, my father," answered White Fox. "I talked to him the night before he was put to death." Long Legs inhaled with a moan and rocked backward and then forward as though in pain. The women started to whimper again. White Fox gave them a stern look and continued to speak. "I would like to take the time to grieve with you, my family, but I have no time. I have made some promises to Little Wolf, and I will keep them."

White Fox's eyes went to Robin's Nest and rested on her. "Robin's Nest and Bald Eagle, Little Wolf asked me to find your little one's body, near the town of Henderson, and to bury it properly. He was worried that the white men would find it and mistreat it. I did find it, and she has been buried."

Robin's Nest reached out to White Fox and grasped his hand, the tears running freely down her face. "You have always been a good brother to me."

"I made one more promise to Little Wolf. He wanted you, Chickadee, to come with me to the north country. He wants you to be with your mother, and he wants his son to be raised with my son, Sparrow Hawk."

Everyone turned to look at Chickadee. Their surprised expressions told White Fox that they knew nothing of the baby. Chickadee turned to Walking Woman and said faintly, "Little Wolf was supposed to have the honor of telling you."

"I understand," Walking Woman replied. "But I already knew there was a baby. You cannot keep such a thing from a grandmother."

Long Legs turned and looked into White Fox's eyes. "Did my son die with honor?"

"Little Wolf died as he lived, with no fear and much honor." Everyone sat silent, thinking about what they had just heard. Finally White Fox said, "I wish I could take all of you from this place, but I am not sure that I can even get Chickadee out. The spirits have given me a plan. Maybe you can tell me if it can work."

Burnt by Fire leaned forward. "Tell us your plan. We will do anything to help you. If Little Wolf's wife and child can escape from here, it will make the grief of losing him a little less."

Woodchuck wriggled closer to the fire and said, "Your friend Grey Wing escaped from this camp just two days ago. He made friends with some of the traders who bring in the supplies, and they smuggled him out. So many of our people are dying every day that the soldiers cannot keep count of us. They did not miss him."

"My friend is waiting for me up on the rise above the camp," White Fox replied. "The Great Spirit helped us to find each other on the trail between here and Mankato. He was on his way to help Little Wolf."

Chickadee reacted to this. "I knew that is where he would go."

"He is going to help me get you out of here," White Fox said to her. "You must put away your grieving for now and help us to save you and your child from this life of imprisonment." White Fox leaned close to her and gently touched her cheek. "Can you do that for Little Wolf?"

"I am strong, you know that, White Fox," she answered.

White Fox nodded. Then he turned to Long Legs. "Do you know if the white soldiers have any guards posted inside the wall?"

"They have none," Long Legs answered.

"A small group circles the outside of the enclosure day and night." White Fox looked around the group. All eyes were on him. "I have a plan," he said. "If I throw a rope over the wall at a point just about straight out from this lodge, do you think you could help Chickadee to climb over it?" His eyes rested on Chickadee. "Do you think you are strong enough to climb a rope over the wall?"

The familiar, fierce little-girl look returned to his cousin's face. "You know I can climb a rope as well as you can," she sputtered.

"Don't forget there are two of you now."

Chickadee patted her stomach and replied, "He is still tiny and is safe right where he is."

Long Legs shifted his position. "What time of the night will you come?"

White Fox thought for a moment. "It will be soon after total darkness. I will give the call of the night owl."

Long Legs nodded. "Do you have a rope to use?"

White Fox's brow furrowed. He hesitated, then said slowly, "I will have one by tonight." He looked around the group, taking in each of the faces that looked back at him so intently. He felt his throat begin to close as he realized how much he loved this family. He drew a deep, ragged breath. "Do you know where they are going to take you when you leave here?" he asked softly.

Long Legs answered. "One of the friendly soldiers told me they are going to move us down the Great River on one of the big steamboats. He did not know where they will take us. He knew only that they had mentioned St. Louis as the first stop."

"Listen, all of you!" White Fox interrupted. "If you should ever regain your freedom, come to the north country and find us. I want for us someday to be together again. You will have family there." Yet, even as White Fox said these words, darkness settled over his heart, and he knew that he would never see most of these faces again. "I must say my good-byes to you before the white soldiers come looking for me," he finished quickly.

White Fox stood up, and the others followed suit. He went to Walking Woman and Long Legs first and put his arms around them, pulling them close. "Do not grieve too much for Little Wolf. His spirit is here among you. I have seen his spirit helper the little wolf with my own eyes and already have had his help to get this far. I will miss you and will remember you always."

The rest of the family moved in tightly around him. White Fox put his arms around each one, giving as much comfort as he could until he came to Chickadee. "You I will see tonight," he said. Then he clutched his rawhide bag close and stepped out through the tepee doorway. He walked away quickly. The men stepped outside to watch him, but he did not turn to look back.

As White Fox neared the gate, he used the fabric of the coat sleeve to brush the tears from his face. "Did you find your man?" the shorter soldier asked.

"I found him," White Fox answered. "Where is the nearest trading post?"

"There is one across the river, but the ferry does not run every day. The river closes up with thin ice one day, then opens up the next when the weather warms. We have had unusual weather lately," the little man added. White Fox did not answer and walked away as though in a hurry. "Not very friendly!" he heard the soldier grumble.

White Fox came to a fork in the trail and followed the path leading to the river. He saw that the water was open and the ferryman was sitting on the ferry. The man's lower face was hidden in the collar of a wool mackinaw coat. He heard the man mutter, "Want to cross?"

White Fox stepped onto the ferry and answered, "I have no money. Will you take my hat?" He did not want to give up the warm cap now that he had grown used to it, but he thought it an offer the ferryman might accept.

The man poked his head out of the coat and smiled a toothless smile. "I would not take a man's cap on such a chilly day, but you wouldn't have some tobacco in that bag you carry?"

White Fox pulled the rawhide bag open and removed the smaller tobacco bag. He handed it to the old man. The ferryman slowly turned the decorated bag in his hand looking at the designs. "Where did you get this?" he asked.

"Took it off a dead Indian," White Fox grunted shortly.

The man looked hard at the younger man then began to pull on the rope to move the ferry across the river. Again he looked closely at White Fox. "Will you want to cross back later?" White Fox nodded. "You've got it," the man affirmed. "This little decorated bag is purty, worth more to me than the tobacco it holds. I like the way those Injun women trim their men's things." White Fox could hear the old man grumbling as he pulled on the rope. "My woman would never do such a sweet thing for me."

He moved away from the man, not wanting to make any more conversation than he had to, but that did not stop the ferryman from talking to him. "You are lucky to get across the river today. Yesterday the ice covered it. Too thin to walk on but too thick to pull the ferry through."

White Fox nodded but said nothing. Then he felt the flat bottom of the boat scrape the sand as it touched the shoreline. "I will be here when you return if you don't stay too long."

"I will not be long."

White Fox walked quickly up to the trading post door and pushed it open. As he entered, a man with a full beard looked up from an open book he had been writing in. "What can I help you with today?" he said in greeting.

White Fox looked around the room, then answered, "I need a long rope."

"Over here," the man replied, walking to the back of the building. "How many feet do you need?"

White Fox stopped and looked down at his feet. Then he remembered that "feet" was also a term of measurement in the white man's tongue. He brought his eyes up slowly, hoping the trader hadn't noticed his actions. The man was unrolling rope from a big roll. White Fox stepped quickly to his side and picked up the end of the rope. "I will unroll as much as I will need," he volunteered. He walked across the room and hooked the rope around a barrel, then walked back. "This will be enough."

The trader let out a deep laugh. "What do you need that much rope for?"

White Fox hesitated. "I must lead my cows behind the wagon when I move my family. It is better to have too much than too little."

"You're right about that." The white man seemed to accept his explanation. He started to loop the rope, measuring it as he went along. "One dollar will cover the cost," he said, laying it on the counter.

White Fox thought for a moment, then reached into the rawhide bag. He brought out the deed paper and handed it to the man. "I will trade this deed for the rope. My wife will not live on that place anymore."

The trader shot him a look of surprise. He seized the paper and stepped to the window to look at it. After examining it carefully, he asked, "Where exactly is this land located?"

"It is not far from the Redwood Agency," White Fox answered.

"If you folks escaped from that area during the uprising, you are very lucky to be alive." White Fox nodded, saying nothing. "I am a notary public and can make out a sales sheet on this land. But I must insist that you accept some money for it." The trader disappeared into the back room and came back with a paper. He carefully wrote between the printed lines and then handed the paper to White Fox. "Sign here." He pointed his finger at the line at the bottom of the paper.

White Fox looked hard at the paper, trying to understand what the man wanted him to do. "If you cannot write, put your X right there." White Fox carefully put an X on the line, hoping he was doing the right thing. The trader seemed satisfied and grabbed the deed from his hand. Then the man held out a gold coin and put it in White Fox's hand. "There," he said. "A deal is made. Do you want a cup of brandy to warm yourself?"

"The ferry is waiting for me," White Fox replied, slipping the coin into his pocket and then hanging the looped rope over his shoulder.

"Good luck wherever you decide to go next," the white trader called after him as the door swung shut.

White Fox hurried back to the riverbank and found the old man waiting for him. He stepped onto the ferry, and the ferryman pulled them into the river again. "I see you got what you needed," he remarked.

White Fox nodded, noticing that the tobacco pouch hung around the man's neck. He stepped up to the rail and took the rope from the ferryman's hand. "I will pull us across."

The old man did not argue and sat down on the bench. When they neared the opposite shore, the ferryman pulled himself to his feet, and as White Fox made the last pull on the rope, he tied the rope's end to the railing. Before White Fox could leave the ferry, the old man grabbed his arm. "In my younger days, I hunted and trapped with your people. I lived with them, and I know an Injun when I see one." He paused, then said, "Good luck, young warrior. I wish I could go with you."

White Fox studied his face for a time and then, with a nod to the man, stepped from the ferry. He walked up the trail a short distance and then broke into a trot. He must get back to the ridge to find Grey Wing. The evening dusk was descending.

He moved quickly through the brush and found Grey Wing leaning over a small fire. He was feeding the fire one twig at a time to keep the smoke to a minimum. Two jackrabbits were hung over the flames. Already they looked brown, and White Fox could hear the fat dripping into the fire. He grinned. As he stepped from the brush, Grey Wing spun around to face him. "You are back," Grey Wing said, looking relieved. White Fox slid the rope off his shoulder and laid it next to the lean-to. "I see you have been trading with the white trader," Grey Wing added.

"I have made two white men happy this day," White Fox said as he reached down and slowly turned the spit that Grey Wing had rigged over the fire.

"The spirits have been kind to us. The wind is taking the cooking smells down toward the river bottom, or we would have the soldiers looking over our shoulders," Grey Wing said with a chuckle.

White Fox felt the past two days of emptiness in his stomach and could hardly wait for the meat to finish roasting. He moved closer to the fire, for suddenly the cold seemed to penetrate his coat. He began to shiver. Grey Wing stepped up beside his friend. "You saw Little Wolf's family?"

White Fox looked troubled and said thoughtfully, "The family looked like the animals after a hard winter. Did you not get much food in the prison camp?"

"We got very little, and often what we did get was spoiled. Below the camp, along the river, the graves are growing every day," Grey Wing answered as he pulled the rabbits from the spit. He gave the bigger one to White Fox. They devoured the meat, carefully cleaning every scrap from the bones.

"Did you say your farewells to your father before you escaped from the camp?" White Fox asked when they had finished.

Grey Wing glanced in the direction of the camp. "I told him I didn't think I would ever see him again in this life. He understood. He wanted me to gain my freedom."

"Long Legs will tell him that you reached freedom and are alive and well," White Fox said. "The Great Spirit has been kind to us in many ways this day. The Great Spirit guided me past many obstacles. The things I did today came into my thoughts as I went along."

"Do you have a plan to get Chickadee from the camp?"

"I do," White Fox answered. "It is a good thing we got our sleep last night because we will be getting none tonight."

"Tell me about the plan."

White Fox motioned toward the coil of rope. "Chickadee is going to climb over the wall on that rope. We are going to go to get her as soon as it is dark enough. The men of Little Wolf's family will help her from the other side."

"She is a strong woman. I think she can make it."

"Are you ready?" White Fox asked abruptly.

"I am ready," Grey Wing affirmed.

White Fox stopped short and tipped his face upward. Grey Wing watched, then turned his face to the night sky also. "Great Spirit," White Fox said quietly, "we have no tobacco to smoke. We have no sage to spread in the fire. Tonight we must ask for you help in the simplest way. Send the spirit helpers to be at our side. I must keep the promise I made to my blood brother." With this, he dropped his head and picked up the coil of rope.

He turned to Grey Wing and raised his hand in their boyhood sign. Grey Wing returned the sign, and they moved off to follow the ridge to the edge of the prison camp. The quarter moon shed a pale glow on the meadow and gave the young men just enough light to see.

They soon were settled into a large plum bush along the west wall of the camp. They did not have to wait long. The soldiers came around the corner on their left and marched past them in the same perfect order they had observed the night before, making the same "hup, hup" sounds. The young men watched until the soldiers rounded the corner to their right and disappeared.

White Fox put his hand to his mouth and sounded the hoot of the night owl. They heard nothing from within the wall. He called again. This time there was an immediate answer. The two young men looked at each other. "They are ready on the other side," Grey Wing whispered. Now they had to wait for the soldiers to come by again.

White Fox felt fear tighten the muscles in his chest. He raised his eyes upward for an instant and felt calm flow back through his body. He carefully looped the rope into as small a ball as he could, leaving one loose end. Then he heard the marching boots and watched, motionless, as they came around the corner. It seemed to take forever for the soldiers once again to step off the distance of the west side and disappear from sight.

As soon as the soldiers rounded the corner, White Fox and

Grey Wing jumped silently from their hiding place and raced to the wall. White Fox held the loose end of the rope in his left hand and bent almost to the ground, his right hand holding the coiled end. He flung his arm up and let the rope fly. It swung up almost to the top of the wall but then stopped in midair. He watched in shock as it fell back to the ground at his feet. He snatched it up and quickly looped it back into a roll.

"It got caught on the button of your sleeve," Grey Wing whispered, grabbing the button and ripping it from his friend's sleeve. "You will make it this time."

White Fox again bent down, nearly touching the ground and threw the rope with all his strength. They watched it, holding their breath. This time it rose high over the wall and fell to the other side. Immediately they heard the shuffling of feet. White Fox held the end of the rope and waited.

Someone gave the rope a firm tug. White Fox gave a tug in response. Then he felt the rope tighten and knew Chickadee had started her climb. All this seemed to take forever, and Grey Wing nervously began to look down the side of the enclosure as though expecting the soldiers to appear around the corner.

Then Chickadee was pulling herself up to the top of the wall. She rolled sideways and pushed her legs over to the other side of the enclosure. White Fox held his breath as she struggled to change her grip on the rope. Her weight would be held from the other side now.

Suddenly she let out a soft cry, and they saw her lose her grip and start to fall. White Fox dropped the rope and reached up to break her fall. Abruptly she stopped and seemed to be hanging in midair. Grey Wing gasped. "She's hanging by her dress. It's caught between two logs."

The two young men watched in horror as she gently swung from side to side. White Fox jumped to action. He pulled his knife from his belt and gave the rope a swift tug, relieved to feel that someone still held the other end. He pulled himself up the rope, climbing until he could reach Chickadee. Then he tried to reach around her to cut her dress, but she was swinging too much from her struggles. "Stop squirming!" he hissed. "Take the knife and cut yourself free." White Fox wrapped one arm tightly around her. "Now!" She hacked at her dress and quickly fell free. White Fox held her but felt the rope slipping through his hand until he completely lost his grip and they both fell.

White Fox hit the ground hard. He rolled to the side and jumped to his feet. Chickadee had landed on Grey Wing, and they too were getting up. Without warning the soldiers appeared around the corner. They did not immediately see the three young people and marched directly toward them.

White Fox felt rooted to the spot. He saw one soldier drop from the formation and heard him shout, "Halt!" All four of the soldiers dropped to one knee and raised their rifles to shooting position. The voice shouted again, "Halt! Stand where you, are or we will shoot."

"We must run!" Chickadee whispered. White Fox's thoughts were spinning. His weapon was back in the bushes, and he could see the four rifles pointed at them.

The silence grew heavy as the soldiers watched the three outlines, barely perceptible in the darkness. Swiftly, from out of the shadows, a snarling streak of fur came flying through the air. It hit two of the soldiers and knocked them into the wall. Guns went off. White Fox grabbed Chickadee's hand and sprinted for the bushes. Grey Wing was close behind. They heard more shots, and White Fox felt a bullet whiz past his head.

As they crashed into the plum bushes, he saw his rifle and grabbed it. Spinning back toward the log wall, he fired two quick shots. Then all grew quiet. The three crouched motionless and listened. Finally they heard the soldiers' voices.

"Are you hurt?" one asked.

"I've been bit by a dog!"

"It was a wolf," another said in wonder.

"Where did he come from?"

"I don't know, and I don't know where he went after he bit me."

"The Injuns have guns, and I'm not goin' out der in the dark lookin' for 'em."

"Look, here's a rope. They were trying to get inside the wall. We came in the nick of time."

"Well, we stopped them. That's all I care about."

"Makes me feel kind of creepy to know they're still out there."

"We'd better get back and report to the general. He may want to post more guards around the outside."

The three young people heard their footsteps and knew without seeing them that the soldiers were walking back to the front gate. White Fox pulled Chickadee to her feet. "Are you able to walk?" he asked.

"There is nothing wrong with me. Let's get away from this place," she answered breathlessly.

White Fox led the way, moving along the edge of the bluff. Shortly they entered their camp. The young warrior turned to his cousin and put his arms around her. "That was a close call for us," he said in a ragged voice.

Grey Wing stumbled into the camp and slid to the ground near the campfire embers. Chickadee moved quickly to his side. "Is there something wrong with you?" she asked. White Fox dropped to his knees beside his friend, concern written on his face. Grey Wing gingerly lifted his right arm and his friends saw the dark stain on his shirt.

White Fox quickly pushed dry sticks into the fire to give more light. Then he gently lifted his friend's shirt and found a wound under the young warrior's bottom rib. The blood seeped steadily from the laceration. White Fox pulled off his wool coat, opened his cotton shirt, and removed it. He began to rip the fabric into strips.

Grey Wing spoke faintly to Chickadee. "Get that bag," he pointed. "My father would not let me out of his sight without some of his healing herbs. I will show you which ones will keep the evil spirits from the wounds."

White Fox heard the word *wounds* and moved close with the bandages. Grey Wing turned slightly, saying, "The bullet hit me in the back as I ran. This is where it came out." White Fox was relieved to see that the bullet's entrance point was off to the side. He knew his friend would survive.

Grey Wing selected the herbs as his friends bound his chest tightly, stopping the flow of blood. When they had finished, Chickadee leaned close to Grey Wing, touching his cheek gently. "I am so glad to see you again. White Fox told us that you were on your way to Little Wolf when he met you on the trail."

Grey Wing looked at her and smiled sadly. "I was too late. But now I am glad to be here with the two of you."

White Fox looked from one face to the other. "He was here tonight," he said softly. "He helped us back at the wall." Chickadee and Grey Wing stared at him. "The wolf. It was his spirit."

A smile slowly crossed Chickadee's face. "He is alive and with us," she said.

White Fox leaned over and gently touched her stomach. "Your little one will always have him as a protector. He told me that it is a son."

Chickadee placed both of her hands on her stomach and smiled. "If that is true, he will have his father's name."

The three young people sat silently watching the flames flicker. Grey Wing's eyes had closed, and he seemed to be resting. After a time, White Fox stood up. "We must travel through the night. Once the sun comes up, the soldiers may have a return of their courage and decide to follow us."

As he disappeared into the darkness to retrieve the ponies, Chickadee walked to the edge of the camp and into the darkness. She stood silently watching the stars twinkle in the night sky. Then she said softly, "Little Wolf, I know you are here. I can feel your presence. I want you at my side. But now, tonight, you must go to your mother. Enter into her dreams and tell her that her grandson and I are safe and on our way to the north country. You must do this to make her strong and able to survive." She paused and then added, "I will know when you are with me again."

The two ponies moved along the ridge, angling to the top. One carried two riders in the pale moonlight. As they dropped over the rise, the ponies turned, and the travelers began their long journey, using the North Star to guide them.

CONCLUSION

The Sioux Uprising of 1862 was also known as the Dakota Conflict. It was a bloody and tragic event in Minnesota's history. During the summer of 1862, Sioux or Dakota Indians were packed onto a narrow reservation along the Minnesota River. The Indians were extremely frustrated by broken treaties, and were enraged by deceitful agents and traders, and near starvation because of crop failure and late annuity payments. These Indians were led by Chief Little Crow, and they attacked the Redwood and Yellow Medicine agencies and all of the white settlers living on their former lands in southwestern Minnesota. The warring Indians killed over 450 whites and took some 250 white and mixed-blood prisoners during the thirty-eight-day conflict.

White civilians and the military, commanded by Henry H. Sibley, defended their towns and forts. They pursued the Sioux band and eventually forced the hostile Indians to surrender or flee westward. It is estimated that about fifty Indians were killed during the uprising. Thirty-eight warriors were hanged in Mankato on December 26, 1862, called by some historians the greatest mass execution in United States history.

By the new year of 1863, strong fear was still being felt among the white people in the state of Minnesota. Approximately two hundred Dakota died of starvation over the winter of 1862 and 1863 in the prison camp below Fort Snelling (at the White Cliff). It is not known how many Dakota died of starvation before this time, during their removal from Minnesota, and later, on the prairies of South Dakota and Nebraska.

Chief Little Crow returned to the Minnesota River Valley area in June of 1863. He was shot and killed six miles north of Hutchinson, Minnesota, on July 3, 1863, while picking raspberries with his son Wowinape (One Who Appeareth). His body was brought to Hutchinson, and during the July 4 celebrations, the young boys of the town entertained themselves by mutilating the body with firecrackers. It was then disposed of in a refuse pit. The body was identified twenty-six days later as Chief Little Crow. In 1896, his skull and forearms were donated to the Minnesota Historical Society. Along with his scalp lock, which the museum already owned, these were put on display in the Society's museum, ironically not more than a dozen miles from Little Crow's birthplace. The items were removed from display in the early 1900s. Finally, in 1971, the bones were given to the family and were interred in a family plot in Flandreau, South Dakota.

After his father's death, sixteen-year-old Wowinape fled north to Devil's Lake, North Dakota. He was captured twenty-six days later and was returned to Fort Abercrombie, where he was tried for war crimes and found guilty. He was sentenced to death but later received a reprieve and was sentenced instead to two years in a prison in Davenport, Iowa. There Wowinape became literate and converted to Christianity. He later took the name Thomas Wakeman and is known as the founder of the Y.M.C.A. among the Dakota.

Shakopee and Medicine Bottle were kidnapped in Canada and returned to Minnesota in the spring of 1864. They were tried and sentenced to death on rather flimsy evidence. They were hanged at Fort Snelling on November 11, 1865. Legend has it that as Shakopee mounted the gallows, he heard one of the state's early steam locomotives. Pointing in the direction of the train, he is said to have stated, "As the white comes in, the Indian goes out."

Appendix

Fictional Characters

White Fox

Spotted Fawn

Running Elk

Little Wolf and family

Panther Man

Sunflower

Chickadee

Falling Star

Grey Wing and family

Straight Talker

Smokey Day

Willow Man

FACTUAL CHARACTERS

Little Crow—Taoyatodeuta—His Red Nation

Wowinape—One Who Appeareth

Susan Brown

Pig's Eye

Inkpaduta

White Spider

Standing Buffalo

Mazamani

Medicine Bottle

Shakopee

Cloud Man

Wabasha

Mankato

Big Eagle

Traveling Hail

Little Leaf

John Otherday

Red Middle Voice

Andrew Myrick

General Sibley

General Taylor

Pawn

PLACE NAME REFERENCES

The Great River—Mississippi River

The Small River—Clearwater River, Minnesota

White Cliff—Saint Paul, Minnesota; describes the limestone bluff upon which Fort Snelling was built

Place Where the Water Falls—Saint Anthony Falls—Minneapolis, Minnesota

Spirit Island—below Saint Anthony Falls; a sacred place to the Dakota was submerged after the river was altered by the dam

Land That Falls Away—Badlands of North Dakota

Soldier's Fort— Fort Ridgely, Minnesota